Anthony Esler is a pro William and Mary in Williamsburg, Virginia. He is the author of *The Blade of Castlemayne* and of several history books.

Also by Anthony Esler:

THE BLADE OF CASTLEMAYNE
HELLBANE
LORD LIBERTINE

Anthony Esler

Forbidden City

Futura Publications Limited
A Futura/Jade Book

A Futura/Jade Book

First published in Great Britain by
Hamish Hamilton Limited in 1978
First Futura Publications edition 1979

Copyright © 1977 by Anthony Esler

ISBN 0 7088 1552 9

Printed in Great Britain by
Hazell Watson & Viney Ltd
Aylesbury, Bucks

Futura Publications Limited
110 Warner Road
Camberwell, London SE5

TO HOLLY

FOR ALL THE STORIES

'The Boxer Sect'
CALLIGRAPHY by LIU WEI-PING

FORBIDDEN CITY

Therefore, O Ananda, be ye lamps unto yourselves. Seek no external refuge, but hold fast to the Truth as your refuge and your lamp, and work out your own salvation.

—THE COMPASSIONATE BUDDHA

FORBIDDEN CITY

BOOK ONE

THE
WALLS

1

THEY CAME DOWN FROM THE GRANITE CRAGS OF T'AI SHAN, their faces the color of blood in the setting sun. They moved in silhouette along the ridge, a long ragged line, descending on the hill-girt hamlet below.

Their scarlet headbands were dark with sweat, their legs dusty to the knees. Broad, high cheekbones, flat noses, shaven foreheads glistened in the sunset. Knife blades, spearpoints, here and there a rust-pitted European rifle glittered in the ruddy light.

They spoke little among themselves. But more than one glanced up at the two strikingly mismatched figures who marched at the head of the column. One was a huge, Mongol-featured man with a crooked queue and a new German Army rifle slung across his wide shoulders. The other was a thin, blank-faced boy of thirteen or fourteen.

The village closed round them, close and rank after the clear air of the mountain. It was a huddle of mud houses with roofs of straw. The streets were little more than paths among the huts, narrow lanes littered with garbage, alive with chickens, pigs, scampering children.

They entered the village with no fanfare, but their impact was immediate. Gossiping old men in doorways turned startled eyes upon them and fell silent. Mothers yanked their children out of the street at the first glimpse of the advancing column, the scarlet sashes and the headbands. Beggars shrank back against the walls, into neighboring alleyways. The streets emptied as if by magic.

The gross-featured giant in the lead smiled as he saw the people give way before him. He smiled with his mouth only, the thick, wrinkled lips curving slowly back from his teeth. His pouched eyes did not smile at all.

At his side, the boy shambled along, slack-jawed and empty-eyed. The sudden silence, the people shrinking away to left and right made no impression on him. He paused only once, to stare at a dragonfly on a string, a child's toy abandoned with a wail a moment since. The boy gazed with a faint spark of interest at the gauzy wings hovering in the air before him, and extended a tentative finger. But the big man with the crooked queue touched his shoulder, and the boy moved on.

Then the huts fell away on either side, and they emerged into the dusty village square. The invaders spread left and right in a rough half-circle and stood there, leaning on their spears and guns. The towering leader strode out into the open and looked around him. The women at the village well, the loafers in the shadow of the ancient pagoda stared mutely back.

An old man in a worn silk robe darted through the gate-posts of a somewhat larger house across the square. He hurried toward the big man and the silent semicircle behind him. He was a fat old man with dewlaps and a greying pigtail, and he was twisting a thick gold ring on one finger. He paused perhaps three yards away, looking up at the man who had come down from T'ai Shan.

He looked up at almost seven feet of broad-chested, heavy-shouldered power. He looked at the crimson headband, at the two long swords thrust through the sash, at the barrel of the German rifle rising behind the left ear. He looked, and he went awkwardly down on his knees, touching his forehead to the earth in a reverent kowtow.

The giant spoke.

"Lao Hsiensheng, women shih huiyu." His voice was harsh and deep as sounding brass in the stillness of the village square, yet his accent was purest Peking Mandarin. "We are of the Society, grandfather. We are of the *I Ho Chuan.* Have you food for us?"

"Honored sir," said the man in the dust before him, "this village always has rice for the *I Ho Chuan.*"

The tableau dissolved at once into flurried activity. The men of the Society relaxed and grinned. Many of them leaned their weapons against the nearest housefront and converged on the well for water. The village women disappeared through darkened doorways to reappear in moments with steaming pots of millet, platters of fruit and nuts and fish. A gong hanging under the ginkgo tree in front of the pagoda sounded its echoing summons above the hubbub. Other faces appeared, vanished, reappeared bearing their own suppers for the ragged troop of men and half-grown boys that were the *I Ho Chuan* in that part of Shantung.

The villagers stood and watched their food devoured, smiling and whispering among themselves. Children stared in envy at the red cloth that bound the head or waist, at the occasional red vest or shirt. Red was the color of happiness and good fortune—and the secret symbol of the *I Ho Chuan*. Would they themselves ever be found worthy to wear it?

The visitors squatted in the square, dipping their fingers into the food, talking and laughing freely now. They were dirty and ill-clad. Some wore nothing above the waist, coolie fashion. Some were bare-legged to the knees, without sandals to walk the roads or hats against the sun. But their teeth flashed cheerfully enough as they chattered and laughed and gorged.

Neither the big man nor the boy beside him ate. They stood quietly, the man with his arms crossed upon his chest, the boy gazing dully about him. They were waiting.

When his men had eaten, the big man spoke again.

"People! People who live in the shadow of T'ai Shan!" There was silence once more.

"You all know this lad!" One heavy hand came down upon the boy's shoulder. "This is Tai Chi-tao! This is the boy from T'ai Shan—the boy to whom the gods speak!"

"We know *you*, Feng!" called a young villager from the back of the crowd. "You are Feng Yu-lan! You are he who is not afraid of the hairy ones!"

"You are Feng," cried another exultant voice, "the Phoenix risen from the ashes of China! You are the Fist—the Scarlet Fist!"

"The gods of Old China have spoken to Tai Chi-tao," the giant called Feng rumbled on in his deep, oddly resonant voice, as though there had been no interruption. "The gods have told him that we must purge the hairy ones, the foreign devils and their spirit-slaves from this land!" He looked slowly around, fixing on each villager's face in turn. "Have you any hairy ones for us?" he thundered suddenly, his voice louder and harsher still. "Any second-class hairy ones, that eat the shit of the foreign dogs and piss upon the tablets of their ancestors?"

"Wu Ping-shan!" a voice cried out after a moment of silence. "Wu Ping-shan kowtows to the god of the foreign devils! Wu and all his family!" A finger pointed, all faces turned toward a shivering man in a light-blue robe, a wife teetering on tiny feet, with a huddle of children, aunts, cousins behind them.

"See—see, I will show you!" In an instant the accuser had darted through the door behind the trembling man and re-emerged waving a cheap European print. It was a picture of a pale-skinned foreigner with blue eyes and long brown hair, raising a hand in blessing above some equally pale-skinned children. "See—it is the god of the hairy ones! It is Je-sus!"

The giant Feng raised his arm, leveled it at the hut from which the fatal icon had come.

"Burn!" his voice boomed across the square.

The red-sashed youths flung themselves upon the house and its terrified inhabitants. The children scattered, screaming. The woman first attempted to totter away on her tiny bound feet, then threw herself into the dust in despair. The master of the house was pummeled, kicked, flung down and trampled. In minutes the thatch of his house was aflame and fire was licking out the doorway, garish and unreal in the deepening shadows of evening.

18

"Are there any more spirit-slaves of the hairy ones in this town? Any more who kowtow to the foreign devils and deny the gods of China?"

"Su Chao-cheng!" shrieked someone then.

The fat little headman in the worn silk robe, who had been hovering anxiously on the edge of the crowd, turned at once and made for his own rudely carved gateposts.

"Su has a foreign mirror in his house, and smokes their tobacco, in little paper rolls! He even buys his food in foreign packages! See here, see what Su Chao-cheng eats for his supper!" The speaker, a grinning round-bellied youth, thrust an empty tin reeking of fish and oil under the noses of the giant and the boy. "He gets his fish this way, from a metal box instead of from the sea!"

"Which is his house?"

"There—there, the widest gate in town, right beside the temple of the Lord Buddha!"

Heads turned, just in time to see the grey queue and the silken robe vanish through the gate beside the old pagoda.

"*Burn!*"

Again the outthrust arm, again the rush, the shrieks, the sounds of blows and rending wood. From within the little garden, the howls of the village headman mingled with the screams of his women. Once more smoke billowed up, and flickers of yellow-orange flame.

Feng Yu-lan's head turned slowly, surveying the scene once more. Somewhere beyond the first rank of houses fronting on the square, he saw more smoke funnel up against the sky.

Someone, he thought wryly, was taking advantage of the growing riot to exact some private vengeance. He had seen it happen before; he would see it again. He shrugged his heavy shoulders, irritated that he had even noticed. He had no time for trifles.

"Any more spirit-slaves of the foreigner here?" he shouted.

"We have something better than that for you, Feng of the Scarlet Fist!" a small, mocking voice chimed in his ear. "We have a first-class hairy one in this village, master!"

Feng looked down at a twisted beggar, hunched with his empty bowl against a wall. The little cripple's eyes were glittering with pleasure as he contemplated the swelling carnage.

"What?" roared Feng. "You have a foreign devil right here in your town?"

"Indeed so, revered master of the *I Ho Chuan!*"

"You let him live here among you, polluting the bones of your ancestors with his every step, blaspheming the gods and the Lord Buddha with his every word? You let this happen here in your own village, and no one said anything, no one did anything?"

"It was Su Chao-cheng!" another voice shouted desperately over the sudden quaking silence. "Su Chao-cheng rented him the house for his temple!"

"And had no man among you fire for his thatch?" Feng's gaze swept over the square, till even his own followers looked up from their groaning victims, the blazing heaps of foreign goods scattered about the square.

"The house," someone mumbled unhappily, "his house is that way, just at the edge of town. The one with the little cross nailed to the rooftree."

It was the boy Tai who responded this time.

His thin face contorted abruptly as though in pain. His eyes rolled up in his head till only the whites showed under lowered lids. Saliva glistened at the ends of his mouth. In a high nasal voice he shrieked: *"Sha-shao! Sha-shao! Sha-shao!"* The mob took up the chant: *"Kill and burn! Kill and burn! Kill and burn!"*

With a roar of triumph they began to move, surging out of the square and up the rutty lane toward the house with the cross on the rooftree. Youths from the village itself almost outraced the scarlet headbands in their haste to rescue the honor of the town. All of them were roaring out the slogan given them by Tai Chi-tao, the boy who talked with the gods. *"Sha-shao! Sha-shao!"*—*"Kill and burn! Kill and burn!"*

Feng followed more slowly, at an almost leisurely pace. One large hand rested on the boy's trembling shoulder. Among the scurrying women and children, Feng moved with a certain implacable majesty, like a shepherd among sheep.

* * *

"Thank you, Patience," said the elderly white man gravely. The old Chinese woman ducked her head, smiling a toothless smile, while she laid out the plates of tinned meat, the platter of steamed bread and yellow fruits on the roughly carpentered table.

Her name was not really Patience, Reverend Rowntree knew. She had been Patience for the past four months only, since he had arrived in the village and taken her on, along with the boy Ming. But she was a serious inquirer, and she would soon enough be ready for Christian baptism. Reverend Rowntree had decided to get her used to her new name in advance.

The Chinese woman put the teapot and the handleless cup on the table, bobbed her head again, and backed out of the bare little dining room.

There was genuine reverence, even awe in her manner. It was the sort of respect that white hairs and learning normally commanded in China, but it was more than that. It was the special awe that followed the Reverend Thomas Rowntree everywhere he went now, after forty years in the China missions. He knew they had taken to calling him "the Christian mandarin" in Peking.

Rowntree frowned, tucked a large napkin into the neck of his shirt, and bowed his head.

Thomas Rowntree was a tall, gaunt man in his sixties, with white hair and piercing blue eyes behind his gold-rimmed glasses. His wrists and neck were thinner, the veins in his hands more prominent than they had been even a year before. But his aggressive intelligence was as quick, his body as enduring as they had ever been. They hadn't wanted to let him give up his job at the head of the Protestant Board Mission in

Peking for this isolated outstation in Shantung, but they hadn't been able to claim he wasn't fit for it. And so here he was, back in the field once more.

He had, he decided, never felt better in his life.

The progress of the new mission showed it. Sipping his tea, he looked around him at the whitewashed walls with the Bible prints, the freshly painted spruce beams overhead. His glance brushed over the unadorned cross on the far wall and the open Testament on the reading stand beside the door. Outside the window with its new glass panes—the only ones in the village —he saw the trees beyond the garden wall moving against a yellow evening sky. The trees and something else. Was it smoke, curling up above the roofs, the feathery foliage of the trees?

He had heard the gong, seen villagers in little groups hurrying past his gate toward the square. Some village festival, he presumed. But smoke—lots of it, now, he saw—was no part of any Chinese festival he knew of. And he knew them all.

He would certainly look into it after supper, he decided. He felt a genuine concern for "his" villagers, as he already thought of them.

He took a bite of fruit and turned his mind to the next day's journey. It would be his first trip back to the capital since he had come out here, and he was not looking forward to it. He did not like the reeking, sprawling Babylon that Peking had always been to him. He did not like the younger missionaries who clustered about the Protestant Board Mission, "modern" young men who talked too much about the material progress of China and too little about evangelizing the heathen. Reverend Rowntree chewed almost viciously. Railroads, medicine, modern education, modern science—that was the Gospel to this new generation in the field. Modern science! he thought. As soon give a loaded pistol to a babe in its cradle as give modern science to the Chinese in their present state of depravity!

He was especially unenthusiastic about the next day's journey because of its particular object. He was going to meet his daughter, come to China for the first time.

Bad enough at any time, to take valuable days away from the field, from God's work, for such purely personal concerns. Doubly bad to have to devote a substantial proportion of his energies to saving this particular brand from the burning. What was it poor Grace had said in her last letter? "Headstrong, willful, self-assertive beyond control . . . an ungrateful, un-Christian and—yes, I must say it—immoral daughter."

What had Grace and Benjamin been doing with her all these years? Reverend Rowntree wondered irritably. At his time of life a troublesome daughter was the last thing he needed.

There was shouting outside now, and someone running. Rowntree turned once more to look out into the courtyard. A strange youth was coming into the compound, naked to the waist, waving a pole of some sort. There were two others behind him. No, more than two—ten, a dozen. He couldn't count them now.

The old man stood up, pulling the napkin out of his collar.

There was a crash and a shout from the kitchen hut across the yard. Feet padded in the little hall behind him. Then Ming was in the room, the houseboy, clutching his throat with both hands, blood spilling between his fingers. He wobbled blindly toward his master, veered off, fell against the reading stand and went down with it. The big Bible landed face down beside the boy's cheek, the pages bent and crinkled. Blood spread like water on the scrubbed plank floor.

Rowntree stepped around the table and started toward the dying servant.

A naked fist came crashing through the new glass window, showering the remains of supper with glittering fragments.

There were men in the doorway now, men and half-grown boys, jamming into the room. Flat dark faces, laughing teeth, bare legs and baggy pants. The missionary saw red bands around their waists and their shaven foreheads, long flat spear-points on poles, a long-barreled fowling piece. He didn't need

23

to see more than the crimson bands and sashes to know what he was in for.

"What are you doing here?" His blue eyes were sharp, his voice harsh with authority. *"Ch'u pa!"* he snapped in Chinese. *"Ch'u pa! K'uai-k'uai-ti!* Go away at once!"

A half-naked youth with scarlet ribbons around his knees giggled and poked at the white man's shirtfront with a spear.

"Yang kuei-tzu!" shouted someone through the shattered window. Rowntree's ears translated the familiar epithet, heard so often on the streets of Peking these days: "Foreign devil! Foreign devil!"

A tile fell from the ceilingless roof, just missing him, cracking in half on the floor at his feet. Another crashed behind him, and a yellow face grinned at him through a hole in the roof.

"This is the property of Su Chao-cheng," said Rowntree in precise Mandarin. "It is your own headman's house. You will answer for any damage to him."

"Su Chao-cheng!" The men crowding into the room laughed delightedly and slapped their thighs. The youth who had been poking speculatively at the white man's shirtfront thrust suddenly. Rowntree staggered under the force of it. He felt the skin break and blood soaking the cloth.

"You will answer for that too," he said more loudly, his voice steady still. "You will answer for that to the soldiers from the West whose weapons speak many times for every one of yours!" And then, his reedy voice harsh with contempt: "But you are fools and children! Is there no *man* among you that I may speak sense to?"

A gigantic figure stepped through the door, thrust through the parting mob. He was a seven-foot giant with thick lips and somber eyes. He had a red scarf tied around his shining bald head.

"You may speak to me, hairy one!" The deep voice filled the room from floor to rafter, from wall to wall. "I am a man!"

He reached out and caught the Reverend Rowntree by his

24

silky white hair with one huge hand. With the other, he pulled one of the long, curved swords out of his belt.

The people moved restlessly about in the crowded courtyard, talking excitedly, watching the *I Ho Chuan* swarm like beetles up the walls and over the tile roof of the mission house. An older man in a red shirt was prying the cross off the rooftree. Yellow flames were already licking up from the servants' quarters and the kitchen building. In the thickening darkness by the open gate, the boy Tai stood forgotten, dull-eyed once more in the flickering firelight.

There was a shout from the main house, a dozen men crying out at once.

A moment later came an eddying about the open doorway. Feng emerged, bending to pass under the low lintel. He stood a moment in the sulfurous yellow glare of the flames, looking from one expectant face to the next. Then he raised one hand. A silence, sudden and palpable, washed back over the crowd.

Feng held the head up by the hair. Blood still ran from the severed arteries, flowing over his wrist and forearm. The blue eyes of the murdered missionary still glared fiercely out upon the multitude, but the lips were pale now, and the jaw hung slack.

2

SOMEWHERE A BELL CLANGED, AND THE *Deucalion's* ENGINES slowed appreciably. The rusty steamer lost way, swung ponderously broadside to the swell. The steel plates beneath the girl's feet vibrated still, but much less horrendously than they had done. She was grateful for that.

She stood, balancing herself against the slight roll of the ship, and gazed across Taku Bar into China.

She saw a vast mud flat, divided by the river's broad mouth. East of the river there was an unprepossessing cluster of whitewashed mud huts. West of the river's mouth lay a long, low stretch of fortifications guarding the steaming delta. She made out heavy earthen battlements and a pennon fluttering.

"The Taku Forts, miss," said the white-coated Levantine steward hovering at her elbow. "The Chinese say they are quite impregnable, even to a modern bombardment." He winked and grinned at her, as if to say, *But we know better, don't we, miss?* His greasy face glistened in the sunshine.

"And the little whitewashed village there?"

"Pilot Town, miss. That will be the pilot coming now, to guide us across the bar." A small skiff was in fact knifing its way across the grey-green sea reach that still separated the *Deucalion* from the mouth of the Pei Ho River. "The water is very shallow over the bar."

The girl said nothing more, and the steward darted off toward the other passengers, clustered in the lee of the lifeboats forward.

The American girl stood alone, balancing on the gently shifting deck with an ease born of weeks at sea. She stood with her bags and her small trunk beside her, a slim, attractive figure. Her long dark skirts were brushed with care, her white shirtwaist crisply starched. She wore a light summer jacket and a small straw hat and carried a parasol. She felt clean and crisp and only a little bit excited. Quite prepared, she told herself, for whatever the next few hours might bring.

Over the heave and settle of the sea, the pilot boat scudded hard over toward the waiting steamer.

The girl's heart began to beat faster. She strained her eyes into the morning sunglare. She could see half a dozen men in the boat. There were sailors, and a portly man in a blue coat, and a couple of other men in uniform, she thought. But she couldn't be sure, in the glare off the water. She bit her lip impatiently and settled herself to wait.

The other passengers drifted over. The pallid British missionary smiled abstractedly and bowed, but his gaze shifted almost at once back to the flat coastline across the bay. The two Central European commercial travelers tipped their hats without interrupting their own conversation. They were talking, as usual, about the unlimited future of the China market. Even the bright-cheeked American student, who had been so attentive ever since Nagasaki, gave the girl only a quick smile before his eyes too swung off across the bar toward China.

The pilot's skiff dropped its sail and came bumping and scraping alongside, just below the railing where they stood. Sailors materialized and urged the little cluster of passengers back a step or two, muttering something apologetic in Greek. The girl fixed her eyes on the little gate at the head of the ladder where the first face would appear.

A ruddy countenance with walrus moustaches and a visored naval cap rose suddenly into view. It was the portly man in the blue coat, the pilot. Two other uniformed officials of some sort followed. They trooped off with the Greek second mate toward the bridge. The girl's heart slowed.

Damn, she thought. But what had she expected?

Then another man came off the ladder and swung himself aboard.

He was a wiry, lean man of middle height, his skin tanned

a leathery brown. He wore the coarse grey jodhpurs and tan puttees, the blue flannel shirt and wide-brimmed hat of the United States Marine Corps. There were three wide yellow chevrons on his sleeve.

"Miss Rowntree?" he said, looking around at the little cluster of passengers.

"I am Elizabeth Rowntree," said the girl, staring at him in surprise.

The Marine touched his hat brim. "I am detailed to get your things ashore, ma'am, and to take you to the railway station. The train leaves in less than an hour, miss," he added, without emphasis.

His voice was wooden, his eyes expressionless. She could not even tell what color they were in that leathery face, in the shadow of the thin, wide brim. But the face as a whole was far from handsome, that much was clear. An unprepossessing low-Irish face, she decided, of the sort no proper Philadelphian would expect to see outside of the stables or the kitchen.

Proper Philadelphian! she thought wryly. And when were you ever a proper Philadelphian, Elizabeth Rowntree?

Aloud, she said, "Detailed? And by whom, pray tell?"

"By Mr. Conger, ma'am. The American Minister in Peking. I am on detached service to the American Legation there."

"And your name is?"

"Connor, miss. Sergeant Connor."

"Well, then, Sergeant Connor, if you will have these bags debarked, I will be happy to accompany you." She smiled at him at last, a bright meaningless smile, and unfurled her parasol against the August sun.

After that, the world around her seemed to dissolve into a dreamlike flow of motion, noise, and color.

There was the vertiginous descent of the ship's side into the heaving, sliding boat. There was the last reach of the sea scudding past under the bows of the little skiff. Then there

28

was a stone jetty, and clusters of men with dark-yellowish skins in blue pajamas—and solid earth under her feet once more. She curled her toes against it through her thick-soled sensible shoes.

But the flow of purposeful motion swept her up once more. Sergeant Connor gave orders, half in English, half in what she took to be Chinese, and the men in the blue pajamas scooped up her bags and hurried them off to a waiting cart. Then she was seated next to her taciturn escort in the little two-wheeled donkey wagon, jolting up a dusty road toward a larger town a mile or so upriver.

"Tungku, ma'am," he informed her briefly. "We will take the train there north to Tientsin, and on to Peking."

"And how long will the journey take?"

"You should be at the American Legation in Peking by sunset, ma'am. Barring any interruptions of service up the line."

"Interruptions of service? The Chinese railway service is not up to what we are used to in America, then?"

"No, ma'am. And recently there have been some special problems."

It sounded rather more serious than he was making it, somehow. Derailments? Exploding boilers? She thought about asking for more particulars, but decided against it. She knew nothing at all about railroads, and she didn't like to talk about things she knew nothing about.

Then there was the siding at Tungku, and the little locomotive with its tall smokestack and chest-high drive wheels, half a dozen coaches in tow. There were more olive-skinned men in baggy pajama pants and the wide straw "coolie" hats she had seen in pictures. Sergeant Connor gave orders again. Then there was the cramped interior of what passed for a first-class carriage, and Connor seated at her side.

"Tientsin in two hours, ma'am," he announced in his clipped, impersonal voice. Then he settled back on the seat, tipped his hat forward over his eyes, and went to sleep.

Elizabeth was just as glad to be left alone with her thoughts —joyless though they were.

At the moment she was simply irritated with herself. What had she expected, after all? It *was* very kind of the American Minister in Peking to have sent someone to meet her. And Sergeant Connor was certainly efficient, if a bit surly. She had no right at all to feel the stab of disappointment under her heart.

Had she really expected her father to drop everything simply to meet his daughter at the dock? Of course not! she told herself.

Outside the window the muddy coastal delta turned to yellow grain, ripening fast in the summer sun. Then there were low grey houses, thickening into swarming city streets. A European facade flashed past, and an elaborate pagoda, and she glimpsed the river beyond the grey tile roofs. Then Tientsin Station slowed outside the glass as the train quivered and clanged to a stop.

More coolies, more orders from the laconic Sergeant Connor, and they were standing on a wide, sun-drenched platform. Elizabeth stretched her long limbs secretly under her skirts and smiled. She breathed in the clear air, so different from the grit and smoke of a busy American railway depot.

"The Peking train leaves directly, ma'am," Connor was saying, cool and correct as he had been every minute since she had met him. She felt a sudden coquettish urge to make him smile. "I'll be leaving you here," he added, almost as an afterthought.

"I beg your pardon?" she said, startled once again. The Irish sergeant seemed to have a knack for startling her.

"I'll be leaving you here, miss. I have other work to do here in Tientsin. There is a friend of your father's who will see you the rest of the way to Peking."

"Ah." She looked uncertainly about her at the frieze of moving yellow faces. There was only a single European in sight, just disappearing into an official-looking doorway at the far end of the platform. She wondered if that was her father's friend.

"Miss Rowntree?" inquired a polite, firm voice with just a touch of hesitation about the *r*. She turned and saw a tallish Chinese, grey at the temples and wearing a white Western suit, smiling at her through his glasses. "I am Dr. Chen. Your father asked me to escort you and your baggage to Peking."

Sergeant Michael Connor stood on the station platform and watched the little train chug out of sight. He was glad to see it go.

"Did you get her off then, Sergeant?"

It was Corporal Fitz—Corporal James Fitzgerald, who had been supervising the purchase of the supplies they had been sent for to Tientsin.

"I did," said Connor.

"How was she?" The corporal grinned. He was a more solidly built man than the sergeant, with a melodious old-country Irish voice. "Was she the poker-backed preacher's daughter you were looking for her to be then?"

Connor shrugged. "A swell," he said succinctly, "and a bitch. I've seen lots of 'em. My mother scrubbed the likes of her mother's floors, and she wonders why I ain't shoveling shit in her daddy's stable." He rolled phlegm around in one lean cheek and spat it out on the platform. "Let's go find ourselves a drink," he said.

The two Marines strode off up the platform.

A Chinese in a blue railway uniform materialized almost immediately, broom in hand, and swept the sergeant's spittle into a dark smear, quickly evaporated by the sun.

3

"Marco Polo," Dr. Chen Li was saying, "described Peking as 'arranged in squares like a chessboard, disposed in a manner masterly and perfect.' I don't suppose it looks much like a chessboard to you," he added dryly.

"I'm afraid—not!" gasped Elizabeth as the iron-wheeled cart jounced through the dust and noise and sun-baked ruts of the main street north from the railway station. She could see nothing at all through the turmoil on either side of them but a clamorous bazaar of mat-roofed stalls, with a tangle of alleyways beyond.

"Yet this is one of the most symmetrically designed cities in the world," said the Chinese doctor. "The main avenues all run north to south, east to west, parallel to the ancient city walls."

"I'll have to take your word for it," said Elizabeth politely. "All I can see is dust and confusion."

Swarms of people, animals, and vehicles of all sorts poured up and down the street on either side of the donkey wagon in which they rode, with its swarthy, sweating Mohammedan driver. Flocks of sheep and swine, two-humped camels and silver-mounted ponies flowed around them. Silk-clad students and saffron-robed Buddhist monks with shaven heads mingled with the blue pajamas and wide hats of half-naked coolies, the greasy sheepskin coats of Mongols from beyond the Great Wall. The swirling dust was thick, the heat stifling, even in late afternoon.

"Peking is not one city but four, actually," Dr. Chen went on, as cheerfully informative as he had been throughout the trip. "There is first the Chinese City—the southern half of the chessboard, you might say—through which we are presently proceeding. There is the Tartar City, the northern half of the chessboard, which we shall soon enter. There is the Imperial City, which is located at the precise center of the Tartar City, and which neither of us, in all probability, will *ever* enter. And finally, there is the Chinese holy of holies—the Forbidden City."

"The Forbidden City?"

"The Forbidden City, Miss Rowntree. Where the Emperor dwells—and the Dowager Empress."

"Ah," she said. "It is a very good-sized metropolis," she added politely, as the swaying cart flung her against his shoulder.

"It is indeed. There are twenty-five square miles of it, and a population in the neighborhood of one million."

Dear Lord, thought Elizabeth. She was suddenly irritated beyond measure at the sixteen gates and the fifty-foot walls of old Peking. Chen's flow of information, anecdote, and easy wit had been pleasant enough on the train up from Tientsin. Soothing even, much as she hated to admit that she, an independent-minded young woman of the coming century, needed any soothing. But ever since they had descended in the railway station outside the southernmost gates of the city, she had had other things on her mind. Or one other thing, to be precise, and that with sudden and overwhelming urgency.

Now, swaying through the clamorous streets in this hideous cart, she tried again.

"I hope my father is well," she said.

"Quite well, I believe, Miss Rowntree. Overwhelmed with work, as usual, of course. He would have met you at the coast himself, but he has recently taken up new duties at a mission station in Shantung, and simply couldn't make it. He is due back in Peking today, I believe, or tomorrow at the latest. But the pressure of his work is very great."

Of course, she thought. His work would come first. As it no doubt should. As it certainly always had.

"You have not seen your father recently?"

"I have seen him only once," she said, "in the past twenty years."

"The Reverend Rowntree's intense dedication is well-known," said the doctor judiciously, "and immensely admired. Your mother, I believe," he added politely, "is deceased?"

"She died when I was five. My father brought me home to his brother and sister in America, and then returned to China. I grew up with them—Aunt Grace and Uncle Benjamin—in Philadelphia. My father has only been able to get home once since then, eight years ago, when he came on business for the Mission Board in Boston. But he did manage to spend some time with us in Philadelphia too."

About a week, to be exact. The most brutally disappointing week of her fifteen-year-old life.

Not his fault, of course, she told herself hastily. None of it his fault. But if only he had not been so busy about the Board's business. If only he had spoken, really *spoken* to her at all.

She visualized his face as she had seen it then. The hollow cheeks and the glinting glasses, the frosty blue eyes, the firm New England mouth and jaw. Every inch the Reverend Thomas Rowntree, whose letters were read aloud to his brother Benjamin's congregation at the little church on Pine Street. Every inch the consecrated servant of the Lord—with eyes that looked right through his only daughter as if she weren't there.

"And now your uncle and aunt have passed away in turn, and you have come to join your father in the mission field."

It was really none of his business, she thought. But there was something in his tone that made the interest seem quite legitimate, somehow. Hadn't she been told that in China it was only common courtesy to inquire about other people's relatives?

"Uncle Benjamin died some years ago," Elizabeth ex-

34

plained. "Aunt Grace—just this past spring. And so I have come to see my father." To see whether now, she thought, he might have time to look at her, to speak with her at last.

"You know my father well?" she inquired, raising her voice once more above the strident cries of the street hawkers, the bleating of a passing flock of sheep, their tails dipped red for the slaughter.

"I have known Reverend Rowntree off and on for a number of years," said Dr. Chen carefully. "You will find that in Peking everyone knows everyone else a little. It is a strange city."

The phrase, or the tone in which it was spoken, caught her attention. Elizabeth turned to look at her companion seriously for the first time.

She saw a man perhaps forty years old, well-knit and rather tall, with a skin more bronzed than most of his countrymen. He had full, firm lips, high cheekbones, and straight black hair, crisping to gunmetal grey at the temples. His hair was cut in the Western fashion, the forehead unshaven, without a queue. His slightly rumpled European suit gave every indication of having been comfortably lived in. The eyes behind the shell-rimmed glasses were intelligent and warm.

He has really been putting himself out to be nice to me, she told herself. Even the colorful parade of guidebook information, she realized, had served a friendly purpose, easing her nervous excitement, helping her pass those last tense hours before she reached her destination.

"Have you always lived in Peking?" she asked, rather more pleasantly than she had.

"Again," he said, smiling, "the best answer is—off and on. I was born in a small village northwest of here, at the foot of the Western Hills. In my youth I traveled a good deal, both in China and beyond the seas. But for many years I have lived here and practiced Western medicine, here and in Tientsin. I was lecturing at the Medical College in Tientsin yesterday, so

35

it was easy enough for me to meet you at the station and escort you back to Peking." His smile made tiny crinkles at the ends of his eyes. "I was of course honored to do so."

Elizabeth smiled back at him.

"I am very glad of your company, Dr. Chen," she said. "It is some time since I have been so solicitously cared for."

"Indeed, you American women of the new generation do go about the world with remarkable boldness. But in this case your father was quite right, I think. There have been troubles all along the line this summer." The crinkles at his eyes faded as he spoke, and a somber look shadowed his precisely sculptured Chinese features.

She remembered Sergeant Connor's oblique reference to "interruptions of service" along the Peking railway line.

"But here is the Chien Men Gate, Miss Rowntree!" said Chen Li abruptly, directing her attention forward, past their dark-skinned driver's perspiring back. "We are about to enter the Tartar City of Peking."

She turned to look up at the great red walls, stretching away to left and right beyond the grey roofs of the city. Each of the component "cities," it seemed, had its own ancient walls. They were about to pass through the most famous of them all.

Just ahead of them, beyond the silk merchants' shops on the right and the clangorous bronzeworkers on the left, half the population of Peking seemed to be flowing over a wide causeway across a half-dry moat. Beyond the causeway, flanked by pale-green trees and clusters of small temples, the huge front gate of the Tartar City rose against the sky. Elizabeth looked up at it, a massive complex of iron-studded portals and looming red towers topped by multitiered pagoda roofs of green tile. The whole elaborate complex soared a full hundred feet above the street.

For the first time that day she was properly impressed by China.

Dr. Chen watched her gaze travel up the awesome height

of the Chien Men and smiled. "Some," he said quietly, "call it the Mouth of the Dragon."

"But why is the central archway closed up?" Elizabeth asked as they swept out upon the causeway and swung toward the crowded right-hand arch.

"The central gate is the Imperial Gate," responded Chen. "It is always barred except when the Emperor—or the Dowager Empress—deigns to make use of it. That would be," he added reflectively, "perhaps half a dozen times a year. When the Face That Is Always To The South goes forth to sacrifice at the Temple of Heaven, or perhaps to summer in the Western Hills."

"Half a dozen times a *year?*" the American girl protested. "And in the meantime, the people of Peking are denied the use of a main gate to their city?"

"The *people! Their* city!" Chen Li smiled and shook his head. "Ah, Miss Rowntree, you do have a lot to learn about China."

His last words were almost lost in the din around them. Through swirling crowds and clouds of dust, through the clang of the bronzeworkers' hammers and high-pitched shouts of *"Chieh kuang! Chieh kuang!"* for the blue-and-green sedan chairs of the rich, through a hubbub of animals and men, of chattering women and scampering children, Elizabeth Rowntree passed through the Mouth of the Dragon into the heart of Peking.

4

THE MAN IN THE FANTASTIC MAD HATTER COSTUME BENT over her hand. "Charmed," he murmured, his outsized top hat brushing her chin. He looked up and winked one mischievous bright-blue eye. He had fair hair and a sandy moustache and was quite handsome in a pink-cheeked British way. "Lieutenant Philip Greville, at your service, ma'am."

A slenderly elegant matador replaced him, bowing in turn over her hand. *"Enchanté, mademoiselle."* She took in the narrow black moustache and goatee, the dark, brooding eyes, the sensuous mouth. "Captain Jean-André Lamenière. I hope I may have the pleasure of the dance before the evening is ended?"

"Certainly, Captain," she heard herself responding. She heard and wondered at herself, for the last thing her bone-weary body wanted that unreal night was a dance.

"And this is Sir Claude MacDonald," rumbled Mr. Conger, her guide through this lantern-lit fairyland. "Minister Plenipotentiary of her Britannic Majesty in China. Our host, and the dean of our little diplomatic community here in Peking."

A fiftyish man with a long Scottish face and the longest, thinnest, most stiffly waxed moustaches she had ever seen bowed with Sandhurst elegance. The subdued grace of his evening dress made him stand out among his more colorfully costumed guests.

"I hope you enjoy your stay with us, Miss Rowntree," said Sir Claude. "I am so sorry your father was not back in time to be with us this evening. But then, Reverend Rowntree is never one for frivolity, is he, Mr. Conger?"

"No, indeed, Sir Claude," beamed the bearded Midwestern

politician who was the American emissary to the Celestial Empire. Mr. Conger, Elizabeth remembered, had been a Congressional friend of President McKinley's. Among these sophisticated European diplomats, she thought, he did not cut a very brilliant figure.

"The good reverend," Mr. Conger was saying, "will be back in the city tomorrow at the latest, I'm sure. He is extremely punctual as a rule." Then, in a bluff, straightforward way that had certainly not hurt his political career in Ohio: "I'm a Universalist myself, Miss Rowntree, have been all my life. But I must say no one does better work here in China than the Reverend Thomas Rowntree. Isn't that so, Sarah?"

"It is, Mr. Conger," his wife agreed. "I've heard you say it more than once." She was a fine-boned, motherly little woman whom Elizabeth had taken a liking to at once.

"Do make yourself at home, Miss Rowntree," said Sir Claude. His brittle, aristocratic British voice contrasted sharply with the Congers' flat Midwestern twang. "You're one of us now, you know." He gave her another formal bow and strolled off under a flowering acacia.

Elizabeth felt dazed as she looked around the lantern-lit gardens of the British Legation, with its exotic trees and flowering shrubs, its lacquered pavilions and multitudes of scurrying Chinese servants. "Quite the most splendid diplomatic compound in the city," Sarah Conger had assured her. "You're in great good fortune to have arrived on the evening of the annual fancy-dress ball!" In a hastily pressed gown pulled out of her steamer trunk not an hour since, still feeling vaguely gritty from her journey despite a quick bath, Elizabeth felt anything but fortunate.

She had a sudden ridiculous impulse to ask the way to the Protestant Board Mission. To go there herself, at once, to see if her father had returned yet.

"That's Baron von Ketteler," Mr. Conger was saying, nodding toward a floridly handsome middle-aged man with thick, bristling moustaches. "The German Minister. Rather an entrepreneur of youth activities here, eh, my dear? Organizes all the excursions, picnics, amateur theatricals, and so on." Conger laughed. "He has an American wife."

"Is that his wife with him now?" inquired Elizabeth politely. The red-faced German was bowing over the hand of a frothily pretty young thing in the shadow of an elaborately decorated Chinese tower.

"Ah—no. That's Maude over there." He indicated a plain-looking woman seated on a carved stone bench nearby. "Her father," he added, "is the president of the Michigan Central."

Somewhere among the painted pavilions, a brass band struck up an incongruous, slightly off-key rendition of a recently popular dance tune.

"That's the I-G's Own Chinese Band," said Sarah Conger brightly. "The best Western band in Peking—and the only one."

Elizabeth wondered vaguely who the I-G might be, and how he rated a band of his own.

"May I have you for this dance then, Miss Rowntree?" a cheerful younger voice intruded. It was the Mad Hatter with the sandy moustache, his handsome cheeks even pinker than before, his blue eyes brighter still. "Perfidious Albion, you know—stealing a march on our Gallic friend."

Well, why not? thought Elizabeth. If her father could not come up from Shantung in time to meet his daughter, when she had come halfway round the world to see him—she might as well enjoy the party!

"Why, thank you, Lieutenant Greville," she answered, "I should be delighted."

She danced with Greville more than once, and found him clever and generally charming. She danced with Captain Lamenière as well, the romantically melancholy French officer in the matador suit. She danced with half the young

40

attachés, officers, secretaries, and students there. She had always loved to dance, in spite of all Aunt Grace used to say about it.

"You are quite the belle of the ball," declared Mrs. Conger while the Chinese musicians took a breather. "Lieutenant Greville and Captain Lamenière especially—my! They're the handsomest young men in the legations, and you've quite turned both their heads."

Elizabeth smiled. When Greville offered her a cup of champagne punch, she cheerfully drank it down, and promptly accepted another from the French captain as well. Handing the empty cup back with a laugh, she saw Sarah Conger's lips purse slightly. This was, Elizabeth knew, no way for Reverend Rowntree's daughter to behave.

Being a minister's daughter—and a missionary's at that—carried certain responsibilities. She had known *that* every minute of her young life.

Soon they would notice her skirts, she expected—the fashionable and eminently practical "rainy daisy" length, a full six inches off the ground. And the light, sheer blouses that made her feel so free and cool—and revealed all too clearly the outlines of the firmly corseted young breasts beneath. Soon they would notice—most shocking of all—that she actually preferred the comparatively intelligent talk of men to the aimless prattle of food and servant problems and friends' peccadilloes that made up the staple of feminine conversation. Soon they would notice—and it would be her Philadelphia girlhood all over again.

"May I say, Mademoiselle Rowntree," said Captain Lamenière gravely, "that you are the most beautiful young woman I have seen since I have been out East?"

"And how long would that be, Captain?" she inquired with a mischievous toss of her chestnut hair. She had not had time to bind it up, and much of it hung in a provocative horsetail down her back.

"Ah, too long, mademoiselle." He sighed. His dark eyes brooded mysteriously. "Far too long, I am afraid."

Suspecting that he wished to talk about himself, she made no comment. That was the one sort of masculine talk she could do without! But she responded willingly enough when the I-G's Own struck up another tune, for the Frenchman was a graceful dancer. The touch of his hand at her waist, the rhythmic movement of his body so close to hers kindled a diffuse sort of sensuality that spread deliciously through her.

Let the old nanny goats fret about that too, she thought with another toss of her head. And to blazes with them all!

It was approaching midnight when she overheard the conversation in the Bell Tower.

She had drifted inside, cheerfully exhausted from the dancing, and sunk down on a stone bench to rest, out of sight of the young gentlemen who did indeed seem to have nominated her regnant beauty of that particular ball. No doubt, she thought, they got few enough new young ladies on the Peking Cotillion circuit.

Then she heard Sir Claude MacDonald's voice, only slightly muffled by the head-high marble partition that divided the lower floor of the Bell Tower in half. "Really, Von Ketteler, you are unduly concerned," he was saying in a faintly irritated voice. "Fists of Righteousness! Brethren of the Long Sword! Even the White Lotuses—a rabble, no more."

The answer came in clearly Teutonic accents. "You should take them more seriously, Sir Claude. And you should take action. Firm, aggressive action, to stop this thing before it grows out of hand."

"Stop what thing, my dear Baron? The distribution of a handful of placards?"

"Not a handful—thousands of them, all over Peking, all over Tientsin. And listen to what they say. Read it again, if you please, Mr. Conger."

"Um. Yes," grunted the flat Ohio voice. "If I can read Giles's translations under the characters here." There was a pause. " 'So, as soon as the practice of *I Ho Chuan*'—he leaves it that way, untranslated—'of *I Ho Chuan* has been brought to perfection—wait for three times three or nine times nine, nine times nine or three times three—then shall the devils meet their doom!' Doesn't mean a thing to me, three times three and nine times nine."

"Go on. Read."

" 'The Will of Heaven is that the telegraph wires be first cut, then the railways torn up.' "

"Eh? Has it not happened twice since spring?"

" 'And then,' " the American Minister's voice went on, " 'shall the foreign devils be decapitated. In this day shall the hour of their calamities come.' "

"Poppycock!" Sir Claude MacDonald sniffed. "Banditry—secret society nonsense, that's all. Utterly unrepresentative of the thinking of the Imperial Government. I know, my dear Von Ketteler. I am in almost daily contact with the *Tsungli Yamen* about it."

"The *Tsungli Yamen!* It is the Old Buddha that decides things in China, not the Foreign Office. And how does *she* feel about the Fists of Righteousness, eh?"

"The Dowager Empress," said the British Minister firmly, "deplores any sort of antiforeign outbreak, indeed any breach of the peace at all anywhere in the Chinese Empire."

"So she tells *you*." The German snorted. "She tells everyone what they want to hear. That is how she has stayed in power for half a century. You British don't understand her. She is a monster, sir—a monster!"

"I must say, Baron," said Mr. Conger, bringing the conversation methodically back to the matter at hand, "that I think Sir Claude's in the right of it this time. This placard business does sound like a lot of damn foolishness to me."

"Tam foolishness!" Sitting in the darkness behind the marble screen, Elizabeth could practically see the florid German's face flush redder still as his English grew thicker, his voice harsher. "Tam foolishness! That's what they said when the Taipings rose in the Fifties and tore the whole country apart. Or the Tientsin Massacre in 'seventy, eh? Ask Pichon about that. They were his people—French officials, French nuns. You know as well as I what happened to them."

"Gentlemen, gentlemen, please," said Conger. "How about a cigar and a little brandy outside, shall we? Stuffy in here. And then after a good night's sleep, perhaps we can get together with Pichon and the others and talk it out. No hurry, after all. I don't expect it'll be three times three *or* nine times nine tomorrow. Nine times nine or three times three."

She heard the click of heels—she could imagine the baron's Prussian bow—and Sir Claude's peevish "Oh, very well, if we must spend more time on it—" Footsteps scraped on the stone floor, and then there was silence.

Elizabeth tried to make some sense out of it, resting her head wearily on the carved stone screen in the darkness. But there were too many pieces missing. And it all sounded absurdly melodramatic, somehow. This was 1899, after all— the last year of the nineteenth century, not the Middle Ages. The world was girdled by steam and telegraph, war had been abolished, progressive ideas were spreading around the globe. Bandits and secret societies were something out of dime novels or Gilbert and Sullivan operas.

"My dear Miss Rowntree!" said a tall young man from the Russian Legation, bending through the open doorway. "Come out, come out—it is the time of the last dance."

She laughed and came.

It was late then, much too late for a girl who had traveled so long and so far. The Chinese band had long since vacated the lacquered pavilion where they had played, and a small group of young men were clustered around Elizabeth at the piano in one corner. Their elders and superiors looked on, trying to appear modern, not too disapproving.

"Miss Rowntree," one young officer was saying, "you're a fresh wind from home, and I don't mind who hears me say it."

"Yes, and a veritable mine of the latest tunes as well," another blustered. "Anna Held herself couldn't sing 'em better."

"I say," said Lieutenant Greville, rolling his moustache rakishly between thumb and forefinger, "do you know 'I Just Can't Make My Eyes Behave'? One of Miss Held's classics, I think."

"Why, Lieutenant!" said Elizabeth, flashing him a demure look over the puffed sleeve of her gown. "How would I know such a risqué air as that? But how about this, for a Britisher?" Her fingers flowed once across the keyboard, and she began:

> "I'm a respectable workin' girl, and I've
>   no time to dally,
> I'm none of your flirtin' actresses or
>   loidies of the ballet;
> I'll give you a smack if you are an earl,
>   if you don't leave me go—
> For I'm a respectable workin' girl, I'd—
>   'ave—you know!"

She looked up at the handsome flushed faces grouped around her, nodded and smiled, and they all joined in on the reprise:

> "For I'm a respectable workin' girl, I'd—
>   'ave—you know!"

Then the group was breaking up, and Mrs. Conger was putting a wrap around Elizabeth's shoulders in a no-nonsense way, reminding her firmly that they really must be going if she was to see her father in the morning. Native servants in white coats were extinguishing the last of the paper lanterns as they passed out through the broad gateway and turned south along the edge of the Imperial Canal toward Legation Street.

Elizabeth Rowntree's first day in China was over. She was vaguely surprised to realize that she had so far met a grand total of one Chinese.

5

ELIZABETH ROWNTREE DRESSED CAREFULLY THE FOLLOWING morning, preparing herself for the walk up Legation Street to the Protestant Board Mission. The longest walk, she reflected with an odd tautness in her throat, of her entire young life.

Young? Well, hardly that, she thought wryly. She was a woman of twenty-three, after all—and still unmarried! Much too old, she knew, to be unmarried, to be a girl still. She had been reminded of *that* often enough, as her friends coupled one by one and took on the new status and firm, flounced self-confidence of matrons.

Outside the curtained window of the legation guest room, she could hear the singsong babble of the native servants, washing clothes in the back courtyard. A babble to her, at least, though she supposed from their shrill laughter that they must be saying something. Suddenly she wondered what. There were so many things to wonder about in this strange new world.

She glanced at herself in the mirror that backed the chintz-lined dressing table. Even the young woman in the mirror looked like a stranger to her now.

Her hair was chestnut brown, lustrous enough when brushed, heavy and long. No use at all for the fluffy, curly hairstyles of the Nineties. She wore it partially tied up in a chignon, and let the rest fall in a long dark horsetail to the middle of her back.

The eyes in the mirror were dark blue, alert, and intelligent. Capable of a flirtatious gleam, of laughter and good humor—though there had been too little of that in her life. Capable too of darkening to a midnight blue that was almost blackness when a gust of passion swept over her. Gusts of anger, of outrage, of misery she knew. And of love? She pursed her lips, wondering.

The girl in the mirror pursed her lips too, and then smiled. Her mouth was rather wide, she thought, certainly no Cupid's bow. But the lower lip did have a tempting fullness to it, especially when her mouth softened in that little half-smile.

And that was Elizabeth Rowntree, the Reverend Thomas Rowntree's refractory daughter.

"No!"

She actually said it aloud, startling herself and that other girl in the glass.

No! That was not half what there was to Elizabeth Rowntree!

She raised her hands, turned them over, looked at them. They were strong hands, quick to pick up new physical tasks, eager for work to challenge their dexterity. "Practical hands," someone had once said—intending no compliment. Young ladies who grew up in the town houses and tree-lined streets around Rittenhouse Square had no use for practical hands.

There were other things too that a proper Philadelphia girl was supposed to have no use for. Until she was married, at least, and even then their uses were shrouded in darkness and secrecy, or in the chastest of euphemisms.

Almost defiantly, Elizabeth raised her hands to touch her breasts beneath the fine linen of her chemise. She ran her fingers down to the fashionable wasp waist, the shapely hips and thighs. She felt the familiar tingle flow through her body. The weird gingery sensation, the sensitivity in her breasts, her belly and thighs that had shamed her throughout her wretched teens. The tight hot longing that she had frankly recognized for what it was only in her twenties—the desire to be touched, to be caressed, and to be loved.

Elizabeth Rowntree was not an abnormal girl. She had grown up as other little girls grew up in Philadelphia in the 1880s. She had worn her gums on rainy days, rolled her hoop in Rittenhouse Square, coasted on her sledge down the crisp

48

white hills of Germantown in winter. She had somehow survived her Aunt Grace, a cold, forbidding woman with wrinkled cheeks and hands rubbed red and swollen with too much washing of them.

Her father she had idealized and dreamed about, and even loved in a romantic little-girl way. But she had lived from day to day with the crushing burden of responsibility his dedication laid upon her. For she was "the Reverend Rowntree's daughter" always.

His daughter, sitting very straight in church to listen to his letters from the mission field read aloud from the pulpit. His daughter, doing just a bit better than the others at Miss Erwin's School. His daughter, eschewing the little frivolities that her playmates indulged in with such cheerful heedlessness because their fathers were only lawyers, or doctors, or officers of banks.

It grew worse as she grew older. She had to fight her aunt to learn to dance, to go to parties, to join her young friends for boating excursions up the Schuylkill on summer afternoons. She had to storm and shout and defy all authority to get permission for such daring activities as picnics or bicycle trips with other laughing boys and girls. It was not seemly, Aunt Grace informed her, for the Reverend Rowntree's daughter to laugh too much in public.

At fifteen she was troublesome. At nineteen she was wild. At twenty she had gone for her first moonlight buggy ride alone with a young man.

But worse even than her flagrant defiance of Philadelphia respectability was another passion totally unsuited to a young woman raised in the tall old houses around Rittenhouse Square.

She wanted to work.

Her superabundant energies had longed for this outlet as far back as she could remember. She wanted to contribute to the bustling life around her. She wanted to serve. She wanted to join in facing the challenges of the modern age, of the new century coming on. Other little girls read manuals of conduct for young ladies, or *Faith Gartney's Girlhood*. Elizabeth read Horatio Alger.

"Work" in her level of Philadelphia society had a very special meaning. It was something the heads of families did—Biddles and Whartons and Cadwaladers and Ingersolls—portly gentlemen who strolled down daily to their law offices on Walnut or Broad, or to the marble-fronted facades of the great banks and trust companies on Chestnut. And this wasn't what Elizabeth meant by work at all.

She wanted to work with her hands.

Not heavy physical work, of course. But something that would genuinely challenge the eye and the hand, the physical self that was so important a part of her. The physical self that was so totally denied by the standards and taboos of her Philadelphia world at that time.

She thought about the decorative arts, or even journalism. She imagined herself rushing around the city gathering "stories" for the *Evening Telegraph*. Then she came upon a picture in an illustrated magazine of the first women medical students ever accepted at Bellevue Hospital in New York.

It was a stiffly posed photograph of half a dozen young women in flowing skirts and high-piled hair grouped around a chastely sheeted cadaver. A bearded instructor, holding some sort of dissecting instrument, stood behind them. These young ladies, the caption explained, would join the small but growing numbers of female doctors who were currently swelling the ranks of the medical profession, especially in gynecological practices and children's hospitals.

Here was service, she thought. Here was challenge. And there was already a Women's Medical College right there in Philadelphia.

After a dozen stormy interviews with Aunt Grace, Uncle Benjamin tut-tutting in the background, she won the right to try. And try she did, for almost two years, before her labors were suddenly and brutally interrupted. Before Aunt Grace broke her niece's determination at last by the simplest and most direct of means, and an embittered Elizabeth had begun to spend even more of her time on those moonlight buggy rides.

There was, it became increasingly obvious, only one real exception to the rigid prohibition of work for a decent Philadelphia girl—most particularly for the Reverend Rowntree's daughter. One sort of work was certainly open to Elizabeth, if she felt the calling for it: God's work. If He spoke to her in her heart, if He urged her to take up the cross her father had borne so long and selflessly, she would be more than welcome in the mission field.

She lay awake on moonlit nights in her white bed, looking out at the silvered leaves whispering beyond her third-floor window, and waited with tears for that call to come. Somehow it never did.

And yet here she was, in Peking, about to set out for the Protestant Board Mission and the father she could only remember clearly seeing once in her life. The life that she was starting over at twenty-three—in the mission field.

Elizabeth pressed her lips together and smoothed the chemise down over her slender body. Then she turned away from the mirror and reached for the black satin corset that lay, with the petticoats and the long white frock, spread out across the bed.

6

"YOU ARE MISS ELIZABETH."

A small, slender Chinese girl stood in the arched gateway of the courtyard. She had a round face, perfect porcelain skin, shining black hair pulled back tightly into a Manchu bun behind her head. She wore a black silk Chinese gown and trousers, with only a single ornament—a small silver cross on her breast. Her smooth-lidded eyes were perfectly expressionless.

"I am An Lin. Please come this way."

Elizabeth followed, breathing quickly. Her heart felt as though it was beating at least twice its normal rate.

She had hurried off up Legation Street to the Protestant Board Mission immediately after breakfast. The grey-walled legation compounds, the handful of Western shops, the European bank or two which lined Peking's only paved, lamplit street had blurred to her oblivious eyes as she hastened on her way. She had not even noticed the splendid Hôtel de Pékin, two whole stories in height, or the famous stone lions in front of the French Legation. Her nose had scarcely registered the reek of the Imperial Canal, which intersected Legation Street at the heart of the Quarter, as she hurried along, her parasol aslant against the morning sun.

Her ears echoed Sarah Conger's meaningless injunction to "stay out of the *hutungs*, my dear"—the tangled maze of Chinese lanes and alleyways that opened out on all sides of the Legation Quarter. Her eyes were fixed on the sunglare off the metal roof of the mission church at the far end of the street, well outside the confines of the Quarter itself. Deaf to the chattering of the Mongol market, blind to colorful robes and the coolies' hats, she had hurried on her way.

Now she was there, and she was terrified.

She followed An Lin through a whole series of small court-yards grouped in the shadow of the tin-roofed brick church. They paused in one whitewashed yard as a procession of Chinese schoolgirls paraded by, chanting a hymn in sweet, high voices. Another walled court was lined with blank-faced Chinese mothers and stoical children, waiting their turns to enter a low door that seemed to lead to some sort of dispensary. Then they were inside the mission buildings, passing reading rooms and offices, entering at last what seemed to be a corridor of private apartments. An Lin rapped on a door at the end of the hall. A voice, clear and friendly, told them to come in.

Feeling as if she were walking in a dream, Elizabeth followed the Chinese girl across the threshold.

A man was sitting behind a worktable at the end of a long, book-lined room, sorting tracts. He was a slim, youngish man in a clerical collar, with prematurely grey hair and the bright smile of one who is genuinely eager to please.

"Miss Rowntree!" he exclaimed, rising and extending a bony hand. "I'm so happy to meet you at last. My name is Rogers, Manson Rogers. Reverend Manson Rogers," he added, almost as if he were unsure of his right to the title. "I hope you're comfortable at the Congers'?"

"Quite comfortable, thank you," said Elizabeth mechanically.

"Good, good. Your father thought you might stay on there for the time being, if you don't mind. Their facilities are so much better than ours, you know."

"Yes, of course."

There was a moment's awkward silence.

"May I see my father now?" said Elizabeth.

"Oh, but he's not here," the young minister answered, startled. "Didn't you know? An Lin, didn't you send that boy up to the American Legation with the message?"

"I sent him before breakfast," the Chinese girl replied in her precise, almost too clear intonation. And then, with the slightest edge to her voice, the faintest slurring of the final consonant: "He shall be punish."

"Not here?" said Elizabeth. She felt a sudden emptiness growing inside her. "My father is not back yet?"

"Oh, he will be here soon enough, of course," Manson Rogers assured her. "Any day, next week at the latest. I have his letter here"—he patted a long envelope lying behind the pile of tracts on his left—"right here, assuring us he will be back to—to receive you."

"I see," said Elizabeth.

"He was very deeply involved in setting up a new outstation near T'ai Shan in Shantung—that's the next province south of here. He wasn't absolutely certain precisely when he could get away. He did hope to be home by today, but"—Reverend Rogers shrugged helplessly—"you see he hasn't made it."

Abruptly, Elizabeth began to feel more than a little ridiculous.

"Well," she said more briskly, "if you will let me know as soon as he does arrive—"

"Of course, of course we will. For now, though," Rogers added, his face brightening, "your father did suggest in his letter that, if you seemed suitable—suitably disposed, that is —you might care to take up some of your duties here in advance of his return. Just to get used to the place, and to the sort of thing that we—" He hesitated, his face suddenly anxious. "You were planning to work here, weren't you, Miss Rowntree?"

Well, Elizabeth Rowntree thought, smothering the sense of emptiness and betrayal, that *is* what I came for, isn't it?

"Yes, of course," she said, in her best professional voice. "If I may have a day to recuperate, I shall be in in the morning."

"Splendid. Splendid. You can begin by helping An Lin with the girls' school. Bible school, you know, and reading."

He ran a thin hand nervously through his greying hair, obviously relieved. "An Lin, why don't you—"

He brushed past the American girl to speak to the young Chinese woman. As he passed, Elizabeth saw another long envelope in the clutter on the worktable, this one not from but *to* the Reverend Thomas Rowntree. It was addressed in a tight, crabbed hand that Elizabeth knew only too well. Impulsively, scarcely thinking, she reached out and picked the letter up and popped it into her reticule.

"If you will come this way, then," Rogers said, nervously touching her elbow, "I'll show you out myself. You get a good afternoon's rest at the Congers', and a good night's sleep, and then—"

Feeling even more dreamlike than when she had entered, Elizabeth Rowntree allowed herself to be led out of her father's workroom and back down the hall toward the alien sunshine that blazed in the courtyard beyond.

"We all vastly admire your father here, you know, Miss Rowntree," Reverend Manson Rogers assured her as he showed her out through the maze of corridors and courtyards. His eyes sparkled as he warmed to his subject. "To think he has spent more than forty years of his life in the China mission! Almost all of it, until very recently, in the most isolated outstations, the most desolate and unprofitable vineyards to labor in. And they bloomed under his hands, Miss Rowntree —they positively bloomed!

"Oh, there are those that say he is a bit autocratic. A bit old-fashioned, too much perhaps for the letter of the Gospel, too little interested in the *material* welfare of the Chinese. But there are Chinese like An Lin who would die for him, quite literally."

"She seems quite devoted," said Elizabeth without enthusiasm.

"Indeed, indeed. He baptized her, some twenty-odd years ago—long before my time. She was a foundling, parents carried off in some epidemic or other. He has been father, mother, teacher, spiritual counselor to her all her life. She is his right hand here at the mission, and a dedicated Christian. I'm sure the two of you will get along famously."

Elizabeth made no comment. Somehow, remembering those black, implacable eyes, the faint edge to that voice—*he shall be punish*—she had her doubts.

Then, as they passed through the glaring whitewashed court that served as a waiting room for the mission dispensary, Elizabeth heard a familiar voice through an open doorway. A familiar voice speaking in Chinese. With a quick "Oh, wait!" to Manson Rogers, she darted in at the door.

"Miss Rowntree!" said Dr. Chen Li, looking up from the mother and thin-faced child before him. "So you have found your way here."

"Yes, of course. But I did not know that you worked for the mission too, Dr. Chen."

"I do not, Miss Rowntree," he answered, smiling. "I have my own practice in the city. But I do stop in two or three times a week, to help out."

"Dr. Chen is too modest," said Reverend Rogers, following Elizabeth in out of the sun. "He handles all the more serious cases. Anything more difficult than a simple cut or a clean break is quite beyond our medical orderlies, I'm afraid. Without Dr. Chen's help, we should be quite lost."

Elizabeth's eyes moved quickly about the room, taking in the crude examining table, the rudely made cabinets, the simple equipment. Philadelphia Women's College at its most deprived had been better equipped than this, she thought. But there was something immensely reassuring about this familiar apparatus of glass and metal in the general overwhelming alienness of Peking.

"Our facilities are very limited, I'm afraid," said Dr. Chen, following her eyes. "We can handle worms and skin diseases, but when the smallpox or the typhoid strikes—we must seek outside help." His eyes were suddenly somber, as they had been at the Chien Men Gate, when he had spoken of the "troubles" along the railway line, or the autocratic Empress who lived behind the red walls of the Forbidden City.

Then his smile warmed again, and he was speaking to her once more. "Pardon me, Miss Rowntree, but have you yourself perhaps had some medical experience?"

"Why, yes," she said. "That is, I attended medical school —for a year and a half. But how did you know?"

"You seemed to be looking in the right places," he answered, "for things that aren't here but should be." Then, turning more thoughtful once again, the Chinese doctor added, "I hope we can persuade your father to put your training to good use here in the dispensary. Your God surely knows," he concluded with a nod to Reverend Rogers, "that we seldom get such a useful talent here in Peking."

"That's true enough," said Rogers ruefully. "We get salesmen from the West in plenty, and diplomats to dicker for them, and poor missionaries like myself, and soldiers to defend us all. But few enough doctors, for a land that sometimes seems to be beset by all the plagues of Egypt at once."

The mother and her emaciated child had been waiting patiently through all this, and Elizabeth knew it was time to go.

"I shall speak to my father about helping here," she told Dr. Chen, "as soon as he gets back to Peking."

"He has not returned?"

"Why, no. Not yet." She looked Chen in the face, and all her uneasiness rushed back. "Should he have?" she said quickly.

But Chen merely smiled, as Rogers had, and said: "Your father, Miss Rowntree, will be where his duty takes him. But he will be back soon, I'm sure."

Elizabeth was just emerging from the mission gate when

she almost walked straight into Sergeant Michael Connor.

"Sergeant!" she gasped, as he materialized out of the dust and jabber and swirling color of the street.

"Ma'am," he said, touching his wide-brimmed hat.

"You startled me." She opened her parasol against the oppressive noontime heat. "When did you get back from Tientsin?"

"This morning, ma'am."

She studied him as she set her umbrella at the proper angle against the sun. There was something about this unprepossessing Irishman that irritated her profoundly.

He was certainly less the spit-and-polish Marine this afternoon than at their first encounter. His puttees were dusty, the sleeves of his blue shirt with the yellow chevrons rolled to the elbows. But his responses, though clipped and brief, were polite enough. He stood quietly before her, his wiry frame seemingly at perfect ease, his lean features calm.

He was, she realized abruptly, simply waiting for her to dismiss him! It was part of his job to be formally polite to her; it was no part of his duty to be forthcoming, friendly, even human. So he answered all questions crisply and courteously —and waited for the inevitable moment when she would grow tired of the game and let him go.

"Well," she said shortly, "I expect I shall run into you again then, Connor."

"I expect so, ma'am. I'll be on regular duty with the marine guard at the legation every other day from now on."

"Marine guard? Isn't that a bit unusual?"

"It is not common, I believe, ma'am."

"Would it have anything to do with the disturbances along the railway line?"

"I couldn't say, Miss Rowntree." With spiteful pleasure she saw that she had shaken his composure at last. He was obviously uncomfortable under this line of questioning. His boots shifted restlessly in the dust of the street.

It was a small victory, but it was something. And in her

"It is all most disturbing, certainly," the British Minister answered the German's challenge somewhat more briskly. "Most disturbing. I shall of course take it up with the *Tsungli Yamen*."

Von Ketteler barely troubled to conceal a snort of disgust. The *Tsungli Yamen*—the Chinese Foreign Office—was staffed by vaguely pro-Western bureaucrats who were known to have almost no influence whatever with the Dowager Empress of China.

"And I am sure," Captain Lamenière murmured sardonically close to Elizabeth's ear, "that the *Tsungli Yamen* will pass on his Excellency's protest to *les messieurs de l'I Ho Chuan*!"

She had heard that label before, in the darkness of the Bell Tower just the night before. She put down her cup of tea. "Will someone please tell me," she asked with unnecessary sharpness, "just who or what this *I Ho Chuan* might be?"

There was a moment of uneasy silence around the table with its white napery and sparkling silver, its little sandwiches and cakes and tea. Then a white-haired old man with a benevolent twinkle in his eyes leaned toward Elizabeth to speak. It was Sir Robert Hart, Inspector General of the Chinese Imperial Customs Service. He was reputed to have lived in Peking longer than any other European.

"The *I Ho Chuan*," said Inspector General Hart, "is the Society of Righteous and Harmonious Fists. Jocosely known among knowledgeable Europeans as the Boxer Society, owing to their odd pugilistic exercises. It is one of a large number of secret societies that have flourished among the peasantry of China throughout her history."

"They're a fantastically superstitious lot, aren't they?" Lieutenant Greville interjected. "Still believe in the old gods spirits of the earth and air, all that rot."

"The lucky Feng bird—the Phoenix," Sir Claude said nodding, "and the Dragon that brings rain for the crops. Gods and spirits far older than Buddha or Confucius." But he did

61

not look at all happy over the direction the conversation was taking.

"The secret societies of today," Hart went on, "the Fists of Righteousness, the White Lotus, the Red Lantern and the rest, are most notable—and most dangerous—for their fierce antiforeignism. They would cheerfully throw every last one of us into the China Sea, and all our noisy locomotives and subversive mission schools with us. A primitive peasant attitude which, unfortunately, jibes all too well with the attitudes —and ambitions—of some of the most highly placed persons in the Forbidden City itself."

"You mean," said Elizabeth, "that the Emperor supports these—Boxers? But didn't I hear that he was some sort of reformer? Quite willing to take advice from his more westernized Chinese advisers?"

"The Emperor Kuang Hsu was in fact a reformer until about a year ago," said Hart, "But in 'ninety-eight he went too far for the reactionary tastes of the princes and mandarins around him—and for the Dowager Empress, Tzu Hsi. She had the reformers executed and the Emperor himself confined to an island prison in the Imperial City. There he is to this day, alas." The Inspector General paused to savor his tea. "Some say he has opium and concubines to console him, and some that he is near death from starvation. But one way or the other, his power is the Dowager Empress's now."

"And that's where the trouble comes, you see." Captain Lamenière took up the tale. "The old Buddha—Tzu Hsi— refuses to disown the Boxers. She's as superstitious as they are, and she hates all of us at least as much as they do. And the miserable princes and mandarins who surround her are trying to advance their own ambitions by encouraging her in this nonsense. Prince Tuan in particular—the worst of the lot."

"Prince Tuan?"

"Tzu Hsi's special favorite. His oldest son has actually been named Heir Apparent to the throne."

"Tuan's the charming fellow," said Lieutenant Greville, "who swears he'll have his sedan chair re-covered one of these days—with our skins. That's all just jingo talk, of course. But it certainly doesn't do the Boxers any harm to have that kind of support at court."

"Precisely so!" exclaimed Von Ketteler loudly. "It is what I am saying all along!" His smooth, plump cheeks were flushed, his *kaiserlich* moustaches bristling. He looked, thought Elizabeth, like a living caricature of German belligerence.

"I think," said Minister Sir Claude MacDonald firmly at last, "that this is not a subject for the luncheon table. Ethel, my dear," he added, turning to his doughy-faced Scottish wife, "did you not have something you wished to say about next week's racing meet?"

The Russian Minister Plenipotentiary began at once to speak about a wonderful Mongol pony which his *mafoo* was training for the next race.

To Elizabeth, his words merged meaninglessly with the *thwock* of tennis balls on the club courts. She let the conversation blur once more in her ears and gazed out the window at the looming grey mass of the Tartar Wall with the clutter of pungent ginseng shops along its base. She wondered why these people all worked so hard to ignore the world they had come so far to live in.

Dr. Chen Li finished up his day's work at the dispensary in the Protestant Board Mission at about three that afternoon. He tapped an emaciated old woman's chest, murmured polite questions, pronounced a familiar prescription, and bowed the last of his patients out the door. Watching her teeter off on her tiny bound feet, Chen found his thoughts suddenly going back to Elizabeth Rowntree, who had passed that way three hours before.

American women, he decided as he washed and cleaned his instruments, were very strange.

Chen Li had known many foreign women on his travels,

when he was a young man. He had studied medicine first at Hong Kong, then in Japan. Thereafter, thanks to an uncle's wealth and his own insatiable curiosity, he had ranged much farther afield. He had studied in Leyden and Edinburgh and London, where he had taken his medical degree. He had journeyed across yet another ocean to study rare Asiatic diseases where they could best be studied—in the United States. And everywhere, on side trips to continental Europe and stopovers on the islands of the Pacific as well as in Britain and America, he had found these amazing American women.

He ticked off remembered instances as he washed his hands in the iron sink. There was the literary lioness in London. There was the temperance crusader in New York. There was the lady missionary in the Hawaiian Islands, carrying on the good work alone on her little atoll with three villages full of seagoing savages. Dr. Chen shook his head and dried his hands on a fresh white towel.

The young lady who had visited him that morning was the purest American type: aggressively self-confident on the surface, restless and unhappy underneath. No doubt a doctor in her own country would pronounce her neurasthenic, he thought with a sigh. Indeed, the diagnosis came naturally enough to his own mind. Such Western concepts were as much a part of him now as his rumpled Western suit.

Beneath that steady flow of alien ideas in a foreign tongue, another drift of thought moved just as steadily and surely. For the mind of the Manchu Chinese he had been raised to be was very much alive beneath the thick overlay of Westernness he had acquired down the years.

The Chinese Chen Li had watched Elizabeth Rowntree walk off across the courtyard that morning and thought of the white birch trees at the end of his father's garden. The graceful curve of the trees, their slow swing in the breeze off the river had been there, in the girl walking away from him.

Their pale beauty was hers too. The pale loveliness—he realized with a sudden pain under the heart—of his own dead wife.

Almost twenty years it had been, he thought, taking off his glasses, cleaning them carefully on his handkerchief. He stood there, shoulders straight, lips slightly compressed, remembering.

Strange that he could not think of Mei Ling without pain, even after so many years.

He had not even been there when she died. He had been in Japan, at the beginning of all his travels, though he did not know it then. He had received his father's letter in his little room in Kyoto, near the university, on a beautiful autumn day. A letter replete with formal condolences, of course, with admonitions to bear the will of heaven with Confucian fortitude. One would never have gathered from the letter how much his father and his mother, his entire family indeed, had hated his wife.

Then suddenly, as though he had crashed through an invisible barrier in his own mind, there was Mei Ling herself. Mei Ling's laughing eyes, full of mischief and quick intelligence. The angle of her head, the curve of her neck. Her voice, like temple bells, and the brush of her mind on his as she spoke. As they spoke together of the life they would have, of the new China they would help to build.

He remembered her as he had not remembered her for years, a living, laughing presence. With a shudder of exquisite pain, he felt again the warmth of her body, the closeness of her in the dark. He felt the two of them together, yang and yin, light and darkness, merged and blended as never man and woman had blended before.

His cheeks were filmed with moisture, his temples beaded with it. Mei Ling, he said her name over to himself. Mei Ling.

"Are you through for the day then, Doctor?" the Reverend Manson Rogers inquired, sticking his head in at the door.

"Yes," said Dr. Chen. "Through until Thursday. I will need more of the Santonin Lozenges for roundworm, if you have any."

"Certainly, certainly. And thank you again, Dr. Chen. I honestly don't know what we would do without you."

The doctor shook Reverend Rogers' hand and went out, across the sweltering brick-walled courtyard, into the city.

"Saw her again today," said Sergeant Connor that afternoon, setting his third cup of pale-yellow rice wine down on the table.

"Who would that be, Sergeant?" asked Corporal Fitz, his eyes bleary, his face flushed with the powerful drink.

"*Miss* Elizabeth Rowntree. The reverend's daughter I ferried from Taku to Tientsin yesterday."

"Ah. The Boston society lady off the ship." Fitz nodded heavily. "And is she still as taken with your Irish charm as ever then, boyo?"

"Philadelphia," corrected Connor. "She's from Philadelphia. Or her old man is, at least."

"That bloody Bible-thumping old puritan! Smell the bridegroom's breath at the wedding, he would, and send his daughter to her marriage bed without the key to her chastity belt." The corporal laughed and reached for his half-empty cup. "But here, you haven't answered my question. Is she still as taken with you as ever?"

Connor shrugged irritably. He let his gaze wander over the dim little dogmeat restaurant with its flayed canine cadavers in the window, its silent Chinese proprietor behind the counter, its half-dozen somnolent Chinese customers. Charlie Dog's, they called it—one of the few places in the godforsaken country where a man could get a drink. In the alleyway outside, a half-naked child wailed, and swarms of flies buzzed over heaps of decaying fruit.

"Does this place remind you of Five Points?" Connor

asked Corporal Fitz. "Or Fulton Street, with dead fish to draw the damn flies instead of rotten fruit?"

"It's much the same," Fitz agreed, turning on his stool to look out the door. "But it reminds me more of that street in Manila. Back of the Luneta, you remember, where the Russian cantina was."

Connor drained his earthenware mug and set it down. "Charlie," he called sharply, without bothering to look at the silent proprietor behind the counter. *"Hung-chiu."* And then, resting his bare forearms on the table and looking Fitz in the face: "Those are the streets we've lived in all our lives, boyo —am I right?"

"You are."

"And for a swell like *Miss* Rowntree, it's been roses all the way. Roses. Not flyblown fruit and crying kids."

Fitz nodded gloomily over the brimming cups which Charlie placed carefully in front of them.

"She's got the world on a string," said Connor bitterly, "and she'd have you and me on a string too, if she could. Like two pet poodles on a leash, strutting up Fifth Avenue ahead of her, or prancing on their hind legs for table scraps at Delmonico's!"

The corporal emptied his cup with a single backward jerk of the head.

"Well, not this paddy, Fitz! Not this Five Points boyo. She'll never get me to prancing for her table scraps."

"And quite right too," snorted Fitz, his cheeks reddening as the fumes of the potent Chinese liquor rushed to his head. "And no more than she deserves."

It was two or three cups later before he realized that Connor had never yet answered his question.

8

IT WAS THE HOUR BEFORE TEATIME, THE HOTTEST TIME OF the afternoon, when the ladies of the legations were all expected to be resting in their rooms. Elizabeth sat bolt upright on the edge of her bed, as she had that morning. But then she had been full of hope and determination. Now she was gripped by a hopelessness, an aloneness so great that it made her want to cry aloud.

She had just read the letter she had taken from her father's desk at the mission. Aunt Grace's last letter to Reverend Thomas Rowntree.

The act itself was revealing. She had never in her life done such a thing before. She did not know why she had done it now. She had simply seen her father's name, and reached out for it, as she had reached halfway around the world to touch his person, to see his face. So she had taken the letter, and now she had read it. And she was sitting on the flounced bedspread, and the hand that held the unfolded sheets was actually shaking, and there were tears forming on her cheeks.

"In spite of everything we could do, her behavior these last years has been absolutely unbelievable." The words blurred and ran. But Elizabeth blinked away the moisture and read on.

> I have always tried, dear brother, to keep you informed as to Elizabeth's general course of life. Yet I have until this present time endeavored to spare you the terrible fears, the horrifying conjectures which have riven my own heart. I could not bring myself to draw your mind even for a moment from your larger spiritual commitment for so small and personal a misfortune as an ungrateful daughter. An ungrateful, unChristian and—yes, I must say it—immoral daughter.

Then it came, shrill and harsh as though from Aunt Grace's own wrinkled lips. The whole torrent of rumors, lies, garish half-truths that all the proper Philadelphians had thought it their duty to bring to the attention of Elizabeth Rowntree's guardians. To dear Grace above all: Pastor Benjamin Rowntree was so busy with his own congregation, and so—unworldly, really—so incapable of thinking evil of anyone. Aunt Grace, thought Elizabeth bitterly, was made of sterner stuff.

I have written you of Elizabeth's insistence on taking up gainful employment despite the generous allowance you have always made her from your own meager remuneration. I have told you of her unladylike passion for the study of medicine, and of my own grave misgivings at her enrollment in the so-called Women's Medical College on Twentieth Street. But I have thus far scrupulously refrained from soiling your ears with any account of the people and of the moral climate with which this mad venture has brought her into contact from the beginning.

Moral climate, my God! thought Elizabeth. A moral climate of disinfectant and anesthetics and formaldehyde, of books with shiny pages, endless sheaves of notes, endless hours of study, till her head ached and her eyes blurred, even as they did now.

Year after year it has grown worse. Dear brother, there has never been a clearer case of the path to perdition taken one small step at a time. From dining out—and drinking wine—at a downtown hotel to supping and drinking I shudder to think what at unprepossessing hostelries on the edge of the city. From bicycle excursions up the Schuylkill by day to rented rigs by moonlight. From the self-proclaimed freedom to work and move as an "independent woman" in the world to—God only knows what unspeakable liberties with the straw-hatted, cigar-smoking young men who come to call for her.

Elizabeth remembered them well enough.

She remembered the straw "boater" hats on the backs of their heads and the cigars between their teeth as they bore her triumphantly off in their livery-stable buggies. Young doctors, young interns from Pennsylvania General, where the girls from the Women's College toured the wards, did their dissecting and most of their laboratory work. She remembered the heavy country meals, sunshine and cider and much laughter of a Saturday afternoon. Then jogging horses along country roads and fireflies over the river in the evening. She remembered heavy arms around her, husky whispers, and the smell of cider and tobacco on their mouths as they kissed her cheek, her half-parted lips.

It had never gone further than that: whispered words, and ardent kisses, the occasional daring caress along a country lane. But that was more than enough, she knew, to earn her eternal damnation in her aunt's theology.

"Dear Thomas," the voice rasped on,

> I have fought this awful collapse with all my strength, and I have failed miserably. She is headstrong, willful, self-assertive beyond control. She has defied me, she has defied you through me, she has gone her own arrogant way. I pray God that you may have that success which we have so terribly lacked—that you may succeed where Benjamin and I have failed.

Failed indeed! thought Elizabeth bitterly. She cut off the funds, didn't she? She put an end to the "so-called Women's Medical College" for Elizabeth Rowntree—if not to the stupid cigar-smoking young men.

Oh, Aunt Grace had won, all right. Won completely and unequivocally in Philadelphia—and now here? Was that censorious old woman to win here too, halfway around the world and six months after her death—through this, no doubt the last letter she had ever written in this world?

70

May God keep you always, and bless you, and help you with this new and terrible burden upon your later years. Until we meet again, dear Thomas, in the fullness of the Lord's eternal mercy, I remain—

Elizabeth crushed the letter savagely in her hand.

So that was why. So that was why.

She remembered her father's brief note, written within hours of receiving the cable announcing Aunt Grace's death—and no more than a few days, clearly, after the reception of this final letter from his sister: "I grieve with you over your Aunt's sad passing." The girl's lips shaped the words silently, as though the note were there before her still. "Under the circumstances, I think it would be best for you to join me here in Peking as soon as possible. I shall dispatch at once funds sufficient to cover rail fare to San Francisco and steamship tickets across the Pacific."

That was all. Not an affectionate word in it for his only daughter, whom he had scarcely seen these twenty years. Yet those words had turned her world upside down.

She remembered opening the envelope in the window seat overlooking the rain-swept square, expecting no more than pious condolences over Aunt Grace's death. She remembered the bolt of joy that had shot through her as she realized what she held in her hand, and what it could mean to her future.

She remembered how she had raced up the stairs, up to the attic at the top of the house, to tug out the huge, dusty old brassbound trunk. It was her legendary grandfather's trunk, brought back from the gold rush days in California fifty years before. She could still feel the sting of her scraped knuckles, the jarring bumps as she dragged the trunk down the stairs. Still hear Mrs. Patterson's amazed warnings to be careful, and her own noisy rejections of any help. And how she had laughed aloud when she had got the thing to her room at last and could begin, dusty and perspiring, hands clumsy with excitement,

71

to pile her gowns and petticoats and skirts and shirtwaists into the ancient silk-lined receptacle.

And this was the reason then. She looked at the crumpled letter in her hand, her aunt's last venomous tirade, reaching across the world to rouse her father to do his duty at last, after so many silent years. Rousing Thomas Rowntree to take up where Grace Rowntree had left off.

No, she thought. She could not, she would not believe it. Her father was not like that, and that was not the way it was going to be.

She had come so far to work at this man's side. To work usefully, productively, using what medical training she had for the cause to which he had dedicated his life. She had traveled all these many weeks, these thousands of miles, to talk to him, to speak to him warmly, trustingly, as she had never spoken to anyone in her life. To see again the half-remembered stranger of her childhood, with his white hair and frosty eyes and sharp New England chin. To feel his hard, unfamiliar arms around her at last, holding her, filling her with faith and hope and strength as no young man's arms had ever done.

She had come so far. She would not give up now.

She would go to the mission in the morning. She would work and she would wait for him. And when he came at last, she would show him she was nothing like the girl Aunt Grace had warned him of.

She drew a deep breath. The fragrance of a plum tree in the courtyard beyond the slatted window filled her nostrils. She smiled to herself, for the first time since the morning. It was going to be fine, she told herself. She *would* begin a new life here in China at her father's side.

9

IT WAS A BEAUTIFUL DRAGON. ITS EYES FLASHED, ITS TONGUE darted, its taloned claws curved artistically. Every scale was executed with meticulous care. It filled the three-foot scroll perfectly, an impressive symbol of imperial power.

The Emperor Kuang Hsu, hunkered back on his heels with the wet brush still in his hand, looked down at the scroll stretched out across the floor and was momentarily pleased with his own handiwork.

The Face That Is Always To The South was a thin, long-headed young man with moist, dark eyes and a weak mouth. His tapered hands held the brush gracefully. He could also paint turtles, and some flowers. But the Imperial Dragon was his favorite subject. He had made many of them, since he had come to the little lake island called the Ocean Terrace.

As the Emperor crouched there over his picture, the screech of bolts drawn back, the rattle of keys echoed through the dim, drafty room. Kuang Hsu rose and turned, drawing his robes about him. He would match the guards insult for insult this time, he told himself, though his lower lip trembled at the thought. The food was execrable—coolie food. He would demand to see the single eunuch who was left him, and complain. He would demand—

A heavy door swung open, admitting a flood of light and the fragrance of many flowers. In the doorway stood the short, squat figure of a woman.

The Emperor dropped to his knees and touched his shaven forehead three times to the floor.

"Venerable Mother," he said.

"How is your health?" The voice of the old woman standing in silhouette against the open door was harsh, her gaze pitiless. "Shall we call the physicians once again?"

"No, Holy Mother. My health is good now. Better than I deserve, Majesty."

"You have no other complaints to make to me today?"

"No, Venerable Mother. Your Majesty's benevolence is more than so wretched a one as I am deserves."

The old woman nodded and flicked her peacock fan. Her small, sharp eyes were full of contempt for the abject creature at her feet—the nephew whom she had adopted as her son, whom she had put upon the Dragon Throne of China—and who had dared to betray her to the foreigner.

She grunted, satisfied, and turned with a rustle of silken robes to go.

"Venerable Mother!"

She stopped, looked back at the frail figure still bent double at her feet.

"Venerable Mother, I am not fit to rule. My punishment is most richly deserved."

She waited, her face stony in the semidarkness.

"Yet out of your most bountiful mercy, Venerable Mother, grant me one consolation. One only."

She waited, knowing what was to come.

"Grant me to have one loving heart to share my confinement, Holy Mother. Grant me—" the voice broke, "grant me to have the Pearl Concubine, Mother. She will come, she wants to come. If Your Majesty will only relent on this one—"

The silken robes rustled once more, and the stocky silhouette was gone. The door slammed shut, the bolts banged into place.

The Emperor rocked slowly back on his heels, staring at the locked door.

The fragrance of the gardens outside faded once more into the odor of must and mold that filled these cell-like rooms. Kuang Hsu turned back to his dragon scroll. He picked it up, examined it carefully, from the flashing eyes to the lashing tail. Then, with a sudden jerk, he ripped the scroll in half. With the same meticulous care that he had lavished on the picture

74

itself, he now tore it to shreds and sprinkled the fragments over the floor.

The old woman stood alone on her marble balcony, fanning herself vigorously and watching the sun go down in a blaze of gold over the lotus-covered lake known as the Northern Sea. She disliked these interviews intensely.

Her gauzy summer robes, embroidered and beaded, bright with flowers and lucky symbols of every sort, almost rivaled the setting sun in brilliance. Her hair was pulled up into the elaborate headdress of a Manchu lady, square-cut, encrusted with jewels. Though she was a widow and forbidden by immemorial custom to wear makeup, her face was thickly powdered, her sagging cheeks and lower lip garishly rouged.

She was a small woman, no more than five feet tall, with a round, sallow face under the powder and a stubborn, mulish cast to her unprepossessing features. With what teeth remained in her head, she was chewing loudly on a mouthful of betel nuts.

Tzu Hsi, the Dowager Empress of China, often paused to watch the sun set over the Imperial City on her way back from these visits to her nephew and her son. She found it soothing to gaze out over the private fairyland which she had ruled with an iron hand for the better part of half a century.

But it was no balm to her today. Neither the lotuses on the water nor the tinkling of the wind-bells under the temple eaves could bring peace to her irascible soul that day. She flicked her peacock fan and glowered over the balcony, one gnarled hand clenched upon the balustrade.

Tzu Hsi wondered spitefully what had happened to the manhood of the Manchu warriors of old. Surely the ancient blood had thinned since her fierce ancestors had come thundering down from the north on their stocky, long-maned Mongol ponies, sweeping all before them in their pride. What had happened to that martial vigor, that proud virility?

Three men had ruled over China in her time—or tried to

rule. Three emperors—her husband, her son, and now this Kuang Hsu, this pitiful creature whom she had personally appointed to sit upon the Dragon Throne. Wretched, puling creatures all of them, miserably undeserving of the awesome mantle that had descended upon each in turn.

Her husband had expired at twenty-nine, beaten by Western armies, his vast realms torn by revolt. Her son had died of smallpox at nineteen, his frail body fatally weakened already by wine and opium and the diseases spread by the transvestites of Willow Lane. And now this wretched Kuang Hsu, with his weak lungs and feeble body, his spirit enslaved to the subversive ideas of the Westerners. Kuang Hsu, whom at twenty-six she had had to imprison for the rest of his life on an island in a lake in the heart of his own Imperial City.

When in three generations of Manchu emperors not one could rule past thirty, something was clearly happening to the blood of the ancient conquerors. That she herself had wrenched power from each of these weak vessels in turn— that her own absolute power was built on their weakness— these things did not occur to the Dowager Empress as she stood there, gnawing her lower lip vindictively and watching the sun set over the Northern Sea.

Tzu Hsi was facing a problem—something she very seldom did.

Most commonly, this sallow-faced old woman thought about herself, her own pleasures and personal vanities. Which of her thousands of gowns, her hundreds of handmade shoes should she wear today? What play should she have performed tonight? What colors should she dress the court ladies in for the public ceremonial next week? These were most often Tzu Hsi's problems. These, or more somberly: What was that nervous tic in her cheek? Should she see that fool of a physician? Why had the moon risen red-orange last night? She must consult the astrologers!

In earlier years, in the vanished years of her youth, of course, there had been the endless intrigues of the Forbidden

City to preoccupy her. And, the gods well knew, there was enough of that still.

Three thousand fat eunuchs and three thousand shrill women, all swirling and fluttering around the spineless jellyfish whom the gods in their inscrutability had placed upon the Dragon Throne—that was the Imperial Court at Peking. Intrigue of every kind flourished here like vines and creepers in the jungle. From the pettiest deceptions of kitchen servants to the bribe-taking of mandarins to the power struggles of the imperial princes themselves, the court was always seething with plot and counterplot.

Tzu Hsi had been through all that. From the day in her fifteenth year when the yellow carts and heralds had come to her father's house to fetch her for a fifth-rank concubine in the imperial household, she had had to claw her way through the jungle of the Forbidden City. From the night when the eunuchs had come to her chamber, stripped her naked, wrapped her in the scarlet rug, and carried her for the first time to the Emperor's bed, she had begun to win. But all that was behind her now, as she strolled on her marble balcony. She had beaten them all. Hers was the hand that wielded the vermilion pencil now, hers truly the Face That Was Always To The South.

And yet there were problems still, irritating intrusions into her private fairyland like the difficulty which tormented the Dowager Empress this day.

It was the problem of the secret societies. The problem of the *I Ho Chuan*.

The imperial princes were for them, the ambitious Prince Tuan especially. Some of the mandarins liked them, some even of the generals. "The secret societies are a patriotic militia," they said. "The *I Ho Chuan* are the people themselves, taking up arms against the foreigner."

"Against the foreigner"—that was fine. But "the people themselves, taking up arms"? Tzu Hsi did not like that. Phrases like "a people in arms" smacked of banditry at best, rebellion at worst. And there were no worse plagues upon the land than banditry and rebellion.

Tzu Hsi remembered the terrible Taiping revolt of her own girlhood. There was a people in arms indeed. The Taiping rebels had ravaged South China for years. They had even borne their dragon banners north, almost to the gates of Peking itself, while the Emperor quailed on his throne in terror. Decidedly, Tzu Hsi did not want the Taipings back again.

And still—and still, there were the foreigners.

Could anything be worse than the foreigners?

Secret societies were bad. But secret societies had not invaded her country three times—four times—five times in her own life's span. Secret societies had not forced their treaties upon her, snatched her tributary states away from her, pried open the doors of China to their merchants and their missionaries down the years. The foreigners had done that to her—to Tzu Hsi and to China.

The Westerners, the barbarians from beyond the seas—they were the great evil. And if the *I Ho Chuan* could dislodge these intruders? Might one not make use of a lesser evil to drive out a greater one?

The *I Ho Chuan* claimed that the gods themselves marched with them. The spirits of wind and water, the great gods of China. What if *that* were true? Tzu Hsi's small eyes glistened at the thought.

She looked up suddenly from the lotus-covered lake, and saw that the sky itself was on fire. The sun was a glowing globe of crimson above the cypress and the pine, the palaces that lined the lakes. The sky should have been darkening to green and blue by this time, fading into the velvety blue of a North China evening. Instead, the dome of heaven flamed scarlet from horizon to horizon.

A blood-red sky over Peking! Did it foretell a bloody sunset for the enfeebled dynasty of the Manchus? Tzu Hsi wondered wildly. Or could it be a bloody end to the foreign intrusion—to all the foreigners in China?

In any case, it was clearly an omen. The Dowager Empress spat the last of her betel nut over the balustrade into the brightly colored flowers below. Decidedly, she must see the astrologers about this.

After that, she would talk to Prince Tuan again about these protégés of his, this rabble in arms that called itself the *I Ho Chuan*.

BOOK TWO

THE
GARDEN

10

ELIZABETH ROWNTREE OPENED THE LARGE-PRINT TESTAment and laid it on the little table in front of her.

" 'The word that Isaiah the son of Amos saw,' " she read aloud in a clear, firm voice, " 'concerning Judah and Jerusalem.

" 'And it shall come to pass in the latter days, that the mountain of the Lord's house shall be established in the top of the mountains, and shall be exalted above the hills; and all nations shall flow unto it.' " She raised her eyes to the rows of Chinese faces, the phalanx of bright Chinese eyes. The girls of the mission school looked back at her, politely attentive. " 'For out of Zion shall go forth the law, and the word of the Lord from Jerusalem.' "

She abandoned the book, stepped around the table, closer to her charges. "Now," she said determinedly, "what do these words of the prophet Isaiah mean to us, children?"

The children waited politely for her to tell them. Two dozen doll-like little girls in black-and-white mission-school pinafores. Two dozen round saffron faces with shiny black eyes and black hair pulled back tight, meticulously braided. What in God's name, she thought, *does* it mean to them, after all?

"In the first place," she began, "it is clearly poetry." Inspector General Hart had told her more than once how much the Chinese revered poetry. "It says that the Lord's house shall be built upon a mountain higher than all other mountains. That is not to say that God lives in a *real* house on a *real* mountain, of course. It means that His teaching, His Gospel is higher than all other teaching, higher than all other wisdom."

"Higher than the teachings of the Lord Buddha, Miss Rowntree?"

It was the small girl in the corner, the one who couldn't

seem to sit still. An Lin had told Elizabeth that this one needed a firm hand. "Very intelligent," An Lin had said precisely, "but slow to learn, slow to accept. You must be strict with her."

Elizabeth drew a deep breath. "Buddha was a wise man, but he was only a man, like other men. You can see that the wisdom of God is greater than the wisdom of any man."

The girl smiled respectfully and said nothing more.

Elizabeth turned with a swish of skirts and stepped back behind the little table. "Now what else do we learn here, children? We learn that the house of the Lord shall be exalted, and 'all nations shall flow unto it.' That is, that all peoples, all the people in the whole world, shall worship the God of Jacob. 'For out of Zion shall go forth the law, and the word of the Lord from Jerusalem.' "

The little round faces looked up at her respectfully, smiling.

"Now I will put the passage on the chalkboard. Get out your composition books, and we will practice writing it."

In the room next door, separated from her own classroom only by the thinnest of partitions, the Reverend Manson Rogers was teaching the boys' class. They were doing a hymn now, in a high singsong chant:

> "Unthinking, high Heaven's just wrath we
>   call down;
> Choosing error for truth, sure we merit
>   His frown.
> If the world its vain customs will
>   never forgo,
> There's a fiery dungeon awaits them
>   below."

The song ended. Reverend Rogers' voice asked a question, called a name.

"And who are the Three-in-One?"

"God the Father, sir. God the Son, sir. God the Holy Ghost. . . ."

* * *

Elizabeth had been three weeks in Peking, waiting with growing apprehension for her father's return. Sometimes she wondered if she would be able to hold out that long, in so uncongenial a role as hers at the mission. She particularly wondered how much more of the rigid tutelage of An Lin she could bear.

The small-boned Chinese girl was a hard taskmaster. Elizabeth's work consisted largely of An Lin's former chores: the girls' school, the servants, the petty daily details of mission life. And An Lin had very definite ideas of how these things should be done.

"You must not let Ping and Yu-Mei slack off, Miss Elizabeth!" she would say exasperatedly. "They think you do not know what they are suppose to do, so they will let small things go undone, you understand? This is very bad for servants. You must be strict with them—must be." Her precise English slipped sometimes under the stress of her irritation. "If small things not done, soon big things not done too. You understand?"

Elizabeth would look at the Chinese girl's creamy skin and dark almond eyes, with the tiny crease between them, and her own temper would flare up. But she would master it. She would press her lips tight together and take a deep breath.

"Yes, An Lin," she would say. "I understand."

"It's awkward, I know," the Reverend Manson Rogers admitted as they sat over tea under the trees in a back courtyard of the mission. "But you must remember that An Lin has grown up under your father's eye. She knows him perhaps better than any of us, his ways and wants and needs. She does these things automatically, and she expects you to do so too. Completely unrealistic of her, but there it is."

"It's her *tone*," said Elizabeth, tapping a fan irritably against her knee. "She treats me like some sort of slow-witted hired girl. I feel—I can't tell you how it makes me feel."

Mr. Rogers ran his hand through his bristly grey hair in the nervous gesture she had come to know well.

"Yes," he said. "That's a Chinese thing, I'm afraid. Something that even so thoroughly Christian a girl as An Lin can't entirely escape."

"What do you mean?"

"Well," said Manson Rogers, looking slightly embarrassed, "in a Chinese household, you see, the man will frequently take a second wife, or even a concubine, especially later in life. When this happens, the first wife has the—ah—compensation of being senior to the newcomer, and in charge of things. The number-one wife is the straw boss, so to speak. And she can make life pretty miserable for the new girl, I can tell you."

"But she's not his *wife*, for God's sake!" Elizabeth had found that she could let her hair down a bit with the younger man in ways she would never have done with the Congers or the older missionaries. "And I'm certainly not a—number-two wife or a concubine!"

"No, but sometimes I think that's how An Lin *feels* the situation, if you follow me." He creased his thin cheeks in that nervous grin of his. "For so many years she's been the woman who took care of the old man. She has been the woman in charge. And now you're here. There's bound to be some—resentment is too strong a word—"

Oh, no, it isn't, thought Elizabeth. She remembered the crease between the eyes, the tightness at the corners of the perfectly fashioned little mouth. Somehow it made her feel considerably better to realize that even An Lin, with her demurely downcast glances and the eternal little silver cross upon her black-clad breast, had her vices too.

Most of all, she worried about her father.

They had allowed two weeks to go by before any open concern was voiced by anyone. The outstation to which he had posted himself was very isolated, at a little village in the shadow of T'ai Shan, the sacred mountain of China. That part of Shantung was some two hundred miles away, and two hundred miles was a long way to travel. And then, everyone knew how total the Reverend Rowntree's commitment to his work was. If something came up, some clear call of the Lord, he would certainly postpone his departure for a few days, for a week.

After two weeks, they sent a messenger south.

Now they could only wait and worry, expecting news daily and getting none. No one would admit it to Elizabeth—or even to himself, she suspected—but everyone at the mission was fearful of what the news might be. A heart attack, a broken bone, anything might have struck him down, so far from civilization.

Reverend Rowntree's presence hovered over the Protestant Board Mission like a living spirit. His words were on everyone's lips, tracts with his name on them lay on every table. His continuing absence made Manson Rogers absentminded and nervous. It put the edge on An Lin's tongue, the sharp line between her brows. One afternoon she was even seen emerging from a fortune-telling establishment in Unicorn Tablet Lane, where she had gone to see the future in a green stone at an idol's foot—something so passionate a Christian as An Lin had never been known to do before in her life.

Elizabeth herself went around in a state of coiled tension. She did her work as well as she could. But her heart beat painfully fast every time a horse or mule came clattering into the courtyard off Legation Street. She slept fitfully and rose unrested.

She wasn't sure which terrified her more: the thought of a stricken messenger galloping through the gate, or the vision of that gaunt old man with the frosty eyes himself, returning to pass judgment on all their work in his absence. With every passing day she grew surer that when the old man did come again, her own labors would almost certainly be found wanting.

11

It was to get away from it—from all of it, from An Lin and her father's disappearance and her doubts about herself and her own new life—that she joined Dr. Chen on his medical rounds of the villages west of Peking.

She rode sidesaddle on a grey mission mule, Chen Li beside her on his rather more elegant black one. He was more Chinese that day than she had ever seen him, she thought. He was positively resplendent in a dark silk robe with Chinese characters emblazoned front and back and a small black skullcap with a feather. The polished leather trappings of his mount gleamed in the pale autumn sunlight.

He turned to her and smiled, that warm, serious smile that she somehow found so massively reassuring. And quite handsome too, she realized, in his Chinese robes. Quite dashing, really.

"I am glad that you could come, Miss Rowntree," he said. "I hope that you do not find the journey too tiring."

"Oh, not at all, Dr. Chen. It's a beautiful day. I don't know when I've felt so good. So—free." She had the most unladylike urge to stretch her lithe young body against the constricting corsets, the swathing petticoats beneath her skirts. To reach up and take the whole sky in her arms.

She still could scarcely believe it. After weeks of the stultifying routine of the Protestant Board Mission—to be suddenly free, outside the brooding walls of the city, jogging up this rutty country road into the hills on the back of a clopping, swaying mule! She filled her lungs to bursting with the dry autumn air, and smiled in her turn.

It was late afternoon now, and the shadows were long. The yellow immensity of the North China plain, dotted here and there with huddled villages, rolled away to the horizon. The Western Hills loomed close over their right shoulders, brown and boulder-strewn, forested in the more distant folds. Off to the left, Peking was a grey blur on the eastern skyline. Elizabeth and Chen were riding along a tree-lined lane that would take them back into the city well before sunset. They had had a full day.

"I hope you are not too weary for one last house call, Miss Rowntree?" said Chen suddenly. "I have promised an old man, very ill with malaria, that I would stop to see him before returning to the city. He lives in that village yonder, on the river-bank." He indicated a tree-girt hamlet off to the right.

"Certainly," said Elizabeth, "let us stop, by all means." She realized suddenly how much she wanted to prolong the day. "What town is this, then?"

"It is Ta Ho," said the doctor. "I was born there."

It was a typical little cluster of mud huts, a dirty yellowish in color, with shrouding roofs of thatch. There was a reed-choked river winding past, a meander of the Pei Ho, with a square-ended punt to ferry travelers across. The wrinkled massif of the Western Hills seemed to loom closer and more obtrusively here. Elizabeth wondered what it had been like, growing up here on the empty plain, with only the reedy river and the shadow of the hills to break the endless sameness of the days.

They dismounted stiffly before a somewhat larger house than she had expected, its front court facing onto the dusty village square, its back courtyards stretching down to the river. A grey-haired woman tottering on tiny feet led them through a guest hall and into a small sleeping room where the father of the family lay.

Elizabeth sat in the shadows while Dr. Chen listened to the old man's faltering singsong, nodded gravely, spoke sagely. Recommending rest and nourishment, no doubt, she thought. The dimness and the closeness of the little room made her drowsy.

Her first intimation that anything was wrong was the protesting bray of the mission mule, followed by hissed imprecations and the uncertain fall of hooves as the animal was led away. They seemed to be taking both animals around to the courtyard in the rear. Perhaps, she thought, there was fodder for them there, or a watering trough. She was hungry herself, she realized, despite the hamper of food they had consumed in the course of the day.

Then the curtain in the doorway was thrust back and the woman who had received them stood silhouetted against the hall outside. Her voice chirped excitedly at Chen. Elizabeth picked up only a word or two, mostly simplicities like "you" and "go" and "them." And another word which she took for "friends," but which might have been something else.

Chen Li rose, bowed his thanks to the old woman, bowed to the old man. Then he turned to Elizabeth.

"Come," he said calmly, "we must go now."

"I believe they've taken the mules around to the back somewhere," said Elizabeth. "I can't think why."

"We will go into the front court," he said. "Please stay close behind me."

His tone was subtly different, somehow. His voice was stronger, electric too with a kind of tension. She followed him, wondering.

They did not go out the courtyard gate into the village square. Instead, they followed the old woman through a screen of dusty shrubbery to a two-leveled grey wooden structure built close against the front wall. The lower level, reeking of dung and stale straw, apparently provided stabling for a pony or a donkey. The upper level, reached by a ramshackle ladder, looked as though it might have been a dovecote at one time. To Elizabeth's astonishment, Chen began at once to test the rungs of the ladder.

"Dr. Chen," she said, "what in the world—"

"They seem strong enough," he said, speaking almost in a

whisper now. "Please climb, Miss Rowntree, and go through the little door."

"I will do no such thing!"

"At once, Miss Rowntree," he said, his low voice vibrant with command. The old woman was gabbling again, with even more urgency. "Do not ask questions now," the man went on. "I will try to explain later."

His hand was on her upper arm, guiding her firmly toward the ladder. She heard the old woman suck in her breath at the impropriety. She herself felt only his strength and her own bewilderment.

"But my skirts—" she began feebly.

"Quickly!"

She put her hands on the rickety rungs and began to climb.

Then the two of them were alone in the cobwebby darkness, thick with the smell of bird droppings and molted feathers, looking out over the ancient garden wall into the village square.

The shapeless open space among the houses was alive with people. Men, women, and children stood in doorways or squatted in the dust, looking out into the square. There was a county-fair atmosphere about it, Elizabeth thought, wondering where everybody had come from so fast.

But there were only two people standing in the center: a man and a boy.

The man was huge, with heavy shoulders and a neck like a bull. He stood with his back to her, his bald head and bare arms gleaming orange-red in the light of the setting sun. He wore a loose red vest, knee-length coolie pants, and a red scarf knotted around his head. His queue hung crookedly down his back, and he had a shiny new European rifle slung over one massive shoulder.

The boy, who stood facing him, was perhaps twelve or thirteen years old. He wore loose pantaloons and a smock-like shirt, a crimson sash and some sort of scarlet headdress —rather like an Arab burnous, Elizabeth thought, harking back to the biblical illustrations of her childhood. He had a slack-jawed, vague look to him that made her wonder if he was ill, or perhaps mentally deficient.

The big man was speaking, orating in a deep booming voice that filled the tree-fringed square and raised a whirring of birds from the reed-roofed houses roundabout.

"Dr. Chen, *what*—"

"One moment, Miss Rowntree! I must hear what he is saying!" Chen's eyes were fixed on the man below with a burning intensity that she had never seen in him before.

The booming voice stopped. The huge arms rose over the gleaming red-scarved head. Instantly a ring of other men and boys with sashes and headbands filtered out of the watching crowd. They advanced, eyes glittering in the sunset, to form a circle around the pair in the center. All of them, Elizabeth saw with a tingle of apprehension, wore swords or carried spears or antique-looking rifles.

Then the big man stepped back out of the ring, leaving the slack-jawed boy alone.

The silence was absolute across the village square.

The boy's eyes fluttered slowly shut. He folded his thin hands upon his chest, raised his sightless face toward the Western Hills, the glowing orange ball of the sun, and began to chant.

"Dr. Chen!"

He did not answer, did not even glance at her.

In the improvised arena below, the boy's wild chanting rose to a crescendo. He fell awkwardly to his knees and began to scrawl weird cabalistic symbols in the powdery dust. He rose again, shouting, waving his arms toward the east, toward Peking. The adolescent youths and young men in the ring around him began to shout at him. Short, staccato phrases, questions apparently, for the boy shouted back. There was saliva on his chin, and when his head was pitched back Elizabeth could see the rolled-up whites of his eyes beneath the lowered lids.

Beside her, Dr. Chen spoke at last, in a quiet voice.

"They are asking him who he is. He says—he is a great man in history."

Elizabeth stared, mesmerized by the violent gestures, the high, off-key shrieking of the voice.

"They ask what he wants. He says, 'A sword. A great sword. The greatest sword in history.'

" 'And what will you do with that sword?' they ask.

" 'I will defend the great pure dynasty!

" 'I will—exterminate the barbarians!' "

The barbarians, thought Elizabeth with a sudden chill. And we—we Westerners—are the barbarians to them.

The boy was chanting again now, lurching about the ecstatic ring, thrusting and hacking at imaginary antagonists with clenched fists. Elizabeth had never seen a boxing match— such bloody affairs were not for women. But the patterned, ritualized hacking and slashing of the boy's thin fists looked very much like the drawings of pugilists she had seen.

"What—what is it?" she whispered. "Epilepsy? Some sort of a fit?"

"A hysterical seizure, I should say." Chen's voice was expressionless. "Not uncommon among superstitious peasants, particularly in an adolescent boy readily susceptible to hypnosis. His confederate can probably put him under with a secret gesture, a private word." He paused. "I had a case of the sort once. A boy who claimed to be possessed by a demon. Ammonia under the nostrils brought him out of his trance quickly enough."

Elizabeth looked over at him in the dimness of the dovecote. He seemed to be talking to himself as much as to her. To be reassuring himself, she wondered in amazement, that this *is* hysteria and nothing more?

The young men with the scarlet sashes and headbands were gyrating wildly now too, thrusting and jabbing in an ecstasy of mock combat. Suddenly one of them stepped up to the boy in the middle of the ring. He held something between two fingers of his right hand. Something that glittered as he held it up, then thrust it savagely into the boy's face, just below the right eye. The boy, frozen in an almost comically fierce pugilistic pose, did not move.

Another youth leaped in, brandishing another glittering point—a pin, she saw now, or a needle. But bigger, grotesquely larger, the size of a hatpin at least. He thrust it in with a cry, just below the other eye. The boy, rigid in his pose of fierce defiance, did not so much as wince.

Two others leaped forward, waving wide-bladed swords over their heads. One struck at the boy's chest, the other at his back. Neither blow drew blood.

"They—they turned the blades," Elizabeth heard herself saying. "They hit him with the flat. They must have."

Before Chen could reply, the big man's voice filled the square once more. The circle of red-scarved fanatics instantly fell back on every side, leaving the boy alone. At the other end of the square, the giant with the crooked queue unslung his gleaming European rifle.

The boy came chopping out of his pugilistic stance, swung round and faced the man with the gun. His head was back. His thin chest, bare now, was heaving with emotion. Elizabeth looked at the twitching hollow cheeks, at the eyes, open but misted over with exaltation.

Then she looked at the man with the rifle.

Her eyes traveled up the gleaming black barrel, the dull splash of sunlight on a leather strap, the gigantic swell of a shoulder. She saw shadows in the cheekbones, a flat Mongolian nose, a glimpse of a wide, wrinkled lip. She saw the glint of a cold eye below the crimson head scarf.

Then the shot slammed out, echoing from the housefronts, rolling off across the darkening plain. She clearly saw the belch of smoke, the spurt of flame. And she saw the boy, standing not twenty feet away, not the length of her own classroom from that belching black muzzle, raise his arms above his head and stand there, unharmed.

12

"The rifle wasn't loaded," said Elizabeth, somewhat breathlessly, as they urged their weary mules to an approximation of a trot up the moonlit road. "He was firing blank cartridges."

"Of course," said Chen tersely. It was the first time he had spoken since they had slipped out of the village an hour before. "You did not think anything else, did you, Miss Rowntree?"

"No, of course not, Dr. Chen," she said. "It's only that he did it so well—with such a flourish. I've never seen a stage magician do better."

Chen nodded. "He would be good at it," he said.

"He?"

"The big man's name is Feng. The boy I do not know. Someone he found in Shantung, I expect. The rest will be their comrades of the Society." He hesitated over the last word, as though uncertain of his English.

"What Society?" the girl asked.

"The Society of the Righteous and Harmonious Fists—the *I Ho Chuan*."

Chuan, she thought—was that the word she had mistaken for "friends"? Aloud, she said doubtfully: "That's the Boxers, isn't it? I've heard of them in Peking."

"Peking," said Dr. Chen shortly, "is safe enough for foreigners."

As he spoke, they trotted around a bend in the tree-lined road and came in sight of the crenellated walls of the city, perhaps a quarter of a mile ahead, beyond a thickening cluster of huts and pagodas. The Pingtze Men Gate would be closed long since, Elizabeth knew. She wondered how Dr. Chen would get them in. But she was sure he would, somehow.

"Feng," she said doubtfully. "Isn't that the Chinese word for the phoenix?"

"It is," said Chen. "The bird that rises from its own ashes. The lucky bird of China. It also means the spirit of the unburied dead, that walks the land and haunts the living still."

Elizabeth felt again the bolt of reasonless fear that had gone through her when she had seen the boy still standing there, unhurt, after Feng's point-blank shot.

"An—an ill-omened name," she said. She wanted to say more, to ask Chen Li what else he knew about the giant called Feng—and how he came to know anything at all about him. But the Chinese doctor's brooding silence discouraged further conversation. And they were nearing the gates now, anyway, black and hard-edged against the moonlit night.

Getting back into the city proved to be ridiculously easy, despite all the beating gongs and bustle of guards at sunset. Elizabeth did not understand what Chen said to the arrogant troopers at the gate, but she heard the clink of coins changing hands, and it sounded more like copper *cash*—the coins one threw to beggars—than silver *taels*.

Elizabeth's head was nodding, her body swaying in the saddle half an hour later when they clopped down Hata Men Great Street toward the Protestant Board Mission and Legation Street. Chen Li's first spoken words since they had entered the city jolted her awake.

"It is very strange. The mission—"

The arched gates to the outer court stood open. Lanterns moved within, and the tall brick church was lit up as if for a service. There were lights in the inner courtyards too, open doors and people hurrying about. Cries and voices spilled out into the night.

My father, thought Elizabeth. My father has come home.

With blood-swollen eyes and dusty skirts, she dashed across the courtyard. There were people in the church. She veered in that direction, stumbled up the low steps, burst panting through the doors. Her father—her father was home!

But it was the thin, angular figure of the Reverend Manson Rogers she saw at the far end of the nave, lighting candles at the altar. It was the servants, the staff, the half-dozen younger missionaries attached to the Protestant Board who knelt or whispered in the square-backed wooden pews. And it was An Lin who turned upon Elizabeth as she hurried down the aisle toward the altar rail.

An Lin—but an An Lin Elizabeth had never seen before. Her small body was taut, vibrating with fury in her swirling Chinese robes. One braid of shining black hair had come loose from the tight bun at the back of her head, and another black strand swung across her temple. Her mouth was an ugly black gash in her face. Her eyes were pits of bottomless pain, of hatred beyond measuring.

"You!" she said, one tiny, taloned hand reaching out toward Elizabeth Rowntree. "You bring this on us!"

"An Lin!" said Manson Rogers. His tone was shocked, reproving. But his own eyes were as full of misery as hers. "Elizabeth—Elizabeth of all people—"

"She—she have brought this punishment and chastisement upon us!" The Chinese girl spat out the words, spewed them out in her agony. "She, this Jezebel from over the sea—oh, he has told me, he has told me—she with her white mealy face and her dresses that show her body, her smiles and her lies! She bring all this to pass!"

Elizabeth stood staring, swaying in front of the maddened girl, knowing and not knowing, refusing to know.

"An Lin!" Manson Rogers' voice cracked out, peremptory now. "She is his daughter."

"No—not she! I am his daughter! I am his daughter of the heart, his real daughter. He has told me many times—"

Tears spilled over her scrubbed cheeks. She raised her hands, hooked like claws, and drew them down across her cheekbones, trenching them savagely with red. Then she rushed past Elizabeth in a flurry of silken robes, fleeing up the aisle, out of the church.

"Elizabeth," Reverend Rogers began, reaching out to her gently in his turn. "You must sit down. I—it is—"

But she did not need to be told. She could see the rough pine coffin, spattered with the mire of many country roads, laid now across two sawhorses in front of the altar.

"A detachment of German soldiers brought him home this afternoon. We should have heard much earlier. A telegram was supposed to have been sent. But that part of Shantung is so— the message was never—" He was babbling, helpless, tears coursing down his bony cheeks now too.

"How did it happen?" Elizabeth's voice sounded tinny and far away, but clear, and stronger by far than that of the broken man in front of her.

"He—please sit down, Elizabeth. Dr. Chen, can you get her to—"

"How did he die?"

"He was murdered, Elizabeth. Murdered with all his people, and his mission station burned to the ground. By the Boxers in Shantung."

Elizabeth felt Dr. Chen's arms catch her as she fell.

13

THE FUNERAL WAS A GRIMLY SILENT AFFAIR. ONLY THE Western community was present, legation society and missionaries of all persuasions. "He was one of our own, Miss Rowntree," said Sir Claude MacDonald somberly. "We are burying one of our own."

Manson Rogers officiated at the simple ceremony in the tree-fringed back courtyard of the Protestant Board Mission. There were five or six hundred people crowded into that walled enclosure, all dressed in black, or in military uniforms with black armbands, black bands around the officers' caps and the high silk hats of the gentlemen. It was a dark fall day, the clouds low and heavy with rain.

"A man whose commitment—a man whose dedication—" Rogers intoned in a shaken voice. An Lin, standing just behind him, the only Chinese present, looked stricken, as if she were only half recovered from a long, lingering illness.

Elizabeth, standing on the other side of the open grave, wondered why she herself felt so numb, so totally without emotion.

It was her father they were burying there. Or so they had told her. She had not seen the body in the simple wooden coffin. There had been a fire, they said. The remains were only identified by the clothing, and by personal items: a ring, a cross. Her heart had skipped a beat at that. If there was no more identification than such circumstantial matters, perhaps it was not her father at all! There were other missionaries in China.

Not in that part of Shantung, they had told her. And there had been more positive identification. An Lin had viewed the dead man, before the coffin was sealed.

Elizabeth had rounded furiously on them then, demanding her right, her *right* to see her father!

But Sarah Conger had held her tightly, quieting her trembling fury. And Manson Rogers, summoning a steadiness she didn't know he had, had told her firmly that she mustn't think of it. There had been—he froze miserably over the words—mutilation. Mutilation of the dead.

Elizabeth had left the room and the house, straight-backed and unseeing. She had stood with her throbbing forehead pressed hard against the plum tree until the waves of dizziness and nausea subsided. Then she had returned to the Congers and the half-dozen leading missionaries and listened without further protest to the rest of the funeral plans. She had felt nothing at all from that moment on.

Now she stood as though turned to stone, the words of the funeral sermon echoing meaninglessly in her ears. "A man who gave his life to the great work . . ."

Then it was over, and the moist clods were thudding onto the coffin lid.

The faces began to pass in front of her, like a procession of pasteboard masks against the tumbled grey sky.

Sir Claude MacDonald again, meticulously elegant in his black mourning suit: "You cannot know, my dear child, how much this shocks and grieves us all. I shall associate myself most vigorously with Mr. Conger's protest to the *Tsungli Yamen*. Indeed, I shall carry that protest to the Dowager Empress herself!" He smoothed his long moustaches with thin white fingers. "In the spirit of continuing Anglo-American collaboration in the Far East—"

Lady MacDonald, a no-nonsense Scottish woman, plucked at his sleeve.

The thick moustaches and Teutonic blue eyes of the Baron von Ketteler loomed up next. "I assure you of this, Miss Rowntree"—his voice was harsh, almost brutal—"you will be avenged! I have explicit instructions from Berlin. Every village in Shantung shall be scoured if need be, but we shall find them. They shall pay for this crime against civilization."

"I do not think my father," she heard herself answer him, "would wish there to be—any more violence or suffering."

"Miss Rowntree," he said, his eyes opaque, "the German imperial authorities in Shantung are most sensible of this stain upon their honor. You shall be avenged."

The heels clicked, the head bowed as if it were hinged at the neck, and he was gone.

Reverend Manson Rogers was there now, with An Lin like a pale-faced ghost at his side. They both looked lost, Elizabeth thought, like children together, though Rogers was probably twice the Chinese girl's age. Elizabeth felt somehow that she should be offering her condolences to them, instead of the other way around.

"The depth of our loss," Rogers was saying, "you cannot know . . ." Elizabeth stopped trying to follow. His voice was unsteady, his cheeks thinner even than before. "I shall try," he said, "God knows I shall try to carry on for him here at the mission. But no one can ever truly take his place. *For there were giants in the earth in those days*, Miss Rowntree, and he was the last of them." He shrugged his slender shoulders helplessly. "I never aspired to be a giant," he added miserably.

Elizabeth was looking at An Lin. The Chinese girl seemed terribly thin and drained. Her eyes were like black coals, blank and unseeing in her doll-like face. She shivered slightly in the breeze that stirred the autumn leaves above them.

Impulsively, Elizabeth reached out to her, clasped her two small hands in her own.

"An Lin," she said, "I am so sorry. He was—like a father to you, I know." It was the most she could do, the most she could say. Later, she might make more of an effort, but this was all she could manage for now.

The Chinese girl's palms felt dry and feverish against Elizabeth's. Her fingers curled tensely, the bones thin and light as a bird's. There was a moment of silence as she stared uncomprehendingly back at Elizabeth.

"My father is dead, Miss Rowntree," she said woodenly, her eyes still staring. "I have no father."

She pulled her hands away, drew her little body up with dignity, and turned away. Elizabeth watched her pad off, hands concealed in the sleeves of her coat, with Reverend Rogers following unhappily behind.

Captain Lamenière, Lieutenant Greville, the Congers, all the names and faces she had come to know paraded past her, murmuring, muttering, unreal. Elizabeth focused her gaze on the metal roof of the mission church, with its thin cross against the rain-washed sky, and let the faces pass. She was not thinking about the Protestant Board Mission's great loss, or the honor of the German authorities in Shantung, or continued Anglo-American collaboration in the Far East, or even the mutilated corpse in the coffin under the thudding clods. She was thinking about the living man, the man she had never known, and had come so far to find.

I could have helped him, she told herself. I could have worked with him and helped him, and he would have loved me. Now it was over. Mr. Conger would go through the tedious official routine of securing her steamship reservations, and then she would be going home. Home to what? she thought. Home to what?

The last to offer his condolences was Sergeant Connor, standing stiffly outside the mission gate in his uncomfortable-looking dress uniform.

"I'm sorry, Miss Rowntree," he said as he opened the little door in the diplomatic sedan chair that was to take her back to the American Legation, "to hear about your father's death." His voice was as stiff and formal as his uniform. Oddly, she felt that he actually meant the words.

With one foot on the edge of the sedan chair, she rounded on the Marine with all the pent-up fury of that terrible week.

"Don't worry, Sergeant," she whispered through tight lips, "I'll be gone soon enough! Until then, please save your d-damned Irish sentimentality for someone else."

She sank onto the little seat and slammed the door behind her and sat like a statue as the bearers lifted the chair and bore her off.

Sergeant Connor's expressionless eyes followed her, the last of a colorful parade of palanquins and closed chairs, off down the street toward the Legation Quarter.

It was not till she was back in her own little room in the American Legation that Elizabeth got the only real consolation she was to receive that day. It came in the form of a short note from Dr. Chen. A small, businesslike note that did not even proffer condolences at all.

" 'My dear Miss Rowntree,' " she read. " 'I wonder if I might trouble you to do me an extreme favor? Reverend Manson Rogers informs me that you will be curtailing your work at the mission rather considerably. Could I ask you to give me some of that time, to help me with my own work? I refer to my many patients in the neighborhoods of the city, too far from the mission to come in for treatment. They very much need medical help. And it seems a pity to let your talents and your training go to waste.' "

It was, she realized with a rush of gratitude, the very best thing that anyone could have said to her. It was exactly what she had wanted someone to say ever since she had come to China. Exactly what she had wanted to hear ever since she had opened an illustrated magazine at the age of eighteen and seen the photograph of the first women enrolled in the medical school of the Bellévue Hospital in New York.

14

AND SO ELIZABETH ROWNTREE PENETRATED THE *hutungs* of Peking for the first time.

At first it was all a bewildering warren, a labyrinth of winding lanes and grey walls, open-fronted shops and stalls roofed with rough matting, Chinese characters inscribed everywhere—on walls, shops, hanging strips of bright-colored cloth. A clamor of street hawkers' cries and beggars' laments, of laughter and noisy bargaining and shouting children. An endless kaleidoscope of changing smells and shifting sights as she drifted in the doctor's wake from the Sheep Market to Fresh Fish Street, from Eternal Peace Street to Burnt Wine Lane.

Revulsion followed quickly on bewilderment. The pungent odors of leeks and garlic and human excrement, strong enough in the main streets of the capital, were almost overpowering in the narrow *hutungs*. To these were soon added the stomach-turning smells of uncleaned sickrooms. When she sat in the corner of some bare, windowless bedroom, with its cobwebby walls and unswept floors, her nostrils clogged with the reek of unchanged bedding, all her training cried out for elemental cleanliness. She could not understand why the doctor did not call for brooms and scrub brushes, for fumigating pans and floods of carbolic.

Instead, Dr. Chen simply sat there in the long Chinese robes he always wore when he visited his Chinese patients, inanely taking the pulse in *both* wrists, asking pointless questions about the sick person's precise age, stroking his chin and looking wise. Only occasionally, almost casually, did he get down to tapping a chest, gently fingering a swollen limb, asking a sensible question about symptoms. And in the end he would likely as not offer some such judgment as "The element of fire consumes your strength, honored sir. I will prescribe a water compound." And write out a prescription for a horrible treacly mass, to be boiled, decocted, and consumed in half-pint doses.

"What in the world *was* that awful stuff, Dr. Chen?" she asked him as they plodded on to the next shantytown neighborhood.

"Let me see," he said gravely. "For Mr. Hu, whom we have just left, I prescribed four or five kinds of bark, some orange peel, ground walnuts, gentian, and—oh, a number of other roots."

"But why in the world traffic in this—this native herb medicine?"

"The people are used to it," he said. "As they are accustomed to medical diagnosis in terms of the four elements, to taking the pulse in both wrists, to my whole bedside manner —of which, I observe, you do not approve at all." He smiled at her confusion. "If I did not cater to their prejudices and traditional expectations, Miss Rowntree, they would never let me treat them at all."

"But what use is your Western medical training then, if you are not allowed to practice it here?" She was genuinely distressed, and his half-bantering smile faded at once.

"It really matters very little whether you tell a patient that the element of fire is consuming him—or that he has a fever," he explained. "And as for the unsavory concoctions I prescribe—one of the five kinds of bark I sent Mr. Hu's *amah* to the pharmacist for was cinchona. When you decoct cinchona in the West, you call it quinine. It should certainly help him as much as anything can with the malarial fevers that are wasting him."

She asked him no more questions after that, but simply followed him quietly through the narrow lanes, listening to the flow of his talk, absorbing the babble and color of the *hutungs*. She changed the filthy dressings as requested, helped set a broken limb, handed him the European Candy Medicine without demur.

They paused frequently in the streets to exchange greetings with shopkeepers, passersby, old men sitting in open doorways. Chen Li must know half the people in Peking, Elizabeth decided before that first day was over. And he spoke with equal gravity to silk-clad students and beggars on street corners, to portly pewter merchants with rings on their fingers and to emaciated water coolies padding by with buckets at the ends of a long springy shoulder pole.

"You know everyone," she marveled as he paused to exchange a courteous word with the walleyed beggar squatting in front of the Temple of the Sleeping Buddha.

"I told you once," he answered with a smile, "that in Peking, everyone knows everyone else a little. If you stay with us long, you will get to know us all too."

She almost regretted that she would not be staying long.

Chen Li took Elizabeth other places besides the wretched hovels of the city's poor. Whenever his rounds took them near some sight she might enjoy, Chen made a point of showing it to her. He took her to see the dazzling blue dome of the Temple of Heaven in its wooded park in the Chinese City to the south. He introduced her to the hushed marble Temple of Confucius in the Tartar City. He spoke to her more than once of the beauty and vastness and sheer unthinkable antiquity of Peking. "Twelve hundred years before Christ," he told her once, "before Greece or Rome were ever dreamed of, there was a city here on the North China plain. While the Israelites were still wandering in the desert, the city of Chi rose here, and the life of Peking began."

But it was the surging, endlessly varied, incredibly vital life of the city itself that fascinated Elizabeth most.

She learned to love the shifting panorama of its streets that fall. She watched barbers shaving foreheads in the open air,

107

while camels stalked past and passersby paused to offer opinions on the progress of the operation. She ate steaming noodles on street corners and laughed with childish audiences at brightly painted puppet theaters. She watched the endless processions streaming by—weddings, funerals, festivals, with crackling firecrackers and snake-dancing paper dragons. She accepted a cryptic strip of yellow paper from a fortune-teller and listened gravely while Dr. Chen perused the characters and informed her that she would have a dozen children and live a hundred years.

Somehow it was all summed up, brought to a bright, achingly hard focus by the little side-street temple in Seven Wells Lane where they sought shelter from the weather one December afternoon. She followed Chen Li blindly, trustingly as usual into the musty dimness out of a swirl of snowflakes—the first snow of the season.

Elizabeth wiped the icy drops from her eyes, looked around her—and found herself in another world.

It was not a great temple of marble and teak, like many she had seen around Peking. It was only a dusky neighborhood shrine to half a dozen minor Chinese deities. The kind of thing a modern young woman like herself would have scoffed at six months before. But somehow, looking round her now, she did not scoff.

In the center of the dark cavelike room stood several carved and colored idols, mostly of what appeared to be female divinities. Stuck to the walls behind the statues were small, brightly painted images of men and demons, houses, bridges, pagodas, and other objects, indistinguishable in the gloom. There was a kneeling mat in front of each statue, and smoking incense on the altar between the row of mats and the row of idols.

An old man in a tattered robe, with a thin queue dangling down his back, was going through his devotions.

He knelt and kowtowed nine times, pressing his forehead firmly to the ground, before each of the carefully carved statues. Then he took a battered cup from before one of the idols and poured out a slow libation. Thereafter, raising his hands and his eyes toward heaven—or at least toward the cobwebby roof of the temple—he began to chant in a low, surprisingly clear voice.

> "*O mi to Fuh, O! niang niang, ah!*
> *O mi to Fuh, O! niang niang, ah!*
> *O mi to Fuh, O! . . .*"

The snow flurry was over, and they stepped out into the street once more. Neither said a word as they set out upon their way to see what they could do with a case of enteric fever in Cotton Thread Street. But somehow Elizabeth Rowntree felt in her bones that, whatever Western medicine might or might not do, there was help for the sufferer in the little temple in Seven Wells Lane.

15

THEN, MUCH TOO RAPIDLY NOW, IT SEEMED, THE DAY CAME. Elizabeth Rowntree was climbing aboard the little train in the Ma-Chia-P'u station—going home.

Chinese clerks and porters milled about her, Mr. and Mrs. Conger were waving from the snowy platform. There was much clanging of bells and hissing of steam as she plucked up her skirt and petticoat, clambered up the two high steps, and turned to wave once more through the narrow door. Mr. Conger tipped his hat; Sarah actually blew her a motherly kiss. Then the train jolted into motion, and they were gone.

Feeling numbed and dreamlike, as if it were all not really happening, Elizabeth made her way forward toward her seat.

Saying good-bye had been a confused, painful, unreal business. It had been easy enough with the Congers, those friendly, easygoing people who had never really understood why she had come, or why she was going. Sir Claude MacDonald, she thought, had actually been rather pleased to have her go. Her brand of gaiety had been a bit much for the Peking legations, and her recent whim for exploring the *hutungs* with the Chinese doctor had taken her totally beyond the pale.

Lieutenant Philip Greville had bade her a cheerful enough farewell, his bright-blue gaze already seeking among the young and eligible for a new dancing partner. Captain Jean-André Lamenière had brooded over her hand one last time, his darkly handsome eyes clearly implying that they might have meant *much more* to each other than they had.

Reverend Manson Rogers had been harried, but cordial, in his good-bye. He had looked older than that first day when she had come in out of the heat and babble of Legation Street and seen him for the first time standing behind her father's littered worktable. He was older, harder-working, and a great deal more nervous now than she remembered. The attempt to live up to his legendary predecessor was clearly taking its toll.

An Lin, standing just behind his right shoulder, did not look at Elizabeth once during the brief leave-taking. But her presence, paler and thinner, with large censorious eyes, shadowed their every word and gesture. An Lin had neither forgiven Elizabeth nor forgotten her father. She gave all her free time to religious devotions now, and was savage with the mission servants.

Saying good-bye to Dr. Chen had been quite easy, to her surprise. They had in fact never really said good-bye at all. They had simply gone their last rounds together and parted as usual at the far end of Legation Street, at the mission gate. Chen had simply inclined his head in the Chinese way, said the usual quiet *"Tsai-chien,"* and left her there.

It was as though they were not separating at all. As though he would see her the very next day, he in his Chinese robe and padded coat, with the incongruous Western medical bag, she in her long fur-lined redingote, for their regular rounds of the *hutungs*. It was uncanny, she thought, shivering slightly as she put her hand on the door to her compartment at last.

She opened the door and found Sergeant Connor sitting inside, waiting for her.

Elizabeth had seen very little of Connor over the weeks since her father's funeral. He was not an officer: his duties limited their contacts to the front gate when he was on guard, and to an occasional encounter in the street. And they had had little enough to say to one another even on those occasions.

Surprisingly, she found herself welcoming his presence now.

"Sergeant Connor!" she said. "Let me guess. Minister Conger has asked you to escort me to the coast and see me safe aboard. There have been disruptions along the line, and a woman traveling alone—"

"It's partly that, Miss Rowntree," he said, rising awkwardly

111

in the confined space of the compartment. "And then, I have other business in Taku too."

"Ah," she said, taking off her cloak, hanging it on the small brass hook provided, and seating herself on the seat opposite his. "Collecting supplies for the legation, is it?"

"No, ma'am. Marines."

"Marines?"

"Yes, ma'am. The *Oregon* and the *Newark* are at Taku. Minister Conger has sent me down to escort back an additional detachment of Marines from the ships to augment the legation guard."

"Surely," she said sharply, "Mr. Conger doesn't expect any disturbances in Peking itself!"

"No, ma'am. It's just a precaution."

"Well, Sergeant," she said then, looking him frankly in the face, "whatever the reason for your coming, I shall be glad of your company on the journey."

"Thank you, ma'am," said Connor. He settled back in his seat, wondering how the hell he was going to get through the hundred miles that lay between Peking and Taku.

He had not volunteered for this job. But the dozen or so Marines temporarily attached to the American Legation "during the present troubles" included no other noncom with his experience of the Tientsin–Taku line. He and Corporal Fitzgerald had made the trip repeatedly, receiving supplies or running other errands for the American Minister. Connor, furthermore, had an Irishman's gift for language, including other people's: he had picked up enough Chinese to function on his own, without an interpreter. Altogether, there was no one else to send. So here he sat, with Fitz and an honor guard of half a dozen privates in the compartments on either side, trying to keep a gloss on their boots and their uniforms unwrinkled through the daylong ride.

"How many Marines are you bringing back, if I may ask?" said the girl, dabbing the moisture off her cheeks.

"Forty-eight Marines and three sailors, ma'am. Under Captain John T. Myers, U. S. Marine Corps."

"Mr. Conger certainly believes in taking precautions, doesn't he?"

"I believe so, ma'am. The other legations are also strengthening their guards."

"And you, Sergeant? Do you expect trouble too?"

"I hope there won't be any, ma'am. I like the Chinese."

"I agree with you there," said the girl. "I like them too." The bantering look was gone from her eyes. To his amazement, Connor detected a look of genuine friendliness.

Sergeant Connor's mind was more than a little confused.

He had never been in such close proximity to such a beautiful, well-dressed young woman for so long before in his life. He had painful memories of girls in fashionable skirts and pert little hats riding in open carriages up Fifth Avenue—with never a glance for a cloth-capped Five Points Irish boy plodding by on foot. The sudden friendliness of this particular representative of her class left him hopelessly baffled, both in his thinking and in his emotions. He didn't know what to think or what to feel, and he took refuge in silence.

He set his leathery features and gazed resolutely out the window at the snowy fields of Chihli flowing past.

But he felt the girl's eyes upon him, speculative and thoughtful. What was it Fitz had said—"Is she still as taken with your Irish charms as ever?" Now there was a ridiculous thought. That a girl like this, with every hair in place, and the faintest fragrance of lavender—

There was a violent jolt, a jar that almost threw him off his seat, and then a wild squeal of brakes. The whole carriage slanted terrifyingly, apparently askew on the rails, and came screeching toward a stop. He heard shouts up and down the coach, and louder, flatter, more grimly familiar noises from outside. The train came to a swaying, shuddering halt.

The girl struggled to her feet, her eyes wide.

Connor lunged across the narrow space between them, caught her about the waist, and flung her to the floor. They landed in a tangle of limbs and clothing in the awkward space between the seats just as the plate-glass window of their compartment came crashing in upon them.

16

FENG YU-LAN HAD GATHERED THEM AT DAWN. THEY HAD trudged up the gritty railway line from Anping, with its new foreign depot, its ugly brick godowns. They were cheerful enough, bundled up in their padded coats and wadded leggings against the wind. "A six-coat day," one young man observed with comical exaggeration to another, and the other boy's white teeth showed in an answering laugh. Only the red headbands and the occasional gleam of a steel blade revealed that they were more than coolies on the way to a repair job somewhere up the line.

At the bend north of Anping, Feng had halted them.

He looked out over them through brooding, heavy-lidded eyes. His hundred stalwarts, he thought. Ready to fling themselves with knives and spears and ancient rifles against the iron monster. Ready to strike a futile, savage blow almost within sight of Peking, where the foreigners were stronger and more numerous than anywhere else in China. Ready to strike, and ready to die—though they themselves did not know that yet.

Feng Yu-lan's thick Mongolian lips twisted into a smile, half cynical and half proud.

"My brothers!" he called in his deep, vibrant voice. "Look here—at the mark of the foreign devils upon the soil of China!" He slid a long metal pry bar from the folds of his coat and swung it with a clang against the shining rail at his feet. "And there—see how their works challenge the gods themselves!" He raised the grey metal bar and leveled it at the telegraph wires overhead, strumming mournfully in the winter wind.

115

"The track of the fire-wheel carts shakes the ground, fills the nostrils with its reek, pains the ears with its shriek and its thunder. The iron road poisons the fields. It defiles the graves of our ancestors!

"And the wires the hairy ones string across our skies— they are an affront to the gods themselves. Hear the laments of the gods of the lower air!" In the momentary silence, the murmur of the telegraph wires in the wind sent prickles up the spines of his listeners. "And see here, see how the gods that drift through the lower regions of the air are injured by the foreign sorcery—see how they bleed!" The heavy iron bar swung like a wand in Feng's gigantic hand, to point this time at a line of reddish drops of rusty water running under the wire—the blood of the gods of China. In a poetic sense, thought Feng wryly, it is true enough.

"But the fist of the *I Ho Chuan* is raised against the iron monster. Strike, my brothers! Strike hard and mercilessly, that our ancestors may smile upon us, and the gods may laugh once more!"

Feng shrugged off his padded coat and stood a moment, his massive chest heaving under the scarlet vest, his heavy shoulders bare and gleaming in the first red rays of the sun. Then he rammed the point of his pry between the rail and the wooden tie and heaved mightily. At the second heave, the spike popped out like a cork from a bottle.

Shouts of glee rose from the eager young faces around him. Other pries flashed and clanged; the first rail was wrenched violently out of line. Above them, boys were scaling the telegraph poles, swinging long knives against the trembling wires. There were more shouts and a flash of sparks as the first and then the second wire fell. Axes appeared and began to slam with a dull *chunk!* into the tarry poles themselves.

Feng Yu-lan chuckled and turned away, his eyes surveying the snowy terrain on either side of the track, stubbly with the stalks of last year's kaoliang crop. He had so little time. Less

116

than an hour before the train would come shrieking around that bend.

It came, thundering and wailing, spewing black smoke against the sky. It came with a scream of steel wheels on steel rails, with a wrench and a jar and an ear-numbing crash as the locomotive drove into the crude barricade of mangled rails and splintered poles and ties. And there it stood, the engine shuddering and belching steam, slanting across the tracks, the half-dozen derailed cars tilted precariously on twisted trucks.

Feng unlimbered his German rifle and sent three shots slamming through the nearest carriage windows at random. Then he stood up among the millet stalks and shouted for the attack.

In the skewed railway compartment in the second car, Sergeant Connor raised himself gingerly to his knees, shrugging fragments of glass from his shoulders.

"Are you all right, ma'am?" he asked the trembling girl beneath him.

"My God!" she said in a strained voice, "I—I think so." She sat up shakily, plucking a more sizable sliver or two of glass from her skirts. "I can't believe we're not cut to ribbons."

We may be yet, thought Connor grimly, before this shindy is over. He risked a quick look over the edge of the compartment window.

He saw flat snowy fields, the nearer of them thick with dried millet stalks. Men were running out of the millet, climbing the embankment toward the train. Forty or fifty of them, he estimated. And the same number on the other side of the track, to judge from the noise. Knives and some kind of long spears mostly, though: only here and there a rifle waved exultantly in the air. Keep on waving 'em, he thought, and we'll do well enough after all.

"Sergeant!" said Elizabeth, her eyes round with new appre-

117

hension. "What's wrong? What's happening out there?"

"A little trouble outside, miss," said Connor curtly. "If you'll just keep your head down, and stay away from the window, you'll be fine."

He slipped out the door of their compartment, jarred open by the impact of the crash, and took two crouching steps down the slanting corridor to the next compartment. The door was jammed, and he had to jerk it open. Corporal Fitz and three privates were inside, all cramming cartridges into the magazines of the shiny new Lee-Enfields they had brought along to make an impressive honor guard for Captain Myers. There was blood here and there from flying glass, but no one seemed seriously hurt.

"All right in here?"

"All right as rain, Sergeant." Fitz grinned. He levered a cartridge into the chamber of his rifle and turned toward the shattered window.

"Hold it," said Connor tersely. "No firing till I give the word."

Fitz touched his wide-brimmed hat in salute and settled back on his heels under the window, his boots crunching in the broken glass. Around the crowded compartment, other bolts slammed home, impassive faces turning to the gusty rectangle of daylight, the shouts and scattered shots, and now the more terrible sounds of screaming.

The other Marines were in the compartment on the opposite side of Connor's own. When he got there, the place was a shambles.

Only one Marine was loading his weapon, methodically shoving round after round into the newfangled magazine of the unfamiliar Lee-Enfield straight-pull. A second sat hunched over, spilling cartridges drunkenly onto the floor as he tried to load, muttering a stream of shaky curses. The third private sat bolt upright on his seat next to the broken window, a six-inch sliver of glass protruding from his shoulder just below the collarbone. His young face was chalky, his blue flannel shirt soaked with blood.

Kneeling on the seat beside him, carefully wrapping her hand in someone's bandana, was Elizabeth Rowntree.

"What the hell—" began Connor. "I thought I told you to keep your head down, Miss Rowntree!"

"I know what I'm doing, Sergeant!" Elizabeth snapped back, her face as pale as the young private's. "This piece of glass has got to come out. It has chopped right through the subclavian. The man will bleed to death if I don't get this wound dressed properly."

Connor hesitated only a moment. Then he nodded curtly, scooped up the wounded man's rifle, slammed the cartridges into the magazine faster than he had ever done in his life, and stepped back out into the corridor.

A thin, grinning youth was coming toward him, naked to the waist, clutching a long, curved sword. The blade was already stained gleaming red.

Connor jacked a round into the chamber and fired. The big rifle jerked against his hipbone. The boy went over backward, his mouth a round *O* of astonishment, his chest spouting blood.

Before the crashing echo of the shot had died away, Connor was back in his own compartment, risking a quick look out the broken window, left and right, up and down the train.

The Boxers were still milling aimlessly around the shuddering locomotive or the carriages full of screaming Chinese, shaking their weapons in the air and exulting in their victory over the fire-wheel monster. Others were clogging the narrow doorways trying to get into the cars. One or two had apparently been hit by random shots from the train. They were standing or sitting, staring in stupefaction at their wounds. Not so damn invulnerable as they told you, eh, boyo? Connor thought, his grin broadening.

Only one of them seemed to be even trying to impose any

order on the ecstatic victors. "A big bruiser he is too," the sergeant grunted, levering another cartridge into the firing chamber. Big every way. Tall, wide-shouldered, deep-chested, with outsized features even for so huge a man. "And ugly as the very devil, as the old man would say." But the big Chinese was barking orders in a booming drill-sergeant voice, and he held his shiny Mauser rifle as if he knew what to do with it.

Connor brought the Lee-Enfield to his shoulder and laid his sights across the huge, half-naked chest.

"Sergeant, what the bloody hell are you doing?"

He jerked back into the shelter of the compartment and turned to confront a frightened-looking civilian, fiftyish and paunchy, waving a big Colt's revolver. The man's grey walrus moustaches were flecked with spittle, and yellow showed at the corners of his eyes.

"They're chopping the damn Chinamen to pieces back there in the second class, and they'll be on us next! For God's sake bring your men! I know you have some troops—I saw you board them—"

He was babbling and wild, but he was right.

"If you'd bring your people, sir," said Connor, "and hold this car, I'll take my men and clean them out of the train."

"Yes—well—quite right." The civilian disappeared, clattering off down the corridor.

Connor followed him out.

"All right, boyo," he said, sticking his head in at Fitz's compartment door. "Take your men and work back through the cars. You'll find 'em packed in the doorways mostly. Or some may be back in the Chinese cars, cutting up anybody with a foreign haircut."

"Right, sir."

"And watch out for an old lime-juicer with handlebar moustaches and a Colt's forty-four. He thinks he's defending Khartoum singlehanded, and he'll shoot anything that moves."

120

Fitz laughed and trotted off up the corridor, his three silent Marines at his heels.

Sergeant Connor pulled open the door to the other Marine compartment once again.

Elizabeth was kneeling in the blood and broken glass beside the wounded private, knotting what looked like a very efficient improvised dressing into place around his shoulder.

"Williams," Connor snapped at one of the uninjured Marines, "you stay here to take care of the lady. Toomy, follow me."

"Not a bit of it, Sergeant!" said Elizabeth briskly, standing up in her turn. "There is at least one casualty in the corridor outside for me to see to. And then I'll go back toward the caboose. I've heard the most horrible cries that way—many people must be hurt."

Sergeant Connor looked at her standing there in the shambles. She had a smear of blood across one soft cheek, and dark tresses of hair fell loose about her neck and shoulders. Her heavy skirts were red and dirty to the knees, her hands and forearms wet with blood. But her eyes were calm, and the familiar note of authority in her voice was unmistakable.

"All right, Williams," said Connor, "you come with Toomy and me." And then, as they loped off along the precariously slanting corridor: "It'll be like shooting fish in a barrel."

Elizabeth was kneeling beside the half-naked young Chinese with the hole in his chest, confirming her initial judgment that he was dead where he lay, when the sound of the first volley came crashing up the cars. It came in an ear-numbing wave of sound that turned her knees to water. A second volley followed almost at once from the other direction, toward the rear of the train. The howls and the shouts grew suddenly louder, only to be smothered once more by a blast of gunfire.

The massed Marine firepower in the confined space of the railway carriages was louder than anything she had ever heard before. She looked down at the ragged wound in the

121

naked chest before her. For the first time since her first dissection class at Pennsylvania General, she thought she was about to be violently sick.

Then, with a heart that seemed to have gone crazy in her breast, Elizabeth Rowntree stood up. She steadied her breathing with a fierce effort of will. Plucking up her ruined skirts, she went on up the car toward the shooting and the screaming.

17

"IT WAS DAMN FINE WORK YOUR PEOPLE DID, CONGER," SAID Sir Claude MacDonald. "Damn fine work. Everyone in the Quarter is agreed." He sipped his claret meditatively. "Reminds me of a similar instance in the Oil River campaign."

"I trust you will mention this Sergeant Connor in your dispatches?" said Baron von Ketteler. "That sort of initiative must be recognized and rewarded, even in noncommissioned officers!"

"I shall certainly mention him," said Conger, signaling to the Chinese waiter for more whiskey. "But I must say that his superiors here at the legation have surprisingly little use for the man. They say he spends too much time in Chinese drinking shops out in the *hutungs*. No spit-and-polish. No pride."

"Nevertheless," Von Ketteler said, lighting another cigar, "the man's given the damn Boxers a bloody nose. Again, I congratulate you, Mr. Conger. The attack repulsed, a dozen of theirs dead at least, and God knows how many more hurt. All at the cost of one injured Marine and two wounded European passengers. A brilliant tactical triumph—I say it again. Brilliant!"

"There were, of course," said the French Minister, M. Pichon, "a few *chinois* killed and injured in the cars."

"Their own people," said Von Ketteler. "Well—" He shrugged and puffed his cigar.

"One or two things about it all do disturb me, however," Pichon continued. He tented his stubby fingertips and looked judicious. "First, there is the boldness of the raid itself. An attack on a train! And so close to Peking! It is, to put it mildly, disquieting."

Sir Claude, to whom these remarks were primarily addressed, savored a mouthful of claret and swallowed it slowly, saying nothing.

"*Et alors*, there is the matter of the Chinese guards," the French Minister went on. "As far as I can tell, they did nothing at all to protect their own train. And have they been in any way reprimanded? I think not!" He was growing excited, as he tended to do. "It is a very bad precedent to set, *messieurs*. We are largely dependent on the protection of the Chinese Government here in Peking, after all. If that protection is not to be depended on—" He raised his well-padded shoulders eloquently, as if to say: Anything might follow!

"In the pacification of the Oil River," said Sir Claude Mac-Donald heavily, "we faced a comparable situation. And yet, with a force of only—"

Baron von Ketteler excused himself with a stiff bow and hurried off to join the younger officers in the billiard room. Conger and Pichon settled down over their drinks to hear Sir Claude's anecdote out. The British Minister's anecdotes were among the minor tribulations of a posting to this sleepy diplomatic backwater at the farthest extremities of the civilized world.

Fifty feet above the streets of Peking, Elizabeth Rowntree strolled along the top of the Tartar Wall with Sergeant Michael Connor.

They had met quite by accident.

Elizabeth had climbed the long ramp behind the American Legation alone late that afternoon. She had wanted to see the sunset behind the Western Hills, so she told herself. Or to get out of the uncomfortably warm legation buildings. Or simply to clear her head after the bewildering events of the last twenty-four hours.

She had leaned against the square-cut crenellations of the battlements for a while, gazing westward past the pagoda roofs of the Chien Men Gate toward the distant purple hills. Then she had turned restlessly away and wandered off in the opposite direction, toward the Hata Men Gate and the Protestant Board Mission. The top of the great wall was wide as a road, and though grass and even bushes grew rank between the stones, it was ideal for a brisk stroll.

Halfway to the Hata Men, she had seen a dark figure leaning over the inner battlements, looking out over the Tartar City.

"Sergeant Connor!" she called in some surprise as she came up with him. "What in the world are you doing up here?"

"Just looking, Miss Rowntree," he answered, adding, "I'm off duty." The words were as terse as ever, but the tone was no longer stonily defensive. Indeed, he seemed almost glad to see her.

For a moment they stood together on the wall, surveying the twilit city stretched out before them.

Immediately below them lay the Legation Quarter itself, with its stores, banks, post offices, and the walled compounds of the legations. Within these few hundred yards, clustered around the intersection of Legation Street and the Imperial Canal, all the Western life of the city was centered. Just north of the Quarter loomed the red walls of the Imperial City, with the yellow-roofed palaces of the Forbidden City just visible within. On all sides, the teeming miles of old Peking, with its grey-tiled roofs, its walled courtyards, its narrow lanes and alleyways stretched away into the evening haze.

"Is it true," said Elizabeth, "that it is illegal to build any structure in Peking high enough to overlook the walls of the Imperial City?"

"That's what I hear, ma'am."

"I don't suppose you've been inside."

"No, ma'am. Very few Westerners have. Very few Chinese either, for that matter."

"I've heard that it's very beautiful. Parks and gardens and temples and lakes. And the palaces of the Forbidden City at the very heart of it."

"Yes, ma'am. Six square miles of it, cut right out of the middle of Peking."

They were walking now, east along the wall, away from the legations.

"She must be a remarkably strong-willed woman. The Dowager Empress, I mean—Tzu Hsi."

"I expect so, ma'am." Connor drew a deep breath. "And so—if you don't mind my saying so—are you, Miss Rowntree."

"If you mean about that train business—I was scared to death the whole time, and that's the truth."

"Everybody was, ma'am," he said. "But it takes sand to go ahead anyway. And you did that."

She laughed, pleased in spite of herself. "From the hero of Anping, that is a high compliment indeed."

He shrugged, his hands deep in the pockets of his greatcoat. "Fighting is what I get paid for. And then, none of us wanted to get our throats cut either."

"Not the easiest way to earn a living. How did you ever get into it, if I may ask?"

"What—soldiering?"

"If that's what a Marine does."

"That's what a Marine does," he said. He walked on in silence for a minute or two. "Well," he said at length, "if you really want to know, I couldn't get any other kind of work. It was back during the depression seven or eight years ago, in the early Nineties. There was no work anywhere in Five Points then—or anywhere in New York, for a Five Points boy."

"So you found work in the Corps."

"Yes, ma'am. Fitz—Corporal Fitzgerald—talked me into it." He grinned almost sheepishly, remembering.

He could see the poster clearly, as Fitz had flourished it before him, half-seas over in a sawdust saloon on Sixth Avenue:

WANTED:
ABLE-BODIED MEN
OF GOOD CHARACTER
BETWEEN THE AGES
OF 21 AND 35 YEARS

Below this were pictures of men in various exotic uniforms, some in white tropical headgear, some with wide-brimmed western hats. Elaborate belts and drums and an occasional fancy-hilted sword were in evidence. Below the pictures, in large capitals, it said:

SPECIAL INDUCEMENTS
TO RECRUITS

And in smaller print:

APPLY AT U. S. MARINE
CORPS RECRUITING OFFICE

"What special inducements?" Connor had said listlessly, hunched over the last of his beer.

"Bed and board, boyo! And fifteen dollars a month! Have you got that now?"

"I don't," Connor had replied. "But I've got my head on still. And I'd rather keep it on, not get it blowed off in some damn foreign place I've never heard of."

"Foreign be damned!" exclaimed his friend, clapping him on the back. "The only foreign place we'll go to is Brooklyn. We'll be guarding the damn Brooklyn Navy Yard from the strikers this time next year—you'll see!"

That time next year they had been crouching behind a Gatling gun at a railway station in Panama, swatting blood-sucking mosquitoes and hoping a mob of shouting, rifle-waving Colombian soldiers would change their minds. The Colombians did change their minds about attacking, but it was too late for Connor and Fitz to change theirs about the Corps.

Elizabeth laughed and Connor realized to his amazement that he had been telling her the whole story.

"And you've been soldiering ever since," she said.

"Yes, ma'am. Here and there—around the edges of things." The girl cocked a questioning eyebrow, and he elaborated: "Panama. Cuba. The Philippines. And now here in China."

127

"You may have joined up by accident, Sergeant," said Elizabeth, more soberly now, "but it looks as if you've found your work after all."

He thought that over. "You may be right," he said. "I like it well enough."

"Tell me, Sergeant," she asked abruptly, "what do they call you? Surely not Sergeant Connor all the time?"

He shrugged. "Mostly they call me plain Connor, I guess. Back in New York, it was Michael for my mother and the priest, boyo for everybody else."

"Let it be Michael for me, then. All right?"

His neck darkened with confusion—and pleasure. And then he heard himself blurt out: "If you were a Five Points girl, I'd be calling you Lizzie."

"All right, Michael—Lizzie it is!" She smiled.

They had reached the Hata Men, across from the mission. She rested her hand on his arm as they started down the sloping ramp toward the street.

"I have enjoyed this very much," she went on, "you've no idea!" The alternative, though she did not mention it, was one of Mrs. Conger's tea parties, with its endless gossip of servants and scandals. "I hope we can talk again soon."

"That would be fine," he said. "But I don't expect there's much chance of it. The Belgians should have their railroad line back in shape within a week."

"That will be nice for travelers," said Elizabeth. "But I shan't be one of them."

His silence, the slight tightening of his body as they descended together, was interrogation enough.

"I've decided to stay on here in Peking for a while," she explained—realizing even as she said it that she had in fact decided.

"I'm glad of that."

But Elizabeth scarcely heard him. She was remembering the train. She was seeing again the face of a Chinese boy, ten or twelve years old, who had looked up at her so quietly out

128

of his smooth-lidded black eyes while she bound up his wounds. She was wondering too if Mr. Hu's malaria had responded to treatment, and how Mr. Yen's little girl was, who had worms, in Burnt Wine Lane. At the deepest level of all, she was thinking of Dr. Chen Li, who needed her help in the *hutungs*.

When she spoke again, it was as if she hadn't even heard Sergeant Connor's last remark.

"You see," she said, "you have your work, though you didn't expect to find it when you signed on for it. And I think I've found my work as well, here in Peking—where God knows *I* never expected to find it."

"But I thought—it's none of my business, but the general impression was that you hadn't found missionarying to your liking."

"Oh, not missionary work, Sergeant," she said. "Not missionary work at all." She flashed him a baffling smile and vanished into the dimness of the winter evening.

18

ELIZABETH CONTINUED TO HELP OCCASIONALLY AT THE MIS-
sion that winter. But she spent a great deal more time in the
hutungs with Dr. Chen. Altogether, those were the happiest
times she had known since she had come to China.

Sir Claude MacDonald clucked at the "risks"—unspecified
but darkly hinted at—run by a white woman in those dingy
purlieus of the city. The Congers shook their heads, unable to
comprehend how she could thrive on a steady diet of typhoid
and malaria and smallpox, roundworms and malnutrition,
festering sores and broken bones. But thrive she did. Her
medical knowledge, allowed to fade over the years since Aunt
Grace had compelled her to abandon her training, came back
with gratifying rapidity. And she herself began to recognize
familiar faces and oddly pleasant corners in the tangled by-
ways of the great city.

The pleasantest of them all was Dr. Chen's own quiet
garden in the heart of the *hutungs*.

She entered the garden quite casually for the first time on
a blustery afternoon in March. "I have never shown you my
home," Chen Li said quietly as they approached it. "It is perhaps not regular—proper, would you say?—for a young lady
to visit a gentleman's quarters unchaperoned. But perhaps
with a widower far older than you, it will be forgiven? And in
any case, we could both do with some tea, I think."

Elizabeth nodded gratefully. She was weary from the day's
rounds of the *hutungs*, and she had had no luncheon.

Dr. Chen's house, it turned out, was in Seven Wells Lane,
not too many doors up from the little temple where they had
seen the old man pray to the ancient gods.

Chen's garden gate was no different from any other she had

seen in the rabbit warren of the city: a simple, uncarved wooden gate set in a high wall of grey stone topped with tiles. Children played in the street outside, hawkers cried their wares, old men gossiped in doorways. The feathery foliage of trees waved over the wall.

Then Chen Li pushed open the gate and ushered Elizabeth into another world.

It was the quiet that struck her first. There was a gate, an open areaway, and then another gate, leading into the garden proper. Beyond this second gateway, the noise of the city was muted almost to silence. She stood on the flagstones looking around her at trees, pavilions, pools, and rocks. She breathed deeply, filling her lungs with the mingled odors of cold water, moist vegetation—and peace.

The general plan of Chen's home was that of any well-off Chinese home in Peking. There was a sprawling one-story house at the back of the compound, tile-roofed and raised on a brick foundation. There were smaller buildings around the walls, and two or three pavilions scattered through the extensive garden. The garden itself was the center of the home, and of its life.

It was like no American garden Elizabeth had ever seen. There were no dazzling lawns, no masses of bright flowers here. The predominant colors were pale green and grey, accented by dusty tile and the gleam of lacquered beams in the buildings and pavilions. There were ancient trees growing through round holes in the worn paving, and many shrubs and ferns in earthenware pots. There were twisted heaps of rock too beautiful to be accidents. Goldfish flashed just beneath the surface of the lotus pools, and birds sang in the branches, some in lovely cages, some flying free.

Scattered throughout this pastel paradise were carved stone benches and small open pavilions, supported by painted and lacquered pillars, decorated with hanging scrolls inscribed in Chinese characters.

With smiling circumspection, Chen seated Elizabeth in one of the open pavilions beside a lotus pool.

"You can tell the Congers," he said solemnly, "that you have never set foot in my house! And besides, it is quite pleasant out here this afternoon." He clasped his hands in front of his chest in the Chinese way, bowed, and padded off to give suitable instructions to his servant.

Pleasant! thought Elizabeth, settling gratefully onto a smooth stone seat. It is heaven!

That is precisely what it was to be for her in the weeks to come.

Dr. Chen brewed tea for them himself, with rather more ceremony than she had ever seen him lavish on anything before.

"It is black leaf Congou," he explained gravely, "from the Wuning Valley. It is my main extravagance and sole vice. The water," he added, "I have brought from a well in the Western Hills to which I am particularly partial." He poured the water, just reaching a boil, over the dark, wrinkled leaves. "There are connoisseurs," he said, "who feel that this is the best tea in China."

Afterward they talked.

In the days to come, Elizabeth would pour out the entire story of her troubled, frustrated, aspiring life in that little Chinese garden, sitting in the pavilions or on the benches, strolling the worn stone paths. That first day she talked mostly about her father—and the failure of her trip to China.

"I could have been a daughter to him, Dr. Chen. I could have learned to help him in his work. I could have done everything that An Lin did for him. If only he hadn't died—I could have been his daughter after all."

"That is really not true, you know," said Chen Li quietly.

"What?"

"The Reverend Rowntree had shaped An Lin in his own

132

image over all the years of her life. She was his real daughter, Elizabeth, in a way that you could never be."

The words should have wounded her deeply, she knew. But they did not. She knew suddenly and absolutely that they were true. And it no longer hurt her to realize it.

"An Lin has sacrificed a great deal for her faith," Chen went on. "She could have no family, no friends outside the mission. Your father was all these to her, and more. And then you came, and threatened to take him away from her."

"I understand," said Elizabeth. "It's only," she added, looking down into the pool, "that I had no one else either. This journey to China was supposed to solve all my problems. And now it hasn't."

"Do you see that scroll just above your head?" Chen Li inquired abruptly.

The girl looked up at the strip of Chinese characters hanging from the painted roof beams of the little pavilion in which they sat. She had picked up some smattering of spoken Chinese over the months, but the complexities of Chinese brushstrokes still defeated her utterly.

"It is a saying of the Lord Buddha," said Chen. "It reads: 'Therefore, O Ananda, be ye lamps unto yourselves. Seek no external refuge, but hold fast to the Truth as your refuge and your lamp, and work out your own salvation.' Most inadequately translated, of course."

The words echoed in her mind. *Be ye lamps unto yourselves . . . and work out your own salvation.*

"Brave words for the Lord Buddha," she said. "But few among us can do without some external refuge." She thought, but did not say: Like this garden, where I am so safe and happy.

"Perhaps," he answered. "And yet in the end we all do work out our own salvations, I think."

"But how?" she demanded. "How, if we have not the wisdom, not the force? It takes strength to save yourself, Dr. Chen.

And where is the strength to come from if you do not have it?"

His sculptured face was turned full toward her. His mouth and cheekbones, his wide forehead were completely relaxed, without a line, without a wrinkle. His eyes were calm and deep and full of peace.

"The *Tao Te Ching* of Lao-tzu is one of the wisest books I know," he said. "Its answer to all such questions as yours is very simple, though astonishingly difficult for the Western mentality to grasp, apparently." He paused a moment, and then recited:

> "Those who flow as life flows know
> They need no other force."

A goldfish glided among the long green stems of the lotus leaves. Elizabeth could almost feel the spring sap stirring in all the trees around her, as she could feel the quick, heavy beat of the blood in the wrist beneath her fingertips.

The flow of life. If she could only learn to believe in it— to trust it.

"Were the maxims of the *Tao* part of your Eastern upbringing then, Dr. Chen?" she asked, striving for a more neutral tone than she could feel.

"No," he answered. "I became a student of the Way only later in life, when I was a grown man." Again the infinitesimal pause. "Right after my wife Mei Ling died, to be precise."

Looking into that calm face, she saw suddenly, beneath the impregnable strength of the man, such pain and love and passion mastered that she trembled as she sat there. It lasted a moment only, that eye blink of revelation. But for that moment, she was vitally, passionately conscious of the man behind the dedicated doctor to the poor, behind the sage in Chinese robes. A man who had lived even as she lived now, rent by passions beyond his control, torn by suffering such as she had never known. A man who had found his own way back to life, who had made his own salvation.

Right after my wife died . . . my wife, Mei Ling.

Elizabeth returned to the legations that afternoon with her heart in a tumult that she could scarcely put a name to. There was joy and wonder there, and hope. And something more, something she had never felt before.

She almost walked right past Sergeant Connor, dawdling about in the shadow of the Hata Men Gate catty-corner from the mission, without even seeing him.

"Miss Rowntree—Lizzie!" he said as she emerged from Ailanthus Tree Lane, her parasol tilted forgotten over her shoulder, her skirts accumulating quite unnecessary amounts of yellow mud from the unpaved street. "Will you have a bit of fruit? These Peking pears are the best this side of Oregon!" He scooped up a pair of the large white pears from a handy stall, spilling copper coins into a vendor's hands.

"Oh—hello, Michael." She seemed vaguely disoriented. "Why, thank you. That would be very nice."

They strolled together up Legation Street, munching the fruit.

Michael Connor's heart was unaccountably full as they walked along together, not speaking, each lost in private thoughts. He hadn't felt so good since the day his father bought him his first beer in Tom Summer's Saloon.

Elizabeth Rowntree smiled at his occasional sallies. But her mind was half a mile away, in the grey-and-green garden beside the lotus pool.

In the house at the end of the garden in Seven Wells Lane, Chen Li bowed very low before a simple stone shrine. A pointless, even a blasphemous shrine by Chinese standards, since it honored no ancestors of his. It was a tablet set up to the living memory of the woman he had known for three short years so many years ago. A tablet to the bright-faced, eager girl Mei Ling, whose coming and whose passing had scarred his life as no other event in all his forty and more years of living had done.

He spoke to her silently now, there on his knees. Spoke to her as he had in life, easily, confidently, consulting her on a matter of grave importance.

The passing of this girl so long ago had plunged a dagger into his heart. It had been there ever since, transfixing him, paralyzing him, closing his heart to joy. Now another had come into his life. A pale young woman from beyond the seas who had opened his heart again, as it had not been opened since Mei Ling had left him forever.

Had he the right to take such happiness once more?

He stared at the enigmatic carven stone, and wondered.

19

IT TOOK ELIZABETH A SURPRISINGLY LONG TIME TO PUT A name to what was happening to her. When she did, it left her feeling stunned and breathless—and full of trembling urgency.

She was talking to Polly Condit Smith, a new girl in the legations. Polly had come out that spring to visit her fiancé, a young attaché on the American staff. She was three years younger than Elizabeth—just turned twenty—and she had instantly adopted the older girl as her special confidante.

"A girl I know at home," said Polly, dabbing her face gently with a warm cloth, "used to say that kissing a man without a moustache was like eating an egg without salt. Isn't that awful?"

It merely sounded stupid to Elizabeth. She went on brushing her hair, pretending to keep count of the strokes and letting the pretense excuse her from comment.

"But being in love is so much more than that," Polly went on, helping herself to a dab of Elizabeth's cold cream. "Don't you think so?"

It was a moist evening in early May. Polly Smith, who occupied the guest room next to Elizabeth's, had taken to coming in for a talk over the later stages of her preparations for bed every night.

"More than what, Polly?" said Elizabeth absently. She felt good enough these days to tolerate even this gushy girl's prattle.

"More than kissing, silly. Kissing and—oh, you know. I mean, you're a *nurse*, Elizabeth. You *do* know." Polly, a small, plump girl, looked down self-consciously and smoothed her negligée. "But love is so much more, so much finer, than *that*."

Elizabeth remembered the high-flown sentiments the young men with the cigars and the straw hats had murmured to her between kisses. She remembered the powerful surges of feeling that even their clumsy caresses had sent rippling through her body. Was that so little, after all—the earthquakes of feeling she had had only those few intimations of?

"I know I'll be terrified when the time comes," Polly was saying. "But I'll go through with it, and try to please him all I can. Oh, but it's his *eyes* I love, you know, and that little smile of his when I've done something silly." She laughed. "He thinks I'm such a goose. I'm not, really, but I let him think so. Do you think that's wrong?"

Elizabeth couldn't remember a thing about the eyes of the young men in the boater hats, or the way they smiled. They hadn't thought she was a goose though, she knew that much. Most of them had been interns or fellow medical students, and she had generally been quicker in her classes and labs than they were.

The only eyes she could remember clearly, even of the people she saw every day, were Dr. Chen's.

And the only smile.

She put down her hairbrush very carefully. It still rattled slightly on the dressing table. She could feel the blood rising in a rush to her cheeks, mantling her throat and breast.

"Good night, Polly," she said, controlling her voice more effectively than she had been able to control her hand.

"What?"

"Good *night*, Polly. I'll see you at breakfast. Or at the race meet, isn't that tomorrow? Or sometime later or earlier or whenever. But for now—good night Polly, good night, sweet Polly, good *night!*"

She pushed the bewildered girl out the door, blew out her lamp, climbed into bed. She lay there flushed and wondering in the darkness, her mind pinwheeling as wildly as her words had done.

I'm as silly as she is, she thought. Dear God, what would he—

She knew she was mad even to think what she was thinking. But she lay there sleepless until dawn, remembering his eyes, his voice, his smile. Basking, bathing in the joy of what had indubitably happened to her. And wondering what in God's name she would do now.

There were five of them in Charlie Dog's that evening, Connor and Fitz and three of the new Marines off the *Newark* brought up from Taku.

"Personally," said one of the new men, "I'd stick to the old Springfield if I had my choice. It may be slow, but it makes a hole you can stick your fist into when it hits."

"And a flash you can see a mile away," said another, younger man. "Give me one of these new Lee straight-pulls the Navy issues. High velocity, and powder that almost don't make any smoke at all."

"The Krag is fine with me," Fitz announced firmly, and began to sing:

> "Damn, damn, damn the Filipino,
> Pockmarked Khadiak ladrone!
> Underneath the starry flag,
> Civilize him with a Krag,
> And return us to our own beloved home."

There was laughter and a call for more *hung-chiu* to moisten Fitz's throat for another song. All the Marines around the table had served in the Philippines, and they were drunk enough to be maudlin about it.

"The bolos," said Fitz fuzzily, "it was the bolos that scared me, and that's the truth. The damn Moros couldn't hit the broad side of a *nipa* hut with those old Spanish rifles. But in close, with those big bolo knives . . ." He fell silent, looking down at his warm rice wine.

"But remember the Luneta on a Sunday, though?" said the oldest of the newcomers more cheerfully. "With a swell *mestiza* on your arm and a month's pay in your pocket? I don't want no better place to be than Manila with a pocketful of dollars and a girl like that."

Sergeant Connor, leaning back in his tilted chair, his wide-brimmed hat slanted back on his head, was thinking about Elizabeth Rowntree.

He thought about her body first, as he sometimes did before he fell asleep—or didn't, if he thought about her too much. He visualized her wasp-thin waist, the curve of her breasts in the light cotton shirtwaists she wore. He saw again the flash of a black-stockinged ankle under her daring "rainy daisy" skirts.

He sipped the warm *hung-chiu* and heard her voice. The words did not come through; they didn't matter. It was the tone, the rich, easy way she had of talking with him wherever they met, her eyes on his, her ears really *listening* to what he had to say. Which wasn't much, maybe—but she really listened.

Through the fumes of the wine, he saw her lips form words, her cheeks soften in a smile. Her slate-blue eyes held his.

Connor, he told himself, you're a mad Irishman for sure! The words passed coolly, half-humorously through his brain. He was, he thought, not completely crazy yet.

But the slate-blue eyes wouldn't go away.

20

CHEN LI HAD SEEN SOMETHING IN ELIZABETH'S EYES, HEARD
something in her voice when they went their rounds of the
hutungs that day. He had determinedly refused to believe
what he had seen. Yet he was not surprised that night when
his white-bearded servant entered his workroom to announce
a visitor.

Chen laid the *British Medical Journal* down on top of an
exquisite edition of the Yellow Emperor's *Classic of Internal
Medicine,* and turned toward the curtained doorway. His heart
was thudding in his chest, his throat suddenly dry. He had not
experienced such symptoms since he was a much younger man.
Their cause, he reminded himself, had been clear enough to
poets when medicine was still in the hands of witch doctors.

"Usher in the honored guest," he told the aged servant.
"And bring tea for us both. Black Congou from the ivory box,"
he added. She will be chilled, he thought. It is a cool night.
And dangerous too, to come so far after dark. She must never
do it again.

The aged servant bowed and was gone. A moment later, a
shadow darkened the silken curtain, filled it, blackened it from
top to swaying bottom. A huge hand pulled it roughly back,
and Feng Yu-lan bent his massive head and shoulders to step
into the room.

Chen Li blinked only once, quickly, and then his eyes were
steady.

He rose, clasped his hands in front of his chest, and bowed
as Feng did, only somewhat less perfunctorily. To the serving-
man hovering in the background, he said calmly: "Bring
tobacco as well, from the cedarwood cabinet." Then he bowed
Feng to the square-backed chair upon his left and settled back

into his own chair to contemplate a man he had not seen—
with a single exception—for fifteen years.

"Have you eaten?" he inquired politely.

"Enough," said Feng laconically, "and recently enough."

"Happiness to my house," Chen continued the courteous
formulas, "from your visit."

"I bring you no happiness, brother of my soul," Feng's deep
voice rumbled back. "I bring you the greetings of the *I Ho
Chuan*."

Chen Li and Feng Yu-lan had grown up together in the
village of Ta Ho. Their fathers had both been impoverished
gentry, living little differently from the peasants around them
and rapidly slipping back into peasant status themselves during the years when the boys were growing up. The fathers were
in fact members of the same clan, and the boys were distant
cousins.

Looking at the huge, disreputable-looking man across the
room from him now, scarred, wrinkled, raggedly clothed, Chen
could scarcely believe those long-ago days of their boyhood.

Feng Yu-lan had been outsized even then, the natural
leader among the village boys despite his unprepossessing ap-
pearance. His ambitions were commensurately lofty and romantic. His head was full of colorful legends of bandits,
generals, and other military heroes who had served their
emperors and carved their own names into history with the
points of their swords. His idol was Feng Tzu-tsai, the bandit
chief, who had helped to crush the Taiping Rebellion, and had
been awarded the Yellow Coat by the Dragon Throne in
Peking. He, Feng Yu-lan, would serve as heroically, he swore.
He too would win the Yellow Coat, and sit at the Emperor's
left hand!

Lounging beside him in front of the fire, watching pebbles
pop and change color in the flames, Chen Li had had much
less to say. Young Li was sturdy and quick, and his alertness
of mind was already noticed by approving elders. But he was

142

the youngest of four sons, and he was in no sense a leader among the village boys. Yet he had already set an exalted goal for himself as well.

It was a simple enough aspiration in the telling. He had decided to become the master of all knowledge.

This could be accomplished, Chen Li knew, by the simple if laborious process of learning all that the Chinese classics had to teach. He would dedicate his life to absorbing the poetry and philosophy, the history and science and religious insights of the Celestial Empire of China, the oldest of human civilizations and the only genuinely civilized people in the world.

"Wonderful, Li!" his gigantic friend Yu-lan had shouted when he heard. They lay chewing grass stems beside the river on a summer afternoon this time. "I shall hack my way to fame with the sword; you will make your way there with the pen! We shall meet in Peking—at the foot of the Dragon Throne!"

Li, a grave boy even then, had smiled but said little. He had watched the swooping dive of a kingfisher over the water, its blue feathers flashing in the sun, and wondered secretly if fifteen years would really allow time enough for him to master *all* the wisdom of the ancients.

The two had gone about achieving their goals in typically disparate ways. Feng Yu-lan had spent many hours in the village's dark little temple dedicated to Kuan-ti the war god, burning much incense and praying ardently that the god might advance his fortunes. Chen Li had begun the long, hard road of learning which would lead to the Imperial Examination Hall in the capital and a chance for a modest beginning in the Imperial Government.

Neither boy had progressed very far along the path he had chosen. But Feng Yu-lan's fall from grace was considerably more spectacular than Chen Li's.

Chen could see his boyhood friend sliding toward a fall even before he himself gave up ancient Chinese wisdom for the newer lore of the West, and set out south to Shanghai to further his new education. He had seen Feng slipping into the toils of low women, cockfighting, gambling. Letters from his sisters had told him how rice wine and then opium had completed the degradation of the village idol. He remembered still the agitated characters in the letter from his youngest sister, telling him how Feng Yu-lan's father had formally disowned his degenerate son, expelling him from the family home and the consciousness of its members forever. The next thing he had heard—Chen was at the British Medical College in Hong Kong by this time—was that Yu-lan had been taken into custody in a raid on an opium den and was in prison in Peking.

He had seen his old playfellow only one more time after that. It was some five years after Mei Ling's death, when Chen himself was newly arrived in Peking, seeking patients for the new Western medicine in a capital ablaze with reaction against all things foreign.

He was taking a solitary meal at the Fortunate Star tea saloon across from the Chien Men Gate when a familiar voice —improbably deep, strangely resonant—had spoken his name. He looked up into the face of Feng Yu-lan. But a new Yu-lan to him, a Feng decked out in silken trousers and a satin coat, with velvet boots and rings of jade and gold on his outsized fingers. A sardonically smiling Feng, flanked by a bulbous eunuch and an effeminate youth in the yellow silks of a Manchu prince.

A very different Feng from the boy who had prayed so long and ardently at the shrine of Kuan-ti in the village of their birth.

"Chen Li, old brother of my soul!" Feng had greeted him on that occasion too. "Welcome to the Fortunate Star. I have not seen you here before."

"Nor I you, Feng Yu-lan."

Chen had risen from his table; there had been bows and introductions.

"So we meet in Peking at last," Feng had said, "though not

yet at the foot of the Dragon Throne." His eyes had glittered with cynical mockery. It was the cynicism of a thoroughly corrupted man who knows what childhood dreams are worth in the harder currency of the great world. "But come with us, Chen Li, and visit my own humble establishment, eh? The prince here finds it much to his liking. Is it not so, your Highness?"

"Your establishment?" Chen had responded doubtfully. He wondered if Feng ran a rival eating house. Looking down at his own threadbare coat, fingering the thin handful of *cash* remaining to him, he doubted that he could afford to dine at Feng's princely table.

"Come to the House of Jade, my old friend," Feng had urged him still, spreading his great arms expansively. "Every pleasure shall be yours to choose from! African girls, Caucasian boys! Every sort of white powder! Come to the House of Jade. It must be experienced to be believed. Is that not so, Prince?"

"Oh yes, it must be experienced!" the prince had tittered.

"His Highness has been much satisfied," the greasily fat eunuch had murmured.

"Will you not join us then, brother of my soul?" Feng had reiterated, his pouched eyes gleaming. "Will you not join us at my humble house of pleasure?"

Chen had declined politely. Feng had led his companions off, roaring with laughter. Many diners had raised their eyes from their steaming bowls and plates to watch his noisy exit with disapproval.

Chen Li had heard of the House of Jade more than once over the years that followed—a notorious opium den and palace of luxurious debauchery. He had heard how it had finally been closed down by the imperial authorities, and how the proprietor had fled from the capital to escape arrest and punishment. But he had not seen Feng Yu-lan again until his startling reappearance in the village square at Ta Ho the previous fall. He had not spoken to him from that day in the Fortunate Star fifteen years ago until this moment.

"You know our cause," Feng Yu-lan was saying. And then, in another uncanny echo of the past: "Will you not join us, brother?"

"Join you?"

"The *I Ho Chuan*—the Righteous and Harmonious Fists, every man of us sworn to protect the Dragon Throne and drive the foreigners out of China."

"The Boxers, in short."

"Foreign phrases come easily to your lips, my friend. But because we know that you spend three days among the people for every one day in the legations, the Society forgives you these unhappy taints of voice and manner. And I ask you once again—will you not join us in the great purging that is to come?"

The old servant returned at that moment, bringing pipes, tobacco, and tea. Feng Yu-lan rejected the pipe, took only a sip of the tea. How abstemious we are become, thought Chen, who once ran the most notorious house of pleasure in Peking!

"You will not be alone in coming over to us," Feng went on as soon as the servant had retired. "Half the imperial princes are with us now. Prince Tuan, the most powerful of them all, is our most passionate advocate. The Empress herself looks favorably upon our actions. The villagers swarm to our cause, and soon we will be here in the capital in greater numbers than ever before.

"The days of the foreigners are numbered, my brother. Join us now, before the great day comes that will separate the true friends of China from those who stand with her foreign enemies. For when that day comes, it will assuredly be too late to protest one's loyalty to the throne and people and the Fists of Righteousness!"

"With such vast numbers of the poor and the powerful alike rallying to your cause," said Chen, "I marvel that the

146

Society should bother about a humble physician. One who has never held a weapon in his hands, and who has neither wealth nor influence to offer in support of your efforts."

"Ah, but you do have something unique to offer, Chen Li." The big man leaned forward slightly, his eyes fixed upon his host's.

"What you have to give," said Feng, "is the whole of your connection with the foreigners! Your knowledge of them. Your unique ability to pass from the *hutungs* into the Quarter with such perfect ease."

"In other words, I might spy for you."

"You know much already which we would know: their hopes and fears, where they are strong and where they are weak. You could learn more—where their weapons and guards are, what plans they have in case of attack. You could save many lives, Chen Li, by telling us these things." Feng's eyes were glittering, his passion undoubtedly real.

"Lives?" said Chen, raising one eyebrow. "But I was under the impression that the magic of the *I Ho Chuan* rendered its members impervious to injury."

The big man leaned back, looking irritable. "Even your Western medical books," he said, "must have taught you that no magic can render human flesh impervious to bullets and bayonets. And common sense has taught me the same. So why do we talk of these things?"

"Perhaps," said Chen evenly, "because somebody seems to have taught many of the young fighters of the *I Ho Chuan* quite the reverse. A number of them have already died under this misapprehension. Perhaps you yourself, Feng Yu-lan, might save a few lives—by telling your people the truth."

"Chen Li," answered Feng, "when we sat together by the river and talked of the future on a day long ago, we spoke of saving the Empire from its enemies. Do you recall that time?"

"I do."

"I have never forgotten it," said Feng. "But I have learned that there is more to raising the people of China against the

147

foreign leeches than swearing valiant oaths and praying to the god of war." He paused. "Young men who are convinced that if they only believe deeply enough they will be magically protected against the guns of the foreigners are much more likely to face the foreigners unafraid. So we tell them this—and build a mighty army to drive the foreign devils out of China."

"And what," said Chen, "do you tell them when they fall before the foreign guns? When they bleed and die like the foolish youths who attacked the Tientsin train? What do you tell them then, Feng Yu-lan, when their friends lie dead around them and their own blood flows?"

"We tell them that their friends lacked faith, that their own belief is not yet deep and strong enough. For if they only believe deeply and strongly enough, they will walk through fire to purge this land!"

Chen Li knew then that the conviction of Feng Yu-lan was as real as his cynicism: that in fact the two had merged and blended in the huge man's soul until even he could not tell the one from the other. The result was a man beyond the reach of evidence or reason. Chen remembered the shadowy rumors he had heard about the man they called the Scarlet Fist of Shantung.

"Feng Yu-lan," he said quietly then, "I have spent half the years of my life serving the people here in the streets of Peking."

"I have not denied it."

"And many of the medicines and almost all the skill I have been able to put at their service have come to me from the West. From Western science and Western schools, in the pages of Western books and the iron holds of Western ships."

"I have said that we are willing to forgive you that."

"We must have that science and those ships, Feng Yu-lan. China must have such schools and such books. Can you not see that we *must* learn from them, if we are to serve and save our people?"

There was a heavy silence in the room.

"I see *you*, Chen Li," said Feng then, his great voice savage with scorn. "And that is enough."

He came suddenly to his feet, his delicately made chair crashing over behind him.

"Look at you! You sit here in this mongrel room, one wall lined with our ancient classics, the other with the chicken scratchings of the foreigner! You sit here without a beard or queue—swathed in the silken robes of our people! Half Chinese and half foreign devil, you are worse than either. You are worse than a eunuch, Chen Li, for it is your soul that has been cut out of you!"

For a moment Chen thought the seething giant might strangle him where he sat. But Feng Yu-lan only looked him once more in the face, a long and bitter look, then turned and surged out the narrow door, leaving swirling curtains behind him.

Dr. Chen picked up the overturned chair and replaced it against the wall. He gathered up the fragments of a broken teacup and placed them on his worktable. He was about to clap his hands for the old man when he realized that that worthy would of course have retired by now. It was the way of Chinese servants, he reflected, to go to bed unbidden, though gongs and clappers, drums and trumpets, might be needed to waken them at dawn. The way of Chinese servants, he thought—and the way of Old China too?

With a sigh and a smile at his own incurable bent for foolish philosophizing, Chen Li went off in search of a broom.

Feng Yu-lan padded off down the lane with hunched shoulders and bowed head, like a weary coolie returning from a long day's work. It was dark in the narrow street, only a candle gleaming in a window here and there to light the way. As he neared the little temple farther up the street, he heard quick footsteps approaching just around the bend. He stepped into the black maw of the temple doorway and waited to see what came.

149

A slender figure swept past him, barely visible in the glimmer of the crescent moon. But there was a flickering orange lantern on a post in front of the little temple in Seven Wells Lane. As the dark figure hurried past, a shaft of lantern light lit up her face. For one brief moment, Feng glimpsed the white skin and wide, eager eyes of a woman of the West.

He watched her go up the lane, saw her stop at the garden gate through which he himself had just emerged, and vanish within.

21

Elizabeth knew very well what Dr. Chen would do. He would serve her tea and send her home again to the legations, with his white-bearded old manservant for an escort. And if she told him? She knew the answer to that too. She could hear his voice grow firm as he told her that she was, after all, much younger than he, that she would soon find someone of her own age and nation. God help her, that would be worse still.

Then she was standing at the gate of the garden in Seven Wells Lane, raising one white-knuckled hand to knock.

Chen Li opened the gate himself, holding a broom in his hand.

"I—" she began, "Dr. Chen—"

He reached out and put his arm around her and led her into the garden.

After that it all flowed like a dream, like a delirium, toward the inevitable climax that she had never dared to foresee.

First there was only his arm, strong about her waist, drawing her quickly in out of the street. Then there was the garden around them both, warm and welcoming with its familiar fragrances—yet unfamiliar too, loud with night insects, lit only here and there with dim paper lanterns. There was the smooth stone path under her feet, and his closeness still, the crisp male smell of him. And the sound of his voice, asking her what was wrong, what had happened to her, why was she here?

She tried to speak again, and burst into tears instead. She put her arms around him and clung to him convulsively, as though the world would end if she let go.

He tipped her head back and looked down into her eyes,

there in the lantern light. His own face was in shadow, gazing down at her. But she could feel his eyes, as she had seen them that first day in Peking, or that afternoon in front of the mission gate when he would not say good-bye. She could feel the warmth, the depth, the caring. And she knew then that he would not send her home.

"Elizabeth," he said quietly. "Come."

He undressed her in darkness, with hands that were intuitively deft over her unfamiliar Western garments. She stood quiescent, letting him do it, wanting him to do it—yet overcome all the while with an overwhelming sense of unreality. It was not really happening, she told herself, even while her body tingled to the brush of his hand, the touch of his breath upon her. It could not really be happening to Elizabeth Rowntree, the Reverend Rowntree's daughter, the little girl from the tall red house off Rittenhouse Square.

Then he laid her gently down upon his bed, stood back in the breathing darkness, and removed his own clothes too.

Momentarily abandoned, cut off from the sense of his closeness, she felt dizzy and lost. A wild feeling of confusion swept over her, as though she had stumbled through a door and found herself suddenly perched over a void. For that instant, terror clutched at her throat. Dear God, she thought wildly, what am I doing here, in this dark room smelling of sandalwood, with this strange-eyed, olive-skinned man?

Then he came down beside her on the high Chinese bed.

He did not speak at first. He only touched her, his body against hers, his hands moving over her, slowly, slowly, with a tenderness she had never known. He kissed her on the eyes and on the tip of the nose, and he chuckled when her nose wrinkled in surprise.

Suddenly she laughed too, and slipped her arms around his neck, and kissed him back. Her body relaxed against his. The lostness was gone, and all her terrors. She felt happy and contented, there in his arms, her body cradled against his smoothly

152

muscled frame. I am safe here, she told herself. It is safe here.

He spoke now, close to her cheek. He reminded her of a ludicrous thing that happened to them once in the pavilion outside in the garden. Of how a bird had snatched a bit of cake from her hand, how the goldfish had rejected her tea. A private joke, close and warm. She laughed with him, and snuggled closer.

Suddenly she no longer wanted to be safe.

For his hands were still moving over her, stroking her breasts, her thighs. He caressed her gently at first and then more firmly, slowly and then more rapidly. And she felt her own body awakening under his touch, tingling to a wakefulness, an aliveness she had never dreamed of. Her nipples unfolded at the drift of his fingers, her belly trembled at it. Her loins longed for his touch, and she gasped aloud when it came.

Then his powerful body came over hers. His mouth and tongue claimed hers. With quick gasps of pleasure, she felt the first satiny probings of his sex against her own.

For Chen Li, it was as though time itself rolled back. Back twenty long lost years, to a summer night in Canton far to the south. Back to a small student's room under the eaves, with easy summer laughter in the lane below, and Mei Ling in his arms. For Chen Li, this was a bridal bed once more, and Elizabeth a bride.

He touched her with a bridegroom's reverence, and called down the aid of whatever gods might be to make it as joyous a night for her as it would be for him. Then, following the *Tao* of the ancient school of Yin, he set himself to give her as much pleasure as was in his power to give.

Patiently, tenderly, he brushed the silken loveliness of her sex with the firmness of his own. But only when her body was hot beneath him, only when her hands slid down his back to clutch convulsively at his buttocks, only when she pulled her wet mouth panting from under his to whisper, "O my love—please—I want you so—" did he come into her at last.

He came then like the master of the house into his home, breaking through into the unplumbed secret parts of her, wringing a cry of pain from her—and then a cry of joy.

* * *

They lay long in each other's arms, in that little room smelling of sandalwood, making love to one another. They lay together in darkness, penetrating and penetrated, their bodies locked in a shared delight that seemed to have no end.

When he slid out of her to rest for a time, she longed for him, kissed him, murmured his name. When he came into her once more, it was like a part of herself come back. They moved together, shuddered with joy together, cried out as their bodies merged in a single common ecstasy.

Man and wife and one flesh truly, murmured Elizabeth silently, washed in a sea of sensuality that was more love than lust, more adoration than either. *One flesh . . . to love and to cherish, till death us do part.*

Sun and moon, light and darkness, Chen Li's dreaming spirit half thought, half visualized in shifting little pictures. *The divided circle of yang and yin, eternally divided, eternally one.*

When they slept at last, they were together as Chen Li had not been for half a lifetime, as Elizabeth Rowntree had never been.

When she awoke in the red light of dawn, he was standing by the high slatted window, clad in a loose silk robe, looking out. She slipped naked from the bed and padded across the polished floor to kiss his shoulder. He smiled and drew her to him, his arm slanting down across her slender back, his hand upon her hip. But he did not take his eyes from the window. Sleepily, she turned her gaze to follow his.

Through the narrow open space between the slats, she saw the trees of the garden, the tiled rooftops of the city. Beyond the silhouette of a nearby pagoda, beyond the distant tower of the Protestant Board Mission, she could just glimpse the looming grey mass of the Tartar Wall.

From somewhere just outside the Wall, a great black column of smoke was rising against the flaming morning sky.

22

THEY HAD BEGUN TO STREAM INTO THE FORBIDDEN CITY well before dawn. They sat stiff and cross-legged in their ornate sedan chairs, passing through the dark streets by the light of horn lanterns, with guards before and on both sides, colorful entourages streaming out behind. They passed on stone bridges over the moat, into the East and West gates of the Forbidden City of Peking.

Within, they made their way through courtyards and up ceremonial avenues to the Chien Ching Kung, the Palace of Surpassing Brightness, the great Imperial Audience Hall of the Forbidden City.

The Audience Hall was vast and gloomy in the pale lantern light. The richness of the scarlet and gold pillars, the five-clawed dragons on the paneled ceiling gleamed dimly in the shadows. Only the golden-yellow glow of the Dragon Throne on its high, fantastically sculptured dais stood out clearly in the incense-laden air. Eunuchs in embroidered ceremonial robes and heavy gold chains of office moved about their mysterious errands, seeing that all was in readiness.

One by one the great men of the Celestial Empire descended from their sedan chairs, mounted the carved marble stairs, and entered the hall. There were Manchu princes in ceremonial military uniforms of lacquered leather, with jeweled helmets and tassels of sable. There were mandarins of the highest ranks, with peacocks and unicorns embroidered on their robes, buttons of ruby and sapphire and lapis lazuli on their velvet skullcaps. There were generals and admirals and heads of all the imperial boards and commissions in Peking. One by one they advanced to their appointed places, each duly marked by a bronze triangle set in the marble floor, in the time-honored order of rank and privilege. One by one they knelt to await the coming of their sovereign.

The floor was cold and hard, and they would have a wait, there upon their knees. The Face That Is Always To The South would not present itself until the stars were at their most propitious, at the very moment the sun rose over the eastern horizon. Some of the older and more corpulent mandarins had small pillows fastened to their knees inside their formal robes of office to ease the waiting.

"He comes!" intoned an invisible crier somewhere in the rear of the hall—one, and then another. "He comes, he comes, the Lord of Ten Thousand Years!"

There was a ripple of movement, a somber gleam of gorgeous uniforms and banners. Four eunuchs of the fifth rank walked ahead, the two principal eunuchs on either side, a dozen more of the sixth rank behind.

Every head struck the floor in a stiff formal kowtow. "Ten thousand years," murmured every voice in the hall, "ten thousand years, ten thousand years." Again and again the foreheads touched the floor. "Ten thousand years," the hoarse voices murmured in the incense and the dimness.

When they raised their faces at last from the ninth kowtow, not one but two people sat on the wide Dragon Throne of the Manchu emperors.

Even the ninth-rank mandarins at the back of the hall knew then that it was a matter of some moment that had called them together. Tzu Hsi did not often trot out the Emperor in person for Imperial Councils anymore.

The Emperor Kuang Hsu sat in a formal, hieratic pose, his tapering hands resting on his knees, his moist dark eyes staring straight ahead. His frail body seemed dwarfed by the elaborate robes of state in which he was encased like a mummy decked out for burial. To the Manchu princes in the front row of the kneeling multitude, their imperial cousin looked extremely unhappy.

The Dowager Empress Tzu Hsi, seated at her pitiful puppet's side, began to speak at once.

"You are summoned here," her rough, scolding voice in-

157

formed them, "to counsel the Emperor on matters of grave import. Particularly on two things. First, on the recent activities of the so-called Society of Righteous and Harmonious Fists, the Red Lantern Society, the Long Sword Society, and similar groups within the Empire. And second, on the new aggressive demands of the foreigners among us."

She paused a moment, sweeping the hall with her beady eyes. She was a tiny, almost doll-like figure on the high gold throne. The robes of imperial yellow satin, stiff with seed pearls and coral, looked too gorgeous to be real. The elaborate jeweled headdress, shaped to the pattern of a bird's wings, drooping in pendants of pearl over her ears, made her white-powdered face look pinched and meager. But the rasp of that voice, the flash of that piercing gaze held every eye and mind in the huge Audience Hall like a bird in the palm of her tiny hand.

"The societies," Tzu Hsi continued, "claim that they are sent of the gods, that they possess supernatural powers, that they are come only to defend the Empire and the glorious Dynasty of Ching from the foreigners. The foreigners assert that the societies threaten the lives and properties of merchants, missionaries, and envoys of their governments dwelling in the Empire. They demand the suppression of the societies.

"Noble princes and honorable officials of the Middle Kingdom, how do you counsel the Emperor?"

Silence filled the red-and-gold hall. Rank on rank of expectant faces gazed up at the Dragon Throne. All waited patiently for the expected lead from the little old woman in the golden chair.

Then suddenly a voice spoke, sharp and oddly echoing in the high-ceilinged throne room. "If the Heaven-Blessed and All-Nourishing Empress will permit?" It was Yuan Chang, an official of the *Tsungli Yamen*, one of the few surviving supporters of Western ideas and reform.

Tzu Hsi indicated with a brusque inclination of the head that he might speak.

"In my humble judgment, then, it would be well first of all to look closely at these so-called patriotic societies that have sprung up among the people. Right understanding of these gangs—for they are no more than that—should provide good guidance in dealing with both the societies *and* the demands of the foreigners."

He paused a moment, then plunged recklessly on.

"For so far as I can tell, these Righteous and Harmonious Fists, and all the rest of them, are not patriot bands at all, but rebels!" There was a hissing and a muttering from the ranks of the Manchu princes, but the speaker went on, oblivious. "Yes, rebels and bandits—violators of order, destroyers of peace in the Empire. They lay waste whole towns; they tear up the fine new railroads. They murder their fellow subjects, who happen to be converts to the religion of the foreigners. They have even dared to attack imperial officials, units of the Imperial Army sent to curb their excesses. And now we hear that they are even here, in Chihli, in Peking itself. In my mind, it is a most dangerous situation, a threat even to the glorious Dynasty itself—"

"Not true! Not true!"

It was Prince Tuan, leaping to his feet, his small, ferretlike eyes blazing, his smallpox-scarred cheeks working ferociously. Only the Dowager Empress's reigning favorite—and a bold, overbearing man to boot—would dare to interrupt an Imperial Audience in such a tone.

"It is not true, what the honorable Yuan Chang tells us!" stormed Prince Tuan. "These societies are a patriotic militia, mobilized to defend their own villages against the depredations of the foreigners. They are brave and worthy, willing to face death in defense of their homes."

"In defense of their homes?" Yuan Chang sneered. "And how do they defend their villages by coming up to Peking? Will the honorable prince tell me that?"

"They come to Peking to protect us all from the nest of vipers that dwells in the legations," thundered Prince Tuan. "They stay as honored guests in my own palace, and in the homes of many of us who hold the safety of the Empire and of the glorious Dynasty dear. Indeed, I myself"—he paused melodramatically—"I myself am proud to be a member of the Society of the White Lotus, one of these very bands that you condemn for rebels and robbers. And I am not alone in that. My noble brother is also of the Society, and so are a number of the honorable generals and other imperial officials gathered here at this moment."

"I do not doubt the patriotic loyalty of the noble prince," another voice broke in—another of the pro-Western officials from the *Tsungli Yamen*. "But surely he cannot support the foolishness of the claims put forth by these societies. That they commune with the gods, that they have magic that protects them from blade and bullet—"

"Even that," Prince Tuan broke in again, "even that may not be as foolish as some think." His small eyes grew smaller still, narrowing like an old woman's telling a ghost story around the cooking fire. "I have myself seen astonishing demonstrations in the camps of the Fists of Righteousness. I have seen European weapons loaded before my eyes— leveled at young initiates to the Society—and discharged no more than the length of my arm from the naked breast!" He struck his own thick chest violently with a closed fist. "And not a mark appeared upon the skin!"

His voice was hoarse with emotion, and he was breathing heavily. Tzu Hsi, looking at his burly frame and flashing eyes, thought for a flickering moment: Perhaps the vigor of the old Manchus lives still—in one or two at least. With the shrewd, rational half of her brain, she knew her favorite for the intriguer he was, with the succession to the Dragon Throne ever on his mind. But her emotional response was nonetheless powerful. Here was a man who did not loll away his life in the palaces and pleasure gardens of the city. Here was a man who had been to the camps of the *I Ho Chuan*. A man who had himself taken the blood oath of a secret society, and stood shoulder to shoulder with these rough, uncouth defenders of her city and her person against the foreign devils. Her heart glowed at the thought of it, even as her superstitious soul tingled at the image of the Western bullets rebounding helplessly from the naked chests of the true believers.

"Are there others who would speak?" she asked, her glance darting over the sea of faces before her.

"I—if I may speak, Revered and Sacred Mother?"

Tzu Hsi turned in astonishment to the slender, listless figure seated on the golden throne beside her.

"Of course his Imperial Majesty may speak!" said the Dowager Empress caustically. "I myself conduct the business of this government only in his Majesty's illustrious name, during his prolonged and regrettable illness. Evidently," she concluded dryly, "his Majesty may speak in his own voice at any time."

The Emperor Kuang Hsu's long jaw trembled; his fingers played nervously with the folds of his robes of state. He moistened his lips to speak.

"I wish to say only—that there is much weight in what the honorable officials of our Imperial Foreign Office have said. That these societies are not after all trained soldiers, but a— a rabble in arms. And that their claim that magic can protect bare skin against the bullets of the Westerners is surely foolishness. How could—how could such a thing be?" His eyes brimmed suddenly with tears, his thin figure seemed to sag and shrink, as though the last of his energy was suddenly gone. He looked unhappily around him, and repeated: "How could it be?"

Tzu Hsi looked at him sharply. There was a febrile glint in his eyes, a dryness to his skin that were more than the effect of his long confinement. He must not fall ill, she thought. Not now. Not with so much already lying in the laps of the gods!

161

Then her shrill voice lashed out again, filling the hall to the farthest shifting shadows.

"I do not myself know the truth of these claims of the societies to divine protection," she said. "Unlike Prince Tuan, I have not had opportunity to go out to their camps, to observe their demonstrations of faith. But I ask this question: If we cannot depend on the supernatural powers they claim— can we not at least depend upon the hearts of these people? For if we lose the hearts of the people, how shall we maintain our country?"

The silence washed impenetrably back.

"And so I say this," the old woman on the golden throne declared, "that if there be criminals among the patriotic societies, they shall be punished, or if there be traitors and rebels, they shall die. But insofar as they are indeed loyal to the Empire and the glorious Dynasty, these same societies shall have our support. Indeed, in their sincere and noble efforts to defend the Middle Kingdom from the foreign devils that ring us round, that gnaw at our vitals from within—in *that* noble effort, they shall have our utmost confidence and our loving protection."

The stillness that followed this declaration from the Dragon Throne was a palpable thing, pulsing with suppressed excitement. Prince Tuan's narrow eyes glittered. A sudden pallor spread beneath the olive skin of Yuan Chang. In that tingling silence, in the dimness and the drift of incense, the Old Buddha looked stonily out over that sea of eyes fixed as though magnetized upon her own. Then the Empress of China lowered her head, and the long jade nail protectors on her left hand flashed as she signed that the audience was ended.

All foreheads touched the floor once more as the imperial party paraded the length of the Audience Hall and passed out into the flaming dawn.

Tzu Hsi was out in the crisp morning air, halfway down the carven marble stairs toward the waiting sedan chair, when she looked up and saw the column of black smoke rising from somewhere outside the city walls. About where the foreign racecourse was, she judged. The imperial protection, she thought half grimly and half gleefully, was going to be claimed sooner than she had expected.

BOOK THREE

THE
STREETS

23

CHEN LI ROSE AND CROSSED THE ROOM TO LIGHT A LAMP. Then he returned to the bed. Elizabeth lay looking up at him, her eyes still clouded with passion. He drew the coverlet aside and kissed each strong young breast in turn. The wonder of her beauty filled him with a kind of awe.

"The Yellow Emperor," he said gravely, "slept with twelve hundred separate women, and so gained immortality. I sleep a single night with you, and am immortal."

"A single night?" she answered him, bantering in her turn. "It has been seven nights, to be precise. Seven separate, perfect, unbelievable nights. Oh, Li"—she savored his name, the given name that only a wife or a lover might use—"I am so happy."

Seven nights in twenty, she thought. Miraculously, incredibly, in the tension and confusion that had engulfed the city, they had been together seven whole nights out of the twenty since she had come to him that first time. Seven nights, and twice that many afternoons. The Congers thought she was helping Manson Rogers at the mission. Like all the other missions in the city, the Protestant Board was flooded with refugees from all over North China. Who would notice the comings and goings of a single American girl in such frantic confusion? Apparently no one had, so far.

Elizabeth determinedly put the terrors of the time out of her mind as she lay in Chen Li's bed that night, looking up at her lover.

Her eyes devoured the firm lips, the shadowed cheeks, the dark eyes looking down into hers. She raised one hand to touch the hairs of gunmetal grey that curled slightly above his ears.

"I feel like that girl in the poem," she said. "How did it go?

'No more strength left in her body,
She feels so weak after pleasuring her lover.'
What was the rest of it?"

He smiled back and said the words, first in melodious Mandarin, then in English:

" 'The flower has fallen from her hair,
And the golden hairpin dropped.' "

"Yes," she said, "that's how I feel. Oh, Li." She took his hand and kissed it softly, inhaling the clean, dry smell of his skin, feeling its texture against her lips. Then she drew him down into the bed with her once more.

"My father," she said to Chen Li the following afternoon, sitting with him in the garden, "would have said this was all so wicked, so evil. And Aunt Grace—all of them. Even little Polly Smith at the legations. Why don't I *feel* wicked then, being here with you like this?"

They sat in the airy, open pavilion by the lotus pool, sipping tea from his fine porcelain. She was wearing Chinese garb herself, as she had done for days now, when they were alone. She had not asked where he had got the loose white cotton pantaloons and the exquisitely embroidered white jacket, but she suspected they belonged to the wife of his youth, Mei Ling. Wherever they had come from, Elizabeth found them amazingly comfortable. She luxuriated in her freedom from the corsets and the heavy skirts and petticoats of Western women's clothing. She wore her dark chestnut hair up for him, in a Manchu bun laced with white flowers. And her heart went molten with happiness to see the warm approval that softened the corners of his eyes when he looked at her now.

"Why should you feel wicked, my dear?" He smiled. "You are not in Philadelphia, or even in the legations. You are in a different world now."

She stretched her legs in the loose trousers, feeling piratical and free, and looked up at the fluttering scroll above her head, the fresh green of the tulip tree beyond. Those who flow as the life force flows, she thought, remembering his words of an eternity before. Surely she was doing that now. And she could not believe that there was so much ardor and beauty in the world. So much life.

From somewhere beyond the garden wall, there came the distant sound of shouting.

Elizabeth had heard that sound before, again and again over those last days. The shrill shouting that resolved itself into a terrible chant: *"Sha-shao! Sha-shao! Sha-shao!*—Kill and burn! Kill and burn! Kill and burn!" Sitting there in the lacquered pavilion, listening to it rise once more, she felt her skin prickle at the sound of it.

The voices grew, reached a chanting climax somewhere up the street, in the vicinity of the little temple. Then they came on again, swelling with a hoarse, vindictive passion, sweeping with a rush of running feet down Seven Wells Lane. She heard them stream, shouting, past the double gates and on, surging toward—what? She closed her eyes and visualized the panting ill-clothed bodies, the fanatical young faces distorted with hate.

She remembered Ping, the head groom at the American Legation, staggering into the compound two days before with his face all covered with blood, beaten half to death. He was a third-class hairy one to the Boxer mob. There were rumors that some second-class hairy ones—Christian converts—had been killed in the city. And hairy ones of the first class, foreign devils themselves?

The burning of the new European racecourse the night Elizabeth had first come to Chen Li's garden had only been a beginning. Night after night thereafter the Boxers had struck. Railway lines both south and west of the city had been attacked. Telegraph lines had been cut, stations burned. The railway works at Huangtsun had been destroyed. A fine new steel span bridge on the Paotingfu line had been dynamited.

A party of Belgian engineers had been ambushed twenty miles from Tientsin, and four of them killed outright.

Granted, the telegraph lines had quickly been repaired, the railway reopened. And a party of Russian Cossack troops stationed at Tientsin had hunted down the murderers of the Belgians and slaughtered half a hundred of them within hours after the ambush. But it was all rather stunning nonetheless. Even the oldest China hands had to admit that there had been no outbreak like it since the Taiping Revolt more than thirty years before. Nothing like it, really, said Inspector General Hart, since the first Jesuit missionaries came to Peking, and the square-rigged caravels of the traders, some three hundred years before.

And now the Boxers were in Peking itself, housed in the courtyards of princes, fed by the Dowager Empress, running riot in the streets.

The screaming voices faded. Then there was only a bird singing in the green-and-grey garden, and the renewed murmur of voices in the lane outside. As if nothing untoward had occurred, Elizabeth thought. As if the terror had not happened.

Aloud she said suddenly: "Chen Li—what is going to happen?"

"If the rains do not come soon," he answered soberly, "God knows. The *I Ho Chuan* tell the people the Heavenly Dragon will not bring rain because the Western barbarians are allowed to live in China, to desecrate the ashes of the ancestors and the altars of the gods. Many people believe them. Even in Peking now, it seems." He put down his teacup on the small inlaid table beside him. "But you are safe enough here," he added. "I have lived in the *hutungs* for many years. I am known and respected here. They will not come into the garden."

"It is not myself I was thinking of, Li. It was—" She fumbled for a word, finally used the obvious one: "It was my people I meant."

For they were her people, she realized, all those far-off strangers in the legation, at the mission. She might sleep on a *kang* in Chen Li's arms, dress in Chinese clothes, drink tea in a Chinese garden—but those others were her people still.

"The *I Ho Chuan* and the other societies swear they will drive the foreigners from China," said Chen slowly. "They are working themselves up to a frenzy with their own loud talk, their chanting, their magic rites—the 'shadowboxing,' as they call it in the legations. And now there are these Moslem troops that Tzu Hsi has had brought all the way from Kansu." He paused a moment, his face somber. "They hate everything Western with a passion which must be very hard for a Westerner to conceive."

"I know," said the girl miserably. "And when people like Von Ketteler speak for us, I understand it. But there must be some accommodation—some compromise possible? Surely this city, this Peking, that has absorbed so many peoples over the centuries, can live with a few hundred Westerners among all its teeming hundreds of thousands? Surely China's millions can tolerate a few missionaries, a few merchants from the barbarian lands beyond the seas?"

Very slowly now, looking down into the lotus pool, Chen Li shook his head.

"I wonder if you know how truly remarkable you Westerners are, Elizabeth. How truly unique in history." He meditated on the rich green leaves, the red flowers just opened on the water. "You are overrunning the globe. That has never been done before—never in all human history. You are everywhere, on all seas and continents, you busy bustling Westerners, with your machines and your money and your passion to change everything, to exploit, reform, transform the world. To make it over in your own image." He paused again, watching the goldfish dart under the lotus pads. "Peking cannot absorb you," he said. "Perhaps the whole world cannot absorb you, you phenomenal, terrible children of the West."

Outside in the city somewhere, Elizabeth heard the far-off

171

roar of a crowd. The Boxer mob, she thought, had arrived wherever it was going. It was doing—whatever it had gone there to do.

"Li," she said, "they have sent for help from the coast. Mr. Conger told us yesterday. The Council of Ministers has telegraphed to Taku for more troops to protect the legations. There are enough Western warships in the harbor there to provide a thousand men, sailors and Marines of half a dozen nations. They'll be coming up by train tomorrow, under Admiral Seymour, the commander of the British flotilla. By this time tomorrow, they'll be here." She looked him squarely in the eyes. "What will happen then, Li?"

He met her gaze. "There will be fighting," he said. "And you must not come here anymore, Elizabeth. Not until all this is over. I have been a fool to let you come so long."

She came to him, and he took her in his arms.

"All right," she said, her face smothered against his chest. "But Li"—she looked up into his dark, smooth-lidded eyes again, and would not let him look away—"Li, this will not—cannot—mean anything to you and me. To us. Do you understand me?"

There was an answer on his lips, but she never heard it. For at that moment there came a pounding on the garden gate.

24

CHEN'S WRINKLED MANSERVANT PADDED ACROSS THE COURT-
yard and vanished through the inner gate. They heard him
fumbling with the outer latch. A moment later he reappeared,
stumbling backward, protesting futilely, as uniformed Chinese
soldiers thrust their way into the garden.

They were not the brass-buttoned men of the Peking gar-
rison, Elizabeth noticed, or ceremonial city guards in their
medieval leather. They were swarthy men in black turbans
and black-and-orange uniforms, with modern-looking rifles
slung across their backs. She remembered dazedly that
Sergeant Connor had pointed some of them out to her from
the Tartar Wall the day before. They were Moslem cavalrymen from Kansu province, the crack new regiments the Dowager Empress had just brought into the city.

They spread quickly across the garden, poking into the
servants' quarters, the cookhouse, the stable at the rear.
Elizabeth heard the fat, cheerful cook—the old manservant's
daughter—squeal as a sun-bronzed face peered in at her. The
trooper laughed, pushed the white-bearded servant in to join
his daughter, and closed the door. Two other turbaned soldiers emerged from the main house itself, their rifles unslung,
and nodded to the officer in command, who was still standing
stiffly by the garden gate.

Chen Li stood silent and placid through it all. He had
stepped out of the little pavilion and placed himself so that
his body shielded Elizabeth's, leaving her half hidden in the
obscurity behind the painted pillars.

"Li!" she whispered urgently now. "What is it? What's
happening?"

He did not answer. His eyes remained fixed on the commander of the troops—and on the gate behind him.

The Moslem officer turned, called something out into the street. Two powerful-looking men in the robes and sashes of imperial eunuchs came through the gate, then stepped to left and right and stood to attention, flanking it. Then another man strode into the garden. He was a short, ugly man, his face pitted with smallpox scars. But he wore the yellow robes of a Manchu prince of the imperial house of Ching.

Chen Li bowed, murmuring ceremonial greetings. Elizabeth caught only a few words, but they were enough: "Happiness to this humble house, Prince Tuan, from your fortunate coming."

No name was more frequently cursed in the legations these days than that of Tuan, the most ambitious of the imperial princes and the fiercest patron of the Boxers in Peking.

"You are the physician Chen Li?" The voice was overbearing and irritable. He sounded like a man with no relish for the errand upon which he was come.

"I am Dr. Chen, honorable Prince."

The prince's close-set, narrow eyes flicked past the doctor, probed the shadowy pavilion behind him.

"Who is that?"

Before Chen could speak, Elizabeth rose and stepped to the edge of the low platform, into plain view.

"My name is Elizabeth Rowntree," she said clearly in English, looking the prince squarely in the face. "I am a guest of the American Legation. And a friend of Dr. Chen's."

Chen Li translated precisely, adding only: "Miss Rowntree is a doctor. She helps me to treat the Emperor's poor subjects in the *hutungs*."

Tuan looked at the Chinese pants and jacket that clothed the girl's graceful figure, at the sandals on her feet and the flowered Manchu bun of her hair. An unattractive smile spread his own lips briefly. But he said only: "She is a physician?"

"She is," said Chen.

"Then she shall come also." The smile was gone, the voice

rude and commanding once again. "You are both to come with me at once."

"May we know where?"

"By order of her Imperial Highness, Auspicious, Orthodox, Heaven-Blessed, the Dowager Empress Tzu Hsi, you are to accompany me immediately to the Forbidden City."

"Is it permitted to know for what purpose we are thus honored?"

"You are summoned. That is enough for you to know."

"Of course, honorable Prince. But if we are, for example, summoned to provide medical assistance, we might perhaps bring some useful drugs or other remedies with us—if we might know what sort of ailment we are called upon to treat?"

Tuan hesitated for a considerably longer period this time. When he spoke, his voice was little more than a whisper.

"You are called upon to treat a most exalted personage. The patient suffers from an indisposition of the stomach. It is due, apparently, to the ingestion of an unknown but clearly deleterious substance which—"

"To poisoning, honorable Prince?"

"To poison."

The Emperor Kuang Hsu lay on an unmade bed in a sparsely furnished, windowless room. His skin was moist, his breathing labored. He was unconscious, though the thin hands crossed on his chest twitched spasmodically from time to time. The cheeks were sunken, and the whites of the eyes showed as narrow crescents beneath the eyelids.

There were two other doctors in the room when Prince Tuan shepherded Dr. Chen and Elizabeth through the door. They were court physicians clearly, portly men with long goat beards, satin robes, and skullcaps. They stood at the head of the Emperor's high brick bed, peering at the patient through gogglelike spectacles rimmed with copper, stroking their beards and murmuring to each other. Elizabeth would not have been surprised to hear that they had prescribed dragon's

175

bones and rhubarb. No wonder they sent for a Western doctor, she thought, looking at the sick man's stertorous breathing, the bluish lips and fingernails. And none too soon either.

It had been dark already by the time they reached the great red walls of the Imperial City. They had passed unchallenged through the eastern gate, and thence through a ghostly labyrinth of gardens and courtyards, through the shadows of half-seen palaces and temples to the far side of the Forbidden City itself. They had crossed a narrow bridge or causeway over open water and passed through one more fragrant garden, invisible in the darkness, to reach this grim, drafty palace, and this ill-lit chamber at the heart of it. Now they stood together, looking down at the hollow cheeks and sagging open mouth of the Face That Is Always To The South.

A perspiring eunuch stood between two imperial guards just across the room, sucking nervously at his lower lip. Chen spoke to him.

"What did his Imperial Highness take?"

"A white powder, sir," said the miserable caretaker. "It is there in the paper on the little cabinet."

Dr. Chen lifted the small square of rice paper carefully to his face and sniffed gingerly.

"Do you know how much of this there was in the paper when he got it?"

"I did not know that he had it, honorable sir," the eunuch protested. "Had I but known—"

Chen nodded. He reached for Kuang Hsu's slender wrist, where the pulse beat with almost visible feebleness.

There was a universal gasp.

"It is forbidden!" squeaked the more corpulent and dignified of the two doctors already in attendance. "It is not permitted to touch the person of the Emperor!"

Chen Li raised his eyes to the portly court physician, then shifted his gaze to Prince Tuan. "Honorable Prince," he said, "I cannot treat any patient that I cannot touch." His tone was neither wheedling nor defiant, but flatly declarative, simply stating a fact.

"Your distinguished colleagues manage well enough," rumbled Tuan.

"In that case, honorable Prince, I shall be most happy to leave the case in the capable hands of my colleagues."

Chen had actually picked up his medical bag and turned back toward the door before the prince stopped him.

"Very well, Chen Li," said Tuan sharply. "If that is the Western way, and since the Venerable Mother has specifically ordered that Western methods also be tried, you may upon this one occasion lay hands upon his Imperial Majesty."

Prince Tuan paused an instant and then, to Elizabeth's surprise, shifted into English. It was a blurred and unsteady English, but English nonetheless. And the uncomprehending looks on the faces of the half-dozen other people in the room made clear the reason for the shift.

"You understand importance of the situation, Dr. Chen. Emperor must live, you understand? Especially at this time" —Tuan darted a vindictive glance at the American girl—"it is essential his Majesty not die. If he die—Auspicious and Venerable Mother have made clear all of you die too."

There was the slightest hesitation before the "you." Elizabeth wondered if he had been about to say "all of *us* die too."

"How did he come to take it?" Chen asked quietly, opening his black medical bag.

"You must know that?"

"I must know as much as possible about the case."

"The Emperor have been most unhappy for recent weeks. He have not been happy with—recent decisions and edicts of Imperial Government. His steward"—Tuan shot a savage glance at the sweating eunuch—"have let him get powder somehow. He took it with cup of flower tea last night. These fools of imperial physicians try all day to heal him. Then Old Buddha—Venerable Mother—says to get Western doctor, but

177

not from the legations." Again the unhappy pause, the suspicious glance around at the blank faces of the guards, the stewards, the court physicians. "All this for no other ears, Dr. Chen Li, you understand? No rumors of Emperor's foolish act must spread outside these walls."

"Of course, honorable Prince," said Chen.

Of course, thought Elizabeth. It would be an evil omen indeed if it were known that at this moment of confrontation with the Eight Powers of the West, the Emperor of China had tried to commit suicide!

"Miss Rowntree," murmured Dr. Chen, "if you will prepare the purgative, we will begin."

By five o'clock the following morning, the job was done. Kuang Hsu was breathing deeply and steadily. The blueness at the lips, the unnatural pallor were gone.

"Thank God," whispered Elizabeth fervently. "Rest and a little chicken broth, and he couldn't die if he tried—as Nurse Sullivan used to say." She nodded toward Prince Tuan, drowsing in a chair. "Shall we tell Old Ferret-face?"

"Not yet," Chen replied in even more muted tones. "You go outside for a breath of air. You've certainly earned it. I shall join you in a moment. But not a word yet, to anyone." His eyes were on Prince Tuan too, but there was nothing flippant in either words or gaze.

Puzzled but willing enough after a long night in the fetid atmosphere of the imperial sickroom, Elizabeth strode out of the chamber and down the hallway to the nail-studded outer doorway. The guards glanced uncertainly at Prince Tuan, but let her pass.

She stepped out of the grim, unsavory palace prison into an Arabian Nights enchantment.

Elizabeth had seen nothing but shadowy silhouettes of the palaces of the Forbidden City as she entered the night before. She had caught no more than a fragrant breath of the gardens and lakes of the Imperial City. But the sun was just rising now as she stepped out into the most sacred precincts in China She stopped in her tracks and stared, enraptured.

Flowering trees and shrubs bright with dew lined the path down to the shore of the island prison. At the end of the path, a marble causeway linked the island to the mainland. Off to her left stretched a wide blue lake, thick with lotuses along its banks, shimmering in the dawn. Gilded pagodas and brightly colored pavilions showed among the trees along the farther shore. Beyond, the yellow glazed-tile roofs of the Forbidden City itself gleamed above the fresh spring foliage.

Near at hand, just beyond the causeway, Elizabeth could see ridgepoles carved with unicorns and phoenixes and dragons, cornices decorated with gold, pillars inlaid with jade. Farther away through the trees, she glimpsed marble terraces, flying bridges, here and there the sparkle of a fountain in the morning sun.

"*Syihwan ma?* Do you like it?"

The voice was harsh, grating on the ear. But the phrase was familiar enough, and Elizabeth answered automatically in her most precise Mandarin: "Indeed, I like it very much!"

Then she turned her dazzled eyes upon the speaker.

An old woman in a flowered gown stood at the far end of the causeway. Her fan was of ivory, her gown of finest knotted silk. Her six-inch fingernails were sheathed in jeweled protectors, and pearls gleamed in her hair. A person of consequence, certainly, thought Elizabeth, wondering where her attendants were and why any Chinese of importance would be up so early in the morning.

The old woman was looking at Elizabeth's own clothing, the Chinese jacket and trousers she had been wearing when Prince Tuan had come pounding on Dr. Chen's door.

"Do the European women all wear our Chinese clothes now?" The woman spoke slowly, pointing to make her meaning clear.

179

"Unfortunately, no," said Elizabeth. "I wish they did. I feel so much more free in this—" She smiled and gestured in her turn.

The old woman seemed pleased. "You would like to see more of my gardens?" she asked. "More of my city?"

Elizabeth went cold at the words. *My gardens. My city.* She wondered desperately if she could have got the possessives wrong. But she knew she hadn't.

Before she could speak again, Chen Li emerged from the aromatic verdure behind her, and froze in his turn.

"Auspicious and Venerable," he said then, bowing stiffly in the European manner. His eyes glowed with the strangest mixture of repugnance and awe, anger and reverence the American girl had ever seen.

"You are the Western doctor?"

"I am, Majesty."

"You have healed his Imperial Highness of his—illness?" Her voice was clipped now, her small black eyes shrewd and hard.

"My colleague Miss Rowntree and I"—Chen inclined his head gravely toward Elizabeth—"have made great progress. I shall, however, have to stay on with his Highness for some few hours yet, I think. In the meanwhile, Auspicious and Venerable, I should like to have Miss Rowntree escorted back to the American Legation. Or to my own house in Seven Wells Lane, if that would seem more discreet to your Majesty."

"No one can leave," said Tzu Hsi, "until his Imperial Highness is well." Her voice was as hard as her eyes now. It was the harsh, domineering voice of one who was used to command. This short, sallow-faced old woman, Elizabeth reminded herself, spoke with the voice of God to four hundred million Chinese.

Chen Li answered the Dowager Empress with perfect serenity. "I regret, Venerable and Auspicious, that unless Miss Rowntree is returned at least to my own home, I shall be unable to continue my treatment here."

180

The challenge was clear. He would trade a guarantee of the Emperor's life for a similar guarantee of Elizabeth's safety. And with one of them safely out of the Forbidden City, what use would there be in holding the other?

Tzu Hsi bit her lower lip petulantly. Elizabeth could see the anger in her eyes. The anger—and the frustration. For there was really nothing she could do but acquiesce. Clearly she wanted her unhappy puppet Emperor kept alive, at least for the time being. Why not, as long as hers remained the hand that wielded the vermilion pencil, hers truly the Face That Is Always To The South?

Then the old woman seemed to relax. A faint smile touched her wrinkled lips. Did it really matter whether they left the Forbidden City or not, after all? Anywhere in Peking, anywhere in China, that little smile seemed to say, they would be equally under her hand.

"I shall see the Western lady to the Gate of Supreme Harmony myself," said Tzu Hsi then, extending a jeweled hand, "and see that a suitable escort is provided. Perhaps I might indicate one or two of the imperial palaces as we go?"

Elizabeth started to protest. But that clawlike hand was on her arm, and she came away, leaving Dr. Chen bowing politely on the causeway.

"A lady doctor," the Dowager Empress murmured. "What will they not think of next in the West?"

25

THE CITY VIBRATED WITH TENSION AROUND HER AS SHE hurried up Seven Wells Lane.

East and north of her, plumes of smudgy grey smoke spread out against the sky. Three times already that morning she had heard the distant roar of angry mobs. Elizabeth remembered how the Kansu troopers who had hustled her through the narrow streets to Dr. Chen's house had swaggered and laughed, boasting among themselves about what they would soon be doing to the hairy ones, the foreign devils from beyond the seas.

She had waited two hours for Chen Li to return to the garden in Seven Wells Lane. But the shouting and the chanting from outside had grown louder, and the first pillars of smoke had begun to rise above the city. And she knew that her presence in his house was the most dangerous thing in the world for the Chinese doctor now. At midmorning, dressed once more in her Western clothing, she had slipped out the garden gate.

There was chanting to the south of her now, between her and Legation Street. But she knew that quadrant well enough. She decided on a detour to the west, around the Temple of the Sleeping Buddha. Nervous and perspiring in her heavy skirts, she turned to the right and plunged into the heart of the *hutungs*.

It took her perhaps ten minutes to become hopelessly lost. Nothing and no one seemed to be where it should be. The barber and the scissors-grinder were gone from their accustomed place. The stone lion, located for some unfathomable reason in Stone Tiger Lane, had mysteriously vanished, and the Temple of the Sleeping Buddha had been swallowed up by the earth.

She slowed her quick, determined pace, trying to think, trying to remember. But everything seemed unfamiliar somehow. Unfamiliar and frightening.

The smells of leeks and garlic and unwashed bodies were sharper than they had been to her since her first days with Dr. Chen. The singsong jabber of the people grated on her ears, and she caught far fewer words and phrases than she usually did. Old men seemed to leer at her as she hurried past. The women, with their shrunken feet and painted faces, looked positively sinister to her.

It is entirely in my mind, she told herself, pausing to catch her breath in the shadow of a ginseng shop. These are the same people, the same streets that Li walks every day. And I with him—every day.

But the difference was horribly clear to her as she stood there, breathing deeply, filling her nostrils with the licorice smell of ginseng. These were Dr. Chen's streets—not hers. With him, she was safe as she would be at Elm and Maple in Philadelphia, half a world away. Alone—

Someone sniggered. It was not the cheerful laughter of children, that she had heard and smiled at so often. Not the giggle of men telling stories in front of their shops. It was a laughter full of scorn for Elizabeth Rowntree, unkempt and dusty now, lost in the *hutungs*.

Li had told her about the contempt so many Chinese felt for Western women with their outthrust breasts and naked, unpowdered faces. He had told her how their "milky" smell irritated sensitive Chinese nostrils. How the very color of their skin jarred Chinese sensibilities—white, the color of death, mourning, and misfortune. Li had told her all these things, explaining his people's prejudices to her in the abstract. Now for the first time she felt the full force of that fierce hatred.

The laughter came again, and with it a half-whispered expletive: *maotzu*—hairy one, long hair, foreigner-without-a-queue. Somewhere much nearer now, two or three blocks away at most, she heard the rolling Boxer chant once more: "*Sha-shao*—kill and burn—"

The American girl began to walk faster still, till she was almost running. She blundered into open shop stalls, stumbled through the ashes of outdoor cooking fires. She banged her head more than once on poles and bars supporting the heavy mats that served as awnings over shop fronts and doorways. Her heart was pounding, her breath sobbing in her chest. Shouts and curses followed her now, as she hurried blindly on from one narrow lane to the next, plunged at hazard up one side street and then another.

"*Maotzu, maotzu!*" The voices followed her. My God, were they going to attack her in the street because she smelled of milk and they of ginseng root?

Then Elizabeth burst out of a reeking alley of wool workers and found herself at last in the familiar purlieus of Stone Tiger Lane. She gasped with relief and slowed her pace at once. At that moment she heard a voice speak her name: "Lizzie!" It was the only male voice in Peking that ever called her that. She turned and saw Sergeant Michael Connor leaning against the ancient stone lion at the head of the lane, a rifle across his arm.

"Lizzie!" he said. "What the—what are you doing out here?"

"I might ask you the same thing, Michael," she answered tartly. And then, with a rueful smile: "The fact is, I was lost. And then that awful chanting started—"

Connor nodded. "We were out half the night, trying to bring in some Chinese converts the Boxers had caught up by the Russian church. They burned the church last night. You could see the fire clear across the city."

"Did you get the Chinese Christians out?"

"Some," he answered. "Some they had—well, it ain't the sort of thing to talk about," he ended lamely. "But we'd better get moving ourselves. That yelling up the street is getting louder."

Elizabeth nodded, still a bit breathless, and took his arm. She knew where she was as well as he did now, and could probably find her way back to the legations as quickly as he. Yet it was comforting to feel his arm under her hand, his body moving beside hers down the dusty, jabbering street.

"What *were* you doing way out here alone anyway, Lizzie?" he asked as they strode along, his eyes darting left and right into every cul-de-sac and shop.

To her own astonishment she told him the truth. "You won't believe it," she said, "but I've just been to the Forbidden City."

Connor chuckled. "Your Chinese doctor friend show you around?"

"Not a bit of it, Michael. The Dowager Empress gave me a tour herself."

He laughed aloud. Elizabeth, knowing she should not have said as much as she had, let it go at that. It would be much too hard for her to explain what she had been doing in Dr. Chen's garden in the first place for her to describe that bizarre night to anyone in the legations. Yet she was glad to have blurted out even so much of it to someone. Obscurely, she was glad that someone had been Michael Connor.

"Really," she said, "this whole city has felt forbidden, closed to me these last weeks. I used to feel as though I was accepted here. Welcome almost, when I went the rounds with Dr. Chen. But lately, today especially, it's all been so different. Do you know what I mean?"

He nodded. "Same at Charlie Dog's," he said laconically. "They don't look at you anymore."

"They did today," she said. "They looked at me, all right. With such hatred, such contempt—"

"That would figure today," said Connor, "with the lid blowing off like this."

She knew she shouldn't ask, shouldn't reveal her ignorance of what must be common gossip in the legations. Far better to wait and pump Polly Smith or Mrs. Conger quietly later.

But she couldn't help herself. "What exactly has gone wrong today?" she asked.

"You don't know?" Sergeant Connor looked at her in amazement.

"I've been up at the mission," she said, "for the last forty-eight hours. We've been so busy finding room for all the people from the outstations, the refugees streaming into Peking—"

"You didn't hear about the fighting at the coast?"

"No—nothing. But what about the troops they were sending us? The relief force from Taku?"

"They ain't here," he answered grimly, "that's all we know."

Elizabeth stopped in the street and stared at him, white-faced. The chanting of the mob had veered away in another direction, and Legation Street was plainly visible ahead, a short block away. They were within sight of safety. But what sort of safety if the troops hadn't come?

"But what does it mean then, Michael?" She felt stupid and melodramatic asking it, there in that dusty yellow lane with shopkeepers staring at her and naked children giggling behind their hands. Once again she had to ask, hoping she wouldn't hear the answer she knew must come.

"It looks like war for certain, Lizzie," said Connor. "And us right in the middle of it."

26

Behind the stone lions of the French Legation, the
Council of Ministers met that afternoon, as it had done so
many times in recent weeks. The room was crowded by the
eleven ministers and their subordinates, secretaries and attachés. The June heat was stifling, tempers frayed.

They had the latest communiqué from the Forbidden City
on the green baize table before them.

It had been delivered to each legation the night before,
each copy in the familiar large red envelope with the seal of
the *Tsungli Yamen*. The very first words had spread conster-
nation and horror across the Legation Quarter:

> We learn that foreign troops have fired upon our forts
> at Taku, near Tientsin. We therefore hereby break off
> all diplomatic relations with your Government.

But the worst was yet to come:

> The Boxer movement is now active in the capital and
> there is much popular excitement. While your Excellency
> and the members of your family, etc., reside here the
> legations are in danger, and the Chinese Government
> is presently in a difficult position as regards affording
> efficient protection.

The terrifying conclusion had sent messengers scurrying down
Legation Street that very night to summon the ministers to
this meeting:

> The *Yamen* must, therefore, request that within twenty-
> four hours your Excellency will start, accompanied by
> the legation guards, who must be kept under proper
> control ["proper control, my God," Minister Conger had
> sworn aloud], and proceed to Tientsin—in order to pre-
> vent any unforeseen calamity.

"But what does it mean?" Sarah Conger had asked her husband as he stood there staring down at the ruled sheets, the precisely lettered thunderbolt from behind the red walls. Conger had tugged at his thick black beard and answered, in a voice as unsteady as her own: "I think it means, my dear, that they intend to get us out on the open road, and then—do for us all."

After two hours of discussion, the Council of Ministers had come to the same conclusion. And yet they could think of no other solution, of nothing else to do, but go.

"But how and when—how and when?" Sir Claude Mac-Donald demanded querulously. "That is the question—under what *circumstances*, gentlemen, are we to depart?" He cleared his throat repeatedly, and seemed rather more concerned with getting the question properly phrased than with answering it.

Questions! glowered Baron von Ketteler, puffing savagely on his big Havana cigar. This was not a time for questions, but for action! Time to show the Chinese at last who it was they had to deal with!

But Admiral Seymour's relief force had not yet come. From the wording of the *Tsungli Yamen*'s message, the promised troops might still be sitting on their ships off Taku Bar, firing at the Chinese forts. What use was that to the Europeans in Peking, trapped a hundred miles inside China? What else could the legations do but obey, and go?

So they sat in the steamy heat and haggled over the details of their suicidal exodus. They argued about the time of departure, the route, about their Chinese escort. About everything but the sheer folly of leaving the relative protection of the legations to march out of the city under the guns of the Chinese—with whom, apparently, they were already at war.

A pink-cheeked young chargé read aloud a note from Reverend Rogers, announcing that he had some seven hundred Christian converts collected in the Protestant Board Mission at the other end of Legation Street who must "on no account"

188

be left behind. All eyes turned sharply to Mr. Conger, Rogers' fellow countryman and a special friend of the missionaries. But Conger merely muttered that he had more vital obligations to his legation staff, that he could not think about Chinese converts until all Americans were taken care of first.

M. Pichon, the French Minister, reminded everyone again that they had only 377 legation guards *in toto* to protect them. "Only three hundred seventy-seven, *messieurs*, think of it!" It was the last thing in the world they wanted to think of.

Baron Nishi, the Japanese Minister, sat stiff-backed, perspiration running down his yellowish cheeks into his tight collar, and said little. One of his eager young attachés had volunteered to cross the Chinese City to the railroad station that morning to see if there was any word of the Seymour expedition. The young man had not returned. Rumor said he had been killed by the Moslem troops from Kansu, who were encamped on the grounds of the Temple of Heaven, between the Legation Quarter and the station. But no one had volunteered to go and see.

At two-thirty, Von Ketteler stubbed out his cigar savagely and stood up.

"You must excuse me, gentlemen!" he snapped. "I have an appointment at three o'clock—at the *Tsungli Yamen*."

Everybody stared up at him, dumbfounded.

"A previous engagement," the German amplified with a tight smile, "made before this ultimatum was delivered." He gestured contemptuously toward the half-crumpled sheet of ruled paper before him on the table.

"But surely you will not keep your engagement now!" protested M. Pichon.

"Really, my dear Baron," said Sir Claude MacDonald, "under the circumstances—"

The offices of the *Tsungli Yamen* were located in Hata Men Great Street, even farther off across the Tartar City than the Protestant Board Mission. For two days this had been no-man's-land for the legation community, terrorized by chanting Boxer mobs, swept by patrolling troops of Kansu cavalry.

"On the contrary, Sir Claude," Von Ketteler replied with relish, "it is precisely because of the present circumstances that I must be absolutely certain of being on time." He stuck his fingers into his waistcoat pockets and twitched his stiff waxed moustaches, enjoying the center of the stage. "I would not want the gentlemen of the *Yamen* to think that any want of courage kept a representative of the Imperial German Government from keeping an appointment!"

It was a brilliant exit line.

The Marine guard at the gate of the American Legation had been tripled. Stepping out into the road in a clean skirt and a fresh white blouse, Elizabeth saw Sergeant Connor standing under a streetlamp, peering eastward up Legation Street.

He was squinting into the sunglare under the broad brim of his hat. His weathered Irish features looked tired. Elizabeth remembered that he had had no more sleep than she the previous night.

"What is it, Sergeant?" she asked, turning her own head to follow his gaze.

"It appears to be the German Minister, ma'am. He's going somewhere."

There were in fact two sedan chairs waiting in front of the German compound, both decked out in the red-and-green trappings that indicated that they were diplomatic conveyances. There were half a dozen German sailors waiting in the sun with rifles, and a couple of mounted Chinese outriders in the livery of the German Legation. And then, while Connor and Elizabeth Rowntree watched, two men emerged from the legation—the man in the lead unquestionably Baron von Ketteler, puffing on a cigar.

"That'll be his secretary with him," said Lieutenant Greville, joining the little group in front of the American compound.

190

"It must be something important, or he'd send the secretary alone."

They watched Von Ketteler step into the lead sedan chair while the second man in mufti climbed into the other. The Chinese bearers lifted their burdens, the Chinese outriders formed up, one on either side. Then, as the sailors shouldered their rifles and prepared to fall in behind, the watchers unmistakably saw the baron lean out of his chair and wave his German escort back. It was too far down the block for them to hear what he said. But Elizabeth could imagine well enough the smug self-confidence of his order. Let them stay behind and find what shade they could, while Baron von Ketteler went out on his Government's affairs with no more protection than his own malacca cane.

"There goes the best man in the legations!" said Greville, with unaccustomed fervor. "The best of all of us, if I do say so, as shouldn't, out of loyalty to my own chief!" He laughed and smoothed his sandy moustache.

Elizabeth was too tired to answer him. She simply stood with Connor, watching the Chinese bearers carry their burdens away into the waves of heat that rose off the macadam of Legation Street.

Von Ketteler drew deeply on a fresh cigar and settled back in the closeness of the swaying sedan chair. He was feeling singularly triumphant.

Action and more action! thought Von Ketteler. That was what was needed. He would be first secretary in Paris yet, while poor old MacDonald was a half-pay pensioner, prematurely retired to the fogs of his native Scotland. The German Minister filled his lungs with tobacco smoke and smiled, enjoying the image. He felt no fear at all.

The little procession swung north along the far wall of the French Legation, east once more along the Chang-an Chieh, then north again under the pagoda-roofed Arch of Honor and up Hata Men Great Street toward the *Tsungli Yamen*.

Out the window of his chair, Von Ketteler saw a low government building, a police station if he recalled correctly, swaying toward him through the pulsing heat. Perhaps two dozen Chinese soldiers were standing in front of it in the sun. The German set his jaw at a pugnacious angle. He doubted that they would try to stop him—he really did have a formal appointment at the *Tsungli Yamen*—but it was well to strike the proper note, just in case.

In front of the police station on Hata Men Great Street, Corporal Chien Hai of the Peking Field Force watched the two sedan chairs and the liveried outriders approaching up the dusty road. Corporal En knew the red-and-green chairs, and he knew the familiar, stiff-backed figure in the first of them. He was trying to decide what to do about it.

Chien Hai was a Manchu Bannerman, entitled to wear the white button and the blue feather in his hat. His ancestors had broken through the Great Wall with the Manchu conquerors of China three hundred years before, and his family had enjoyed the hereditary privileges of Bannermen ever since. But by 1900 the Bannermen of China had fallen upon evil days. Many of them were little more than night watchmen or hangers-on about the houses of the rich. Chien Hai was only a corporal, and not likely to rise higher. Not likely, that is, unless—

The rumors that filtered down through the innumerable ranks of his superiors said seventy *taels* of silver—and a promotion. Rumors only, of course, barracks talk. No one could ever be strictly identified as having made such an offer. Still and all, a chance like this did not come one's way every day. The gods would probably never send such an opportunity *his* way again.

The sun was very hot. The clop of the bearers' sandals, raising a tiny puff of yellow dust at every step, was very close. In the hooded chair, the hairy-faced foreigner expelled a cloud of aromatic smoke and looked away, as though the sight of a detachment of the Peking Field Force bored him ineffably.

Corporal Chien Hai took two steps forward, to within a yard of the sedan chair, swung up his Männlicher carbine and shot the German Minister in the back of the head.

27

CORPORAL FITZ SAT IN CHARLIE DOG'S, STONE DRUNK AT midafternoon on Canton snake wine.

Connor was to join him there later. But Fitz needed a drink now. It was all getting to him a little—he had to admit it.

He couldn't get Company C of the Ninth out of his mind. Company C on Samar, attacked over their breakfast tables by a whole village full of screaming Philippine *insurrectos* with bolo knives. Veteran troopers, the Ninth, who had fought in the canebrakes of Cuba and the jungles of Luzon. They were wolfing their eggs and tearing open their mail that sunny morning when the Moro bolomen hit. In half an hour, the streets of the village were littered with the brains and guts of American Marines.

The bolos, thought Corporal Fitz groggily. The Goddamned bolos, that was what got you.

He picked up his cup of greenish-yellow wine and poured what remained of it down his throat.

"Charlie!" he called, banging on the table with his open palm. "Hey, Charlie. Rice wine this time, eh? *Chiu*—more *hung-chiu!*"

The old men across the room did not look up from their game of dominoes. Neither the owner nor his wife appeared. Fitz swayed heavily to his feet. He fumbled for the Krag leaning against the rough plastered wall behind him. Neither he nor Connor ever went anywhere in the native city without a rifle now.

"Charlie, ye yellow bastard!" he roared in the thick brogue of his shanty-Irish kin from the East Side of New York. The fat, sweating Chinese appeared almost at once, waddling out through the curtained kitchen door, hands upraised, expostulating mildly.

Of course there would be more wine. If the honorable guest would just be seated—and put down his weapon? Fitz nodded at the gestures and the broken English. Certainly he would sit down. He wasn't after trouble, really. He just wanted a little to drink, was all. He was dead tired.

From somewhere over toward Hata Men Great Street—the nearest avenue—came what sounded like a shot. Then another, and after that a whole fusillade of detonations. Then another bang or two, and the preternatural silence of the city settled back down again.

Fitz shifted his gaze painfully up to the round, fat face of Charlie Dog behind his counter.

"Firecrackers, Charlie?" he said dully. "Whazzat—a wedding or a wake?" He shook his head sleepily. "Never can tell difference, with you people."

He raised the chipped, brimming cup groggily to his mouth.

Dr. Chen was taking tea alone in the pavilion by the lotus pool when he heard the frightened voices in the street, and then the pounding at his outer gate. He started up, wondering. He had left the Emperor out of all danger, perhaps three hours before. There should have been no complications since—unless they had let him get his hands on more of the white powder? Chen crossed quickly to the gate, waving his frightened manservant back into the house.

The moment the bar was out and the latch drawn back, a sobbing European fell forward into his arms.

"Dr. Chen," he gasped in passable Chinese. "Thank God." His chest was heaving from a desperate run, his face as chalky as his shirt. The trousers of his white European suit were dark and glistening with blood. "I couldn't believe it when they told me—this was your house."

Chen Li bolted and barred the gate before he half-carried the injured man across the garden and into the house.

"Cordes," the man said huskily, as Dr. Chen lowered him onto the bed in the front guest room and began to open his clothing. "Heinrich Cordes, from—from the German Legation. We have met at various legation functions, I—" He gave a loud cry as the trousers were pulled away.

There were puckered, oozing bullet holes in both thighs, as though a single shot had torn right through both his legs.

"They—they shot his Excellency on the way to the *Tsungli Yamen*. A damned Bannerman it was, I saw the button and the feather. Then they all started shooting at me—all the soldiers—and I ran for my life."

"This was in Hata Men Street?" said Chen, cleaning the wounds as gently as he could. "And you ran all this way with these injuries?"

"Ran and crawled." The German seemed ashamed to admit that he had crawled. "The wildest kind of luck, that I got away. And then to stumble across your house in the middle of the *hutungs!*"

"We will have to get you to better care than I can give you here, Herr Cordes," said Dr. Chen calmly, taking a dressing from his servant's wrinkled hands. "The Protestant Board Mission for a start, I think. And then into the legations as soon as we can procure transportation."

"Can't ask you to do that, Doctor," said Cordes, his voice fading to a whisper. "Your life would be worth less than mine —if you were seen out there with me."

"We will leave in half an hour," said Chen to his servant. "See if you can find us a cart, or a barrow at least. Something large enough to carry Herr Cordes, and spare clothing." For the German was right about one thing: after succoring a wounded foreign devil, there would be no coming back to the house in Seven Wells Lane.

The tolling bells of the Protestant Board Mission jolted Corporal Fitz out of his alcoholic stupor. He shook his head and stared around him. How long had he been sleeping? Where was Connor?

196

The two old men were gone, and Charlie Dog. Fitz was suddenly and absolutely certain that if he stepped through the curtained door at the back, he would find the kitchen empty too, and the living quarters behind. Charlie and all his family had gone away.

Fitz covered his ears, trying to drown out the clanging of the bells. Every echoing chime threatened to split his aching head in two.

"Ye'd best be off, boyo," he said to himself, slipping once more into the soft brogue of his shanty-Irish childhood. He stood up and reached for the rifle leaning against the wall behind him. It wasn't there.

Then he heard the sound of running feet coming up the alleyway outside.

He had a chair in his hands by the time the first one showed his grinning yellow face, jabbing at him with a spear. He took the spearpoint through his arm, but he knocked the man that put it through him galley-west with the chair. He did the same for the next, and sent him reeling back into the others who now came crowding in at the narrow alley door. So the drunken Irishman was going to have his battle after all! Corporal Fitzgerald roared a long-forgotten Five Points war cry as he kicked chairs and tables aside to clear a space in the middle of the room, to make his stand.

Then he saw the big man coming in.

He was a huge, thick-featured Mongol with a heaving chest and a bright red scarf around his bald head. The barrel of a German Mauser gleamed over one shoulder, and there were two long curving knives in his scarlet sash. Across one massive forearm he carried Fitz's own Krag-Jorgensen.

"Yours, soldier?" he said in fuzzy English, smiling.

The Boxer gang that was with him spread quickly back around the walls. A slack-jawed, half-grown boy appeared at the giant's elbow and stood staring blankly at Fitz, like a child contemplating an insect about to be crushed on the sidewalk.

With a pleasure that looked almost voluptuous, the big man slid back the well-oiled bolt, clicked a cartridge into the chamber.

The crash of the shot was terrific in the enclosed space, stunning the eardrums. The impact of the bullet hit Fitz like a fist in the stomach, driving him backward against Charlie Dog's worn counter. Around him, the red-scarved Chinese boys leaped as though they had been shot too, covering their ears against the blast, wrinkling their noses against the stink of cordite that suddenly filled the room.

Fitz hung onto the counter with both hands and stayed erect. He did not look down, knowing the pain would come any second, remembering how he had seen gut-shot men die before.

The big man flung the rifle to one of the grinning youths around the walls and started for the Marine, sliding a long, curved sword out of his sash as he came.

28

ELIZABETH ROWNTREE CROUCHED ON HER KNEES JUST OUT-
side the gateway to the British Legation, pouring dirt into a
gunnysack. "Sandbags," she had been told they were gener-
ically called; but since they had no sand, loose earth would
do as well. Filled bags were already being piled up along the
canal in front of the gate, to serve as a barricade. Elizabeth
brushed her hair back from her damp forehead and poured
energetically, double handful after double handful.

The canalside road in front of her, the vast grounds of the
British Legation behind her were a bedlam of dazed European
refugees, hired coolies, rifle-toting soldiers, and helpless-look-
ing diplomats. Barrows, carts, wagons of all sorts trundled in
and out of the gateway, raising choking clouds of dust, bringing in baggage and supplies, sallying forth to collect still more.
Troops of a dozen nationalities trotted off to hastily arranged
defense posts on the perimeters of the Legation Quarter. Inside, the various legation staffs were being assigned quarters
in the scattered buildings of the British compound—the
Germans and Japanese to the students' quarters, the Americans to the chapel, the Norwegians to the stables. Officials of
the Belgian Railway had their baggage heaped on an outdoor
pavilion, including plenty of tinned delicacies and cases of
wine. The managers of the Bank of Hong Kong shared a rear
pavilion with the headquarters of the military commanders.

Perhaps a thousand people milled distractedly about under
the luxuriant trees, trampling on the flowering shrubs, littering
the tennis courts with bags and chests and blankets.

Confusion was total. The plan of the morning—instant
departure for Tientsin—had been replaced by another in-
stantaneous and equally ill-thought-out scheme: to gather in
the spacious grounds of the British Legation, there to prepare

for a siege. All the women and children, and a considerable number of civilian men, were duly gathering. The legation guards, in the meantime, were being scattered out over the rest of the Quarter to set up strongpoints for defense.

My God, thought Elizabeth, is anyone thinking at all?

"You really shouldn't, miss," said a British Royal Marine, bending to pick up the sandbag she had just filled. "Wouldn't you rather be inside under the trees with the other ladies, preparing the supper?"

"There are quite enough ladies to prepare supper," answered Elizabeth shortly, "but I understand there is a serious shortage of sandbags."

"There is that, miss," the Britisher admitted with a grin. He shifted the sandbag to his shoulder and went off with it. Elizabeth reached for another empty gunnysack.

Columns of black smoke billowed up over the trees and the rooftops across the canal. Above the din around her, she could hear the sporadic rattle of rifle fire. None of it was really happening, of course. Like most of the people bustling around her, Elizabeth was more than half convinced that she was enjoying a particularly detailed and convincing dream.

There was a shout, and Elizabeth looked down the road to see its source. She saw a long procession straggling across the Legation Street Bridge and turning up the canal road toward her. Dozens of missionaries—some with wives and children—led the way, followed by hundreds of Chinese. A score or so of U. S. Marines herded them along. As the shuffling line reached the walls of the British compound, legation officials hurriedly divided Western missionaries from Chinese converts and sent the latter splashing across the muddy, almost empty canal to a commandeered prince's palace across the way.

As the last of the missionaries approached the gate, Elizabeth realized that Manson Rogers was not among them.

"Reverend Moore," she called to the very last of them, "where is Reverend Rogers? I don't see him here."

"He wouldn't come, Miss Rowntree."

"Wouldn't come?"

"We began to toll the bells to call in the Christian Chinese as soon as word came that there would be room for them after all—across the canal, I see," he added with distaste. "But some protection, anyway. Unfortunately many of our people were not back at the mission compound when the Marines came for us. Reverend Rogers told us to take those who had come, and go with the armed escort. He—he and a few Chinese—stayed to wait for those who hadn't arrived yet."

"But it's almost night now. And the smoke and the shooting—"

"No one could move him, Miss Rowntree. He said—he thought your father would have stayed."

Elizabeth bit her lip and looked down. "Yes," she said. "Yes, I see."

When she looked up, Moore was gone. But another familiar figure was approaching now. Her breath burst out in a long, silent sob of joy and relief. Mingled with the last of the Chinese refugees was a litter with a wounded European lying on it. Chen Li, wearing his white suit and carrying his medical bag, walked alongside.

When they reached the dividing point at the canal's edge, there was a brief altercation over which way Dr. Chen should go. But the wounded man raised himself on one elbow, arguing vigorously, the officials shrugged, and Chen came on with his patient toward the legation gateway.

Elizabeth watched him as he approached. His eyes were darker, his face more completely expressionless than she had ever seen it. She wondered if he even saw her, crouching there among the half-filled sandbags. But as he reached her, he looked down and smiled.

"Miss Rowntree," he said, "I understand a hospital is to be set up in some of the legation offices. I expect we could make rather better use of your services there than here—if you could come by later?"

"Of course," she answered hastily, keeping her voice as level as his own. "Of course, Dr. Chen."

"Thank you, Miss Rowntree." He smiled again, nodded to the bearers of the wounded German, and went on into the chaos of the legation grounds.

Thank God, thought Elizabeth shakily. Oh, thank God. None of the rest of it mattered, she thought, if he was safe.

The mob came over the walls of the mission compound before the Marines and the long procession of refugees were out of sight, and began to loot. The Boxers came in at the gate.

The people of the *hutungs*—dirty, lice-infested, jabbering with glee—went like sharks for the neat rows of boxes and trunks and rude parcels of personal belongings abandoned along the walls of the inner courtyards. With almost no transport but their own backs, the evacuees had left most of their things behind them. Now their trunks were pried open, their valises and carpetbags ripped asunder, and clothes, books, jewelry, pictures, scent bottles, a thousand small things broadcast over the stone court. An old man pranced about in a woman's silk dress. A young one drank off a bottle of cologne and staggered about the yard, howling that the gods were within him.

An Lin, watching tensely through a slatted window from the rear of the mission, could stand it no longer.

"Stop it!" she screamed, bursting through the door. "Is this the piety Lord Buddha taught? Is this the decorum of Confucius?" Her small figure was shaking with rage and shame. Rage at the violation of the mission where she had lived all her life. Shame for her own people, savaging the buildings like animals.

They paid no attention to her at all.

Then, out of the same low doorway from which she had come, a dozen or so other mission Chinese who had volunteered to remain with Reverend Rogers came charging, waving homemade pikes. With pointed sticks and kitchen knives on poles, they chivied the looters away from what was left of the bags and trunks. The ragged, pockmarked mob howled curses at them and bombarded them with rocks and bottles and other objects snatched from the shattered footlockers and steamer trunks. But they backed away before the jabbing poles, out of the inner tangle of courtyards toward the front of the mission.

An Lin, oblivious of a bleeding cheek, watched with blazing eyes. Her cheeks were sunken with six months of wasting grief. Her heart was beating like a bird's in her thin chest. Yet she was almost glad that it was here at last—the conflict between her people and her faith that she had always known must finally be faced.

Then the Boxers came.

"Burn and kill! Burn and kill! Burn and kill!"

The rolling chant preceded them up Legation Street. There was a glow of torches in the gathering dusk. A moment later they came through the arched gateway, cheeks and foreheads trenched with frenzy, eyes drunk on rice wine and their own passion. Half naked, scarlet ribbons fluttering, head scarves and pigtails flying, they charged like wolves at the thin line of Chinese sacristans and deacons who defended the mission.

"Burn and kill! Burn and kill!"

Their spears drove savagely in, their swords rose and fell, spattering blood about the walls, spattering their own chests and faces. Torches and lighted lanterns crashed through windows into the dispensary, the storerooms, the tall church itself, and flames licked up within.

"Burn and kill!"

An Lin stood flattened against the wall of the sacristy at the back of the church. Her dark-circled eyes were fixed, seared by the rising flames that clawed toward heaven all around her. Her ears were filled to bursting with the screams of the dying and the more terrible agony of those who had not yet been granted a release. Her lips moved, murmuring the prayers that had been part of her life as far back as her memory reached.

"Come, An Lin." It was the Reverend Manson Rogers' voice. He stood beside her, there in the shadow of the sacristy, his bony bespectacled face white even in the glare of the fires. "Come with me to the church."

The Chinese girl turned her head to look up at him. "No, Reverend Rogers," she said. "I stay here."

"God—God calls us, my child," said Rogers, staring as though hypnotized into the orange flames. "He is taking it all from us—all the years, all the work—and calling us to Him." He put one thin hand upon her shoulder. "Come with me to the altar."

"No," she said again, shaking her small head fiercely. "I stay here to wait God's call—with my people."

Manson Rogers' lips parted to speak again. But a louder voice filled the flame-lit courtyard now, a voice harsh and brazen as a gong's stroke, exultant, triumphant.

"The gods are pleased, my brothers!" the great bass voice boomed. "The Fists of Righteousness strike hard, the Swords of Righteousness bite deep! Kuan-ti drinks his fill tonight, brothers, and the spirits of our ancestors laugh in heaven!"

"Yes, Feng Yu-lan! Yes, Feng of the Scarlet Fist, Feng the Phoenix of China! Yes!"

Shrieks of adulation rose all around the towering figure. His naked chest heaved; his massively muscled arms held two swords above his head. His face was tilted back, looking up at the fires that now twined like vines around the steeple of the mission church.

"Where are the missionaries?" he shouted. "Where are the foreign devils that ran this brothel these many years? Surely the shepherds have awaited our coming, here with their slaughtered sheep?" His voice mocked, his men laughed.

204

Then An Lin stepped out of the thinning shadows, into the yard.

"All the Christians will go to their God, Phoenix of China!" Her voice was shrill, and as triumphant as his own. "The God of the Christians waits for us, as all demons in hell wait for you, Phoenix who will never rise!"

Feng's flat, ugly face turned toward her, nostrils flaring, eyes narrowing with sudden anger.

"There is one missionary left, Feng Yu-lan!" cried a blood-smeared Boxer at that moment. "In the Christian temple—see!"

Through a gap in the blazing walls, Reverend Rogers' thin figure could be seen walking up the aisle, flame already flickering about him, toward the pulpit and the altar rail.

"It is so, O spirit who will wander forever unburied," An Lin baited Feng once more, "rejected of your fathers, condemned of the gods—"

A huge section of the church's tin roof slid free and fell with a crash and a shower of sparks into the court. Boxers danced screaming away as the red-hot metal tilted and fell over on the mangled bodies of several of the mission's defenders. An Lin turned away, revolted at the sight and smell of burning flesh.

And then, out of the swirling smoke, out of the fire and darkness, the gigantic silhouette of the Boxer leader loomed before her eyes. He had neither sword nor rifle in his heavy hands now, but only a square-cornered five-gallon drum, snatched from a burning storage shed.

As he reached her, the rooftree of the church gave way with a rending crash behind him, and half the church collapsed.

"Am I rejected of my father, then? Am I hated of the gods?" Feng's voice was low and vibrant and charged with fury. "And shall I burn forever in the Christian hell, O whore of the Christian priest?"

She saw his bloody hands come up, his shaven forehead

205

gleaming in the firelight. Her mouth was wide with terror, and she could not close her eyes as the hands came up. With her last strength she whispered, "Kill me. Kill me. Please."

He emptied the can of kerosene over her head and shoulders.

29

SERGEANT CONNOR CROUCHED WITH CAPTAIN JACK MYERS and two other U. S. Marine officers behind a parapet on the Tartar Wall. Below them in the darkening streets of the Chinese City beyond the wall, black-turbaned Moslem cavalrymen in black-and-orange uniforms were cantering about, deploying or preparing to deploy. Eastward, toward the Hata Men, a dozen fires seemed to be burning. As Connor's eyes shifted that way, a finger of flame shot up the steeple of the Protestant Board Mission.

"We will have to hold this section of the wall," Captain Myers was saying. "From the ramp at the back of the American Legation *there*"—he pointed—"to someplace across from the French compound that way." He swung his arm back toward the darkening city and the spreading fires. "If the Chinese ever mounted heavy guns up here, they could reduce every legation to rubble in a day."

"It's a hell of a thing to hold, Captain," said one of the junior officers. "The top of this damn wall must be thirty feet wide, and no cover but these weeds and bushes growing through the stone." He kicked a dry bush with a polished boot. "That wouldn't stop a peashooter, let alone a Mauser or a Männlicher."

"We'll build barricades," said Myers, "just like the ones in Legation Street. One by the ramp head and the projecting bastion behind the American Legation, one up there across from the French."

"Have we the men to man them, sir?"

"Not both. I'll see if I can get the French to take the other one."

"I hope they see it your way, Captain," said someone else sourly. "Who the hell is in charge of this business, anyway?"

"God knows," said Myers.

Connor watched the fires spreading over the eastern side of the Tartar City. Over there, he thought, shifting his eyes slightly to the left, would be Charlie Dog's. Suddenly he wondered where Fitz was. He hadn't seen him since the morning. Had he said something then about a quick drink at Charlie's? Surely not.

"Anything to contribute, Sergeant Connor?" Myers was saying. "You've been here longer than any of us."

"No, sir," said Connor. "Except maybe get the Germans for the other barricade. It will be pretty much behind their legation. And the French will have enough to do, holding that city park they call a compound."

"All right," said Myers, "I'll think about that. Anyone else?"

A bullet whined and spanged off the parapet into the thickening darkness. No one said anything.

"Well, gentlemen," said Myers, "let's get at it."

Another bullet ricocheted past as they trotted off at a crouch. Behind the three-tiered pagoda roof of the Chien Men Gate, the red ball of the sun dipped from sight behind the Western Hills. Then, incongruous and unreal against the shouting and crackle of rifle fire, there came the clangor of a gong. It was sunset, and the Chien Men Gate was closing up as usual, sealing the Tartar City of Peking off until dawn.

Captain Lamenière stepped out of the French Legation into the darkened street. He exchanged a sharp greeting with the sentries, looked left toward the incandescent glow that filled the east end of Legation Street, and slapped his thigh angrily with a riding crop. From the roof a moment since, he had seen the French Cathedral to the north burning too. With a muttered oath he turned to the right and strode off toward the canal and the British Legation beyond.

He had done all he could. The extensive French compound —next largest after the British—was an armed camp now, all civilians gone, soldiers garrisoning every building and scattered strategically through the parklike gardens and along the walls. He would report the situation to his chief. M. Pichon was already comfortably ensconced with his staff in a private house on the British grounds. Then Lamenière would return to set up his own military headquarters in the French Legation, one of the keys to the defense of the Quarter.

As he approached the stone bridge over the canal, he saw a familiar figure. It was Lieutenant Philip Greville, leaning against a stone post at the corner of the bridge, a gunnysack hanging from one hand. The British officer swayed slightly, as if he were about to fall.

"Greville!" Lamenière called in a low voice. "You are hurt?"

"No, it's—look here. Look what I found. Took it off one of those bloody—" He gagged, thrust the sack helplessly toward Lamenière. "I got him in the leg, a lucky shot in the dark. When I saw what was in this thing, I blew the yellow devil's brains out with my pistol."

Captain Lamenière shook the sack out impatiently upon the pavement. Seven or eight round objects about the size of cabbages rolled out. It took the Frenchman several seconds to realize that they were human heads.

He stood staring down in the flame-spangled darkness. One or two of them rolled all too easily. They had had their ears and noses cut off. Several looked up with black holes where their eyes should have been.

"And look," said Greville, "look here. One of 'em's white!"

Footsteps were coming up behind them. Nauseated, feeling oddly guilty, Lamenière dropped to his knees and began to stuff the heads back in the sack. "We must bury them," he said through gritted teeth. "At once." A woman's head slipped between his fingers, and he had to pick it up again.

"What is it, Captain?"

It was Myers, the American Marine captain, with two or three junior officers in tow.

"Relics," said Captain Lamenière, getting awkwardly to his feet, fumbling for the English word. "Remains of Boxer victims. Lieutenant Greville recovered them. He—I will have them buried."

"God!" said one of the American officers.

"One of 'em's white," mumbled Greville again, still leaning on the stone post, looking down into the canal.

"Yes," said Lamenière. He held it up, the face still largely intact. "I wonder if you know—"

"Yeah," said Sergeant Connor, staring hypnotized at the sagging jaw and jellied eyes. "It's Corporal James Fitzgerald, sir. U. S. Marine Corps."

It was Fitz. And Connor couldn't even bring himself to touch him.

30

THE DOWAGER EMPRESS TZU HSI SAT STRAIGHT IN HER undulating sedan chair as her eunuchs bore her up the steep path. Orange lanterns bobbed ahead and behind, and her flat nose wrinkled with pleasure at the strong smell of firs and cedars on either side. The great white Dagoba loomed palely through the darkness on her right, but she paid it no heed. In a moment she would reach the summit. In a moment she would see it all.

The old woman's eyes glittered with excitement in the light of the nearest lanterns. Her face, unpowdered for once beneath the elaborate Manchu hairdo, was sallow and pouched with shadows. Her jaws moved rather more rapidly than usual, crushing and grinding betel nut.

The swaying sedan chair bore her over the crest of Prospect Hill, the highest point in the Imperial City. All of Peking lay spread out before her under the stars.

"Will the Blessed of Heaven descend here?" inquired the Chief Eunuch, bowing his head just level with her heel.

"Yes. Oh, yes."

Tzu Hsi's eyes were shining as the Chief Eunuch had never seen them shine before. Her bony hands clutched the carven arms of her chair like claws. She sat like a woman possessed, gazing out over the extraordinary midnight panorama of Peking in convulsion.

Her heart was molten with joy and gratitude that heaven had allowed her to see this night.

From her point of vantage on top of Prospect Hill, the Dowager Empress could see the southern half of the Tartar City, with the Legation Quarter just to the left of center, and the entire Chinese City beyond. There were no streetlights except for those—now extinguished—in the European Quarter. But there were enough cooking fires, enough lanterns hanging in front of temples or the garden gates of the rich to make the great grid of the city clear. And in the left foreground there were now a dozen towering beacons burning brightly enough to light up whole sections of Peking.

"There, that is the French church!" she exulted, "and that the Russian one. And there—there at the end of their fine paved street is the American Protestant mission, a finger of fire in the sky!" She crowed with glee, like a spectator at a particularly spectacular fireworks display. "There, that is a legation, is it not? Which one? Who can tell me which one?"

"I do not know, your Majesty," said the Chief Eunuch. He had scarcely passed beyond the circumference of the red walls since he had submitted to the scissors forty years before. He knew no more of the world outside than she did.

"You do not know!" Tzu Hsi hissed at him. "Pah! Get me someone who does know. Get me—get me General Tung—at once. I must know all the glorious things I am watching, that I may treasure them up in my heart for all the days to come."

The Chief Eunuch retreated, hands clasped upon his wrinkled bosom, and snapped an order to an underling who fled at once, down sliding stones into the darkness.

The Empress sat rocking and crooning in her gilded chair, her eyes leaping from fire to fire across her city. That is for the Opium War, she thought, her memory racing and tumbling back to her earliest childhood. That is for the Arrow War. That is for my beautiful Summer Palace burned, and that for the Taiping Revolt—

Rocking in her seat like an excited child, cackling with glee, she ticked off the wrongs of her long lifetime. For lost provinces and tributary states that were China's no longer—for Burma and Annam and Tonkin and Korea and all the rest. For Manchuria, where Russian Cossacks burned her villages, and Shantung, where the Germans ruled down the barrel of a Mauser. For all the insults and degradations down the years—let them pay now!

"It is General Tung, Bountiful Mother," murmured the Chief Eunuch, materializing at her side once more. "And Prince Tuan also," he added apprehensively, "with two others. He assures me that he was sent for to come to your Majesty here."

"Even Tuan's insolence shall be forgiven tonight." Tzu Hsi laughed. "Send them to me. Send them all to me."

They emerged out of the darkness of the evergreens and the aromatic shrubbery, and came forward to the lanterns on the hilltop. Prince Tuan, the greatest patron of the Boxers in Peking. General Tung Fu-hsiang, the commander of the Kansu Moslems. And two others, unknown and half-seen in the rear.

Prince Tuan, garish in rough wadded clothing and a scarlet coat and head scarf, insignia of his Boxerism, strode foremost, the reigning favorite. But it was to the swaggering old Moslem general behind him that Tzu Hsi called first.

"General Tung! Come quickly and tell me, what is that burning just beyond the Chien Men in the Chinese city? I know of no foreign installations there."

Tung Fu-hsiang was a swarthy, savage Moslem from the remote province of Kansu. Like most of his cavalrymen, Tung was uneducated, only half civilized, and more than half a bandit. But he and his men had fine new European rifles slung across their backs and the single-minded ferocity of generations of hard-riding ancestors beating in their veins. General Tung knew that, for this night at least, he was indispensable to the Empress of China.

He turned with one hand on his hip, and swung the other in a seeking gesture over the flame-lit city.

"In the area just beyond the Chien Men Gate, your Majesty, the leaders of the *I Ho Chuan* have sworn to burn out the shops that dispense Western medicines. There are many of them there, and they spread evil and disease among the people under the guise of healing."

"There are also a number of other shops in that area,"

213

grunted the old woman. "Shops which dispense silks and furs, tapestries and lacquer ware and jewelry. Unless I mistake, there are more than fabricators of Western medicines burning there."

"That may be, your Majesty," said General Tung boldly. "They are all shops heavily patronized by the foreign devils."

"They are also patronized by mandarins and imperial princes." Sometimes Tzu Hsi had serious doubts about the judgment of these wild men from the hills who called themselves the Fists of Righteousness. But once more she shook her head, rejecting its counsel. Nothing should be allowed to dim the glory of this night.

"Tung Fu-hsiang!" she said sharply. "Do you remember an offer you made to me years ago, when first you came to Peking?"

"I do, Illustrious and Worshipful."

"You said then that you would take your soldiers from Kansu province and purge this city of the foreign devils. Is that not so?"

"It is so, Majesty."

"And I told you then that the time was not yet ready for so doing."

"I abide in the judgment of the Heaven-Blessed."

"But that time, Tung Fu-hsiang, is come now!" Tzu Hsi's eyes were hard black beads, her mouth a sharp line of resentment in the folds of her chin and jowls. "The soldiers under the English Admiral Seymour who set out from Taku two days ago have been stopped at Langfang. They are surrounded there and will be annihilated. The foreign installations and forces in Tientsin itself are under siege at this moment.

"Everywhere they are stopped, surrounded, Tung Fu-hsiang! Stopped, surrounded, annihilated. Now is the time to deal with the heads of the monster—the foreigners in Peking. That task is for you, General Tung—for you and the *I Ho Chuan*, the people of China risen against the foreign devils."

214

The Dowager Empress turned imperiously in her chair. "Prince Tuan—come here!"

Tuan, his pockmarked face working irritably at being ignored so long, thrust himself forward with a bow that was almost peremptory. "Your Majesty summons me?"

Tzu Hsi held out her old hands, jeweled six-inch nail protectors gleaming in the light of the distant fires. "I summon you both," she rasped, "to a glorious task—the destruction of the foreign devils in Peking!"

Both men clasped their hands before their chests and bowed very low.

"And these behind you, Prince Tuan?" Tzu Hsi added, almost gaily once more. "Who are these that you bring? Jugglers and sword dancers for my entertainment? Or what?"

"Ah, better than that, Heaven-Blessed—far better than that!" He drew the ill-assorted pair in out of the darkness, and they both prostrated themselves at once in a reverent kowtow. "These," said Tuan proudly, "are my comrades of the *I Ho Chuan*. This boy is named Tai. He comes from T'ai Shan the sacred mountain, and is known to the people as The Boy To Whom The Gods Speak. And this man is Feng Yu-lan, whom the people call the Scarlet Fist. These are among the great leaders of the Society, and they have come to bow in gratitude before your Majesty for allowing them this day of vengeance on the devils from beyond the seas."

"Feng!" the Empress exclaimed. "Feng, you say? Feng the Phoenix, that rises reborn from the ashes—as China shall rise from the ashes of the foreign devils! It is an omen—a very good omen indeed." And then, to the prostrate giant: "Rise, Feng Yu-lan, that I may look upon the people—the people of China, who have taken upon themselves the extirpation of the foreigners."

Feng rose and bowed once more, his thick hands clasped upon his chest. He did not trust himself to speak.

"Feng," said Tzu Hsi. "Yes—there was another Feng that

215

served me well once. Feng Tzu-tsai, the outlaw that fought the Taipings so bravely, and again against the French. I gave that Feng the Yellow Jacket thirty years ago as a token of my gratitude for his good service. Do you know of him, Feng Yu-lan?"

"He was the hero of my childhood, Bountiful Mother," the big man answered huskily. "I prayed every day in the temple of Kuan-ti the god of battles that I might be allowed to serve the throne as he did."

"Indeed! Another omen, certainly. And a big man too, is he not, Tuan?" She stretched forth gnarled fingers to squeeze Feng's massive arm. Feng quailed to feel the sacred hand, like a nervous white spider clutching at his bronze flesh. "Yes, he is a man. The vigor of the Manchus of old is not dead after all. You have done well, Tuan, to bring me such a one."

This was the greatest moment of Feng Yu-lan's life. As he knelt there on that hilltop ringed by the flaming pyres of the foreigners, trembling under the gaze and the harsh, rasping praise of his Empress, he thought his laboring heart might burst under the burden of its joy. Feng the pleasure merchant, the debauchee and the degenerate, was gone forever now, burned away in the flames that devoured other men's flesh. He was the boy Yu-lan once again, the boy who had prayed to Kuan-ti in the village beneath the Western Hills. For did he not kneel now in the shadow of the Dragon Throne, even as that boy had sworn to do?

"Feng Yu-lan!" said Tzu Hsi then, so sharply that he could not help but raise his deep-pouched eyes to hers. "The foreigners are like fish in a stewpan down there, Feng," the old woman said in a voice that cracked with emotion. "For forty years I have lain on brushwood and eaten bitterness because of them. Will you not cook them for me now?"

"With scallions and garlic, Bountiful Mother!" Feng Yu-lan burst out. Abashed at his own presumption, the master of the *I Ho Chuan* buried his face once more in the wet grass. Above him, he could hear the old Empress cackling with glee.

"Your Majesty," whispered the Chief Eunuch at that moment. "Your Majesty—look! The Chien Men!"

"What?" snapped Tzu Hsi, irritated at having her mood of exultation marred once again. "What is it?"

"Look, your Majesty—the Chien Men Gate itself has caught fire!"

The old woman swung round. "Impossible!" she snapped—even as she saw that it was so.

The entire section of the Chinese City just south of the main gate of the Tartar City was a raging sea of flame. Shops full of beautiful lacquered cabinets, gorgeous silks, embroidered hangings, pearls and precious gems set in gold and silver, all were going up in sheets of yellow flame. And now the towering Chien Men itself was blazing too. She could almost hear the bright-green tiles cracking and sliding from the three-tiered pagoda roof to crash into the streets below.

Tzu Hsi sucked her wrinkled lips back from the jagged yellow teeth. This was a bad sign indeed, an evil omen for the throne of the Manchus. As she had so often in recent months, she remembered the ancient prophecy, that the rule of a woman should bring down the Dynasty of Ching in ruins.

"Come," said the Dowager Empress sharply, "we will go in. I have seen enough."

As the imperial sedan chair swayed back down the gravel path into the darkness, the magnificent south tower of the Chien Men—the Mouth of the Dragon itself—crashed in a shower of sparks and a noise like an explosion into the street a hundred feet below.

BOOK FOUR

THE
BARRICADES

31

THE EARLY JULY HEAT HUNG HEAVY AND MOIST IN THE ROOM. It was a palpable presence, like the odor of wounds and disinfectant. Like the buzz of the flies which the best will in the world could not seem to keep out of the little warren of offices that served as the legation hospital.

The heat and the dampness beaded the foreheads of Dr. Chen and Elizabeth Rowntree as they bowed together over the wound. A rifle bullet had smashed through the tall young Austrian's thigh, shattering the femur, severing the femoral artery, and doing a good deal more damage before exiting just above the knee. It was a desperate case, and their hands worked with desperate urgency over it, cleaning, tying, binding, splinting. The young officer lay unconscious under their hands, his cheeks dead pale, drops of perspiration standing out on his face as on theirs.

Elizabeth and Dr. Chen worked together like a carefully drilled team now, after months of fellow toil in the *hutungs* and weeks of siege. It was clear to Chen, as to the other doctors, European and American, who happened by them as they labored together over torn bodies and shattered limbs, that Elizabeth's skills went far beyond even those of an operating-room nurse. Most important of all, this was increasingly clear to Elizabeth herself.

The Austrian soldier began to make a helpless moaning noise in his throat. His head rolled from left to right and back again on the table. His thin yellow moustache glistened with sweat.

Chen Li completed the dressing, nodded to Elizabeth. She was already loosening the tourniquet.

He signaled next to two volunteer orderlies, civilians in their shirt sleeves, and they hurried over with a stretcher. A moment later, Chen and Elizabeth stood alone in the smelly, flyblown little office-turned-dressing station. It felt very strange indeed. They had scarcely had a moment alone since the siege of the legations began, three weeks before.

Elizabeth looked at the man in the stained surgical gown standing across the table from her. The sculptured cheekbones were the same, the deep, half-hooded eyes only a little wearier. The nearest sound of voices was Dr. Poole's, lecturing Nurse Lambert a couple of offices away. Impulsively, Elizabeth leaned forward and kissed Li quickly on the mouth.

From somewhere up toward the North Bridge, there came a sudden burst of rifle fire.

Chen's eyes crinkled briefly at the corners. He touched the girl's cheek. Then he turned away to pack up his instruments.

"I hope the firing stops directly," he said. "It's time for us to cross over to the Fu to see to our—other patients." There was a touch of bitterness in his voice that made Elizabeth herself feel a pang, sharing his hurt.

"The Fu" was the common label in the legations for the commandeered princely palace across the Imperial Canal where some three thousand Chinese Christians had been assigned their place of refuge. These Chinese victims of Boxer terror were thus within the legation defense lines, yet safely segregated from the European community in the British Legation. Dr. Chen was one of the few who went over periodically to give them medical care. Elizabeth, chin held high, defying the stares of her own people, always accompanied him on the hurried, dangerous crossing.

"Will you come over to the Bell Tower for some tea first?" she asked. "The shooting is bound to go on for a while yet, before it peters out."

"No," said Chen, "no, I think I'll get a little rest. You go ahead, Miss Rowntree," he added in a slightly louder voice as Dr. Poole appeared in the doorway, "and have your tea. I'll stop for you when things have quieted down outside."

Elizabeth nodded, smiled briefly at the head doctor, and

222

stepped out into the tree-shaded grounds of the British Legation.

It still amazed her to see how little the British compound was changed after twenty days of siege. The trees which gave the grounds their parklike beauty also provided cover from enemy fire. If one stayed away from large open areas like the tennis courts, it was quite possible to move about with no worry whatever about enemy sharpshooters.

But there were differences, even within the British Legation. Walls had been thickened and raised on all sides, sandbags deployed strategically over every gate and connecting alleyway. The place was vastly overcrowded, men and women of a dozen nationalities drifting aimlessly about with the glazed look of people who had had little sleep for weeks. Exhausted soldiers and Marines slept in open pavilions or on the grass. Wounded men sat or lay everywhere, trying to get a breath of air in the smothering heat of high summer. The smell of wounds, the stink of the sizable additional latrines dug at the rear of the grounds were constantly in everyone's nostrils. And always in the distance there was the savage crack of rifle fire, the boom of a cannon.

The rest of the Legation Quarter was little better than a no-man's-land. Some of the foreign buildings had been captured already, some burned, all of them attacked repeatedly, pocked with bullets and pounded by light artillery. Soldiers were quartered in all the legations still in Western hands, and civilians hurried here and there on specific errands. But there was always the nervous fear of the hidden sharpshooter or the sudden Boxer sally.

Beyond the shrunken perimeters of the Legation Quarter itself, there stretched acres of burned-out *hutungs* and gutted shops. The Boxers had set dozens of fires, many of which had gotten out of hand. The charred ruin of the Chien Men Gate was a towering reminder of the mindless fury of the Boxer mobs. But General Tung's disciplined Moslem troops had kindled their share of blazes too, hoping the flames would spread into the Quarter. The Hanlin Academy behind the British Legation was a blackened wreck, centuries of ancient manuscripts destroyed in a few hours. British Royal Marines and turbaned Kansu troopers alike were using some of the surviving codices to stuff crevices in their sandbag revetments.

In almost every direction around the Legation Quarter, desolation spread like a stain. Roofless houses and trees burned to charcoal where they stood offered mute evidence of the fury of the siege.

Everywhere and always, finally, there was the fear, sapping the strength of the besieged as no privation could. They ate well enough still, though they were eating their own racing ponies and even mules now, and rationing the tinned vegetables. But there were white heads already on poles in front of General Tung Fu-hsiang's headquarters, and they had all seen the bloody, terrified Chinese rescued from the hands of the Boxers. Fear of torture, violation, mutilation filled the silences of every conversation and haunted all their dreams.

But Elizabeth was too exhausted that blistering July day even to think about what might happen to her in the days and weeks to come.

She sank gratefully into a lawn chair beside the ornate stone Bell Tower and reached for a cup of tea, kept always available by the ladies of the legations. One such, a matronly Britisher, wrinkled her nose and averted her gaze as she passed. Too late the American girl realized that she had forgotten to remove her long, stained nurse's apron.

But there were other reasons for the wrinkled nose and the averted gaze, Elizabeth knew. Rumors had been spreading about her and Dr. Chen all spring. Now that they were in daily contact under the very eyes of the entire legation community, the rumors had become certainties. To half the women there, she was, quite simply, "the Chinese doctor's concubine," a shame to her nation and her race.

They were the old Philadelphia rumors all over again. This time she found that she didn't care a jot.

She had her work to do this time. Her work——compelling, totally involving, vastly more important than her precious reputation. And she hadn't noticed any of the wounded men who lay on the table before her day after day pushing her morally tainted hands away!

She smiled almost tranquilly after the departing matron's back, and drank her tea, and waited for the firing to stop so that she and Dr. Chen might go together to the Fu.

32

CONNOR CROUCHED IN THE LEE OF THE ROUGH BRICK BAR-
ricade, rain dripping off his wide-brimmed hat, and squinted
through the darkness along the top of the Tartar Wall. His
flannel shirt was soaked to his shoulders, and he doubted very
much that the revolver strapped to his waist would fire. It was
after midnight on the third of July.

That made it the fourth, he realized suddenly. Happy glorious Fourth.

The rains had begun that very day. The long drought was
over. Connor wondered how the Boxers would explain it, since
a good many of the Westerners were still alive, in Peking at
any rate. No doubt they would claim that, the good work of
massacre once begun, the gods had relented and opened the
floodgates of heaven upon the parched fields of the Celestial
Empire.

A flash of lightning blazed across the sky, illuminating the
wall and the city below. In the spectral glare, Connor could
see the new Chinese barricade, no more than twenty-five yards
down the wall. Just behind it loomed the tower. It was fifteen
feet tall already, almost high enough to give Chinese sharpshooters a clear field of fire over the entire area behind the
American barricade.

They worked fast, these damn Chinese. It had all been done
in a single day.

"What it comes down to, men," Captain Myers was saying,
"is that the Chinks have got to be dislodged from that new
barricade, and that tower has got to go. You all know how
important this wall is to us. If the enemy get ahold of it, they'll
mount artillery here and pound the legations to pieces. And
they're sure as hell going to get ahold of it if we leave that
sharpshooting tower intact. So we're going to go for it. At
once."

Connor saw that there were a couple of dozen Americans in the shuffling, dripping cluster around the captain, plus a slightly larger contingent of British Royal Marines and considerably fewer Russians. A thoroughly mixed force—bad news to start with.

"This is going to be a bad business," Myers went on, "and I want only willing volunteers. Any man whose heart is not in it had better clear out now."

Officers always did talk too much, thought Sergeant Connor, even good ones. He bent over, sheltering his Lee-Enfield as well as he could with his body, and checked the rifle's mechanism with quick, nervous fingers.

Myers assigned the Russians a diversionary attack along the right-hand parapet. The Americans and British would charge straight for the Chinese barricade. There would be no shooting until they were in hand-to-hand contact with the enemy. Fix bayonets.

As the men moved up to their own loosely built barricade, lightning flickered eerily once more. In the muted roll of thunder that followed, Connor heard the captain's voice call out the single word *"Go!"*

He clambered over the wet bricks and dropped into the weeds of no-man's-land.

It seemed to Feng Yu-lan that he had not slept for weeks, perhaps for months. What rest he had had came in bits and pieces, odd moments snatched from the battle in whatever corner came handy. His head had not touched a pillow since the Empress of China had charged him, and the *I Ho Chuan* through him, with the exalted task of frying the foreigners like fish in a pan.

He had roamed impatiently from one side to another of that embattled rectangle, less than a thousand yards on a side, where the Westerners cowered under Chinese shot and shell. Sometimes with the exhausted boy Tai stumbling along in his wake, sometimes striding alone through the smoldering ruins that ringed the Legation Quarter, he had prowled like a tiger around his trapped and dwindling foes. The brass-buttoned Peking Field Force and the black-turbaned Moslem troopers alike knew his tall, heavy-shouldered figure. Even the fierce Moslems swore that "the big Mongol" was a man and gave him a weird ululating cheer when he rallied them once more to the assault.

That was his sole message: Attack, attack, and attack again. Press the foreigners night and day. Give them no rest, no hope, no quarter. Build the pressure till their defense lines crack and splinter like old glass, and the last white face is crushed under a Chinese heel.

When he heard of the planned assault along the Tartar Wall, when he saw the rickety tower and the advance barricade outlined against the setting sun, he had come at once. He was drowsing fitfully in the rain, his back against the base of the tower, when the crash of gunfire and the caterwauling screams of the attackers brought him to his feet with his rifle in his hands.

Connor teetered for an instant on top of the Chinese barricade, squinting into the muzzle flashes and the deafening bang of the guns. In the darkness at his elbow, a Royal Marine caught his breath with a grunt and went over backward off the barricade. At the same instant, Connor launched himself forward into the shouting tangle of bodies in the blackness below. As he leaped, the lightning blazed over the wall once more.

Half a dozen things etched themselves into his memory in that flash-lit moment. Captain Myers down and rolling with a spear jammed halfway through his leg. Chinese backs and loosened queues breaking from the fight, scattering over the top of the wall back toward the Chien Men Gate. Marines wading knee-deep through the dead and dying, almost all of them with rain-streaked Chinese faces.

And one Chinese who was neither dead nor in flight. A seven-foot giant at the base of the unmanned tower, his gleaming Mauser raised and ready. Slitted eyes and heavy Mongol features that Connor had seen before, through a train window against a snowy field of kaoliang.

The instant the lightning revealed his enemies to him, the big Chinese began to fire. Once, twice, three times. Connor saw another Britisher go over backward and Private Yancy collapsed like a crumpled scarecrow, blood spurting from his neck. He felt his own rifle shatter violently in his hands. Then the night closed around him, and the Mauser was silent.

Connor dropped his broken gun and clawed for Yancy's, came up clutching the fallen weapon in numbed fingers. He ran in a low crouch toward the looming outline of the Chinese tower and the shadowy figure of the man beneath it.

But the rain was sluicing into his eyes, and he was half blinded by the last dazzling flash. He thrust and thrust again into the vibrating blackness, and hit nothing. Then out of nowhere a paralyzing blow slammed into his stomach, doubling him up with pain.

He tried to cry out, tried to shout *"Here he is—the big bastard's over here!"* But his thin lips worked soundlessly in the darkness as his lungs fought for air.

"Yang kuei-tzu!" hissed a low vibrant voice in his ear. "Foreign devil!"

Then a huge pair of hands caught him at the neck and the crotch, swung him high into the air, and hurled him over the crenellated ramparts off the top of the Tartar Wall.

33

HE WOKE UP TO THE REEK OF CHLOROFORM AND THE SOFT
moaning of wounded men. A lantern was shining in his eyes.
His head hurt horribly, and his whole body ached.

"You are one of the most fortunate men alive," said the
voice of Dr. Chen.

"What happened?" said Connor, astonished at the feebleness of his own voice.

"Three broken ribs and at least one concussion," Elizabeth
Rowntree responded from somewhere beyond the lantern light.
"And apparently nothing else."

"How—?"

"You went over the inner rampart of the wall. You fell
through a ginkgo tree and the roof of a ginseng shop. And
thanks to the luck of the Irish—or the thickness of the Irish
skull—you'll probably be back on the wall again before the
week is out."

"Huh," said Connor groggily. "Where'd you find me—in
the middle of somebody's bed?"

"We didn't find you at all," said Dr. Chen. "You walked
out of the shop, wandered half a block up the lane, and collapsed in the middle of the tennis courts at the Peking Club.
We found you there."

"First time I've ever been inside the Peking Club," grunted
the sergeant as Chen Li raised his torso slightly from the table
and Elizabeth expertly bound up his ribs with strips of torn
sheeting. First time Chen has ever been there too, he thought,
remembering that the club was as closed to Chinese as it was
to noncoms and enlisted men.

Dr. Chen said something in Chinese, and the lantern suddenly dipped away. "If you'll come this way, Sergeant," he
murmured. With surprising strength, he lifted the Marine off

the long dispatch table and stood him rocking unsteadily on his feet. "Miss Rowntree will find you a bunk in the hall."

Connor took a hesitant step and almost fell. His head throbbed painfully. Then he felt Elizabeth's arm around his body, her hip against his in the darkness. "Just lean on me," she said cheerfully. "I'm stronger than I look. And you are considerably weaker at the moment."

With eyes quickly accustomed to the dark, Elizabeth led the wounded Marine through the tangle of uneasily sleeping patients, dodging the mosquito netting draped from the ceiling. She found their way out the door and up the main hall of the Chancery, past men that groaned and men that snored, till she came at last to an empty straw mattress on the floor.

"Here you are," she said, lowering him as gently as she could. This must hurt terribly, she thought, trying to keep her hands high under his arms and off the bandaged ribs. But he went down on the mattress without a whisper of pain.

"Thank you, ma'am," he said in a low, dazed voice as he rolled over on the crackling straw.

"*Sergeant* Connor!" she said with a little laugh. "Do we have to go back to ma'am and miss? I thought we were better friends than that."

"I hope so, ma—" he said. "I hope so, Lizzie."

"Good," she said cheerfully. "I'm looking forward to your stay." He felt her cool fingers brush his forehead, smoothing back the loose dark hair. Then a blanket settled down over his body out of the blackness. "If you need anything in the night, call for Sister Marie. She's the night nurse—just down the hall, where you see the slit of light."

He tried to answer and couldn't, for the booming pain in his head.

"Good night, Michael," she said. She squeezed his hand in the darkness and was gone.

Connor spent four days in the hospital.

The first day was unadulterated misery, a fog of pain and

231

heat, stinging insects, the stench of chemicals and wounds. The second day he was sitting up and noticing the world around him, joining in the jocular conversation up and down the hall. By the last day he was up and making himself useful around the enlisted men's wards, despite continuing headaches and the dull pain in his ribs.

Corporal Toomy came to see him twice. He reported that the wall was for the moment cleared of Chinese. The big Mongol who had thrown Connor over the ramparts had got clean away, but a dozen of his mates had been killed and the rest routed, at a cost of two American lives and less than half a dozen wounded, mostly Britons and Russians. Captain Myers was recovering nicely in the officers' ward. They were all heroes, particularly the Americans. Minister Conger and the entire legation staff had worn little red-white-and-blue flags in their buttonholes on the Fourth of July in their honor.

Connor shrugged and asked how many of the men were down with dysentery, which had been sweeping through his platoon in the days before the attack.

"Nobody's *down* with it," said Toomy, spitting accurately into a strategically located earthenware jar. "Everybody's *got* it."

Connor told him where the rice water could be had in a corner of the legation kitchens and urged him to take as many quarts as he could get away with. Toomy nodded and went away.

But Connor's overwhelming preoccupation during those four days was Elizabeth Rowntree.

He had never been so close to her for so long. The sound of her voice, the click of her footstep on the polished floor became part of his life during those days and nights. His heart beat like a boy's when she passed, spoke, knelt beside his pallet to take his temperature or adjust his bandages. He absorbed her face by day—the dark-blue eyes, the straight nose and wide, generous mouth. He dreamed of her at night.

Elizabeth's affection for him was real enough, he could see

232

that. And it was a warmth that went beyond mere friendship. Her smiles, her glances across the ward, the occasional touch of her hand told him more than she perhaps even knew herself of her feelings for him. It was incredible, yet it seemed almost possible that the Philadelphia minister's daughter might actually come in time to care for the Irish immigrant's son from the bad side of New York.

Or so at least he dared to hope as he swatted at flies and watched her move about the cluttered, steamy, makeshift hospital.

Elizabeth herself was not in fact oblivious to Sergeant Michael Connor. Connor to his friends; Michael to his mother, his priest, and Elizabeth Rowntree.

She saw the quick hunger in his eyes the first day of his stay in hospital. She took it for fever at first, but then that was gone, and the look remained. It was a look of lust and longing mingled that she had seen more than once on the faces of the young men in boater hats who had taken her buggy riding up the Schuylkill. She wondered she had not noticed it before on Michael Connor's unprepossessing Irish features, in all their easy talks and strolls up Legation Street.

They were not such unprepossessing features as she had thought, really, once you got used to the Irish type. It was a tough, bony face, with a mouth not made for smiling. But there was an uncompromising honesty in his eyes, and courage in the set of his mouth and narrow jaw. Somehow, quite irrationally, she believed that, beneath all the differences their vastly different worlds had bred into them, she and Michael Connor were two of a kind.

She thought these things with a smile of genuine gladness as she hurried about the wards. Thinking about it seemed momentarily to ease the weight of the wrenching, tragic passion that still bound her to Dr. Chen Li.

34

THE COUNCIL OF MINISTERS MET THAT NIGHT AS IT ALWAYS had, in an atmosphere of indecision and disunity.

Sir Claude MacDonald sat as usual at the head of the green baize table. Three weeks into the siege, sandbags covered the windows and everyone looked a little more wilted than was their wont. Herr von Bülow, the urbane German chargé d'affaires, had replaced Baron von Ketteler as chief spokesman for the subjects of the Kaiser in Peking. Otherwise all was the same. Pichon was as nervously apprehensive, Conger as slow and stolid as ever. The paroxysm that was shaking the Chinese Empire was the subject of all their discussions—was in fact the sole reason for the Council's existence. But it seemed to have done little to fuse the besieged into a unified body dedicated to the single goal of survival.

Sir Claude shuffled his papers unhappily that steamy mid-July evening. The news, he was sorry to report, was unrelievedly bad.

Admiral Seymour had definitely been turned back at Langfang—had perhaps even been annihilated, if you could take the crowing of the Chinese seriously. The allied column had abandoned the railway, which the Chinese had torn up both before and behind them, and had tried to take the river route back to Tientsin. But the barges and sampans they had commandeered had moved pitifully slowly, under heavy fire from both banks of the river. Whether they had survived the retreat to Tientsin was unknown.

The Western community in Tientsin itself, furthermore, was under siege. A tremendous battle was raging around the city, and God knew how that would end. At the far end of the line, the allies had certainly launched an attack on the Taku Forts. But whether the forts had been taken or not, no one knew. Even if they were in Western hands, they represented no more than a tiny foothold on the coast of this vast continental empire. How long it would take the Powers to expand that foothold and begin a second march on Peking was anybody's guess.

"All most discouraging," he concluded, "most discouraging." His long Scottish face looked suddenly bleak and bony behind the elegant moustaches.

"If they only realized how perilous our situation is," said Mr. Conger, tugging at his beard, "they'd send troops fast enough."

"It is not at all certain, of course," MacDonald felt obliged to remind them, "that the outside world is aware that any of us have survived at all."

"What?"

"I say, that if none of our messengers have reached friendly lines, it is quite possible that the world assumes that we have all long since been massacred. In which unhappy eventuality, I do not think we can look forward to the imminent arrival of a rescue column."

"But it is even more reason," protested Herr von Bülow, "to send an expedition if they think the Chinese have murdered us all!"

"An expedition, yes—but a punitive expedition, not a rescue force. And a punitive expedition will want to be very sure of itself. It will take time to build up sufficient strength to be absolutely sure it does not share Admiral Seymour's unhappy fate. It might not start the march north until autumn, or even later. By which time—"

The British Minister coughed delicately. There was a silence around the table.

"It all comes back then," said Von Bülow, "to the messengers."

"It does," said Sir Claude.

Half a dozen Chinese boys had already been sent to inform the world that the legations were still holding out. Some had

235

been lowered from the Tartar Wall in wicker baskets. Some had gone scuttling out the water-gate through which the Imperial Canal flowed out under the wall. They had gone in a variety of disguises. None of them had ever returned.

"What hope?" M. Pichon shrugged tragically. "They have all been caught. Why should the next get through?"

"My legation," said Baron Nishi, the Japanese Minister, "promised a thousand *taels* of silver, and still the boy we sent did not return."

"I really don't think," said MacDonald, gently reproving, "that silver is the answer here. Mr. Conger and I have quite another notion, actually."

The ministers hunched forward with a flicker of interest. Every one of them felt in his heart that the end was not far off. But they would rather go out scheming than in this torpor of despair.

Michael Connor had never believed in love. Love was something in popular songs and storybooks, he thought. Something only the most self-deceiving swells could ever take seriously. He had had to travel halfway around the globe, it seemed, to find out that he was wrong.

He thought about Elizabeth Rowntree's body, of course. Who could help it? She was the prettiest woman in the wards. He watched the way she moved, the way she smiled, the way the hair curled up on the back of her neck and under the little makeshift nurse's cap. His eyes drank in the slimness of her ankle as she passed, the smoothness of her arms as she drew his blanket over him. The thought of the slender young body under the long skirt, the thin blouse and blood-smeared hospital smock inflamed him almost beyond bearing.

But he saw other things now too, as he lay dreaming through the days on his straw tick mattress on the floor. Things that stirred feelings in him he had never felt for any woman before.

That she had grit he knew, had known since he had seen her coolly tending the wounded under fire on the Tientsin

236

train. He now discovered other traits as well—a stamina, a determination, a sheer calm competence that he had never known in one of her sex before. She never seemed to tire; she never lost her head or her temper. And she did her job. Every broken man in the wards knew that, and respected her for it.

Elizabeth Rowntree was no fairy-tale Florence Nightingale to Sergeant Connor, no Lady with a Lamp moving distantly and perfectly through a sea of suffering. Her hair was seldom in place after ten in the morning. Her brow was as damp with sweat, her smock as pungent with chemicals and less neutral odors as any patient's. She was a hundred times more real than any tabloid saint, and commensurately more magnificent.

It was on his last night in the makeshift hospital that he collected the courage to speak to her.

The night was hot and moist as usual, loud with insects, punctuated now and again by the soft cry of a wounded man. Connor stood up quietly in the dark and pulled on his battered grey jodhpurs. Barefoot, naked to the waist save for the bandages around his rib cage, he padded up the hall toward the slit of light that marked the night nurse's station. He had heard Elizabeth say that afternoon that she would be taking Sister Marie's place this evening.

Michael Connor's heart throbbed painfully within the band of broken ribs. If she was busy, he told himself, he would simply turn around and go back to bed. But if he didn't speak now, didn't tell her at least something of what he felt, when would he have another chance?

It was this night or never. He reached the half-open door.

"But, Li," Elizabeth's voice whispered in the small, lamplit office, "what in the world can they want so late at night? Can't it wait until morning? You need rest so badly."

"So do we all, my dear," said the Chinese doctor's voice. "I shall not be long."

"Stop and tell me what it's all about on your way to bed?"

"I will, Elizabeth."

There was a silence. A silence louder than the crash of

237

artillery to Sergeant Michael Connor. He thrust a leathery cheek, a single eye up against the gap between the door and the doorframe.

He saw a clutter of filing cabinets, a long dispatch table draped with a darkly stained sheet, a tangle of mosquito netting over the sandbagged window. An oil lamp burned smokily. Next to the window, the upper part of their bodies lost in shadow, Elizabeth Rowntree and Chen Li stood with their arms around each other, their faces together in the darkness.

There was a mutter of gunfire somewhere off to the south. Connor turned around and went back down the corridor.

35

Elizabeth sat alone in the crowded little office turned into a receiving ward, waiting for the orderlies to come and take the dead man away. It was much later that same night. The *crump* of the Peking Field Force's light artillery reached her through the sandbagged windows. The corpse lay under a reddening sheet on the dispatch table, its carefully shined black boots gleaming dully in the lamplight.

Elizabeth's cheeks were tight. Her clasped hands showed white at the knuckles.

The outer door opened and closed quickly, and Dr. Chen was back.

"Li!" She rose, one hand reaching out to him. "Thank God you—" She stopped. "What is it, Li?"

Chen Li's eyes were opaque. His smile was as warm as ever, from the corners of his mouth to the wrinkles at the corners of his eyes. But the eyes themselves were inward-focusing now. With a pang Elizabeth realized that even after all that had been between them, Chen Li was still capable of shutting her out, of retreating into depths she could not reach.

"What is it, Li?" she repeated more slowly, searching his face with her own distraught blue gaze.

"I am going to Tientsin tomorrow," he answered, as if it were no more than a matter of a six-hour train trip. "You will have to take my rounds in the morning. And keep as many of our patients as you can while I am away. I think Poole has enough sense to utilize your talents as they should be."

He poured himself a tiny cup of tea from the small pot he kept on the filing cabinet, beside the big European coffeepot. Elizabeth stared at him in disbelief.

"You're going to Tientsin?" she said. "You?"

"The Council of Ministers think I would be an appropriate person to carry out word of conditions here. And of course an urgent plea for relief as soon as possible."

"You, Li? But why? You of all people are needed here!"

"You are becoming quite adept at bullet wounds, Elizabeth." He smiled. "And Dr. Poole is after all a military surgeon."

"You have more surgical skill than Velde and Poole and the rest put together! For God's sake, why can't they send another student, or someone else from the Fu? Why you?"

"The students have been very brave, but they are only boys. They must be given written dispatches, or no one would believe them in Tientsin. And written dispatches, however cleverly secreted in clothing, may be found when they are stopped at the gates—or at any village between here and the coast. I will carry the words of Minister Conger and Minister MacDonald in my head only. And I am well enough known in Tientsin that I will be believed. The odds are much better that I will get through." Chen Li sipped his tea. "That is Sir Claude MacDonald's reasoning, at any rate."

"But it's insane!" said the girl. "No one can get out." There were tens of thousands of Chinese troops in Peking alone. The Boxers controlled the entire province, as far south as the war zone itself. No one could pass out through that tormented city, let alone cover the hundred miles of open road to the coast. "It's insane," she said again.

"The chances are not at all bad, actually," he replied, still in the withdrawn conversational tone in which he had spoken since he entered the office. "I know the *hutungs* better than any student. And I have made regular tours to the villages every—"

"How can you do this, Li?" said Elizabeth shakily. "How can you leave me—leave *us*—for what is waiting out there?"

"It's the only thing I *can* do, Elizabeth," he answered quietly. "Can you not see that?"

She shook her head numbly.

"I cannot take up a rifle against my own people, Elizabeth. I must find other ways to keep them from staining their hands with the blood of the hundreds of us trapped here, the thousands across the canal in the Fu. I have done my best as a doctor. I have treated the sick and injured on both sides of the canal. I have bound up the wounds of the captured attackers as well as defenders of the legations—what few wounded prisoners are brought in," he added, with a touch of acid bitterness. It was well known that neither side took many prisoners.

"Now the ministers are asking me to try at least to get word through that the legations still live, hoping help will come the faster for that knowledge. I do not know about that. But I do know that the sooner the legations are relieved, the sooner the killing will end. The sooner this mangled city will cease to bleed."

"And what about *us*, Li?" she asked again. "What about you and me?"

He turned quickly to her. "I will be back, Elizabeth," he said. "You know that. Whether the Powers can get here in time or not, I will come back."

"Heroes!" she said. "You're all such b-bloody heroes." She stopped a moment, holding the tears back. "You, and my father, and Manson Rogers at the mission. And here—here's another of your bloody heroes tonight." She turned blindly to the dispatch table and yanked back the sodden sheet.

The face was largely shot away. One of the soft-nosed bullets that both sides commonly used had burst open against the bone. Caroming away, it had carried a substantial part of the flesh with it.

"His name," she said, "was Lamenière. I don't think you knew him. I scarcely knew him myself, really. Just another flirtatious young officer in the legations. But they say he died heroically tonight."

"Many die gallantly every night, Elizabeth. On both sides of the lines. It is to stop the dying that I must go."

241

"And die yourself, like the rest of them." She looked him in the face, her eyes hot and brimming. "Oh, Li, don't go. I've needed you, waited for you all my life. Don't leave me now. Don't give me another dead hero to love."

"I have to go, Elizabeth. You know it."

She knew it. She felt her heart grow cold, but she knew he was going to do what he had to do. She stopped fighting then, and let the tears flow silently down her cheeks.

But she did not fling herself into Chen Li's arms.

Dr. Chen replaced the wet sheeting over the ruined face and turned back to Elizabeth. She has the strength, he told himself as he watched the healing tears flow. The strength of hopelessness now, but soon the strength that is in herself. Soon she will have that too.

36

THE GIGANTIC SKY OF NORTH CHINA TOWERED ABOVE THE Tartar Wall, black and blazing with stars. A rocket arched up across the Milky Way, then burst in a fountain of white fire. It cast an eerie glow over the crenellated wall and the roofless city of the dead outside, threw fingers of shadow across the broken rooftops of the Legation Quarter. A moment later, two Krupp guns banged and flashed from somewhere in the gutted ruins outside, and shells whined over the wall to fall with a roar into the American compound just below.

Sergeant Connor flattened himself against the six-foot outer crenellation and waited till the light of the rocket faded from the night sky. Out on the broad bastion they had taken from the Chinese on that rainy night a week ago, two Marines were nervously stamping out what remained of the flight of fire arrows that had hit just before the rocket went up. Fire arrows —the Boxer contribution. While the Peking Field Force blasted away with Krupp light artillery and the Kansu cavalry peppered the legations with new Männlicher carbines, the tatterdemalions who had started it all attacked with spears and bows and arrows. Connor shook his head—and winced at the pain that was still there.

The last white light had faded. The sergeant slid his head around the stone merlon to peer through the slit, down the steeply angled wall into the dry moat sixty feet below. Had he seen something move in the darkness there?

"Toomy," he said softly, "come here and take a look."

The tall, lantern-jawed corporal rose from behind the barricade and moved quietly over to the sergeant's side.

"See anything down there, in the ditch?"

Toomy pushed back his wide-brimmed hat and leaned forward, gazing almost perpendicularly down the smooth stone wall. In the shadows and the starlight, it was hard to see anything at all. Toomy scratched his nose.

"Can't say that I do, Sergeant."

Connor nodded and passed a hand across his aching forehead. Twenty-four hours after reporting for duty again, he still felt rotten.

"Okay," he said. "Send the Chinaman over."

Toomy trotted off, bending low behind the barricade, toward the head of the ramp. Connor waited, not thinking, listening to the accelerating crescendo of rifle fire from up north of the Fu. The Japanese were catching it hot and heavy up there. It sounded as if an attack was brewing. But then it always sounded that way at night.

The Krupps banged again. This time the shells whistled on across Legation Street to explode in the Russian compound, just across from the American. "Pegging away, pegging away," murmured Connor to himself. Even those little nine-pounders could do a hell of a lot of damage, pegging away day after day and week after week.

"Here he is, Sergeant," said Toomy, materializing out of the darkness. A hunched figure in Chinese pantaloons and robes appeared close behind him. "The basket's ready, on the other side of the bastion."

Another rocket arched upward, splashed the sky with light. All three of them dropped to a crouch behind the head-high battlements, waiting for the glare to fade, the shells to pass over.

They had done a good job on him, Connor thought with icy detachment. Chen's face looked old and dirty and dry as parchment. They could not give him a beard, but his forehead was shaved and he had a false queue bound up in a knot behind his head. The wrinkled robes he wore had obviously been worn for a long time. He was Chinese to the core, from battered thonged sandals to the untidy grey hair at his temples. Not a shred of the white-coated Western doctor with the shining black hair and impeccably clean hands remained.

The glare of the rocket faded once more.

"You ready?" said Connor tersely.

"As ready as I'll ever be, Sergeant." Connor knew Chen was smiling in the darkness.

"This way then. Quick as you can. We want to get you down into the ditch before the bastards decide to send up another roman candle."

They ran out across the rubble-strewn, weed-grown bastion to the corner where the deep wicker hamper lay, bound in a net of heavy rope. Toomy and two privates helped the doctor into the basket and slid the container cautiously through a gap in the battered stone crenellations. The two privates braced their feet against the stone and wrapped the ropes around their wrists.

Just before the awkward container tipped to the vertical and began its descent, Dr. Chen extended his hand gravely and said, "Good-bye, gentlemen."

Connor froze. He couldn't do it.

Mother of God, he told himself, *the man is going out to get himself killed!* He knew that Chen Li would probably be caught and tortured to death before the night was over. He knew that this man was running this terrible risk for him, for all of them. And still he couldn't do it. He couldn't take the hand of the man that he had seen in Elizabeth Rowntree's arms not twenty-four hours before.

Toomy stuck out his own big-knuckled hand and gave the doctor's a perfunctory shake. "Good luck," he said laconically.

Chen nodded. He turned his head toward Connor in the obscurity, seemed about to speak. Then he settled deeper into the ungainly hamper, and the privates began to lower him down the wall.

" 'Good-bye, gentlemen,' " Toomy mimicked softly with a

shake of the head. "Sounds like a real lime-juicer, doesn't he?"

Connor remembered that Dr. Chen had learned his English at Hong Kong, and had lived for years in London.

He watched the two Marines pay out the rope until it went loose in their hands. The shelling and the rocketing seemed to have stopped for the time being—there were no more *crumps* or flares. They waited quietly a minute, listening to the crackle of rifle fire around the perimeters, breathing as calmly as they could out here on this exposed position on the bastion. Then Connor nodded, and the privates began to reel in the rope.

The basket came back empty.

Chen emerged from the hamper on his hands and knees, on the inner edge of the moat that ringed the Tartar City. He adjusted a straw coolie hat on his head, and descended quickly into the deeper darkness of the ditch, out of sight of anyone watching from the ruined houses and shops beyond. At his third step, he stepped on a corpse.

He stepped back, murmuring the apology to the dead that came automatically to his lips. He tried another way, and tripped once more over a stiffening human body. He realized then that they must have lowered him over the section of wall where the corpse detail threw the enemy casualties every night. In the confined space of the besieged legations, this was an essential sanitary precaution. The Westernized physician in him approved entirely. The Chinese half of him, imbued with centuries of respect for the ancestral dead, was revolted beyond measure.

Murmuring prayers for the wandering souls of the unburied, he picked his way through the stench and the carrion and clambered up the outer bank of the moat, into the Chinese City.

He paused briefly at the top, listening for the footsteps of any wandering patrol. Then he hurried forward into the shadows of the nearest burned-out building. Moments later, he was making his way slowly and quietly through the ruins of what had been the Bond Street and Fifth Avenue of Peking, the gutted shops of dealers in silk and bronze and lacquer ware and jewelry whose work had been the glory of the city. The fanatical Boxers, so it was said, hadn't even bothered to loot them.

Off to his right, as he worked his way along roughly parallel to the wall, the blackened skeleton of the Chien Men Gate loomed up against the stars.

A year ago, almost to the day, he had passed through that gate with Elizabeth Rowntree at his side. Gently but firmly, he filed that memory away with all the others, against the hour when he would need it. When he would need every recollected moment of their brief time together to steel him for what must surely come.

37

MORNING, MIRACULOUSLY, FOUND HIM WELL ON THE ROAD to Tientsin.

The dead were everywhere. They lay unburied on the verge of the dusty highway. They littered the streets of ruined villages, blackened and bloated, covered with flies. Even their relatives would not go near them. Most of the living had deserted their homes in any event, and were hiding in the fields in terror.

Chen Li found it surprisingly hard to determine just who the killers had been in any particular case.

In one little hamlet less than an hour's walk south of Peking, he came upon a gutted building with a dozen charred corpses lying among the ashes. It had been a Christian temple, a wooden-faced old woman assured him, and the Society of the Righteous and Harmonious Fists had burned it down when the spirit-slaves of the foreigners had run there to hide. But there was a blackened Chinese idol in the ruins too. Chen Li could only wonder.

He continued southward through the day, and through the day after.

In the fields of golden kaoliang around Langfang, the soldiers lay steaming in the sun. This was where the great battle had been, the peasants told him, and where the foreigners had been turned back. They showed him the abandoned trains, the twisted rails torn up on either side. They did not have to show him the corpses. Dead soldiers in the bright-colored uniforms of half a dozen nations lay heaped among the railway carriages, or sprawled in the head-high millet as far as the eye could see. Dead Chinese imperial troops and dead Boxers were mingled indistinguishably with Russians, Frenchmen, Englishmen, Americans.

In the little mud-walled villages south of Langfang, the corpses were all Chinese. They were peasants, most of them, who had come in the way of charging Cossacks or fallen before the train-mounted machine guns as Seymour's column chugged up the line toward the debacle at Langfang.

The Maxim guns had pocked the mud-walled houses in geometric lines, marching across smashed window slats and splintered doors. Against the walls, heaped in the shrubbery, the shrunken mummies of women and children lay staring with pecked and rotted eyeholes up at the sun.

North of Langfang, the Boxers were everywhere, strutting about with scarlet headbands and long knives on their hips. Farther south, it was the imperial troops who swaggered about the streets of the larger market towns, boasting of the foreign blood they had shed.

At a noon stop more than halfway to Tientsin, Chen watched a round-faced Bannerman display his most prized trophy to his envious mates—the head of a Japanese soldier. The Bannerman was going to take his trophy to the Viceroy Yu Lu himself, to claim his reward. A hundred *taels*—some said a thousand. For a white head, even more.

How much for a Chinese collaborator, a spirit-slave of the foreigners? someone asked. The Bannerman shrugged. Second- and third-class hairy ones were not worth much anymore. It was the foreign devils who must be killed, killed or driven into the sea. He wrapped the head carefully away and went back to his meal of beans and millet.

Everywhere, Chen went carefully, keeping his eyes on the dust before his sandaled feet. He stayed away from inns, ate little, slept in the fields or in cemeteries, where even the Boxers would not go. Before long the dirt rubbed so carefully into his skin, the slope-shouldered weariness he had affected since he left Peking were real enough. His feet were calloused and bleeding the first day, and he had fierce stomach cramps the second. When he awoke on the morning of the third day, he thought he saw Mei Ling standing by a wooden grave stele, smiling and beckoning to him.

Elizabeth sat under a huge, umbrella-shaped tree by the Bell Tower, drinking her tea. The Bell Tower and the nearby trees were all plastered with notices, rosters, stern injunctions in all the languages of the legations. Off-duty soldiers slumped on the steps or in the grass. Pale-faced ladies in straw hats and puffed sleeves sat about in pairs, saying little. The intermittent crash of gunfire not two blocks away made conversation almost impossible even if anyone had had the heart for it.

Elizabeth was exhausted.

It had been more than a week since Chen Li had gone. A week almost without sleep, without rest from the brutal exigencies of the makeshift hospital. There were never less than fifty wounded men crammed into the little rooms and hallways of the Chancery. Everyone was using improvised sawdust dressings now, and only the most serious surgical cases got chloroform.

If the days had been filled with grueling labor, the nights had been sheer agony. She had spent them tossing and groaning in her sandbagged little bedroom, weeping for Chen Li. *Dear God*, she told herself as she collapsed into bed each midnight, *this can't go on much longer*. Every morning it began again.

"Elizabeth," Lieutenant Greville broke in upon her meditations, "may I join you for tea?"

"Of course," she answered, dully amazed that he should even ask. She never ceased to be astonished at the proprieties and punctilios that continued to flourish in the legations even after weeks of siege.

Philip Greville sank down on the peeling lawn chair beside her. Like everyone else, he had lost weight, and the ruddy glow had gone from his cheeks. His sand-colored moustache looked almost wispy against those pale cheeks. A ricocheting bullet fragment had caught him in the right forearm, and he

250

wore his right arm in a narrow black sling. He was also, she noticed with an elevated eyebrow, smoking a long black cigar.

"Cigars before supper, Philip?" she asked. "I never thought you would join the utilitarian school."

He shrugged nervously. "Old school manners are dead," he said. But he offered to extinguish the cigar nonetheless.

"No, no," she responded with as much of a smile as she could muster. "Unless the supply is running low, of course."

"Not much chance of that," he answered sourly. "That's the beauty of being besieged in the diplomatic section. We've all the Havana cigars and champagne we could possibly want. It's only the necessities we're running low on."

And that was true too. They were down to a pound of mule meat per person per day on their side of the canal, and a single cup of fermented rice in the Fu. Enough to keep body and soul together certainly—on the European side, at least. But what would they do when that was gone?

"Much discomfort from the arm?" she asked, raising her voice to be heard above a sudden crackle of rifle fire from the German barricade

"No, of course not," he came back quickly. "This damn sling is as much for show as anything, you know that." He blew smoke into the wind. "It's practically shameful to go around here with a uniform on, and not a mark on you."

Elizabeth looked into his unhappy blue eyes and said nothing. Every vestige of his old gaiety was gone, and ten extra years at least seemed to have come down upon his shoulders.

"If you have anything for nerves, now," he added, in a lower voice, "I'd be only too glad to have it." He gave her another darting look, and she saw that he wasn't joking anymore.

Nothing we don't need more for more important purposes, she almost snapped at him. But then she didn't. For she saw the look in his face she had seen in Captain Lamenière's before he went back to his post of honor in the battered

251

French Legation. Or in the plain, doughy face of Baron von Ketteler's American widow, before she had wandered out onto the open tennis courts with bullets rattling around her like hail. The look of a person tottering toward the breaking point.

"People like Lamenière," he said, as though he had read her thoughts, "they don't have any trouble with nerves. Or your Marine friend, Sergeant Connor. Absolutely amazing, those men up there." He looked up through the foliage, toward the Tartar Wall. "That place is a deathtrap, you know. Yes, and they know it too. Captain Myers has told Sir Claude so, and his own chief, Conger. But they stay up there. They must have no nerves at all."

He went on puffing at his cigar, staring at the foliage and seeing nothing at all.

"You do look a bit done in," said Elizabeth carefully. "We need an officer in the wards. Perhaps I could—"

"Don't be silly." He spoke jerkily, still not looking at her. "Why should I get off the line and let a better man have my bullet?"

"Philip—" she began, leaning forward, trying to speak firmly. But Greville flung his cigar into a flower bed, rose with a muttered excuse, and hurried away.

Elizabeth looked around her at the straw hats and summer dresses, the bandaged men in uniform stretched on the grass beneath the trees, and wondered if she had the strength to stand up herself and make her way back to the hospital.

38

EVEN BEFORE THE SUN ROSE ON HIS EIGHTH DAY SOUTH FROM Peking, Chen Li began to pass tattered remnants of the Chinese Army, fleeing north.

All through the morning, the rutty road north of Tientsin grew more crowded with carts and wagons, walking wounded and dispirited troops. Some of the men were sullen and angry, some laden with loot from the city they were abandoning. Twice Chen Li was made to strip beside the road while loud-talking soldiers searched him. They claimed they were looking for messages from the foreigners. But they showed real disappointment only when they found he was telling the truth when he assured them that he had not a single *cash* on his dishonorable person.

Other soldiers, equally dispirited, were considerably friendlier to him. Some shared their meager noon meal with him, and earnestly urged him to stay away from Tientsin. By the time he came in sight of the low, dark walls of the city, late that afternoon, Dr. Chen had a hazy idea at least of what was happening.

It was what he had expected, what he had known must happen sooner or later. The Western Powers had landed more troops at Taku and rushed them north by train. With a massive artillery barrage, they had broken the siege of Tientsin, sent the Chinese besiegers fleeing north in confusion. Most of the city was now in Western hands. British, American, Japanese, and Russian troops now surrounded the walled Chinese inner city. Their guns were pounding away at it, preparing for a mass assault.

The attack might even have begun already, the retreating troops told Chen. The artillery barrage last night had been something they had never dreamed of, something beyond belief.

Chen Li lamented with them and went on south. His body was wracked with eight days of exhaustion and hunger, his heart ravaged by the pain of this passage through his torn and bleeding land.

The attack was being mounted from the south side of the city. That was where the Western armies were gathered. That was where he must go. Leaning heavily on a wooden staff, placing one bloody foot in front of the other, he worked his way through the muddy outlying villages around to the south.

Chen felt the fever parching his cheeks and clouding his brain once more, as it had so often those last days. He had caught something, somewhere back along the dolorous road from Peking. He did not know what, and he had no time to think about it now.

He tried several times to approach units of Western troops.

The Japanese fired on him the minute they saw him, across a stubbly field of newly cut kaoliang. He plunged face first into a shallow irrigation ditch and lay absolutely still in the mud until they had disappeared.

The Russian infantry he fell in with to the west of town paid no attention to him at all as they worked their way around the walls, watching for any Boxers or imperial troops who might try to escape their way. Chen Li did not speak Russian, and none of them spoke any language he did.

It was almost dark when he gave it up and decided to try the front gate of the city itself.

There seemed to be a wooden causeway along a canal leading up to the gates, dark and high above him in the gloaming. He made his way slowly up the causeway, his body aching, his mind drifting from dreaming into delirium and back again.

It was foolish to go this way, he knew. There would be no Western headquarters in the city while the fighting still raged. But he had heard English voices out of the obscurity ahead of him, English and American, he was sure of it now. They were off somewhere to the right, firing up at the wall. Answering shots were still flashing down at them, long streaks of white and yellow, with the lurid glow of larger fires showing above the walls.

But Chen seemed to have gotten confused, because the English-speaking voices were in his rear now. He saw that he was very close to the wall, much closer than he should be. And was that not Mei Ling's voice he heard now, his dead wife's voice, calling him back to her?

But Mei Ling was dead, he thought abruptly. Dead long ago. Elizabeth was alive still, trapped behind the barricades in Peking. Chen stopped, trying to order his thoughts. Elizabeth was alive, and he must bring help to her. He must tell someone—the English, the Americans—that they were still alive in the Peking legations.

He was teetering on the very edge of the causeway, reflections of ruddy fires above him flickering in the muddy water at his feet. Bullets were snarling around him like angry insects. American bullets. Chinese bullets. He saw his own reflection as the flames flared up behind him.

He must get off the causeway, out of the open. He turned and started back the way he had come.

He felt the shot that struck him only as a jar, a painless blow that spun him slowly around and toppled him with infinite gentleness off the causeway. He wondered vaguely whose bullet it was as he fell sideways into the waiting waters.

39

WHEN ELIZABETH ROWNTREE BROKE AT LAST, IT CAME VERY suddenly, without fanfare or preparation.

She stepped out of the improvised hospital into the rain that night, the usual warm drizzle that came at sunset almost every evening now. She was no more and no less exhausted emotionally and physically than she always was. But this time, something happened. Something very quiet and very ordinary—and totally insane.

Instead of turning left toward the MacDonalds' official residence, where all the American ladies were quartered, she turned to the right, passed out through the sandbagged gates of the legation, and strolled off down the Imperial Canal.

The men behind the sandbags were crouching at their loopholes, peering up toward the North Bridge, where one of the countless alarums of the night was developing. They did not notice the girl who passed behind them and turned in the opposite direction, south toward Legation Street. In moments she was swallowed up in the gently falling rain.

She had gone this way often with the Congers on other evenings, returning to the American Legation after festivities at the British compound. She was walking now almost in her sleep. She tilted her head back and let the falling drops patter against her cheeks and forehead. After a day in the hundred-degree heat and the incredible stenches of the wards, a quiet walk in the rain was pure bliss. She brushed the tight cap off her head and let the water get at her hair, unwashed since God knew when. This really was what she needed, she thought as she turned left and strolled across the Legation Street Bridge over the canal. She wondered why she had not thought of it before.

A sullen flicker of lightning lit the scene for a brief moment. It revealed a nightmarish panorama—low, boiling clouds, the roofless rubble of the legation buildings, broken lampposts, the shell-pitted macadam of Legation Street, and on the right the looming shadow of the Tartar Wall. She wandered on through this gutted wilderness as though it had not changed at all. A slender girl in a grey ankle-length gown, going for a walk in the rain.

"What the *hell?*"

The voice came from her left, out of the deeper darkness that followed the lightning. From the gateway to the French Legation? she wondered, turning her head to peer through the gloom. She really wasn't sure where she was. The vaunted gaslight of Legation Street, the only gaslight in Peking, was not working at all.

"What the hell are you—ma'am, what are you *doing?*"

Someone was loping toward her. Not from the French compound—there were the stone lions, farther on. From the steps of the Hôtel de Pékin, then. The hotel too was unlit, as though no one at all were staying there. Surely they couldn't all be in bed so early?

"Lizzie—my God, it's you!"

"Hello, Michael," she said. "So you're one for an evening stroll as well?" She put an Irish lilt in it. She was suddenly feeling quite gay, even flirtatious. It felt good. She hadn't felt like a flirtatious girl for a long time.

Connor caught her by the arm and hustled her at a stumbling half-run back into the shadow of the deserted hotel.

Of course it was deserted, she thought, staring at the shell-scarred front, the broken door swinging loose on its hinges. It had been empty for weeks, ever since the Chamots had given up and retreated to the British Legation with the other civilians. She felt suddenly dazed and terribly confused as Sergeant Connor sat her down in a sheltered embrasure lined with sandbags in front of the door.

"Miss Rowntree!" he said in a crisp, military voice he had never used toward her before. "What are you doing out here?"

She shook her head. Her gown was soaked to her body, her hair falling dankly over her neck and shoulders. She was shaking as though she had an ague even on so warm a night. She heard the desultory bang of the guns now, mostly at the other end of the street, the other side of the legations. She saw in the next flicker of lightning that the French compound, toward which she had been strolling so casually, was half demolished, the stylized Chinese stone lions standing before an almost nonexistent gate. There was a burst of firing from the corner of the rain-soaked gardens where the French still held their own.

"I'm—damned—if I know, Michael," she answered him finally, in her own voice again. "I seem to have wandered away." She hugged herself to control the shaking.

"Are you all right now?"

"I think so. Except for being wet through. What are you doing here?"

"I just came off the wall. I stopped to wait out the rain here."

"I seem—I really seem to have gone off my head for a moment." She smiled ruefully at him. "You seem to be making quite a career out of pulling me out of tight places, Sergeant," she added, remembering his strong arm under her hand as he led her out of the *hutungs,* a month or an aeon ago.

"Lizzie—you got to rest." The military crispness was gone from Connor's voice now, replaced by a tone of fierce tenderness. "You stay away from the hospital tomorrow, Lizzie," he said. "Or so help me God, I'll report this whole business to Dr. Poole."

"Michael, I can't, I—"

"I'm not arguing with you, Lizzie, any more than you argued with me when I was lying on the floor of your hospital. I'm telling you." He gestured brusquely toward the lunar landscape and the churning clouds above the Tartar Wall, illuminated once again by the fitful lightning. "These are *my* wards out here. And you just walked into them."

258

"I guess I did," she said. She raked the wet hair back from her forehead with trembling fingers. "I still can't understand why—"

He heard the distant *crump,* and he knew it was not thunder this time. The premonitory whisper of the coming shell had him up and moving instantly, pulling her back with him through the doorway into the littered hall. Then there was the red flash in the street, the tilt of shredded sandbags, the jarring impact of flying debris against the wall outside, where they had been sitting.

Bits of rock and metal caromed off the walls of the darkened hallway. Elizabeth sat up in a tangle of what seemed to be lace curtains and elegant tablecloths. 'Collected for sandbags, she thought, and then left behind as too flimsy for the purpose. Then she realized that her left arm didn't work.

"Are you all right?" said Connor, silhouetted against the paler grey of the open door.

"I think so," she answered, "except for my arm. It seems to be—no, it's coming back." For the sensation and the function were rapidly returning now. She could feel a tenderness at the elbow.

A match rasped and flared, and Connor was bending over the arm. Together, awkwardly, they unbuttoned and rolled back the wet cotton sleeve. The skin was already darkening and swelling about the elbow, but it was only a bruise.

"You see," she said, "it's quite all right."

Their eyes met for one moment before the match went out. She saw the hunger there, the love and the longing she had seen on his face that first afternoon in the wards.

Then his hand slid up her naked arm, tearing the puffed sleeve open. His other hand-caught at the back of her neck through her thick hair, and his mouth came hard against hers in the darkness. With a sob of mingled breaths, they slipped clumsily down together among the drapes and tablecloths.

She smelled the wet flannel of his shirt, felt the hardness of his hands through her thin cotton frock. She realized that her own arms were locked tight about his neck, that her lips were parted, her own mouth working desperately against his. She knew that here and now, in this collapsing world with violent death as close and certain as tomorrow's sun, she needed him as much as he needed her.

He drew back from her slightly.

"Well, Lizzie," he said, "but this was a long time happening."

She nodded wordlessly, not trusting herself to speak. She was thinking what she had thought in the wards: Two of a kind. Under it all, we're two of a kind after all.

"I think," he said, "we'd better go upstairs."

Again she nodded, slowly, still unspeaking.

With their arms tight around each other's waists, they went up the staircase together into the darkness.

40

SHE SAW HERSELF MOMENTARILY IN A SHATTERED MIRROR, as a fading flicker of lightning glimmered through the window. She did not recognize herself.

She stood all but naked in front of the cracked glass, a black, beribboned chemise dangling from one hand. But she was not the same Elizabeth Rowntree who had stood in front of a similar glass in her room at the American Legation one year ago, examining herself with a critical eye—but an eye full of hope. That slender, large-eyed girl, poised on the brink of a new life, was not there anymore. The room where she had stood lay roofless to the falling rain now, just down the street, a rubble heap of stone and broken tile. The father who was to give her that new life at his side was dead, and the life that had seemed so exciting to her then, a long-forgotten dream.

The man who had given her the life she lived now—he must be dead too, she thought. Chen Li, who had rekindled her faith in her own hands and brain, who had given her as his parting gift the care of a dozen broken bodies—and all the dozens that came after them—was himself a broken corpse by now, somewhere in that rain-washed night. How many nights had she wept for him? How many days carried his death like an unhealed wound beneath her heart? But that Elizabeth Rowntree was gone now too.

The woman who looked back at her from the broken mirror was the ghost of that vanished girl. Her body was twenty pounds lighter, angular at shoulder and hip, with hollow cheeks and eyes lost in shadow. Her dark hair, unbound, twisted lank and lifeless about her shoulders. Her mouth was wide and generous still, but it was a mouth that did not smile.

Then Connor came up behind her and put his arms around her and cupped her breasts in his hands.

The glimmer of lightning was gone, and he was a shadow only, embracing the shadow that was herself in the riven glass. But she felt his rough palms against her flesh, and her nipples rising to meet them. She felt his breath and the scrape of his chin against her bare shoulder, and then his lips at the base of her throat.

With a cry like an animal in pain, she twisted around in his arms and clamped her mouth on his.

He had never known a woman like her. The intuitive passion of her lovemaking, the ardor of her clutching hands and writhing body shook his soul. This was the woman who had strolled up Legation Street twirling her parasol with elegant gloved fingers. The woman who sipped champagne in legation gardens and stroked the keys of the piano while officers with ginger whiskers sang Broadway airs and strutted to her tune. This was—God in heaven—this was his Lizzie!

Her head strained far back into the pillow, moaning.

Beneath him, she felt the final release burst from her loins, shaking her whole body. Her legs rose up and locked around him, her fingers taloned convulsively. All the tensions of those weeks of labor and loss exploded in her at that moment. Exploded and were gone in a cascade of weeping.

"Lizzie—what is it? Have I—"

"No, Michael, no, no. Nothing that you—it's nothing that you have done. It's just that I—I almost feel alive again. Here with you."

It was scarcely true, yet. But somehow she knew it would be. Clinging to him there in the darkness, pressing his body against her own, with the drip of rain and the rattle of gunfire in her ears, she felt the possibility of life like a tiny spark kindled somewhere deep within her. A spark the horrors of the siege had smothered, a glimmer that had died as Chen Li turned inexorably from her. A flicker that lived still, and was growing once again.

She lay on the dusty bed and felt the hotel shake beneath her as a shell slammed into the Fu behind it. She lay and stroked the man's shoulder and let the spark of happiness spread like a cordial through her veins.

BOOK FIVE

THE
HOLOCAUST

41

Impeccable in a fresh gown emblazoned with flowers and five-clawed dragons, the Motherly and Auspicious Dowager Empress of China strolled on the tile-roofed balcony of her North Sea Palaces.

Ladies-in-waiting in chrysanthemum gowns strolled on either side of her, and silent eunuchs followed behind.

The distant sounds of firing swelled and faded in the drowsy silence of the Sea Palaces.

"There has been enough shooting these last few weeks to kill off every foreigner in China a dozen times over," the Empress snapped crossly. "And see how little there is to show for it!"

The nearest lady-in-waiting, taking the remark as addressed to her, clasped her hands and bowed, murmuring hasty acquiescence.

"Prince Tuan and General Tung have not done as they promised," Tzu Hsi went on petulantly. And then, elevating her flabby, stubborn chin imperiously: "*I* shall have to do something about it myself!"

Reports from the battlefront and from the siege lines, memorials from her southern viceroys, dispatches from her embassies abroad were filled with evil tidings. All across the Western world, it seemed, a single strident cry had gone up: "*Save the legations!*" And then, when all contact was severed between the coast and the interior, when shocking news and more shocking rumors filled the newspapers of London and Paris and New York, a still more furious war cry: "*Avenge the martyrs of Peking!*"

The Powers were massing to do just that. And Tzu Hsi, who was no fool, knew it.

The troops that manned the farthest Asiatic bastions of the

Western empires were rallying for the assault. Russians from Port Arthur, Americans from the Philippines, British regiments from India, Japanese troops from the home islands poured through the captured forts at Taku. Tientsin had fallen, and every report indicated that the Eight Powers were preparing to march upon Peking itself.

That, at all costs, must be prevented.

The best way, the only way the Dowager Empress could conceive of accomplishing this was to remove the legations as a bone of contention. That morning she had taken the first step toward that end.

Over the preceding days, she had tongue-lashed Prince Tuan publicly. General Tung had been forbidden the Imperial Presence. Published edicts had referred contemptuously to the Boxers, the darlings of the court not a month since, as bandits and vagabonds. Now she had taken the final step. She had taken up the vermilion pencil to write, and what she wrote would be done.

But how much better, she thought with bitterness, how much more glorious indeed if the Boxers had accomplished what they set out to do!

They had talked so confidently, so passionately of the will of the gods, of saving the glorious Dynasty and purging the land of all things foreign. They would extirpate the foreign devils before they took their morning meal, so they said. They would eat their flesh and sleep upon their skins. And she had been so sure they could do it.

She wondered what had happened to Feng Yu-lan. He was no Prince Tuan, that fellow, no devious intriguer beneath his protestations of patriotism and loyalty. He was the voice of the Chinese people incarnate. The people who loved her, Tzu Hsi was sure, and hated the foreigners as she did.

The people whom, in fact, she had hardly seen for fifty years.

Tzu Hsi would dine as usual that night, seated alone before

a hundred dishes, that she might pick and choose what pleased her.

Beyond the red walls, guns would flash, men would cry out, ashes would sift into the ruins of the legations. Chinese would groan over bone-hollow bellies in the Fu, and Europeans writhe in dreams filled with torture and bloody death.

In the morning the Dowager Empress would rise to a bowl of hot milk flavored with honey and almonds, with crushed pearls added as an elixir of long life.

In the legations they would have another sort of surprise awaiting them.

42

ELIZABETH CAME AWAKE SUDDENLY, IN A DISORIENTING tangle of dreams and realities. There was hair in her face, and she lay in her austere little room at the top of the house on Rittenhouse Square, with a sleepy bird chirping in the dark outside her dormer window. Except that the room was the wrong shape and the bed the wrong size, and there was a man in it with her.

In the grey predawn, she recognized M. Chamot's garish French-provincial wallpaper, the pitcher and washbasin on the stand, the Chinese cabinet that served in lieu of a chest of drawers. The sleepy bird's chirp she knew now for a high-pitched challenge in Chinese, coming from someplace in the gardens of the Fu. It was followed immediately by a desultory pattern of half a dozen shots. This in turn was echoed dimly by scattered firing from the Russian sector on the other side of the Legation Quarter, and by two shots close together from the Tartar Wall. It was an hour at least till sunrise, but another day of siege was already beginning.

She swept the mass of dark-brown hair back from her face and looked down at the man beside her. Michael Connor still slept, lying on his back with his mouth partly open. He could sleep through anything, he said, except a direct order to get the hell up.

Elizabeth, feeling dizzy with hunger and damp with the heat that never left Peking in summer, smiled down at the gently snoring figure.

"Connor!" she said sharply. "Get the hell up!"

The eyes were open and looking at her at once. The snoring ceased; the Irish mouth smiled.

"Lizzie," he said, his voice thick with the old-country accent of his childhood, "ye're lovely this morning." He stretched out an arm and drew her gently down to kiss her.

"Michael," she answered presently, disengaging her soft lips from his harder, more demanding mouth, "you are a constant and congenital liar."

"Well," he admitted, stroking the tightly drawn skin under one prominent cheekbone, "I have seen ye looking better, and that's a fact."

They laughed together, with her head on his bony shoulder, and kissed again.

This was the fifth time Elizabeth had awakened in bed with Michael Connor. She felt as much at home with him in this dreary room in a deserted hotel as though they had been married for years.

Three times they had made love. Twice they had been too physically exhausted, too emotionally drained to do more than cling and murmur and fall asleep holding each other. Even the three short, violent explosions of passion they had experienced together had been ominously flawed. On two occasions their lovemaking had been accompanied by bursts of gutter language from Connor which had startled Elizabeth as nothing else about him had done. On the third there had been sentimental whispers from the girl which she knew left the East Side immigrant's son distinctly uneasy in her arms.

And yet she could imagine no greater happiness than these feverish awakenings in bed with Michael Connor.

He stroked her flank with one hand now and moved his stubbly face against her cheek. "We'll have to fatten ye up, lass," he said. "Ye're not fit for an Irishman's woman, that's sure."

"And what are the onerous duties of an Irishman's woman, pray tell?" she asked him archly.

"Why, to stir his pot and bear him sons, I reckon. My father was never too clear about it. But that was what my mother seemed to do, mostly. When there was anything to put in the pot, that is."

"You've never been to Ireland, have you?" she said thoughtfully, tangling her fingers in the hair of his matted chest.

271

"Nor ever want to go there. It's a poor place from all I hear, run by lime-juicers and priests entirely. America's good enough for me."

Ridiculous, she told herself. America's meant nothing to him but poverty, and he's scarcely been back in the country these ten years.

"Connor, you don't make any sense at all, do you know that?"

"Lizzie, you talk too much—do you know that?"

He put his hand on her body under the bedclothes, and she felt the gingery surge rise once more in her loins.

Connor could scarcely believe his luck as he drew Elizabeth into his arms.

She had begun as a challenge, almost as a dare to him. She had become an obsession. She was certainly the gamest, sharpest, squarest girl he had ever known, and just about the most fun in bed. But she was more than that, he thought as their bodies clove together, blended into one. Oh, but she was more than that.

They made love with nervous passion in that predawn hour, knowing they must leave for the quick, dangerous passage back to their respective quarters before sunup. It was not a matter of being seen. Neither had any illusions that their meetings were unknown to the sentinels and barricade troops who were everywhere. It was a matter of getting behind protecting walls before it was light enough for Chinese sharpshooters to see them clearly on Legation Street, or crossing the canal.

The defense perimeters of the Legation Quarter shrank steadily, almost day by day. The northeastern corner of the Fu was gone, despite all that the tough little Japanese contingent could do. The French Legation was more than half lost. The Russian compound on the west was notoriously soft, likely to crumble at any major effort by the Moslems from Kansu.

Within the legations everyone went glazed and terrified about his business. In the British compound they ate mule meat, and that voraciously. The few surviving Chinese Christians in the Fu ate leaves and bark off the trees, plus what dogs and cats they could catch. There was much talk of Khartoum and Lucknow and other famous massacres. If the barricades buckled anywhere, every adult was to have a weapon—for self-defense or suicide at his or her own discretion.

Everyone lived from hour to hour. Nobody really believed anymore that the long-awaited relief column would find anything more than bones and ashes when it came at last.

Connor and Elizabeth lay gasping beside each other now, their hearts fluttering rather more than hearts in healthier bodies should have done. They caught their breath and kissed each other again, and then rose to dress rapidly in the thinning darkness. They descended the stairs together, and he prepared to venture out first into the shell-pocked street. That was when they heard it.

It was a sensation their ears had not enjoyed for many days and many nights, a sensation they had never expected to revel in again. It was the sound of silence.

The guns had stopped.

43

ELIZABETH CLAMBERED WITH DIFFICULTY UP TO THE TOP OF the sandbags at the British Legation gate. Feeling light-headed, she shaded her eyes and looked up the canal toward the North Bridge. All around her, the brazen call of the long Chinese trumpets rang out hoarsely over the ruins. Above the Chinese barricades on the bridge, a large placard inscribed with scarlet Chinese characters showed plainly.

"The general purport," a dry voice observed at her elbow, "is that all firing will cease immediately, and that a message will be forthcoming." It was old Sir Robert Hart, Inspector General of the Imperial Customs. "All," he added, "by imperial command, no less. I wonder what her Majesty has in mind now."

Elizabeth turned away and began to concentrate on what her own eyes could tell her.

It was the first time she had ever stood upon a barricade. After thirty days of almost incessant fighting, it was a weird and frightening spectacle. To the north she could see the blackened ruins of the *hutungs* stretching almost to the foot of the walls of the Imperial City itself. Closer in, less than a block away, the solid-looking fortifications set up by the besieging troops loomed threateningly, loopholed everywhere, with red and black and purple pennons flapping overhead, inscribed in black characters with the names of generals. Faces were beginning to show over these fortifications now—the dull-yellow faces of the Chinese, the weathered brown faces of Tung Fu-hsiang's Moslems. Down the long muddy stretch beside the canal, the litter of four weeks of fighting lay: rifles, swords, spears, bits of uniforms, here and there the glint of spilled cartridges. In the dead center of this no-man's-land, out of reach of either side, a few partially decomposed corpses lay, bones half bared by the sharp teeth of the pariah dogs that roamed the city now.

Elizabeth, for all her recent experience with dead and dying men, shivered in spite of herself.

Chinese soldiers were climbing up onto their barricades. Some sat and grinned at the white faces staring at them from the legation forts. One or two stretched out on top of their own fortifications and began to take the sun.

There was an especially loud blast of massed trumpets, and an unsteady figure appeared on the enemy sandbags. He was Chinese clearly, and not young as he worked his way slowly down on their side with a piece of white cloth on a stick. He began to make his way across the grisly tract between the two lines.

"It looks like that old chap the Ministers sent out last week," said Sir Robert. "Through the Hanlin, wasn't it? In any event, it looks as if they caught him." He sighed. "They do seem to catch them all."

Two British Marines went over the sandbags to help the old Chinese in. Sir Robert stepped over and spoke briefly to him before the Marines led him off into the British compound. Elizabeth could not catch the words, but she could see that the old fellow had trouble speaking and blinked continually as though the sun hurt his eyes.

"He says he was beaten for two days at General Tung's headquarters," said Hart, returning, "then fed up handsomely for three. After that they gave him a sealed note for Sir Claude and bustled him off to the lines. Perhaps," he added, "I'd better go on in and see if they have need of my services." The Inspector General hurried off, looking quite dignified despite the two heavy revolvers hanging at his sides.

Before the afternoon was over, soldiers and Marines from the legations were over their own barricades and mixing with the men they had been shooting at in the wasteland between the lines. Some of the civilian volunteers, who happened to have a smattering of Chinese, were even taken on tours of the massive fortified bastions, which now enclosed the entire Legation Quarter, by cheerful Chinese soldiers.

At sunset, after a day of mounting tension, there was a military review of sorts, parading in plain view along the base of the walls of the Imperial City. The people of the legations lined their own defenses to gaze at the multicolored jackets and tunics and pantaloons, brightly bordered, emblazoned with black dragons or red Chinese characters. Massed horns blared; terrible two-handed swords were shaken aggressively. Only the Kansu horsemen in their black-and-orange uniforms and black turbans swung silently, almost sullenly along, their gleaming carbines slung. They did not, as Greville uneasily observed to Elizabeth, look at all happy with the situation.

The ragged, red-sashed Boxers, the spark that had set the city aflame, were conspicuously absent from the review.

By nightfall everybody in the legations knew that a truce had been offered. Negotiations were to begin at once between the Council of Ministers and the *Tsungli Yamen*. Pending agreements, all firing was to cease. After a solid month of fighting, they would sleep that night without the incessant clatter of the guns.

The diplomats were jubilant. Mr. Conger bustled about among the Americans in their corner of the British compound, rubbing his hands and talking about a "return of sanity" at last. But M. Pichon still wrung his hands—literally, and considerably thinner hands than they had been five weeks before. And there were doubters still among the younger men. "We'll be having bullets for breakfast in the morning," Lieutenant Greville declared, "mark my words."

But the next morning dawned as silent as its predecessor. A silence broken almost at once by an even more incongruous sound: the creak and squeal of iron-wheeled carts, the clop of donkeys coming up Legation Street.

There were four cartloads of watermelons, four more of vegetables, fresh fruits—and even ice. All came with the best wishes of her Majesty the Dowager Empress of China. Her

Majesty hoped they were all in health, and that these poor gifts might provide her Western friends with some relief from the abnormal heat which prevailed that July.

"Poisoned," said Greville, "I shouldn't wonder."

"A peculiarly Chinese gesture," said Sir Robert Hart, "to begin a negotiation with such a gift."

"What do you think, Connor?" Elizabeth asked in the casual tone she always assumed with him in public.

Sergeant Connor, chewing methodically on a wad of tobacco, looked around him at the pinched cheeks and loose flab of even the best padded Europeans, the hollow bellies of those who had had less to start with. His gaze flicked to the skeletal Chinese huddled in the gates of the Fu. Then his narrow eyes rose to the looming red walls of the Imperial City.

"I expect," he said, "that the old lady's having herself a fine laugh at us all, up there." He turned and slung his rifle and went back to the Tartar Wall.

44

THE BLACK BIRD FLOATED AGAINST THE HOT AUGUST SKY. Just about over the water-gate, Connor judged. He watched Toomy sight his rifle from the rubble of an abandoned barricade. The pulsing air off the top of the wall made the barrel ripple like a reflection in water in the heat of the afternoon.

The bang came flat, the flash almost invisible in the blinding sunlight. The crow jolted and fluttered and then came spiraling down. Connor, leaning on the inner battlements, turned to watch it land with a puff of dust just at the edge of the canal a dozen feet inside the rusty bars of the water-gate. In seconds a dozen Fu Chinese, spidery in their gauntness and their rags, had popped out of the nearest ruined shops and fallen savagely upon the still feebly fluttering bird. In seconds they had torn it to pieces and were eating it raw.

"Good shot," said Connor, as Corporal Toomy sauntered over to join him at the ramparts.

"Jesus," said Toomy, looking down at the brownish-yellow skeletons kneeling in a litter of bones and feathers.

"Daly got a dog for 'em yesterday," said Connor. "He swears they tore it apart still yelping."

"The poor damn Chinks don't get anything anymore, I guess," said Toomy.

"We're not going to be doing much better soon. They killed the last mule yesterday."

They had not in fact been doing well for weeks. Neither man had much fat on him normally. Now, after so many weeks of siege diet, they looked like a pair of sloppily assembled scarecrows. Shirts open to the waist beneath slanting cartridge belts revealed prominent ribs and hollow bellies. Rolled-up sleeves and hats tilted forward over their eyes showed skin burned dark as Kansu cavalrymen by the sun.

"What about Curtiss, Sergeant?" said Toomy, abruptly

changing the subject. "He's just about plastered now, and it ain't even suppertime yet. Hall will have a fit."

"Curtiss ain't the only one either."

The two noncoms shifted their positions slightly to look at the four Marines sprawled shirtless in the shade of their barricade some twenty yards away. As they watched, Curtiss tilted the whiskey bottle over his mouth, took a swallow, and passed it on. Their rifles were leaned more or less within reach. But no one at all was standing to the barricade, watching the Chinese fortifications facing theirs a mere fifty yards up the wall.

"Cap'n Hall says Curtiss called some British sergeant-major a fucking lime-juicer yesterday. They want him thrown in the stockade, or some damn thing." Connor stroked the stubble on his chin. He had stopped shaving only the week before. "As if we had any stockade. Or could afford to spare him if we had."

"He's a good enough Marine," said Toomy, "when he ain't drunk. But with all this heat and nothing to do but look down the Chinamen's gun barrels, it ain't surprising the boys do a lot of boozing."

"It ain't surprising," said Connor, "but it ain't smart either. Let 'em have another round, and then you better go over and take the bottle. And if Curtiss feels like telling a sergeant to go fuck himself, tell him to come and tell me."

Toomy grinned and slouched off.

Elizabeth applied the ointment as gently as she could to the ugly, inflamed sores around the woman's neck. She knew it hurt, but her patient did not so much as wince. None of the celebrated Chinese stoicism in that, Elizabeth thought. The woman, thirty and looking fifty, was simply too drained of energy even to groan.

"Chinese medicine?" the woman croaked suddenly, in halting English. She had seen the jar with the Chinese characters on it.

"Yes," said Elizabeth.

"Dr. Chen's medicine?"

"Yes." It was the last of it, mixed with all the incredible mess of herbs and nuts and less savory ingredients Chen Li's Chinese patients had expected. As the stock of European medicines ran low, Elizabeth had drawn increasingly on Chen's meager stores for her daily visits to the Fu.

"Good," said the woman feebly. "Good."

Elizabeth was glad something was.

The Fu was an inferno. The children wandered naked from one compound to another, looking as thin as mummies. Their parents, all but naked themselves, lay helplessly in what shade they could find. Their eyes were darkly lidded and feverish, their bones straining to burst through their parchmentlike skin. Their chests rose and fell in quick, shallow breaths, like a dog panting in the sun.

Every day Elizabeth closed the eyes of the dead.

She moved sluggishly herself now, putting away her instruments, closing up her bag, Dr. Chen's instruments, and Dr. Chen's bag. Li, she thought, as she rose with ridiculous difficulty, Li, I hope to God I'm not losing too many that you could have kept alive. She spoke to him directly that way, in her mind, a good deal now.

She made her way slowly toward the gate, patting a child as she passed, inclining her head to the venerable gentlemen and honorable ladies who sat looking like twitching cadavers in the roofless pavilions. They always clasped their hands upon their chests and bowed back.

They were certainly dying with dignity for their faith, she thought.

Outside of the Fu, walking south toward the stone bridge at Legation Street, she looked up at the Tartar Wall to see if she could catch a glimpse of Connor. She saw very little more of him than that these days. Now that the uneasy cease-fire had opened all the streets and alleys of the Legation

Quarter to free passage, there was almost nowhere that Elizabeth and Connor could meet in privacy.

They had managed two meetings, both during the early days of the truce, in the ruins of a ginseng shop behind the shell-smashed American Legation. They had been brief, unsatisfying encounters. Neither of them had the strength for passion. Their lips were dry as paper, their skins almost painfully sensitive to each other's touch. He had loosened her shirtwaist and touched her breasts, and she had kissed him tenderly. But she had been terribly conscious of the boniness of her own body, of her stringy hair and the perspiration that plastered her blouse to her skin even hours after sunset. She had found herself crying helplessly, weakly, against his shoulder.

She saw him now, briefly outlined against the afternoon glare on the top of the wall, just above the water-gate. But he did not see her, and he walked away, up toward the American barricade.

She wondered if he really cared about her at all. Or if it was just siege fever.

What they had come to call siege fever took every form imaginable, and it struck the noncombatants even more frequently than it did the men on the walls and barricades. Like poor Maude von Ketteler, who now had to be watched twenty-four hours a day to keep her from wandering off into the *hutungs* and showing up as a head in a cage over the Hata Men Gate. Like the Norwegian missionary, old "Nearest-to-God" Nestergard, who had gone mad and raved about Armageddon and the coming of the Anti-Christ. Like the hollow-eyed German who hunched hour after hour over the piano in the ballroom of the British Minister's quarters, playing "The Ride of the Valkyries" over and over, waiting for the end in a proper Wagnerian ecstasy.

It was siege fever that turned the slenderest rumor into a fiery conviction, over which red-faced colonial officials were frequently ready to come to blows. The Yangtze Valley was in open rebellion, Manchuria was up in arms, Tientsin had finally been taken, Tientsin had not been taken, the relief column was on its way, the relief column would not leave till the end of August . . . everyone knew for sure—and no one really knew anything.

Was it only siege fever, Elizabeth wondered, that brought the soft Irish brogue into Michael Connor's voice when he took her into his arms?

And what was it then—she stopped in the street at the thought—what was it that had flung *her* gasping and clinging up against *his* chest? What but a sort of madness, she thought ironically, could have brought a minister's daughter from Rittenhouse Square to bed in a tawdry hotel with a low Irish tough? Could she really be Connor's Lizzie, treated with as much cheerful disrespect—and honest affection—as any shopgirl or lady of the chorus? She certainly could be! Elizabeth smiled to herself.

She rested her hand momentarily on the stone railing as she stepped off the bridge and turned left up the other side of the canal toward the main gate of the British Legation. She had Connor on her mind now. She would have to see him soon. She strolled slowly up the canal bank, wrinkled skirts swinging about her ankles, scattered filaments of hair blown across her forehead, and thought about seeing Michael Connor again.

Her eyes rose casually from the mud of the canal to the sandbags of Fort Halliday. There, just passing through the legation gateway, was Chen Li.

45

"THE CHINESE DOCTOR? NO, MISS, WE 'AVEN'T SEEN 'IM."
The British sentry behind the sandbags flashed a gold tooth
in a grin.

"There have been a couple or three Chinese through, Miss
Rowntree," a massively moustached young officer added, "but
only the usual contraband traders, smuggling in a peach for
the price of a melon. Coolies and barrow pushers, you know
the sort I mean? No one of Dr. Chen's class. Besides," he
added artlessly, "didn't Chen go over the wall several weeks
ago? And never been back since, I believe."

"Yes," said Elizabeth, "yes, of course. That's why I—"
She breathed slowly in and out, fighting down a surge of
hysteria. "I must have been in error then."

The officer sniffed. She knew him now. He was one of the
priggish holier-than-thou sort, who had always let her know,
by word and tone and look and gesture, that they were quite
aware of all her peccadilloes. From her first ventures into the
hutungs to her most recent clandestine meeting with Sergeant
Connor, they had sniffed their disapproval, turned an icy
shoulder as she passed. She looked at the carefully combed
moustache, the bland, self-satisfied eyes on this putteed and
stiff-backed perfection. She wondered angrily what his reaction would have been—how they all would have felt—if
her doctor had not been Chinese, if her soldier had been an
officer.

She was suddenly, violently sick of them all.

"You ought to 'ave one of the other doctors take a look
at you, miss, if I may say so," the sentry urged politely.
"You are the American lady doctor, aren't you, miss?"

"Yes," she answered precisely, "I am." Without another
question she turned her back on the legation and walked
rapidly back the way she had come.

It had been Li, she was sure of that. Li's gait, Li's shoulders, Li's face in sudden profile under the wide straw hat as he turned to pass through the pagoda-roofed gateway into the compound.

It had been Li, or she was really off her head this time.

She had best go and see Connor now, she thought with rather more precision than she should have. Connor on the Tartar Wall. She hurried back along the canal bank toward Legation Street.

Their Excellencies the Ministers Plenipotentiary clustered eagerly about the green baize table. The thin, wrinkled piece of paper passed almost recklessly from one elegantly manicured hand to the next. The latest carefully lettered missive from the *Tsungli Yamen* was thrust impatiently aside, some copies even trampled on the floor.

"Gentlemen," said Sir Claude MacDonald, clearing his throat more than once, "gentlemen, I really think that, for the record if for no other reason, the communication ought to be read aloud."

The paper was passed reluctantly up to him, and he read, keeping his voice as steady as he could:

> " 'The foreign settlement at Tientsin has held and has now been relieved. A mixed division consisting of twenty-four hundred Japanese, four hundred Russians, twelve hundred British, fifteen hundred Americans, fifteen hundred French, and three hundred Germans leaves Tientsin on or about August first for the relief of Peking.'

"Crisp and to the point, gentlemen, I think," he concluded exultantly.

"Better than seven thousand men, by my reckoning!" said Mr. Conger, tugging excitedly at his beard. "The American division alone could finish this business off in jig time, by God!"

"On or about August first, the message says," purred Herr von Bülow. "And it is the eighth today! That means they may be here within the next few days, does it not? Within the next few days!"

"If we can only extend the truce," Pichon urged eagerly, his sagging cheeks and little moustache moist with perspiration, "if we can but prevent them from resuming the assault until the column arrives, we are saved."

"Yes, yes, the truce must by all means be extended."

"By all means!" Sir Claude was positively jolly, rubbing his hands together as he looked about the table. "Here, where's that latest chit from the *Yamen?*"

"If I may offer a suggestion, gentlemen," said a tired voice from a corner of the room. "I should not put too much faith in the truce holding much longer."

Every head turned toward the messenger, the bringer of their new hope. Every face was bent with sudden unfriendliness on the thin Chinese face that gazed placidly back at them.

"Eh, what's that, Chen?" demanded Conger aggressively. "The truce not hold? We've been dickering with 'em for weeks now, and it's held up fine. Why can't we stall 'em another few days, then?"

"We are immensely grateful to you for bringing us this first word of rescue, Dr. Chen," said Sir Claude MacDonald discreetly. "But with all due respect, negotiation is our business here. And I believe my colleagues will agree with me that lines of discussion have been opened up in recent days which give real promise of leading to some fruitful results. Or which should at least serve, in the words of my American friend"—he permitted himself the faintest of smiles—"to 'stall 'em another few days.'"

Chen Li sat quietly, listening. The blue pantaloons and

smock of a water coolie hung loosely on his body. He held himself stiffly in the rattan chair, his torso and left shoulder still bandaged. His smooth-lidded eyes were dark and quiet, almost meditative.

"I have of course no wish to question the honorable Council's diplomatic skills," he said when Sir Claude was finished. "But I have spent the past two days in this city, attempting to find a way through the siege lines into the legations. In that time I have heard and noticed one or two things which I would be happy to share with the Council of Ministers, if it would be of any use to your deliberations."

There was a momentary uneasy silence.

"Better let him talk," said Conger then, irritably. "Chen's no fool. And he does speak the language, which is more than most of us can say."

"Well, of course, the doctor's firsthand experience—" said MacDonald doubtfully.

Chen Li braced himself up between the wide cane arms of his chair and began to tell them.

Connor squinted up the wall toward the Chien Men, trying to see in the blinding light of the declining sun. There was something different about the Chinese redoubts that barred Legation Street up that way, beyond the American and Russian compounds. And over there, something odd in the barricaded, rubble-strewn Mongol Market behind the British legation too.

There had been more marching and countermarching than usual over the last couple of days, but they had all gotten used to that. More trenching too, it seemed, though it was hard to tell about that even from his vantage point on the wall. But there was more than that today. Then the grey cloud cover mounted over the sun, preparing for the evening rains. With the sun-dazzle gone, Connor saw instantly what was wrong.

The banners were different. There were new flags, new

pennons fluttering from the enemy sandbags all around the legations. And there in the western quadrant, up Legation Street and back of the Mongol Market especially, there were gaudy new uniforms too.

Tung Fu-hsiang's Moslems held that sector, that and the north. Connor scratched his jaw unhappily.

A tall, lean shadow fell across his shoulder. "You notice all that work up by the North Bridge barricade?" said Toomy laconically.

Connor looked. He hadn't noticed it. They were busy as beavers back there, he thought. Damn unlikely in the heat of the day.

"What do you make of it?" said Toomy.

"Not much," grunted Connor. "But I tell you what. Let's get out the cartridge boxes for the Colt. And put a couple of those drunken bastards to pulling this inner rampart here apart. That will widen the Colt's field of fire to take in Legation Street, and the canal and the North Bridge too."

"Open a field of fire for the machine gun right into the legations?"

Connor knew what Captain Hall would say when he got wind of it. He knew what even Captain Myers, down with typhoid now as well as his wounds, would say about it. He squinted once more up at the strange uniforms milling about behind the Legation Street barricades.

"Put 'em to work on the rampart," he said. "It'll sweat some of the liquor out of their hides anyway."

He strolled away himself, to get the cartridge boxes out from under the tarpaulin.

It was at that moment that Elizabeth emerged from the Fu and looked up and saw him walk away.

Twenty-five minutes later, the bray of the Chinese war trumpets sounded from one side of the Legation Quarter to the other.

Chen Li was still speaking earnestly, urgently in the steamy

287

little room where the Council of Ministers met. Four cursing, sweating Marines had just torn out about half the inner ramparts in front of the Colt's machine gun on the Tartar Wall. And Elizabeth Rowntree had just set foot upon Legation Street.

46

THE NEW SHANSI INFANTRY DIVISION TROTTED SMARTLY UP
to the sandbagged, loopholed redoubts that ringed the Legation Quarter on the west and north. They were Tung Fu-
hsiang's reinforcements, their uniforms spotless, waving their
new rapid-fire rifles at the Kansu troopers they were joining.
They were fresh and eager. And they had come to fight.

The entire Shansi division had taken a mass oath to wipe
out the legations, "leaving neither dog nor fowl alive." As the
afternoon sun declined through streamers of grey rain cloud
toward the Western Hills, the division pressed in swelling
numbers up against the redoubts, now less than a stone's
throw from the European barricades. Under the sudden
screaming of the trumpets, the familiar chant began to rise:

*"Sha-shao! Sha-shao! Sha-shao!" "Burn and kill! Burn and
kill! Burn and kill!"*

To the east up Legation Street, just outside the walls of
the French compound, sappers of the Peking Field Force
emerged, dripping with perspiration and smeared with dirt,
from the mines they had been laboring at for the past two
weeks, ever since the truce began. A smartly uniformed
Chinese officer took the report, nodded briskly, and issued
orders in a singsong voice, tremulous with excitement. The
men stiffened briefly and then dived like moles back into the
ground once more, this time carrying matches and fuse. The
officer turned on his heel and strode off to make his own
report.

To left and right of him, rows of trumpets tilted up against
the sky and began to blare their brazen challenge. In the
burned-out houses all around him, men of the Peking Field
Force crouched with weapons in their hands. Their war cry

rose now to meet the Shansi chant across the rooftops of the legations:

"*Sha-shao! Sha-shao! Sha-shao!*"

In the blackened ruins of the Protestant Board Mission at the end of Legation Street, Feng Yu-lan rallied the remnant of the Boxer horde he had led that first night, when the city had been on fire and the foreigners seemed helpless under their hands at last. Some of them had been with him as far back as the Tientsin train, as far back as Shantung. But it was the other end of the revolution now, and they were a wretched-looking lot of men. Feng's wide nose wrinkled with distaste as he confronted them, dirty and evil-smelling, with sullen cheeks and eyes that shifted constantly, like boys caught stealing from their masters.

Since the heroic early days of the movement, the *I Ho Chuan* had fallen upon bad times. They had taken in too many vagabonds from the streets of Peking, thought Feng. And how long could the country boys he had brought up with him be expected to resist the temptations of the capital? They had burned the foreign buildings and slaughtered the spirit-slaves of the foreigners passionately enough in the early days, but they had seldom pressed to the front lines. The imperial soldiers had begun to laugh at them, demanding to know why, if they were proof against blade and bullet, they hung back so conspicuously from the foreign guns. Now they did little but drink rice wine and loot and lounge defiantly around Prince Tuan's palace, where they ate and slept and collected the pay Tzu Hsi had decreed for them in her early enthusiasm for their cause.

Feng had sworn, kowtowing through the night before the altar of Kuan-ti, that he would himself lead these men to the heart of the Legation Quarter—with Tai Chi-tao, the boy with whom the gods spoke, at his side.

He had never risked the lad before, the magic voice of

the spirits of earth and air that gave his own vibrant bass its power over the people. But some dramatic gesture was necessary now, if this hangdog mob that had been the Society was to make this final effort.

So he had talked long and earnestly with the feebleminded boy through the night, kneeling beside him at the incense-clouded altar. He had told Tai over and over that the gods were calling him to greatness, that tomorrow was his hour of destiny. Tai had been terrified at first, when he was told that he must go out the next day and face the horrifying clatter of the foreign guns. Now he stood quiescent at Feng's side, his jaw sagging slightly, his eyes staring out at the hundreds of swaying faces. His half-formed adolescent mind was full of the night before, of the smoldering incense and the vibrant voice of Feng Yu-lan, which was the voice of the gods to him.

That voice was speaking now, in powerful gong-like phrases. Feng stood on a pile of rubble in the Reverend Rowntree's ruined church, its broken brick walls rising around him. He stood with one huge hand on Tai's shoulder. The heap of stone and brick and charred wood accentuated his great height; the ruined walls behind him seemed to broaden his wide shoulders. He spoke directly into the sullen, unresponsive faces, the sunlight gleaming on high sweaty cheeks and shaven foreheads, the red headbands and sashes, the hands clenched almost petulantly around swords and spears and rifles. He spoke, and the eyes began to moisten once more with excitement, the hands to swing the weapons with almost jaunty confidence once again.

Then the horns began to blare, and the old chant to go up: *"Sha-shao! Sha-shao—"*

"Who sang that song first, brothers of the *I Ho Chuan?*" demanded Feng Yu-lan. "The noble Bannermen, that were night watchmen and street beggars this time last year? The Peking Field Force, that have sat on their guns these two months? The turbans from Kansu?" His big hands were on his hips, his tone grating with sarcasm. The men laughed, hefting their spears and swords, half intoxicated already by the braying of the trumpets, the booming chant. "It is strange, brothers, but I do not remember seeing a single tea-colored Moslem face down there in Shantung! Not a single Peking voice raised for the purging of this land when you and I were listening to the voices of the gods and fighting the foreign devils all alone!"

Men who had never been any nearer to Shantung than the Yung Ting Gate nodded their heads vigorously, eager now to get out and prove themselves worthy of their fine new scarlet sashes. Veteran fighters of nineteen or twenty, who *had* been in the hills of Shantung, felt their eyes mist over with sentimental memories and renewed enthusiasm for the cause.

"The Emperor calls upon us to fight in his sacred name! The Heaven-Blessed Empress Dowager has laid her hands upon my own unworthy person and upon Tai Chi-tao beside me, and has charged us all with this glorious task! And we shall accomplish it, brothers—for do not all the gods of China march at our side?"

There was shooting from the Mongol Market now, and the sound of the trumpets challenged even Feng's gigantic voice.

"Save the glorious Dynasty! Finish the foreigners forever!"

His massive chest, naked beneath an open crimson vest to receive the bullets of the enemy, heaved with the passion of his words. He unslung his long-barreled Mauser and held it up against the crystalline sky. Then, touching Tai lightly on the arm, he leaped down from the rubble and strode out of the ruins of the Protestant Board Mission and down Legation Street. Three hundred of the *I Ho Chuan* came chanting and whooping after him.

* * *

A T'ang poet, thought Chen Li, would have done something exquisite with it.

He had just completed his somber report on the results of two days of desultory conversations with coolies and carters and tea-shop operators, all the best-informed gossips in Peking. He had told them what he had seen of new troops in the city, and of the new spirit of the Boxers. He had told them what the blind beggar at the Temple of the Sleeping Buddha had said about the auguries for the first days of the seventh month of the Year of the Rat—the Month of the Hungry Ghosts in the Chinese calendar.

At this point there had been actual chuckles and smothered groans from the Ministers Plenipotentiary. They fidgeted in their chairs. They were like children, totally swept up in their new hope, irritated and resentful at any caveats from their elders. What was he boring them with this nonsense for? Did he not know they were about to be saved?

Patiently he told them what the relatives of the great eunuch Li Lien-ying had told him—after first proudly displaying the shriveled genitals that had made the family's fortune. How the Old Buddha closeted herself daily with her soothsayers and augurs now. How Prince Tuan had lost face, and Tung Fu-hsiang had only one chance left to save his. How the very defeats of her generals in the south and the advance of the relief column on Peking drove the old woman with increased desperation back once more to the Boxers . . .

How all things, in short, gave promise of one last cataclysmic effort to crush what remained of the legations into the dust and mud of Peking.

Mr. Conger was looking pointedly at the big gold watch hung on a gold chain across his vest, and Sir Claude was just clearing his throat, preparing to cut off the polite, exhausted Chinese voice. *"Mais vraiment,"* murmured M. Pichon to his neighbor Herr von Bülow, *"mais vraiment, tout ça, vous savez*—" He rolled his eyes and spread his expressive Gallic hands, an eloquent comment on the Chinese doctor's doom-crying.

And then the trumpets began to sound.

Truly, thought Chen Li, a T'ang poet could have done wonders with it.

For Connor on the Tartar Wall, there was nothing poetical about it.

One moment it was a quiet late afternoon in the uneasy truce time. There was the usual sprinkling of people picking their way through the shell holes on Legation Street. A slow-motion game of cricket was under way on the open lawn of the British Legation. On the steps of the legation chapel, Connor could just hear the voices of a missionary choir raised in a chorus of "Tramp, Tramp, Tramp, the Boys Are Marching." Behind the chapel, he could see a small honor guard stiffening to attention around the newly closed grave of an Austrian captain, recently dead after lingering for weeks in the hospital.

Then suddenly the trumpets sounded, and the terrible chant rose once more.

The chorus on the chapel stairs was washed away in that blast of sound. The cricketers stumbled to a halt. The people on the street darted for cover toward the nearest garrisoned legation buildings. And in the Mongol Market, where Connor had seen so many of the new banners and unfamiliar uniforms, the crackle of gunfire swelled to an ear-stunning roar.

"That ain't no sharpshooter," grunted Toomy. "That's a Goddam attack!" He spat his wad of chewing tobacco into the alleyway below and leaned forward over the parapet to look.

An instant later a storm of rifle bullets scythed across their position. Private Curtiss, peering out through the gap they had been ripping in the inner rampart, went over backward with the top of his head blown off. Toomy spun away with

294

a splash of blood where one ear was and his left arm swinging rag-doll loose. Conner felt something sting his face and a jolting blow in the right shoulder that flung him headlong among the weeds and tumbled stones.

In the street below, Elizabeth, stumbling toward the ruins of the American Legation, looked up and saw him fall.

47

ELIZABETH'S FIRST THOUGHT HAD BEEN TO GET OUT FROM under the screaming of the trumpets, the rain of brazen sound. She felt naked and terrified out there in the middle of the shell-pocked street. She had been walking toward the American Legation anyway, because the ramp that led to the top of the wall—and Connor—was behind the American compound. Now she darted toward it to get under cover. Even broken walls and shattered buildings were better than the open street. The horns were sounding all around her, and the hate-filled chant was rising and rising.

Then she heard the crash of gunfire from the Mongol Market, from the Chinese redoubts just up Legation Street. And she looked up at the Tartar Wall and saw Connor fall.

Russian soldiers in their white-belted tunics were rushing past her now, hurrying to man their barricade. The American Marines who garrisoned the legation were tumbling out from the other side of the street, with cartridge belts flung over their shoulders and rifles in their hands. She was close to the Russian and American barricades that closed the street at this end. Too close, she knew, as she heard the familiar whisper past her head and saw one of the Russians stumble awkwardly and fall.

"Not here, ma'am!" A white-faced Marine officer caught her by the shoulder, pointing back toward the stone bridge. "Back to the British Legation, ma'am," he shouted above the din, "as fast as you can!"

But Connor! she thought desperately. *Oh, Michael—*

She could see it happening over and over, as if it were burned into her retina. The two Marines leaning on the ramparts, silhouetted against the sky. Others bending to some sort of work at the parapet. And then, in the sudden, crescendoing hail of gunfire, the whip of invisible bullets across the little group, flinging them back like marionettes, sweeping the wall clear in an instant. And Connor too—Connor too—with that awful jerk of the head as he fell . . .

"Please, ma'am," shouted a Marine with a heavily bandaged hand, running past her, "we'll be needin' you back at the hospital!"

They would, of course. They were already rolling the bleeding Russian onto a litter. Russians and Americans were lined up side by side firing through their loopholes—and there was an American Marine sagging, turning a stunned face toward her as he slid down the rough brick barricade.

Of course, she thought numbly, she must get back to the hospital.

She ran as fast as she could up the street, head down, clutching skirts and petticoats up around her knees. The sound of the guns had all but drowned out the trumpets now, and the chanting seemed somehow to be coming from the wrong direction. Not from the west, from the barricades and redoubts behind her, but from the east—from the direction in which she was running!

She looked up as she ran, and saw what looked like half the French Legation blown into the air.

Connor felt the wall move under him, like an earthquake. He rolled over and pulled himself to a half-sitting posture with his good left arm. He saw a column of black smoke boiling up over the French compound. He rose to his knees, saw flying debris littering the street. In the compound itself, two buildings at least were settling into spreading clouds of dust and smoke.

"A mine!" he said over his shoulder to Toomy. "There ain't much left of the French Legation." And then, as his gaze swept back from east to west: "And the Royal Marines are sure catching hell over there in the Market!"

But Toomy only groaned. Connor looked down at him. His

left arm was all but severed at the shoulder, and the left side of his head was covered with blood.

Connor cursed and touched his own cheek. His hand too came away bright and red.

"Sarge!" someone was screaming at him. "There's all bloody hell down there. What do we—"

The whine and spang of a bullet sent them both tumbling—Connor with a blinding flash of pain all up and down the right side of his body. When his head cleared, the man beside him was still yelling at him. Private Williams it was, one of the New Yorkers, like himself and Fitz. And Curtiss, whose brains Connor had come within inches of rolling into.

"Sarge, for God's sake, what—"

Connor sat up, balancing himself carefully so that he wouldn't fall over, and slapped Williams across the face with the back of his closed fist.

Anger replaced terror instantly in the private's face. Anger and rationality.

"Get the Colt over here," said Sergeant Connor, loudly enough to be heard, not loud enough to generate any more panic. "And you bastards help him," he added sharply to the other two shirtless Marines who had been helping Curtiss open the gap in the wall. Both of them were lying flat, looking sick with liquor and fear.

"Move!" snarled Connor again, and they moved. After a last quick look at the blood that was soaking his torn shirt all down the right side, they scuttled off after Williams on their hands and knees.

Connor moved on his own knees over to the low inner parapet. Inching up to the gap, he rested a shaking hand on the stone and peered cautiously out.

A blue drift of gunsmoke was rising over the Russian and American barricades. In the opposite direction, smoke was billowing up from the French compound. A rough bucket brigade had been established from a well to the burning build-

298

ings, and other French troopers were strung out under the smoke, watching for a rush across the gardens. In the street in front of the famous stone lions, the barricade was almost deserted.

A ricocheting bullet showered him with rock dust, and he ducked down. But not before he had seen one more thing.

On up Legation Street beyond the French barricade stood the first Chinese redoubts. Over and around these fortifications, a horde of shouting Boxers now came streaming. They were waving swords and shaking spears, their red ribbons, sashes, headbands fluttering as they charged. Connor saw the huge figure of their leader pause for a moment on top of the redoubt, a skinny adolescent boy scrambling up beside him. The giant stood balanced momentarily on top of the rocks and sandbags, as though defying Western bullets to strike him. Then he leaped into the street beyond and led the mob in a pell-mell rush upon the almost unmanned French barricade.

Connor had seen that gross, ungainly figure before. It was the man from the Tientsin train. The man who had thrown him off the Tartar Wall.

When he risked a second look, the Boxers were into the French position, chopping down the last of its defenders. The giant and the awkward boy, who ran leaping like a rabbit at his heels, were charging on with half a hundred of their screaming followers into the heart of the legations.

Elizabeth was almost to the stone bridge before she saw them. Fifty, a hundred of them, piratical in their wide pantaloons and scarlet head scarves, many naked to the waist, shouting and brandishing their antique weapons. The swelling chant of *"Sha-shao! Sha-shao!"* rose louder than the guns. And at the head of them, she saw a face that she had seen before, behind a gleaming rifle barrel on a village street, almost a year ago.

They would be over the bridge in a moment. They would cut her down long before she could make the long run up the canal bank to the safety of the British Legation.

Then a drift of black smoke from the dynamited buildings dimmed her view of them—and theirs of her, she thought suddenly. She veered, stumbling, to the right and flung herself down behind a Peking mule wagon, lying on its side with a broken axle in a pile of fallen roof tiles. She lay there panting, her eyes wide with terror, watching them come on.

She fully expected to die in the next few seconds. A slashing blow with one of those long, ugly knives, a single thrust with a wide-bladed spear would leave her choking on her own blood among the hot tiles and shreds of canvas in the shadow of the overturned cart. Her eyes hurt from staring, her mouth came open to scream in spite of herself. She had never felt so helpless as she did then, as those pounding feet and flashing blades came rushing toward her up the street.

Then, miraculously, they were passing her by.

Bare feet and running sandals surged past her. The whole mob seemed to be continuing on up Legation Street at a dead run, missing her entirely in her scanty refuge. In a minute the last of them would pass her, and she could get up and make her run for the gates of the British compound.

Only a minute more.

They had done it—they were going to win!

The two thoughts pounded in Feng Yu-lan's pulsing brain. They had broken through the lines. They would take the Americans and the Russians in the rear, sweep Legation Street. If the Shansi regiments could only be brought in—quickly, quickly!—to hold the street, it would be all but over. The French, German, American legations, the Tartar Wall would all be cut off and taken, what was left of the defenders driven back in pandemonium into the British compound.

It would be over before the sun went down that day.

Feng ran like a rolling juggernaut at the head of the wave of screaming Boxers, invincible, unstoppable. The great bellows in his chest swelled with life; his heart pumped cataracts of blood through his swinging, straining limbs. His bare skin *was* impregnable! His life *was* charmed and proof against all foreign steel! He believed it at last, believed as he had never believed anything before in all his life.

He ran laughing and shouting up the wide street, the boy with whom the gods talked scampering at his side, a hundred throats roaring behind him. His gross-featured, hideous face glowed from within with a childlike happiness.

"They're dead game, I'll say that for 'em," said Williams, settling behind the big, ugly-looking gun.

In the street below, the Boxers were stretched out from the French Legation over the bridge and halfway to the American. Fire from the German and Japanese compounds was already beginning to pepper away at their rear. American Marines and Russian soldiers were turning around, seeing what was coming, and bringing their own rifles to bear on the charging, shouting van. The Boxers had left a trail of their own dead and wounded from one side of the Legation Quarter almost to the other side, and they were still coming.

"Cut loose," said Connor, setting his teeth against the pain. "Get the big son of a bitch if you can." He braced himself against the broken stone and stood up to direct fire.

Then he was choking on cordite, his ears stunned to deafness by the jolting power of the machine gun. The Colt was pouring four hundred bullets a minute into Legation Street. Connor, with a Chinese bullet in his body, stood and watched the Chinese go down like ripe grain under a scythe.

The first arc pocked the macadam at Feng Yu-lan's feet. Tai Chi-tao, the boy who spoke with the gods, running just behind him, took three bullets through his narrow belly and was thrown six feet away, almost cut in half. Behind him, the incredible hail of flying metal chewed its way through the front ranks of the rampaging host.

When Feng faltered and turned at last, he saw a slaughter-house where his army had been.

Elizabeth had just risen to her feet, still gasping for breath, her legs shaking under her, when the shredded mob broke and turned and came stampeding back up the street. She gauged her chances of making it across the wide road before the first of them reached her—and knew she had no chance. But there was shooting from the German Legation, just across the bridge. She could reach that. She plucked up her skirts and began to run as she had not run since she was a little girl racing bare-legged after her hoop across Rittenhouse Square.

But the gates of the German Legation were barricaded, and bullets were driving inch-deep holes into the brick walls. Box-ers were streaming past her now, jerking and tumbling under a merciless fire from both sides of Legation Street and from the Tartar Wall. She ran on, frantically seeking a way out, an escape from the butchery all around her.

She found it. A narrow alleyway led around the German Embassy, back to the Peking Club behind it. She ran, sobbing for breath. A dozen panting, terrified Boxers jostled around her.

Then there were the tennis courts and the half-finished new clubhouse. And still the whine of bullets everywhere. There was another alley, twisting and littered with bricks and blackened wood. There was a rickety barricade, and she was clambering over it, jabbering Chinese boys before and behind her.

When her sanity returned—when the bullets and the screaming were behind her at last, and even the sound of shooting muted by the intervening houses—she was half a block into the *hutungs*, surrounded by the bloodied remnants of the *I Ho Chuan*.

48

EVERYTHING CONSIDERED, IT COULD HAVE BEEN A GREAT deal worse, thought Sir Claude, smoothing his moustaches in the mirror.

There had been casualties, of course, killed and injured in every sector of the shrunken Legation Quarter. The French had suffered particularly. But they had held onto their sliver of a legation in the end. The Royal Marines in the Mongol Market had had to face the new repeating rifles the Shansi troops had brought with them. But they too had held on, and bloodied the Shansi boys properly when a Chinese barricade unexpectedly collapsed in front of them. And the damn Boxers had been decimated on Legation Street.

He applied the moustache wax with care to produce the flaring beauties, half again the width of his narrow face, that were his hallmark in the legations. He patted his cravat. You could always tell a gentleman, Sir Claude was fond of saying, because he *looked* like a gentleman. On such a night as this, he was bound to look his best.

It was to be a small dinner party for the ministers and their ladies only. There would no doubt be a mild round of applause, and some formal expression of appreciation for his leadership in this hour of testing. He meditated an appropriate response as he slipped into his tailcoat.

There were undoubtedly those who would condemn the whole affair as premature. Rifles were still banging furiously on the perimeters, after all, and the shelling had recommenced, this time from several ancient cannon located on the walls of the Imperial City itself. Sir Claude's own tree-shrouded home had suffered several hits: he glanced disgustedly at the sifting of plaster and broken glass in one corner which his stupid Chinese boy had somehow missed.

There were those who would scoff at champagne and candlelight while the guns still sounded, right enough. Well, let 'em! It was time civility returned to Peking.

He got his expression of appreciation and his applause. The champagne was the best in the cellars, and the Chinese chef produced as succulent a horsemeat steak as even M. Pichon had ever tasted. With impeccable self-restraint, they avoided the topic that was uppermost in all their minds. They avoided it, at least, until the ladies had left the room to the gentlemen for their port and cigars.

"Tell me, Sir Claude," said the acting German Minister Herr von Bülow then, putting a match to a long black Havana, "exactly when do you expect the relief column?"

"Ah, the famous relief," Sir Claude responded with a dry twinkle, "when indeed?" He smiled toothily into the uneasy round of laughter that followed.

"But, seriously, Sir Claude," said Von Bülow gently. The urbane Rhinelander was not to be put off. His predecessor had been the only Minister Plenipotentiary killed in the entire siege.

"Seriously indeed," MacDonald agreed then, straightening his shoulders with the air of authority that had carried him so triumphantly through the Oil River campaign. "Seriously speaking, after further consultations with our heroic messenger, and after discussing the matter with such of our military commanders as have been available during the recent emergency—I honestly can't tell you any more than we knew before. According to Dr. Chen's message, the troops have long since left Tientsin. But then, if Admiral Seymour's unhappy experience last June is any indication of what they will have to face, the new relief column will not have an easy time of it."

There was no laughter at all, only an impatient clearing of a throat or two. Sir Claude decided to save his analysis of the military situation for question time, and got on with it.

"My best estimate, gentlemen," he concluded, "is three more days. Three nights from tonight, we should be drinking champagne with our liberators!"

"And meantime?" inquired M. Pichon.

"Meantime," replied Sir Claude succinctly, "we hold our ground. Risk nothing, hold everything, stand fast—and we're saved!" The last words came out in an unintended rush of emotion that stirred an answering throb in every heart around the candlelit table.

"Risk nothing." Herr von Bülow smiled. "My sentiments precisely."

"Only sensible damn thing to do," grunted Mr. Conger, reaching for the nearest decanter of port.

"And what about the prisoner?" demanded an unexpected voice from outside the circle of candlelight. "What about the American girl captured during the Boxer attack this afternoon?"

Chen Li, in his rumpled old white suit, advanced slowly into view. He looked totally out of place in that ambience of tailcoats and tall white tapers, cut-glass decanters and silver cuspidors. The Europeans were obviously not happy to see him.

"Dr. Chen!" said MacDonald. "I was under the impression that you were acquiring the rest so richly merited by your recent exploit. Indeed, I really think you would be better advised—"

"Miss Elizabeth Rowntree," Chen cut him off. "Your guest and compatriot, Mr. Conger. And something of a heroine to the wounded of all nations, so I understand. A German soldier and two American Marines saw her swept off the street in the battle by a retreating detachment of Boxers, and subsequently bundled over a barricade into the *hutungs*."

"A tragic business," said Conger, shaking his head. "Tragic. My wife has been quite distraught. They got along very well, you know, in spite of the young woman's—escapades."

"All of us," said Sir Claude, "share our American colleague's sorrow at the young woman's misfortune. Despite her —ah—eccentric behavior, Miss Rowntree had performed yeoman service at the hospital in this time of trial. None of said eccentricities," he added firmly, "will of course be mentioned in dispatches to the outside world. She shall go down as an unsullied heroine of the siege!"

There was a vigorous rumble of approval around the table.

Chen Li looked from face to face. Pale, flaccid, ill-nourished they were, but blind and arrogant as only Western faces could be. The Chinese doctor looked them each in the eyes in turn. Then he asked the question one more time:

"You do not, then, plan any sort of effort to rescue her from the Boxers?"

"We of course hope very much that she *will* be rescued," said Sir Claude testily. "At the same time the rest of us are, by the International Relief Force."

"Which you expect in three days."

"Approximately so, yes."

Three days.

The eminent orientalist who had gone over to exchange a word or two with the Chinese troops on the first evening of the siege had been tortured through the night, his head thrown back into the legations the next morning. The feebleminded priest who had wandered away during the recent truce had been cut to pieces and his head mounted on a pole in front of General Tung Fu-hsiang's headquarters before noon the next day.

"The Boxers," Chen Li began again, "are undoubtedly demoralized by their defeat this afternoon. A vigorous sweep through the *hutungs* where they—"

"Out of the question," snapped MacDonald. "It would only serve to irritate the Chinese further, when our whole object now must be to keep them calm, to minimize the fury of their attack until help comes. Any rescue expedition of the sort you suggest would be suicidal, not only for those who undertook it, but for the Legation Quarter as a whole."

"Really, Chen," said Conger through a cloud of cigar smoke, "it'd be damn silly to risk it all now, when we're—so close to home."

Chen clasped his hands before his chest in the Chinese way, and bowed, and went away.

A dark figure detached itself from the shadows as he stepped out the front door of the British Minister's house. Dr. Chen recognized the set of the shoulders, the aggressive angle of the head silhouetted suddenly against a bursting rocket behind the trees. The shelling and the shooting had if anything intensified since afternoon. A light rain was falling.

"Sergeant Connor," said Chen wearily. "You must get back to hospital at once."

"Doc," said Connor, "what are they going to do about her?"

"About her?"

"About Lizzie."

Even in the darkness, staring at a silhouette, Chen Li knew that there was none of the flaccid arrogance of the men inside in this man. And the American Marine had, he remembered, been a special friend of Elizabeth's.

"Nothing," he said flatly.

"They aren't going to do a thing?" Connor swayed slightly on his wide-planted feet. He was evidently sedated, if only with brandy while they took the bullet out. "Not a Goddam thing?"

"No. Now come back to hospital before you have to be carried."

"The bastards," said Connor, slurring the words. "The Goddam fucking—"

Dr. Chen took him by the left arm and led him off. It would be out of his way, a detour past the Chancery. But there would be time enough to get the sergeant back to the hospital and still do what he must do. Somehow he was quite sure of that.

49

FENG YU-LAN DREW THE OPIUM DEEP INTO HIS LUNGS, HELD it, and let it slide slowly out again. The world was beautifully distanced now, like a play, or a puppet show in the street. He could bear it now. He opened his eyes and looked about him.

They had pretty well torn the place apart, house and garden both. The pools were fouled outside, and some of the trees and one lacquered pavilion had been chopped down for fire-wood. The floor was caked with mud and cluttered with dirty clothes, weapons, remnants of food, broken furniture. The *I Ho Chuan* were peasant folk, not used to the niceties of city living.

The room where he sprawled in a chair tilted back against the wall had been the study, Feng remembered. They had ostentatiously used the Western books and journals to start fires with, or for toilet paper. The Chinese classics they had left reverently on the shelves—rather as icons than anything else, thought Feng wryly, since none of his brothers of the Society could read.

The Scarlet Fist of China slowly surveyed the room. Each separate thing stood out with preternatural clarity, jewel-like and distinct. There was the rumpled, dirty cot where Tai had slept, with a litter of mineral-water bottles around it. There was his gleaming, black-oiled Mauser leaning with the long spears in a corner. Chen's worktable was littered with spilled cups, the half-full bottle of *shamsu,* bowls of uneaten noodles. The long, elaborately carved opium pipe hung loose in Feng's outsized hand, a wisp of smoke curling up.

On his own mattress, in the farthest corner, lay the girl.

They were laughing drunkenly in the guest hall outside the curtain. The *shamsu* was going fast around, though his coun-try lads would have been shocked at the opium. How long had it been since he had touched the pipe? Two years?

The girl moaned on the bed.

Two years at least, he decided. From the day he had committed himself to the movement, the Society, he had eschewed all forms of intoxication, all sexual indulgence, all sins of the flesh whatever. He chuckled and shook his shaven head. His crooked queue hung over one shoulder, sloppily braided and loose. Truly, his purity had been amazing. There was nothing like an old pander for piety.

He looked at the wrinkled, dirty sheets where Tai Chi-tao had slept. For two years he had even kept his hands off the boy, though he had always had a predilection for boys. Tai had had a fine, lean body too, he remembered, for all his feebleminded awkwardness.

This girl, now. His eyes shifted slowly back to her. Was she worth raping? Had she been raped already?

She was trying to sit up. She was a scrawny Western woman, her face bruised, her gown torn in several places, her hair all over her shoulders in disgusting disarray. Her dark-blue eyes, open now and watching him, were filled with terror.

Feng's gaze traveled drowsily over her taut, trembling body.

Fleshless knees, he thought, thin shanks. And that baleful paleness of the skin. White skin—white, the color of death! Why should he, a connoisseur, who had run half a dozen pleasure-houses and enjoyed women of every shade and nationality, bestir himself for this? He settled back heavily and knocked the embers of the opium out against the wall.

He doubted if the lads who had brought her in had raped her either. They were good shamefast peasants, quicker to cut a woman into pieces than to take her sexually.

A Japanese girl, now—there was happiness! He closed his pouched eyes to dream.

Elizabeth stared at him. The Chinese seemed huge to her, a gigantic brownish-yellow statue of a man in the lantern light. The slablike, hairless pectoral muscles of his chest glowed with a faint film of moisture. The thick, uptilted lips, the flat nose and pouchy eyes seemed to embody more blatant evil than any face she had ever seen.

The eyes were closed now, as though he was drunk or asleep. Perhaps if she— But before she could gather her limbs under her, she heard laughing Chinese voices from beyond the curtained doorway. Glancing quickly up at the slatted window, she saw darkness outside, and cooking fires, and moving figures in some sort of garden.

It was only then, as she looked around the room in desperate search for a way out, that she realized where she was.

Chen Li's workroom.

She knew the scrolls on the walls, the ruins of his worktable. There on the floor was his American medical degree, and the photograph of him with his friends at the London Hospital— the frame broken, the picture stained and smeared. Around two sides of the room ran his bookshelves, half empty now. For all the filth and litter, it could be nowhere else.

She covered her throbbing eyes with her hands and tried to think.

Her head hurt terribly; her whole body ached. She remembered the hysterical laughter, the sudden anger of her captors. She remembered knives flourished in her face, and fingers tugging at her hair. Then a sudden stunning slap across the face. Hands upon her body—and her own hands flailing, striking out wildly, fighting them. More blows then, and falling, and being kicked and beaten until she couldn't remember anymore.

And now she was here. They had turned her over to their leader—the face behind the rifle in that village street last autumn, the face that had led the charge up Legation Street that afternoon. When he woke up, this hideous giant would do whatever occurred to him to do with her.

She sat there on the mattress on the floor, curled in a tight ball, listening to the laughter behind the curtain, an incongruous burst of song outside in the garden. It was raining outside now, the usual gentle evening drizzle. She rocked very slowly back and forth, her arms hugging her breasts, and never for a

310

moment took her eyes off the gleaming shaven head and the crooked queue.

She was still rocking, still staring fixedly at the big bald man two hours later, when they jerked back the curtain and flung Dr. Chen Li into the room.

50

FENG HAD FUNNELED FAR BACK THROUGH TIME ON THE curling blue smoke of the drug. Back to the river of his childhood in the shadow of the Western Hills. Back to Chen Li's boyish face, with its wind-hollowed cheeks, turning slowly to watch a kingfisher dive. *We shall meet in Peking,* Feng had said to that Chen Li of his boyhood, *at the foot of the Dragon Throne.*

Feng opened his eyes and saw the Chen Li of twenty-five years later, wiping the blood off his face and taking the scrawny Western girl in his arms.

The sculptured forehead was still there, and the dark, serious eyes. But the black hair was slashed with grey, the strong body stiff with a weariness the boy's lean limbs had never known. The forehead was shaven—recently, it seemed —but Li had long since cut his queue, and the battered Western suit he wore fitted him as naturally as his skin.

The girl was touching him shamelessly, and they were gabbling in the English tongue.

"Welcome to your house, Chen Li!" said Feng loudly. He continued to lounge in the delicate teakwood chair, tilted back against the wall, but his eyes were glittering, his voice harsh and aggressive. "We have made ourselves completely at home, as you see."

Chen smiled tenderly at the Western woman once more, then set her from him, back into the corner of the mattress, and turned to Feng. "You honor my humble house by your presence, Feng Yu-lan," he said formally, dabbing a continuing trickle of blood from the corner of his mouth. "Many happy days will no doubt come of it."

"I regret only that my friend Tai Chi-tao may not be present for this meeting, Chen Li," Feng continued sardonically. "Alas, he is gone to join his revered ancestors. He was cut into two pieces by the guns of your friends the devils from the West this afternoon in Legation Street."

"I regret his passing," said Chen, inclining his head, "though all must go."

"He was a good enough lad," said Feng, "a peasant boy from the slopes of T'ai Shan. Something of an idealist, like you and me when we were boys, Chen Li." His wide, wrinkled lips spread in a grin. "Except that poor Tai was weak in the intellect."

Chen said nothing.

Feng tipped his chair forward off the wall, brought the front legs crashing down upon the polished floor.

"Do you know, Chen Li, what it is like to want all your life to believe?" His voice was harsher, louder. "To want to believe, and to find nothing anywhere but corruption and degradation, panders that sell and mandarins that buy? Ah! If you had seen princes of the Imperial House fling off their yellow robes to wallow in the arms of Shanghai Caucasian girls and Willow Lane transvestites—perhaps you too would have enlisted under the banners of an idiot boy from T'ai Shan!"

Still Chen said nothing. He sat quietly, dabbing at the blood that oozed from a broken lip, the gap where a tooth had been.

"But you—you never knew my exaltations!" Feng was leaning forward in the delicate skeleton of a chair, big-boned hands clenched on his knees, eyes blank with the glistening opium stare. "You never knelt a day and a night together at the altars of the gods as I did, Chen Li, weeping and praying to believe. Your soul was always a coolie soul, for all your brushes and rice paper. You were not born for greatness. While I—I might have worn the Yellow Jacket!" He raised one arm and brought it down, smashing one slender arm of the chair to ivory-colored fragments.

"I confess, Feng Yu-lan," said Chen quietly, "that I have

never known your exaltations, or lusted after true belief as you have done. I am a doctor only. I pick up the pieces of those your exaltations scatter like chips across the land."

"You are a fool and a whore, Chen Li," said Feng, unclasping his great fists, his eyes clearing, "as I told you when last we met in this room. What are you doing here now?"

"I have come to trade."

"To trade what for what?"

"To barter my own person for the release of this unworthy Western woman."

"Unworthy she certainly is." The wide, flat grin was on Feng's face once more. "But why do you feel that you yourself are worth any more to me?"

"To cut this woman into pieces would no doubt give some pleasure to your people in the courtyard yonder," said Chen evenly. "To do the same to me would perhaps give them more. And it might also reflect considerable honor upon your own head, Feng Yu-lan."

"Indeed? And why would that be so?"

"I am a well-known running dog of the foreign devils—anyone in the *hutungs* will tell you that. My death would be an exemplary lesson."

Feng shrugged. "There have been many such exemplary lessons these last two months."

"I am a purveyor of foreign medicines. A poisoner of the living, a plucker of eyeballs from the dead. A pickler of Chinese babies. Whatever else you will."

"Not good enough," said Feng, raising and spreading his hands in the merchant's gesture of rejection of a completely unacceptable offer. "You have troubled me for nothing, I think."

"I think not, Feng of the Scarlet Fist," said Chen. "For I am also the messenger who has just returned from Tientsin with the first heartening word the foreigners have had since the siege began. Word so heartening that I think you will never overrun them now, so strengthened are their spirits by the news that I have brought them."

Feng straightened slowly in the chair, uncoiling like a powerful hunting animal at the sight of prey. "And what news is that, Chen Li?" he said softly.

"News that is undoubtedly known well enough in the palaces of the Forbidden City, Feng Yu-lan, though it has probably not yet reached the fighters in the streets. Word that the foreign armies are at last marching upon Peking."

Feng laughed. "They came in the spring, Chen Li—have you forgotten? Chinese valor routed them, drove them back upon their ships."

"That was no army, Feng. It was only the scrapings of the foreign naval vessels that happened to be anchored at Taku Bar. What comes now is an army. Thousands upon thousands of soldiers. Maxims and Gatlings and cannon that even the walls of Peking cannot stand against. All the Eight Powers of the West in arms, closing upon this city."

The big, heavily muscled body settled slowly back, like a hunting cat whose prey has passed. "And does it give you pleasure, old friend of my youth, to contemplate the Western cannon bringing their muzzles to bear upon Peking?"

Elizabeth heard, and understood.

She had tried desperately to understand, ever since she had overcome her stupefaction at seeing Li once more, at his arms around her and his whispered reassurances, before he turned back to the Boxer chief. She had strained every bit of the Chinese she had picked up over a year in Peking. But the flow of words came too rapidly, the inflections were strange to her fatigued mind. She had caught nothing continuously until this last exchange.

A Western army closing upon the city! A wild hope for life, after so many weeks of living with the certainty of death!

She felt the blood rush to her cheeks and lowered her eyes

315

quickly, in order that the sparkle she knew must be there might not betray her excitement. Life, hope, a future after all. Her breast hurt with the joy of it, and her breath came quickly.

And then, strangely and quite irrelevantly at such a time, the weight of the Boxer leader's question settled upon her: *Does it give you pleasure, the Western guns leveled against Peking?*

The question was asked of Chen Li, and he was answering, in short, vehement phrases. But Elizabeth answered it too, in her heart. And the answer, amazingly, in a city that had become an iron ring of enemies to her and all her people, was a heartfelt *No—my God, no!* Not Western guns against these temples and walls and pagoda-roofed gates, shattering the blue dome of the Temple of Heaven, leveling the fairy-tale loveliness of the Forbidden City that she had seen only once in her life, and never would see again. Not Western shells exploding in all these winding lanes and alleyways, with their garbage and scavenging dogs and laughing children, their beggars and fortune-tellers and hot soup and noodle stalls, the gossip, the heat, the flies, the life—the life!

She remembered the ruin that stretched out over the *hutungs* around the Legation Quarter. The siege of the legations had done that. Must a vastly greater assault now do the same to all those teeming miles of Peking? In her joy at her own reprieve, she longed for a reprieve for the city as well.

Almost at once, she realized with chilling certainty that neither the one nor the other was really going to happen at all.

Chen Li knew also that he had lost. He could see it in the sag of the giant shoulders, the collapse of the great cat. Feng Yu-lan no longer cared. The news of the coming of the Eight Powers in arms had finished him. He no longer cared what happened to Chen or to Elizabeth or even to himself. He would give them both to his brothers of the *I Ho Chuan* in the morning, and he would watch through drug-filmed, indifferent eyes what his brothers did.

So Chen Li answered the question Feng had asked succinctly and with no more guile. "They are not my people, Feng, who bring their cannons and their Maxim guns against Peking."

"Indeed? And are we your people, then?"

"No, old friend of my youth," said Chen, "you and your brothers are not my people either."

"You have no people then, Chen Li, as I said when last we talked." Feng's smile was easily triumphant, like a man scoring a key debating point over an unimpressive opponent. "You are some sort of mythic beast, I think. A queueless Chinese, a yellow-skinned European—something surely without kith or kindred in this world."

"My people are real enough, brother," Chen answered slowly. "My people are the broken ones. The small unimportant pieces you and the white mandarins in the legations play with and flip off the board."

"You cannot be doctor to the legations and to the *hutungs* too. Not now. Not anymore."

"Then I shall choose the *hutungs.* When they will have me once again."

"They will not have you again!" Feng's face came momentarily to life again, full of sudden vindictiveness. Vindictiveness—and was it jealousy as well? "We have seen to that, Chen Li. We may pass, we may die to the last man—but the *hutungs* will remember. The foreigner and all his spirit-slaves will yet be driven from China!"

"It may be, Feng. For my lifetime, the foreigner will prevail, I think. And the people of Peking will need me."

"They will not have you again. We shall not let them. We shall bring such a shower of fire down upon them that they will curse the West and all its works for the rest of their lives."

"Those that live? Those that survive the fire you bring down upon them?"

"Those that live. The survivors will be ours!"

Chen shook his head. "Those that live will be their own people, brother. They will seek their own accommodations with life. They will be neither your spirit-slaves nor those of the foreigners, but lamps unto themselves, and work out their own salvation. As they have always done."

But Feng's interest had passed; his flare of sudden caring was over. His wide mouth wrinkled in a frown as he pawed about for his opium pipe.

"We have talked too long, brother of my youth," said Chen then. "I told you why I came here. Will my body not satisfy your people? May not this woman go?" He gestured toward her casually, contemptuously, as if she were not worth his glance.

"Li, Li," sighed Feng in his deep vibrating voice like the wind in the reeds of childhood, "you know I will not let either of you go. Could not if I wanted to"—he smiled sardonically —"for the brothers of the Society would undoubtedly put me to the torment in her place if I were to do anything so foolish."

"One favor, then, friend of my childhood."

"And what is that?"

"Allow me to spend this last night with the Western woman." He paused a moment. "It is little enough to ask. And I ask it in the name of better years, when we were young and clasped hands upon our brotherhood."

"A woman for your last night on earth, Chen Li!" Feng chuckled. "And a skinny Western whore at that. I should not have thought it of our philosopher, our village mandarin."

"Nevertheless, I ask it."

"And I grant it," said the Boxer chief cheerfully, with only the faintest hint of peasant guile in his voice. "Oh, yes, Chen Li, you shall have your last night alone." He chuckled again and slammed one elbow against the wall to bring his drunken followers stumbling into the room.

Chen Li bowed his gratitude, hands clasped upon his chest. He did not need the whole night, he thought. He had the dagger close to hand, and it would be only a moment's work to set Elizabeth free before the morning sun.

51

THE ROOM WAS SMALL, WINDOWLESS, AND COMPLETELY dark, smelling of clay and moldering fruit. Or so it had been the last time Chen Li had entered it, in company with his servant, to select what remained of the winter storage of fruits and vegetables. He caught new odors now the minute the thick plank door swung open: the smell of stale blood, the lingering pungent stench of vomit. In the first flickering shafts of lantern light, as they stumbled down the stairs, he saw half a dozen wooden collars, three chained to each wall left and right. Splintered bamboos jutted from one of the empty fruit bins in the rear. The back-garden fruit cellar had obviously been used for other purposes in recent weeks.

"Here is your chamber for the night, Chen Li," said Feng, bending to pass through the low doorway, but coming only a step or two down the stairs. "I trust you and your white concubine will enjoy your last hours together." The drunken youths in red sashes and headbands who accompanied him giggled at their leader's joke.

Chen was hustled over to the left-hand wall, Elizabeth to the right. The wide square wooden collars with the circular holes for their necks were slipped into place, closed and locked. They had four feet of chain. Their fingers would not come within six feet of touching if they strained to the limits of their reach.

"I wish you joy of each other," said Feng again, blurring the softer consonants. "The caresses of the last night must be sweet!" And then, turning once more in the squat doorway: "Eight cuts in the morning, eh, Chen Li, old friend? Eight cuts only. Or as well as we can approximate them!"

He thrust the door open and passed out into the starlit garden, followed by his laughing entourage.

The door closed. Chen heard the bar slam into place. Then the two of them were alone in total darkness.

"You will find that you can sit down," said Chen's voice out of the blackness. "It is a blessing. Frequently the *cangue* does not allow the prisoner to sit or lie. And at least we are spared the cage."

"Yes," said Elizabeth mechanically. "It is a blessing." She had seen the full *cangue*, the vertical cage with the criminal's head sticking through the wooden collar at the top. This Chinese version of the stocks was often so designed that the condemned had to stand on his toes or hang half-strangling by his chin.

The girl sank to the damp earth now, exhausted and aching still. The wooden collar was thick and heavy and smelled abominable.

"Li," she said presently, "why did you come?"

"I told you," his voice answered, "that I would never let you face this alone. That when the end came, I should be with you."

"But help is coming!" she said desperately. "Didn't I understand that much?"

"The relief force is coming. They think in three days. Nobody really knows when."

How close she had come, she thought, to living after all! A wave of anguish washed over her. It really did feel much worse to have come so close.

"Oh, Li," she said, "I am glad you came to me. It is terrible —I did not know I could be so selfish. But I am so glad."

"I am glad too, Elizabeth. You know that." She could almost feel his smile in the darkness.

"I wish I could touch you, Li."

Again she felt the smile, reassuring, strengthening. "And I you, Elizabeth. But our voices will reach out and touch. That they cannot take from us."

"Yes," she said miserably.

Then abruptly, without preamble, for no reason but the

321

sudden urgent necessity to do so, she was telling him about Connor.

It all came tumbling out in a rush of words. That first night at the deserted Hôtel de Pékin, her sudden need and his, and what came after. That night and all the rest—the passion, the tenderness, the closeness they had shared. All that, and the final uncertainty that had gripped her that very day about herself and Connor and what they might or might not have been to each other if they had met anywhere but this doomed city.

"I think I love him, Li," she said finally. "I think I love him as much as I do you."

There was a silence.

"Love is a good thing, Elizabeth," said Chen's voice at last. "I have not had enough of it in my life. It is good that you have found so much in yours."

"There was none before you, Li. I could not—I don't think I could have loved him before I loved you."

"I am glad. You know how much happiness you have given me." And then, with the faintest of chuckles: "I am half a westernized Chinese, so I am half furiously jealous. And half very glad for you."

"And for him?" My God, she thought, I am actually bantering with him. I can actually joke—here and now.

"Not for him," said Chen Li. "Half Chinese, half Western I may be—but I am all flesh and blood. And that is too much to ask of flesh and blood."

They laughed together in low voices, and for one moment were at peace.

But the far-off rattle of the guns penetrated even through the thick earthen walls. The rough wood of the *cangue* scraped her neck; its weight hurt her slender shoulders. And there was one question she had to ask him. Something she thought she had caught in the Boxer leader's last words, as he left them in their darkness.

"Li," she said, "what are the eight cuts?"

322

Chen Li thought very fast. But not fast enough, he knew. There was a fraction of a second's hesitation before he answered: "It is decapitation, Elizabeth. And the quartering of the body."

"Afterward?"

"Afterward."

But that answer came too quickly, he knew, and he cursed himself for his ineptitude.

Chen Li had witnessed few executions. But as a prospective mandarin, before he turned to Western medicine, he had studied the law. He could see the characters now, running vertically up the page: *The first class of punishments for capital offenses—to be inflicted for treason, parricide, matricide, murder of the husband, uncle, or tutor. The criminal is bound to a scaffolding and cut into pieces by the imperial executioner. With imperial clemency, into eight pieces only: the first two cuts to remove the eyebrows—the third and fourth, to sever the arms at the shoulders—the fifth and sixth, to cut off the breasts—the seventh, to pierce the heart—the eighth, to sever the head.*

In practice, betel nut or wine was usually provided by friends or by the jailers themselves, to prepare the condemned for death. Chen Li doubted that the Boxers would have wine to spare for foreign devils.

"Elizabeth," he said firmly, "I have something for you. If you speak, I will throw it toward the sound of your voice. It is very important that you recover it. Do you understand?"

"Yes," she faltered, "but what—"

Something hard and heavy struck her knee, bruisingly even through the skirt and petticoats. She leaned as far forward as she could against the chain and the weight of the *cangue* and felt about on the pounded-earth floor, until her fingers encountered cold metal. A six-inch blade, a handle of bone or ivory.

"Have you found it?"

"Yes."

"I meant to do it for you, Elizabeth. I could have done it quickly. Now you must do it for yourself. The edge is keen —it will hurt only a bit. Do you understand what I am saying?"

"Yes. Oh, but, Li, I can't—"

"You must. Do you hear? *You must.*"

She tried to speak, and could not. She felt the thin, cold blade with her fingertips. She could not see it even when she held it almost against her eyes.

"You are a doctor, Elizabeth. You know where the radial and ulnar arteries flow, and the median vein of the wrist. You can find them even in the dark." The voice was stern, commanding, yet dry as if he were reading an anatomy lecture in the old brick medical building at Twentieth and North College, in an incredibly far-off place called Philadelphia.

"Yes," she said numbly. "Yes, I can find them."

She felt with her fingers, not her thumb. Found the ridges. Felt the pulse of life.

"I will talk to you, Elizabeth," said the voice out of the dark. "I will tell you about the little temple up the lane. Do you remember it, the temple in Seven Wells Lane, that we stumbled into that snowy afternoon last winter? Do you remember the six carved gods, and the bright little pictures in the darkness?"

She felt the flow of life beneath her fingers. The pulse beat steadily, waiting for the stroke that would save her from the far worse horror that lay beyond the night. Waiting for the stroke that she herself must give.

"Do you remember the lamps, the incense, and the song?" the insistent voice went on. "Do you remember the song the old man sang? . . ."

"O mi to Fuh, O! niang niang, ah!
O mi to Fuh, O! niang niang, ah!"

THE OLD MAN KNELT ON THE MAT BEFORE THE POLISHED idol, chanting into the incense. Around him, the cavelike room was silent, full of shadows where the light of the scattered candles did not reach. Pictures of demons and pagodas gleamed on the nearest walls.

The old man's face was a network of wrinkles. His sparse grey queue hung untidily down his back. He kowtowed seven times, eight times, nine times before the first of his six idols, poured out a slow libation. Then he moved on to the next. Behind him, the low door stood open to the street. The drizzle had stopped outside.

The temple in Seven Wells Lane had stood open throughout the Boxer troubles, as it had through fire and war and civil discord for more centuries than the old priest knew. He himself had tended these six haughty divinities for almost fifty years. Soon, he hoped, the gods would send him a successor to train in the exacting rituals, so that he himself might think of laying down the heavy burden.

He poured out another libation and moved on.

A lanky youth in the jodhpured uniform and wide-brimmed hat of the U. S. Marine Corps stepped quietly through the door behind him. The intruder took three quick steps across the packed-earth floor and cracked the old priest across the side of the head with the butt of his rifle. As the old man toppled, the Marine reversed his weapon expertly and raised the bayonet.

"Skip it!" said Sergeant Connor tersely, stepping into the temple just behind Private Williams. "We'll be long the hell gone by the time he wakes up anyway."

"Hell, Sarge," said Williams, "I hear the Boxers sacrifice people alive in places like this. This old bastard—"

"I said skip it!" Connor spoke through a jaw set tight against the pain of his wound, against the weakness that oozed with the blood beneath his bandages. "The next Chinaman that wanders in here would see the wound and holler bloody murder. This way, they'll just think the old guy keeled over himself. They'll put him to bed for the night, and forget it. It's those sons of bitches with the red bandanas we're after. Come on."

It was the longest speech he had made that night, and just about as long a one as he could manage. He jerked his head toward the doorway, turned on his heel, and went out. Williams shrugged and followed.

There were a dozen men waiting outside in the little courtyard, where the ancient lantern still flickered and swayed in the wind. About half of them were American Marines, the rest volunteers from the guards of other legations, plus a civilian or two. They were all there, deep into the enemy-held *hutungs,* entirely without permission or authorization by their superiors. They had agreed to come with Connor when he had told them that the Council of Ministers intended to do nothing at all to rescue the American lady doctor. Many had fresh scars that Elizabeth Rowntree had tended. All of them were determined that no white woman should be left in the hands of the Boxers.

"Any sign?" whispered Lieutenant Philip Greville nervously as they came out. Greville still didn't know where he had found the courage to join the volunteer party. But he thanked God that Connor's vastly superior knowledge of the *hutungs* allowed him to defer command of the expedition to the American sergeant.

Connor shook his head to the Britisher's question.

"Which way now?"

"North," said Connor. "There's a bigger temple a couple of blocks up that way—a Buddha temple. They might have

326

taken her there. There's nothing else in this street."

It was like looking for a needle in a haystack, he knew.
But what the hell else could he do? Leave Lizzie—his Lizzie
—in the hands of that Mongolian giant, to be hung up in
front of General Tung's tent in the morning? He would look,
and go on looking, until he dropped.

"Come on," he said huskily, and led the way on up Seven
Wells Lane.

The old woman must be mad, thought Prince Tuan irritably
as he swayed along in his sedan chair, fingering the yellow
cloth folded across his knees.

To be roused in the middle of the night, to be summoned
peremptorily to the Dowager Empress's chambers in the Forbidden City—that was unusual and unreasonable enough. To
be ordered then to set out at once to scour the sleeping city
for one particular chieftain of the *I Ho Chuan*—one out of
the dozens of would-be generals who strutted about Peking
these days—was worse than unreasonable. It was insane. The
Old Buddha was sinking into her dotage at last.

Prince Tuan scratched a smallpox scar and thought what
this would mean to the succession of his son to the throne—
of his family to the dynastic mastery of China. If the Eight
Powers really were marching on Peking, the Dragon Throne
might not even be worth having. Tuan felt vaguely cheated.

He sat cross-legged in the curtained darkness, brooding.
The sedan chair bounced gently to the rhythmic trot of the
bearers. Before and behind, a small escort of Manchu Bannermen loped along. A lantern bearer preceded the little
column, but there were no drums or gongs, no officious shouts
of *"Chieh kuang!"* to announce his coming. Prince Tuan was
one of the most powerful men in the Empire: he was not
proud of being sent as an errand boy to carry a gift from that
senile old harridan in the Sea Palaces to a shirtless Boxer in
Seven Wells Lane.

It had been easy enough to trace him, actually. The huge,

ugly man with the German rifle was perfectly known to everyone in the siege lines, it seemed. "Feng!" they would say with an almost respectful smile. "Ah, yes!" He was the big devil that was at them every day to attack, attack harder, attack now! The worst of it was, he was more than willing to join them in any assault, at any time, no matter how suicidal. A big fool, truly. He really must believe he was proof against the bullets of the foreign devils! A big fool—but a juggernaut in action, added those who had seen him charge. "Why, this very afternoon—"

Tuan had cut them off with a question, and had got his answer. In Seven Wells Lane, at the house of Dr. Chen . . . Then the sedan chair and its little entourage was on its way again, careering off into the darkness.

Prince Tuan did not want to hear again about this afternoon. He would not be here now if it were not for Feng Yu-lan's fantastic charge into the heart of the legations. For Tzu Hsi herself had seen that wild rush from the high walls of the Imperial City. Using a pair of German binoculars, held and adjusted for her by the trembling hand of an old eunuch, the Dowager Empress had followed it all, and crowed with triumph as the red-sashed irregulars surged up Legation Street. When bullets from all sides had begun to cut them down, she had thrust the binoculars from her and turned away. But as she turned, she had rasped out an order: that if the big master of the *I Ho Chuan* named Feng survived, she was to know of it at once.

She had been praying at the Temple of the Imperial Ancestors in the Forbidden City when that word had come. She had retired at once to her apartments in the Sea Palaces to meditate and confer agitatedly with her astrologers. It was the middle of the night before she reached her decision, and sent for Prince Tuan.

None but he, she had told him, her soft trembling chins raised arrogantly, was fit to convey her sacred gift to the man Feng, who was destined to crush the foreign devils in the

328

Legation Quarter at last. None but a Manchu prince, the noble father of the Heir Apparent, should bear the gift of the Yellow Jacket to her new Feng.

"But, Bountiful Mother," Prince Tuan had protested in vain, "his men are all gone! All but a handful shot down in the street today. And most of the rest drunk in my own palace yard. He has only a small bodyguard of his own—"

"It is enough. If not one man remains to him, yet shall he save China. What happened today is an omen, a sign from the gods. I have ignored them too long, to my peril."

"An omen, Bountiful Mother?"

"Of course—of course! the Phoenix bird has always been my lucky symbol—see it here, embroidered with the five-clawed dragon on every curtain in this room. And did I not say myself, two months since, when you first brought this man to me, that he was my old Feng reborn? Now the gods have shown me what he can do."

Her eyes were glittering dully in her sallow pudding face.

"He shall be summoned to the Forbidden City in the morning. I shall consult with him about this wretched siege, which you and that famous General Tung cannot seem to bring to a conclusion. And then we shall see how the gods smile upon us at last!"

And so there he was, the father of the Heir Apparent, jouncing up Seven Wells Lane with the Yellow Jacket across his knees. He had pain from too much wine in the back of his head and bitter gall at all this folly in his heart.

The ambushers hit the prince's party from both sides of the lane at once—the American Marines from the left; two Britishers, two Germans, a Frenchman, and a Russian from the right. They used bayonets and rifle butts, and they struck with all the fury of their desperate isolation in a city full of enemies. The sleepy Bannermen outnumbered their attackers, but they never had a chance.

Only two shots were fired, both by Lieutenant Greville,

329

shooting into the dark after their fleeing enemies. Connor swore under his breath.

"See who's in there, Williams," he said in a slightly louder voice. He gestured at the fallen sedan chair. One bearer still lay under it, the others had fled with the guards.

"My God," breathed Greville, as the squat, pockmarked man in the yellow silks of the imperial house stepped from the chair. "It's Prince Tuan." And then, with a quick glance at the sedan chair: "It doesn't appear that he has got around to having his palanquin covered with our skins yet."

One of the German officers stepped forward, drawing his pistol. It was widely rumored among the Germans that Prince Tuan had been the one who offered the reward for the head of Baron von Ketteler.

"Wait a minute," said Connor sharply. "Get Simpson over here. He speaks their lingo like a native. Let's find out what the hell a swell gent like this is doing out here this time of night."

Simpson, the other Englishman, worked for Hart at the Imperial Customs Service. He spoke quickly to Tuan, who answered in brief monosyllables. He turned then to another, lesser prisoner who, kneeling with a bayonet at the back of his neck, was considerably more voluble.

Sergeant Connor waited impatiently, narrowing his eyes against the darkness all around them. He could feel observing eyes upon them now, could hear footsteps scuttering up nearby alleyways. Off to the east, Greville's two shots were echoed by shooting that seemed more than sporadic now.

"What does he say?" he demanded, throttling down the pain.

Simpson, in his imperturbable lime-juicer way, bent over and pulled something out of the abandoned sedan chair. He held it up in the lantern light. It was a lemon-yellow coat made of shimmering satin. Only then did he look at Connor with excitement shining in his eyes.

"Well?" snapped the Marine.

330

"Sergeant," said Simpson, "is the man we're after, the one who took the lady, a Boxer named Feng?"

"How the hell would I know his name?"

"But it is the chap who was out front this afternoon?"

Connor spat into the muddy lane. "Damn right. What does hizzoner here know about it?"

Simpson told him.

They let Prince Tuan and the other prisoners go, despite the guttural objections of the Germans. "We'll find him when we want him," said Connor grimly. They did not even take time to finish the two or three Bannermen who were still lying in the road. For the crash of gunfire seemed to be spreading, and there was shouting now. Even Connor managed an agonizing double time up Seven Wells Lane to the house with the large garden that had been Prince Tuan's destination.

As they clustered silently about the gate, trying to estimate the numbers inside by the sounds of drunken revelry within, Williams edged up beside Connor.

"Sarge," he whispered, "don't that shooting sound like Maxims to you?"

Connor reflected momentarily. "Sounds like a Maxim in with the rifles," he said. "We'll get in and out of here as fast as we can."

"That ain't it, Sarge," said Williams. "I was just wondering where the Chinks got a Maxim gun from."

Where indeed? thought Connor. And why so much shooting to the east? The legations were the other way. He looked up the lane and saw the first ruddy glow of flame rising against the midnight sky.

53

"ALL RIGHT, CAPTAIN," SAID GENERAL VASSILEVSKI, WIPING his saber with calculated coolness on his dark trousers, "bring up the field guns."

The general stood, with a handful of picked troops, just inside the stone vaulting of the Tung Pien Gate, on the east side of the Tartar City. Their white-belted tunics and the white caps of the officers moved like restless ghosts in the gloom. At their feet, the last of the Chinese sentries rolled over and lay still. General Vassilevski, the Russian Chief of Staff, had himself led the short, savage charge across the bridge over the moat to cut down the guards. The surprise attack had been eminently successful.

The next problem was the massive gate itself, locked and barred at sunset, not to be opened until dawn. With the help of the two field guns his men had dragged with them through the night, Vassilevski intended to get through the iron-studded gate considerably before then.

The International Relief Force had set out from Tientsin ten days before. The reality was even more impressive than Chen Li's message had indicated. An army of more than twenty thousand men, followed by a supply fleet of junks and sampans six miles long, moved northward up the Pei Ho toward Peking. Ten thousand Japanese, five thousand Russians, five thousand American and British troops made up the bulk of the relief column. But there were others too: French Zouaves in bright red-and-blue uniforms, Germans with pointed helmets, Italians with plumes, Sikhs in colorful turbans. Russian Cossacks and units of the famed Bengal Lancers fanned out across the front of that flowing ocean of men. North up the dusty roads, through head-high fields of kaoliang under the August sun they ground their way, day after blazing day. And mile by bloody mile, the Chinese gave ground.

General Gaselee, the solid Victorian Britisher in overall command, drove his men relentlessly. And the Chinese retreat turned into a rout.

Under the yellow summer sun, choking on dust, eaten alive by mosquitoes, the Western host had moved like a plague across the flat North China plains. Under the crushing weight of superior Western armaments, rigid discipline, and legendary invincibility, the vastly more numerous armies of China had simply gone to pieces. Chinese generals shot themselves. Chinese soldiers went wild and looted their own people. With burning villages for beacons and a trail of trampled fields and bloating corpses to mark their passing, the International Relief Force marched north.

The day before General Vassilevski ordered his cannon up against the Tung Pien Gate, the Western horde had rolled into Tungchow, an ancient walled town a dozen miles from Peking. There they had paused to rest, regroup, and plan the final assault on the capital.

But that same night, a Cossack reconnaissance patrol had brought back word to the Russian commanders that there was scarcely a Chinese soldier to be found between them and Peking. Chuckling at the thought of stealing a march on their fellow rescuers, eager to be first to plant a banner on the fabled red walls, the Russian generals had their grumbling men on the road by midnight.

They marched in a fine drizzle, through cornfields and irrigation ditches and over a maze of muddy roads toward the city. Behind them, though they did not know it, the news of their departure had spread, and the rest of the international army was taking to the roads as well. Twenty thousand men under arms were moving through the night, followed by creaking wagons and rumbling artillery, preceded by the nicker of cavalry horses and the laughter of excited young officers. Twenty thousand men, red-eyed with sleeplessness and dull smoldering anger, with lust for battle and for spoil, were converging on Peking.

The rain had stopped. General Vassilevski had his two field guns trundled up through the scattered shanties along the outside of the moat to the end of the wooden bridge and leveled point blank at the Tung Pien Gate. There were already shouts from the wall, from the high pagoda roof over the gate itself. Around the cannon, Maxim guns were being unloaded from mules, and riflemen were seeking points of vantage.

Vassilevski gave the order to fire.

Within half an hour, the gates were a smoking ruin, and the Russians were on the wall. Their Maxims were playing up and down the neighboring streets, while their rifles engaged the Chinese on three sides. A score of shops and houses were on fire already, roof tiles cracking, matted awnings going up in gouts of yellow flame.

Here and there in the shadow of the Tartar Wall, Russian soldiers, clearly distinguishable with their thick beards and white-belted tunics, were already running from house to house with growing armloads of silks and furs and gleaming precious metals.

54

"TELL ME, COUSIN," SAID A SLEEPY NINETEEN-YEAR-OLD youth sprawled against a red-bean tree in a dark corner of the garden, "is it dawn already, and have we drunk the night through? Or is that a fire in the east?" He waved vaguely toward the lurid glow pulsing above the garden wall.

"I think," said his equally drunken companion, "that it must be the sun. Because if it was a fire, you see, we would have heard the alarm bell and we would all have to turn out and fight it." He nodded at his own irrefutable logic and fumbled about for the bottle of *shamsu* among the roots of the tree.

The peaceful garden all around them looked more like a camp of nomads on the Gobi than a pleasure garden in the heart of Peking. The red embers of cooking fires glowed among improvised tents and lean-tos, fitfully illuminating the muffled figures of sleeping men, the roughly bandaged bodies of the wounded. Only a single fire still blazed brightly, by the servants' quarters on the other side of the garden, where a handful of red-sashed youths sat laughing and drinking and telling stories.

Suddenly there was a pounding at the gate.

"You see, Cousin?" said one of the young men under the red-bean tree. "This is how we handle fires in the city!" He rose unsteadily and headed more or less in the direction of the gate.

Simpson repeated his high-pitched demand, in flawed but undeniably excited Mandarin, that the gates be opened so that the fire fighters could get at the wells. The men clustered with him in the muddy lane heard a voice answer from within. Sergeant Connor thumbed Simpson back and set his rifle barrel against the wood.

The gate swung inward and a young, drunken face peered out. Connor jammed the muzzle of the Lee-Enfield into the man's red-sashed midriff and squeezed off.

The shot flung the Boxer back against the inner wall. He bounced off it and crumpled into the darkness. With the crash of the shot still stinging his ears, Connor lunged through the inner gateway into the garden, his volunteers crowding after him.

Everywhere among the trees and lotus pools, he could see sprawling figures starting up at the sound of that first echoing shot. There were a lot of them.

Sergeant Connor braced his rifle against his hip and snapped off a shot at the widest figure hunched about the one fire still burning brightly. The man pitched forward without a sound into the red-orange flames, taking a cooking pot with him. A moment later, half a dozen guns were banging around Connor, and then another half-dozen as the rest of his people poured in shooting.

In seconds all the men who had been drinking around the fire went down, falling into the flames, rolling on the flagstones. Then the merciless guns turned on the rest, on men just stumbling to their feet, or clawing blindly for weapons in the dark. The attackers had fanned out along the wall and scarcely moved from there. They simply stood or crouched in a ragged line, half hidden in the night, and fired till their long guns clicked on empty magazines, then dropped them and yanked out revolvers. They had come heavily armed into the *hutungs.*

The din was terrific. Gunsmoke swirled through the garden like fog. And still the guns flashed and banged out of the darkness, and stumbling, half-risen figures crumpled, toppled, pitched into unseen pools or windmilled into collapsing tents.

The Europeans fired until not a movement, not a groan could be detected anywhere among the trees and ferns and flowering shrubs. Perhaps three or four darting shadows made it to the shelter of the buildings at the rear.

"All right," said Connor then, "let's get into the house and the outbuildings back there. And look before you shoot now. There's a white woman back there somewhere."

Pushing clips and cartridges into their magazines, the rescue party advanced in a rough skirmish line. Connor headed straight for the wooden pillars and scrolled doorway of the main house just ahead.

Just before he reached the steps, a door flung open and the biggest man in the world came charging down upon him.

Feng Yu-lan had seen the glow of the fires against the eastern sky through the slatted window of Chen Li's workroom. Dull though he was with opium, he too had detected the crackle of the Maxim guns, and parsed out their meaning.

He sat for what seemed to him to be many minutes, watching the fires spread. Watching the beginning of the end of his city. How did the verse go? The silly bit of verse their schoolmaster had welted into them in the mud-walled schoolhouse of his childhood? *"The Phoenix must to ashes come—"* He couldn't remember the rest. He sat and watched the pulsing glow in the east, and listened to the guns.

Then he heard a much louder shot, followed at once by a fusillade that seemed to tear the garden apart.

Feng dropped his pipe on the mattress beside his chair and pulled himself slowly to his feet. He stood for a moment, his immense height bulking enormous in the small, book-lined room. Then he took the two curved swords off the shelf just behind the broken chair in which he had been sitting.

The drug throbbed heavily through his veins, slowing the world, filling him with a great peace. The glow beyond the bullet-splintered slats of the window pulsed like an unfolding rose, beautiful beyond expression. Outside in the garden, the shooting had stopped.

Feng turned and bent his head and passed out through the door into the hall, a sword swinging from each outsized hand.

At the front door he paused and peered out, accustoming

337

his eyes to the greater darkness. He saw a shadowy skirmish line moving on the house. The man in front, an American Marine, was only a couple of yards from the short flight of steps that led up to the pillared porch.

Feng Yu-lan filled his lungs with air, whispered an invocation to the warrior gods of old China—and kicked open the door.

Sergeant Connor was advancing with his heavy service revolver held uncomfortably in his left hand. His right arm, the whole right side was numb with pain now. Even so, he managed to get off two quick shots before the big Chinese was on him. The first missed entirely, the second struck but scarcely jolted the oncoming giant. Then one of the swords came down, ripping across Connor's shirt and chest. A second later the whole weight of the big man's body hit him and sent him sprawling.

The sergeant rolled over, wracked with pain, the cold flagstones heaving and pitching under him. Above the red roaring in his ears, he could hear the crash of rifle and pistol fire all around him. Through a pulsing haze he saw the giant's wide-planted legs, solid as pillars, straddling his own fallen body. Then there was a rush of Western boots, the flash of bayonets, and a spiraling into total blackness.

Then Connor was sitting up in Williams' arms, and Simpson was holding a small silver flask to his lips. He choked on the brandy and sat up straighter.

The thick, Mongolian features of the big Chinaman were looking straight at him from three feet away. He lay propped up against the steps, bleeding from many wounds, only a flicker of life left in his glazing eyes.

"That's a game man, Sarge," said Williams.

That's a dead man, thought Connor. He looked at the blood pulsing out of his own chest and wondered if he was a dead man too.

55

CHEN LI HEARD THE RATTLING OF THE LATCH, AND THEN the uncertain scraping of the door across the stone threshold. He turned his head toward the doorway, his neck chafing under the heavy weight of the *cangue,* his eyes straining to see in the darkness.

He had heard the explosion of gunfire in the garden. Then there had been silence, no more singing, no more half-heard bursts of laughter. Even the faint rattle of gunfire from beyond the garden walls seemed momentarily to hesitate. Chen stood very still, listening and waiting.

Then he heard the footsteps on the flags outside, and the first fumbling at the door.

At least they would not find Elizabeth. There had been no sound from where she sat against the wall, invisible in the darkness not ten feet away, for at least an hour now. He had long since ended his soft, hypnotic monologue, and she had not spoken, not answered when he gently called her name. It was done. She at least would be spared the death of many cuts.

The door was open. Shadowy figures filled the doorway and a lantern shot yellow beams of light into the cellar. Hard heels came clumping down the stairs.

In the swaying lantern light, Chen saw sandaled feet and knee-length pantaloons. But close behind them came gleaming leather boots, puttees, the sheen of a leather holster. Military boots, military puttees, and then a pair of civilian legs in white mufti. The first voice he heard spoke not Chinese, but the precise, clipped English of Eton and Oxford:

"I say, Miss Rowntree," the voice demanded anxiously, "are you all right?"

The light spread across the floor to touch the huddled figure against the opposite wall. The girl sat slumped forward under the weight of the square wooden collar, head bowed, hair spilling in heavy folds over her face. In the open fingers of her right hand, the ivory-handled knife that Chen had tossed her still reposed.

"Miss Rowntree?" said the Englishman again, hastening forward, dropping to one knee before her.

Chen Li saw, as the Englishman did not, how lank and lifelessly her hair fell forward over her bowed head. His eyes riveted upon that limp figure, Chen felt the blade of that ivory-hilted knife plunged like a dagger of ice into his own heart.

The Englishman was shaking her shoulder now. An American Marine was raising freckled hands to unlock the *cangue* from around Chen's own neck. The Boxer who had led them down was backed into a corner, shaking with fear.

All of it was transparently unreal to Chen Li.

He saw instead the narrow, lurching lanes of old Kyoto reeling past him, as they had done that long-past day in his youth when he had learned that his bride Mei Ling was dead. The wrenching agony that had torn him all that hallucinatory day was suddenly upon him once again. All the agony, and all the guilt.

He had killed his love a second time. He had left Mei Ling to the care of a family who hated her, and they had let her die. He had held Elizabeth in Peking by the sheer force of his love, and now Peking had killed her too. And he—he had handed her the knife! Chen Li gave a cry and staggered toward her, arms reaching out.

Elizabeth opened her eyes and saw a face looking into her own. She raised a hand to brush the hair away, and saw Chen Li.

"Oh, Li," she said, "I couldn't do it! I couldn't—"

Then she realized that there were other faces in the room,

and stiff military uniforms. The *cangue* was gone from around her neck. She was free.

"Dear God," she gasped, and burst into tears.

It was Chen Li who led her up the stairs and out the door, while Simpson blinked and the two Marines scratched their heads and watched them go.

"I couldn't do it, Li," she whispered again against his ear. "I couldn't help but go on living, even for a few more hours. Even with what was coming—afterward."

"You were right, of course," he answered as they stepped out into the garden. And then, with half a smile—the last smile she would ever see on his face: "The life force flows more strongly in you, I think, than it ever has in me."

"Connor!" gasped Elizabeth as they rounded the corner of the house and came in sight of the little group in front of the porch.

Connor was sitting on the ground, his shirt pulled off, one Marine supporting him, another attempting to fix a rough bandage around his chest. His shoulder was heavily bandaged, and there was a long gash diagonally across his upper body. His thin Irish face was dead pale in the light of a paper lantern.

Elizabeth plucked up her skirts and ran to him.

"Lizzie!" he said. "I guess they found you."

"The little Chink took us right there, Sergeant," said one of the Marines who had liberated them. "*K'uai-k'uai-ti*—damn quick—just like you said."

"All right," said Connor. "Let the man go—like I said."

"If you can manage to stop giving orders and just be quiet for a while, Connor," said Elizabeth, exploring his wound with experienced eyes and fingers, "you might—just might—live to collect your medals. Or whatever you expect to get out of all these—ridiculous—heroics."

Connor gave her a humorous, affectionate look and crooked his mouth in a resigned smile.

"Okay, Doc," he said. "It's your hospital."

Chen Li knelt more slowly beside the bloody, still breathing body of Feng Yu-lan. There was nothing medical to be done for him. Yet Chen Li knelt and touched the face of the man who had been the Scarlet Fist of China.

Feng opened his eyes and looked up at the fiery glow above the garden walls. It filled half the sky now. The three-tiered pagoda across the lane stood out in sharp silhouette against that wall of flame. It looked as if the whole southeastern quarter of the Tartar City were on fire.

The mouth of the fallen giant moved, slowly and with difficulty. Chen had to bend close to hear.

"What is that verse, Chen Li," the voice whispered, "that verse our honorable schoolmaster set for us, concerning the phoenix bird? I have been trying to recall it, but it has escaped my memory."

"There is a verse," said Chen, "that goes, '*The Phoenix must to ashes come—if he would arise once more.*' Is this the verse to which my friend refers?"

"It is, Chen Li." Feng's eyes were clear now, the effects of the opium blasted out of him by the bullets and bayonets that had killed him. His gaze strayed past Chen's face to the pulsing sky once more. He moved his shining head very slightly, as though trying to get a better view. Then his eyes slid back to Chen.

"It is the very verse, old friend of my childhood," he said with a chuckle that broke in his throat. "You always were the scholar of our village."

His jaw dropped slightly, and he was dead.

Chen Li rose stiffly, feeling a throb in his own weeks-old wound. He looked at Elizabeth, briskly tightening a bandage around Sergeant Connor's chest. He looked past the little group of Westerners to the charnel house his garden had become—or to what he could see of it by the light of the burning city.

There was whooping and laughter from inside his house

342

once more now. The soldiers of the West were finishing up the *shamsu* the Boxers had left, Chen thought. And probably filling their pockets with jades and ivories as well—which the Boxers had not done.

An American Marine staggered out on the porch wearing an embroidered silk robe over his dirty uniform. He was as drunk on violence as on *shamsu,* and his eyes glittered in the light of the fires.

"Ain't this something, Sarge?" he said, raising his arms to show off the intricately patterned fabric. "Some swell coat, I'd say."

"It's Dr. Chen's!" protested Elizabeth indignantly. "Connor, make him give it back!"

"Put it back, Sawyer," snapped Connor, his voice blurring only faintly at the end. "Now."

The Marine blinked, looked at Chen and back at Connor. "Sure, Sarge," he said. He turned and went back inside, shrugging off the robe as he went. But his eyes were already flickering about in search of some other, less blatant souvenir of the Great Siege that might bring him a good price in the hock shops of San Francisco when he got home.

Outside in the ravaged garden, Chen Li drew a long slow breath. Then, summoning what reserves of energy were left in him, he walked out through the garden gate into the blazing streets of Peking.

"Li!" called Elizabeth, looking up from where she knelt at Connor's side. "Where are you going?"

"Those fires will be out of control soon," Dr. Chen answered evenly. "Someone must organize a fire brigade."

He walked on out of the garden. The rest stayed where they were and watched him go.

BOOK SIX

THE
ASHES

56

At two-thirty the next afternoon, Mrs. Conger was passing between the kitchens and the hospital with broth for the most critically injured patients when she saw an apparition. She stopped dead in her tracks, the Chinese girls who minced along behind with the heavy tureens bunching up around her. All of them stared at the astonishing intrusion into the lawn of the British Legation.

It was a coffee-colored man wearing about half a British uniform, sweat shining on his naked torso. He was dancing about on the green grass, waving a rifle and shouting happily *"Oorah! Oorah!"* in a loud voice.

"Hurrah!" Polly Condit Smith answered him, darting out of the Bell Tower. "Hurrah!" And then, to Sarah Conger: "Oh, Mrs. Conger, don't you see we're saved?"

"They came through the water-gate!" called the British sergeant-major on guard at the gate. "Not five minutes ago! I can see the blighters dancing with the Yank Marines down by the wall from here!"

Everybody was running from everywhere by now, all dressed in their best as they had been since they had heard the artillery barrage along the east side of the city begin in earnest that morning. Ladies with parasols, gentlemen in white summer suits, Sir Claude mopping his brow, Lady MacDonald looking, as one sweating soldier put it, "as if she had just stepped out of a bandbox."

The Sikhs came marching into the legation compound, their scarlet turbans bright in the afternoon sun. Then came General Gaselee himself, the commander of the International Relief Force, reining in his great white horse and swinging down upon the soft legation turf. His uniform was dusty, his face wet with perspiration. Peering about him under his bell-shaped tropical helmet, he saw Polly and Sarah Conger staring at him from the front rank of the gathering crowd.

"Thank God, men!" the general called loudly to the officers behind him. "Here are two women still alive!" He strode up to them and kissed Mrs. Conger on the forehead.

Then Sir Claude and his lady were there, and the other ministers, and someone was opening a bottle of champagne.

When the American contingent arrived two hours later, a U. S. Marine saluted them somewhat more laconically from his post on the Tartar Wall.

"You're just in time," he called down, hitching his wide-brimmed hat back on his head. "We need you in this business!"

Weary from battling their way through a sizable section of the Chinese City, the American soldiers and Marines filed through the water-gate into the legations. The American commander, General Chaffee, hurried off to see Mr. Conger. The troops rested only a short time before they joined the sepoys in clearing away the barricades and preparing to move out against any Chinese soldiers who might choose to resist. Signal-corps men hooked up the telegraph wire they had methodically laid all the way up from the coast. By nightfall the liberated legations were in contact with the outside world once more.

In the northern part of the Tartar City, the Russian and Japanese contingents were still fighting when darkness fell. The Russians had been pinned down through the previous night, had only moved out in force into the city that afternoon. The Japanese poured hundreds of artillery shells into their objective—the northernmost gate in the Tartar Wall—before they broke in just after sunset and began to fight their way through the streets of Peking. The roar of their cannon, the crash of their rifle fire almost drowned out the merriment in the dining room of the shell-scarred Hôtel de Pékin, where the European officers drank late, toasting their victory.

Elizabeth stood at the window of the little bedroom she shared with two other young women, watching the rockets arc across the night sky somewhere beyond the Fu.

The other two women were off at the impromptu celebrations that seemed to be springing up everywhere around the legations. Elizabeth was alone, dressed in a ruffled nightgown, watching the distant fighting. She had slept the clock around and was only now coming groggily to herself. She remembered Sarah Conger shaking her half awake in the middle of the sultry afternoon to tell her excitedly that it was "all over!" Gazing out into a night bright with fires and loud with the distant *crump* of artillery, it did not seem all over to her.

She knew the firing was far away, in the eastern half of the city. She knew it was the Chinese who were under bombardment now, not the Legation Quarter. And still the pain about her heart would not go away.

Connor was going to be all right. She had pried that much out of Mrs. Conger before collapsing once more into a sleep of total exhaustion. He was flat on his back in the makeshift hospital, "wrapped up like a mummy in bandages," as Sarah Conger cheerfully put it, and sleeping like a log. But Dr. Poole said he would be fine.

Chen Li had not come back from the battle-torn *hutungs*. But somehow, Elizabeth felt no fear for him either. He was in his place, doing what he could to save what he could of his city. He would survive. She knew that with a certainty that was every bit as real to her as Dr. Poole's scientific prognostication of Sergeant Connor's recovery.

It was what was happening to Peking itself that made her shudder as she stood there in her nightgown, looking out the window.

She remembered the shell burst in Legation Street, that rainy night when she had fallen into Connor's arms behind the sandbags of the Hôtel de Pékin. She remembered the torrent of bullets the defenders of the legations had poured into that same street yesterday, the rain of death that had driven her, blind with terror, into the very arms of the Boxers to escape it. She thought of the shells crashing into the streets, the bullets pocking the walls of all that eastern side of the city at that very moment. She thought of the people there, cowering as she had cowered under the weight of that flying metal.

She would go out in the morning and see what she could do

Tzu Hsi stripped off her gorgeously embroidered gown with her own hands, for there were no servants left to help her. Eunuchs and concubines, servants and ladies-in-waiting had been slipping away one by one for days. Over the past twelve hours, they had fled in hundreds. The ghostly beauty of the Forbidden City lay almost deserted around her now. And it was time for her to leave as well.

She flung aside the gown adorned with flowers and tied with a thousand tiny knots, and reached for the blue gown of a peasant. The rough cotton scraped over her pampered skin. Muttering angrily, she pulled the jeweled combs from her hair until it fell unkempt and loose about her plump shoulders. The grey was showing through the black dye, she noticed irritably as she looped it up into a simple bun on top of her head. She yanked off her long curving nail protectors of gem-encrusted jade and cut off the six-inch fingernails.

She would do well enough, she thought, examining herself in a mirror. Every evidence of her aristocratic status was gone. Only the unbound feet remained to reveal the Manchu blood she gloried in. And her feet would not show as long as she stayed in the cart.

She studied her round, wrinkled face one last time. The sagging cheeks were sallow under the powder and shadowed with exhaustion, for it was long after midnight. But her puffy chin was as mulishly stubborn as ever, her bright raisin eyes as piercing. She would fox them all, she thought. She had foxed them for fifty years, and she would fox them all again.

350

She turned and swept away through echoing halls of rosewood and sandalwood, teak and marble. Artifacts of jade and porcelain and lacquer, curtains of satin, lamps of crystal fled past her and were gone. There was not a guard to salute her, not a solitary concubine to witness her departure from the palaces of her ancestors.

Three hooded mule carts waited in a distant courtyard, with a handful of faithful eunuchs—and the royal party.

The Emperor Kuang Hsu, looking sick and miserable still in a plain black gown and pantaloons, hurried up to her. "Bountiful Mother, what madness is this?" he whined. "We must stay here, in the Imperial City! They will never dare breach the walls of the Imperial City!"

"Get in your cart," she snapped back at him. "And close the screen, so that you will not be recognized." He was left pawing helplessly at the air as she turned to the rest of the little group: the Empress, the Heir Apparent, the Chief Eunuch, a hangdog general or two.

"You," she ordered the pinched little Empress she had selected for Kuang Hsu so many fruitless years ago, "will ride in the third cart, with Li Lien-ying." The Empress and the faithful eunuch bowed. "I shall ride in the first cart myself. And you," she added to the Heir Apparent—crude, hulkingly adolescent, looking totally bewildered—"will ride over the shaft on my cart."

"But where is my father?" the Heir Apparent demanded unhappily. "Is he not to come with us?"

"The honorable Prince Tuan," Tzu Hsi answered acidly, "has sworn to fight to the death. I expect we shall see him in a few days."

Before the boy could think of a riposte, the Dowager Empress of China hurried off to give final instructions to the mule drivers. Within minutes, the humble carts had slipped unobtrusively out through the Gate of Military Glory and were making their way north through the clogged and surging streets of the capital.

351

By torchlight and lantern light, in wagons and litters or afoot, laden with all they could carry of their possessions, half the people of Peking seemed to be fleeing for their lives. There was still artillery fire and the endless banging of rifles to the east, and many fires still lit up the night.

So they are fighting still! the old woman thought, with one last burst of pride. The Manchu spirit is not dead yet in China!

But she knew better. At the bottom of her vain, conniving, arrogant old heart, she knew that more than the souls of slaughtered thousands, the gods of the burning temples, more even than the Empress and her imperial entourage departed Peking that night. In the light of the burning buildings, in the terrified crowds that swirled around her hooded cart, Tzu Hsi knew that the Mandate of Heaven itself was lost forever to the house of Ching.

She would fight—she would fox them all—she would die back in her beautiful Sea Palaces yet! But it was a new century, in the calendar of the foreign devils from beyond the sea. In that century, the Dynasty of the Manchus would sit no more upon the Dragon Throne. They had lost the sanction of the gods, the Mandate of Heaven.

Chewing nervously on betel nut and meditating on her ancestors, the Dowager Empress of China clattered out through the northeast gate of the Tartar City. The sun was just rising as her cart swung to the left along the road toward the Western Hills.

57

IT WAS A BEAUTIFUL AUTUMN DAY IN PEKING, THE SKY bright and cloudless, the air tangy as chilled wine. The blue dome of the Temple of Heaven glowed in the sunlight above the dark foliage of the cedars and the green-tiled roofs of lesser pagodas. On the other side of Chien Men Street, on the grounds of the Temple of Agriculture, Dr Chen stood behind the barrier with a noisy crowd of his countrymen, watching the military review get under way.

It was a parade of the American occupying forces, in honor of the American supreme commander, General Chaffee. Officers from all the other allied forces had been invited to attend. The people of Peking were allowed to watch from a distance.

"I say, Chen, hello there!" said a cheerful British voice from the other side of the barrier.

Chen Li looked up, narrowing his eyes against the dazzling blue of the sky, and saw Lieutenant Philip Greville. The British officer, in full uniform replete with medals and ribbons, sat his horse with the ease of a born fox-hunting man.

"Good morning, Lieutenant," said Chen quietly. "I am pleased to see that your wound has knit so well." The black sling, which Greville had worn through most of the siege, was gone from his left arm.

"It's fine, fine, thanks to you and Poole. But what are you doing over there, Chen? And in that costume?" His ruddy cheeks glowed, his blue eyes twinkled as he surveyed the Chinese robe, pantaloons, thonged sandals. And was that the beginning of a queue knotted behind Chen Li's head?

"This is the reviewing stand reserved for my people, I think," Chen answered calmly, resting one hand on the barricade. "And I feel more comfortable in this clothing. I always have, actually." His dark eyes and smoothly sculptured cheeks crinkled into a smile in their turn.

"Ah—quite." Greville steadied his horse, which was side-stepping nervously in the presence of so many laughing, shouting orientals. "Well—splendid set of men, aren't they?" He nodded toward the first ranks of American troops, just stepping off to a spritely military air.

The American officers rode by, then the flags and guidons. Then came the troops, row on row, arms swinging, rifles slant-ing, booted feet rising and falling in unison. They marched by in a column of companies, heading north up Chien Men Street toward the charred ruins of the Chien Men Gate itself and the Tartar City beyond. The officers of the Eight Powers sat their horses in the shade of the cedars and saluted as the flags went by. They were obviously impressed. Chen saw some of the East Indian officers applaud gently with white-gloved hands.

"Ninth and Fourteenth Infantry," Greville ticked off the passing units for him. "The Marine Battalion. The Sixth Cavalry. And old Riley's artillery—fine new rifled guns, those."

Chen Li, who saw every day what those fine new guns had done to Peking, said nothing.

"The Americans have a future over here, no question of that," said Greville thoughtfully, watching the last of the artillery rumble off up the dusty street. "Damned if I don't think they'll be sharing the world with the rest of us before this century is out!" He turned to see what Chen thought of his daring prediction. But the Chinese doctor was gone.

The massed bands of the parade units marched by last of all. Lieutenant Greville wheeled his mount dexterously and cantered over to the small wooden reviewing stand under the trees, where the Ministers Plenipotentiary and their lady wives were watching the spectacle.

"Splendid show, sir," he said politely to Minister Conger, seated front and center with Mrs. Conger at his side.

"Thank you, Lieutenant," Conger responded, ponderous and dull as ever. But Greville had a question, and he got it out between bleating horns and booming drums. "I was wondering, sir, what the tune is? I don't believe that I know it." He prided himself on being familiar with all the most popular military airs of the great powers.

"The tune—yes," ruminated Conger. "I don't believe it's a regulation military march at all, is it, my dear?"

Sarah Conger turned her birdlike eyes on Lieutenant Greville and smiled beneath her wide flowered hat. "No, indeed," she said cheerfully. "But it's a mighty popular song at home, I understand—Elizabeth used to play it all the time. I believe it's called 'There'll Be a Hot Time in the Old Town Tonight.' "

"Catchy," observed Greville, "very."

"Isn't it?" said Sarah Conger. "Elizabeth said they played it for the Marines when they marched down Broadway to embark for Cuba a couple of years ago."

They watched the bands march off with blaring brasses and rattling drums, in the dusty wake of the artillery.

Chen Li took a parallel route north through the Chinese City toward the Hata Men Gate and the Tartar City beyond. He had his regular rounds that day, and he knew the crowds would make the return all but impossible if he waited longer.

He passed through the Hata Men, crossed Legation Street under the blackened walls of the Protestant Board Mission, and angled up Ailanthus Tree Lane into the *hutungs*.

Almost at once, he was confronted by a funeral procession coming down. People continued to die of their injuries, though it had been two months since the fall of the city. Chen stood respectfully to one side, under the mat awning of a ginseng dealer's, while the wailing and the gongs and the clatter of firecrackers paraded past.

Waiting, Chen's eyes rose automatically to the towering red walls that dominated Peking, the walls of the Imperial

City. He had heard that American Marines were bivouacked in the Forbidden City itself, and that some of the Ministers Plenipotentiary took visiting dignitaries on guided tours of its courts and palaces and temples.

He wondered how much longer they would be there, all these Western diplomats and soldiers. To judge from the lethargic pace of the peace negotiations, it would be a while.

The last white-clad mourners passed by and on down the narrow, crowded lane. The cheerful jabber of gossip and bargaining, shouted greetings, scolding women, easy laughter took up once again. Chen Li filled his nostrils with the rich mingled odors of spices and excrement, fruits and flowers. He turned in the shade of the reed matting to bow his thanks to the ginseng dealer.

Then he picked up his battered satchel—very carefully, so as not to disarrange the gleaming instruments and the bottled medicines that were once again beginning to reach him from the West—and set out on his way.

58

THE RAILING BEGAN TO THROB VERY GENTLY UNDER HER
hand, as the metal plates trembled beneath her feet. In the
bowels of the ship below her, sweating stokers heaved coal,
and the great engines churned. The twin screws began to
thresh their way through the grey-green water. With a clang
of bells and a final heave against the trough as she came
around, the rusty old freighter began to move.

The slender young American girl strolled toward the stern
to take her last look at China.

It was the *Deucalion* once again—an astonishing coinci-
dence, she thought as she accommodated herself easily to the
rolling motion of the ship. The Levantine steward had almost
recognized her—thought he had, in fact, and then had
changed his mind. After a quick, appraising second look, he
had changed his "This way, miss" to a "This way, if you
please, missus," as he led her down the passage to her cabin.

It was the second time that had happened, she thought as
she ducked under a stanchion past a swaying lifeboat. The
customs official who had perfunctorily checked her bags had
also accorded her the honorific "Mrs." She wondered idly
how she had changed since she had passed under these same
official eyes a year ago to merit that verbal symbol of respect.

Much more interesting, she thought, were the soldiers who
had come up to her in the course of the trip down from
Peking and called her "Dr. Rowntree." Four of them there
had been, two Americans, one Frenchman, one Russian, and
only one of them an officer. They had wanted to thank her,
they said, for what she had done for them in the hospital
during the siege. To them she was Dr. Rowntree—and she
hadn't bothered to correct them.

She hadn't corrected them—but she had reminded herself
sternly that she was no such thing.

Not yet, anyway.

She reached the afterdeck and made her way through a clutter of steamer chairs to the rail.

The churning wake foamed away and faded into the brackish chop, the scream of orbiting sea gulls. Beyond that, a whole flotilla of foreign warships lay scattered across the harbor and the river's mouth. Her mouth tightened slightly at the ugly grey silhouettes against the yellowish-brown shore, the pale-green reeds along the river. The low earthworks of the Taku Forts stretched away to the west, the flags of half a dozen nations fluttering in a stiff breeze over them. None of the flags, she noted, was Chinese.

She supposed that was one of the things they were negotiating about in Peking.

"Quite a sight, isn't it?" said a voice from just behind her left shoulder.

She turned and saw Sergeant Connor.

"Quite a sight, indeed," she said gravely. "I don't think I like it." She looked him in the eye as she spoke, and her own slate-blue eyes were smiling.

"I don't expect I'd care much for it either," he answered, "if I were Chinese."

He looked, she thought, more spit-and-polish than she had seen him for many a month. No rolled-up sleeves, no hat pitched back on his head, no borrowed British puttees. His hat brim was strictly horizontal, his shirt and jodhpur trousers pressed, his boots freshly shined. A light sling supported his right arm. Most startlingly different of all, he neither wore nor carried a weapon.

"Connor," she said, her voice softening, "what are you doing on this ship?"

"Going home for a rest cure, Lizzie," he answered, his thin cheeks creasing in a smile. "They aren't so good at getting me back on my feet at the Tientsin Hospital as you were at your clinic in Peking. So they've decided a couple of months in the States would be just the thing to get me fit for duty again." He shook his head, still grinning, and came forward to join her at the railing. "I told them they ought to put you in charge of the case—you'd have me up and back on the wall in no time flat."

"You had three broken ribs that hadn't knit yet, a bullet wound that got so badly infected they almost had to take the arm off, and a bad case of typhus into the bargain. Frankly, I think they've done remarkably well to pull you through at all!"

"Now, how would you know all that, Lizzie?" The pleasure in his face was genuine, if slow and cool as ever.

"I kept in touch with your case," she answered archly. "Through Dr. Chen, mostly—he has taken up his teaching at the Chinese Medical College in Tientsin again. When he can find the time," she added, her eyes growing somber. "He's so desperately needed in Peking."

"You were mighty fond of the Chinese doctor, weren't you, Lizzie?"

"I still am," she answered, looking him levelly in the eye. "One of the things I intend to do when I get home is try my best to arrange for medical supplies for him. For a clinic in the *hutungs*, not in the missions or the legations."

"But you are going home yourself," said Connor.

"Yes," she said, "I'm going home."

They both turned their eyes to the frothing wake and the receding coast of China. The *Deucalion* was well beyond the bar now. The pilot boat was knifing back through the flickering whitecaps toward shore.

"What'll you be doing then," Connor asked, "in Philadelphia, is it?"

"In Philadelphia, yes," she said, holding her small straw hat against a gust of wind. "Believe it or not, I'm going back to school. Medical school, to be precise, at the Women's Medical College of Philadelphia. And then the Pennsylvania General."

"You're going to be a doctor."

"I'm going to be a doctor."

The sea breeze was freshening considerably now, and the two of them turned away from the exposed after railing and strolled back into the lee of the nearest peeling grey superstructure. Without a thought, as naturally as breathing, she put her hand on his arm as they walked along.

"And you?" she asked, as they paused once more in the lee of the swaying lifeboat. "What will you be doing after you've properly recuperated?"

"Report for duty in the Philippines, I reckon—that's where my regiment's posted. Go back to chasing Aguinaldo through the forest. Though I got to say," he added with a shake of the head, "I'd be damned surprised if we ever catch him."

"And what after that—when your enlistment's up? Enlist again, and drift around the world once more?"

Connor thought about Toomy, buried only a week ago in the yellow earth of China, and Fitz, swallowed up forever in the rebellion, and Curtiss and so many others. Oddly, he found himself thinking also of the *insurrectos* that had fallen under his gun in Samar, and the Boxer charge up Legation Street under the hammering fire of Williams' Colt machine gun.

"Well," he said reflectively, "after this tour is over, I may just come home myself. Had enough of drifting, I guess."

He looked at the girl to see how she took this. Her eyes met his, frank and warm and steady, and she smiled.

She was certainly the most elegant woman he had ever known, he thought, by a long shot. He tried to keep it at that as he looked at her, in her fluttering white skirts and sheer shirtwaist, the flared jacket and the little straw hat perched on her dark-brown hair. But he could not help remembering that hair spread across a dusty pillow in a plaster-strewn bed in Peking. He could not help remembering that wide, soft mouth against his, those large, intelligent eyes closing gently against his cheek.

"In that case, Connor," said Elizabeth, still smiling, "we may be seeing something of each other yet."

"That we might, Lizzie." Connor grinned back. "That we might."

A bell clanged somewhere once again, and the ship jarred slightly, slowly and ponderously gathering speed for the long voyage home.

THE HAVERSHAM LEGACY
A TROUBADOUR SPECTACULAR

Daoma Winston

The saga of a powerful, passionate family whose riches concealed a mesh of corruption, bloodshed and madness, this is also the story of Miranda Jervis, who left her mother's seedy boarding house to claim a share in the dazzling Haversham inheritance – and began the stormiest era in all that family's troubled history.

'A wonderful gothic, full of jewels, flowers, love, envy, murder, childbirth, suspense and intrigue . . . a fiery tale that should find a wide audience.' *Publishers Weekly*

LOVE'S TENDER FURY
A TROUBADOUR SPECTACULAR

Jennifer Wilde

The story of a turbulent English beauty, sold at auction like a slave, who scandalised and captivated the New World in her fight to conquer her masters.

Marietta Danver was a woman wronged – seduced by her employer, charged with theft by her jealous mistress and shipped to the colonies to serve fourteen years as bound servant to the man who bid highest. But Marietta was also beautiful, educated and resilient and she was determined to prevail over the handsome silent planter who bought her to be his housekeeper; over the dashing entrepreneur who supplied girls to the New Orleans red light district; over the wealthy sadist who used her in his madness.